Dark Cindy

Dark Cindy

M. Apostolina

Simon Pulse
New York London Toronto Sydney

This book is a work of fiction. Any references to historical events, real people, or real locales are used fictitiously. Other names, characters, places, and incidents are the product of the author's imagination, and any resemblance to actual events or locales or persons, living or dead, is entirely coincidental.

SIMON PULSE
An imprint of Simon & Schuster Children's Publishing Division
1230 Avenue of the Americas, New York, NY 10020

Designed by Karin Paprocki
The text of this book was set in Weiss.
Manufactured in the United States of America
First Simon Pulse edition December 2006
2 4 6 8 10 9 7 5 3 1
Library of Congress Control Number 2006926731
ISBN-13: 978-1-4169-1769-4
ISBN-10: 1-4169-1769-1

For Billy
and for all the residents of Chuckieland

Acknowledgments

Many thanks to Anjali Ryan and Kristy Scanlan,
for always being there when it counts most; Jason Agard,
for introducing me to strange consciousness thingies and
multilayered something-or-others; Lori Grapes, whose words
and thoughts continue to inspire; and Julia Richardson, Ellen
Krieger, Siobhan Wallace, Jennifer DeChiara, and FL-Dawg
(the man, the myth) for their boundless enthusiasm and support.

And as always, many thanks to my family, and a special thanks
to Ricardo Moreno and Demanda Maraschino
for their helpful translation notes.

Dark Cindy

November 3

Dear Diary:

I had a nightmare this afternoon. But right before that, I was in a real-life waking nightmare. I was on a small private plane, calmly gathering my purse and my belongings. Everything was normal. See, I thought we were landing, I thought we were safe, but I was wrong! When we headed down toward the landing strip, the plane's wheels suddenly retracted—and then we veered straight up into the air at what seemed like a ninety-degree angle. Oh my God, oh my God, oh my God! The force of the plane's upward motion slammed me back into my seat. I gripped both handrests, and I may have even squealed, because next to me, Mamacita chuckled and muttered, "You're such a candy-ass."

Okay, so maybe I am (at least on planes) (especially small private planes that shake a lot) (and this was a stolen Sugarman private plane, after all, so that probably didn't help). After a moment, the pilot came on the speaker system, and in a surprisingly calm and grandfatherly voice, he informed us that there was a bit of a backup at Corpus Christi International Airport. We would be circling the airport until we got the okay to land. My waking nightmare was over. Mamacita yawned and pulled out a Montecristo Platinum cigar.

"Can you smoke on a private plane?" I asked. She shrugged.

"Probably not." Then she clipped one end of the cigar with a

1

small silver guillotine cutter, flicked a gold-polished beam-sensor lighter, and contentedly puffed away. I inhaled a bit of the smoke. And it calmed me down. It reminded me of Dad and all the road trips we used to take when I was a kid. In the wintertime, we would drive for hours to get to Grandma and Grandpa's house for Christmas, and because it was so cold out, the windows were rolled up, the heat was on full blast, and Dad's cigar smoke lingered.

On the plane, I leaned back in my seat and allowed Mamacita's cigar smoke to curl around me. We would be landing soon, I would be safe. I closed my eyes, took a deep sigh—and then a savage jolt of turbulence woke me up. Oh God, I hate turbulence so much. I braced myself, turned toward Mamacita. But she was gone. Vanished. There was no one in the seat next to me. I looked around the plane. It was completely empty! What was happening? I felt another jolt, and the lights flickered ominously. On the speaker system I heard static, and then a song blasted. A really awful song by JC Chasez:

> *All day long I dream about sex . . .*
> *And all the time I think about sex*
> *With you, with you*

I knew I had to do something. I couldn't just sit there (someone had to turn JC Chasez off). I reached down to unbuckle my seat belt and half-glanced out the window. My eyes nearly popped out of my head. Just outside the plane—and only a few hundred yards away—was a ginormous tornado. Holy crap! I screamed, but I couldn't hear myself; the sound of the wind and the whirring tornado drowned out everything around me (including JC Chasez) (the one bonus of a tornado) (that I know of). *I've got to tell the pilot,* I thought, so I flung aside my seat belt, bolted up, and heard a scary popping sound. The lighting console above me was sparking—and it set off a sudden terrifying chain reaction. *Pop-pop-pop.* All the lighting consoles on the plane sparked and then they extinguished. I was plunged into darkness. The plane jerked to the side. I reached out blindly, steadying myself with the seat backs. Then *blink-blink-blink.* The emergency aisle lights illuminated on the floor, blinking on and off erratically. It wasn't quite like a strobe-light effect, but it was close, and it was definitely freaking me out. I took a breath, realizing in that moment that my heart was beating outside my chest and tears were streaming down my cheeks (I didn't even want to know what my hair looked like). I had to make it to the cockpit.

I took a gulp and carefully stepped forward, holding the seat backs for balance against the still-rocking plane and looking down at the aisle lights so I could see where I was going. They blinked off, then they blinked on—and I couldn't believe what I saw. Quick as lightning, a raccoon ran between my legs and up the aisle. What the . . . ? The lights blinked again, and right before me on the floor was a baby. A dead baby! The lights blinked again, and—*poof*—the baby was gone. *I'm imagining things,* I told myself, *I'm totally stressed by the tornado* (and, really, who wouldn't be?). I mean, what the heck would a dead baby be doing onboard a plane? I glanced out the window. The tornado was getting closer. The lights blinked off again. And when they blinked back on, I saw a series of objects lined up on the aisle floor, one in front of the other, as if they were bread crumbs charting a path. I stepped carefully past each one. There were several large aerosol cans, which were oddly spinning and hissing and spraying all on their own, and then I saw a golf club, a fishing pole, a screwdriver, a telescope, a wrench—and, oh my God, it just went on and on—a tiny toy train, a syringe, a necktie, a drill, an umbrella, and countless loaves of French bread (which kind of made me hungry).

Ka-boom! A plane window blasted open. *Oh, now I'm in for it,* I thought. *Whoosh!* Everything in the plane abruptly levitated, spinning around wildly, including me. The tornado was upon us, and everything was going to be sucked out of the window. I cried in vain, and yet in that split second I thought, *No, I'm not going to die this way.* I bravely (I thought) lunged forth and grabbed an armrest. The force of the wind was incredible; my entire body was perpendicular, my dangling legs were being pulled right toward the gaping open window. Everything in the plane was being sucked out—papers, magazines, anything that was loose. Ouch! I was bonked on the head by the tiny toy train, then *whoosh!*—it was sucked right through the window hole, followed lickity-split by the fishing pole, the screwdriver, the telescope, the drill, the umbrella. I could barely hold on to the armrest. Objects were madly gyrating around me, including a spooky, glowing, spinning globe.

And that's when I lost my grip. Oh no! I flung my arms and hands forth in vain, desperate for a handhold. But it was too late. The force of the tornado was too strong. I could feel it pulling. I was going to be sucked right through the gaping window hole. Good-bye, world. Please don't let Lisa sing at my funeral, and please tell Mom and Dad I love them, and please, oh, please tell Patty to lay off the Skinny, and tell Keith (my love, my sweet, my everything!) that I still love-love his six-pack, and tell Bud to keep it clean (or at least try), and tell Lindsay to learn to say no to Bud on occasion, and tell Shanna-Francine that it's time to hang up the PC crap, and please, oh, please don't forget to tell Meri Sugarman that I said, "Die, bitch, die!" And I know, I know, that's way harsh, and I'm really not that way, but in these final moments, that's how I really and truly feel. The plane suddenly dipped, and I felt the tornado upon me. *Whoosh!* This was it. I was going to be sucked out of the plane. Then I heard *thump! thump! thump!*

And I fell to the aisle floor. Nothing was moving. Well, the plane was still moving, but everything that was spinning and levitating (including me) had fallen to the floor. A large cluster of French bread loaves had jammed and sealed the open window hole. Disoriented, I stood up—and nearly fell face-first when the plane bumped up and down. The tornado was still out there. I had to be careful. Then *blink-blink-blink*. All the emergency aisle lights went out. Permanently. I could barely see in front of my nose. *Just one foot in front of the other,* I told myself. *You have to make it to the cockpit.* With the noise of the tornado now muffled, I could hear it again:

All day long I dream about sex . . .
And all the time I think about sex
With you, with you

Ignore it, I thought (admittedly hard to do when it comes to JC Chasez). I took one step after another (was I even going in the right direction?) (who could tell?). Then I saw light. I nearly yelped with joy. The airplane's bathroom door had swung open, and the light inside was splashing out. My throat was dry, I was thirsty. If I could make it to the bathroom, maybe I could have a sip of water from the sink before going to the cockpit. The plane was still jerking and vibrating, so I stepped to the door cautiously. Oh my God. I found myself face-to-face with none other than Keith, and he was naked, and he was, well, I don't how to say this politely, but he was fully aroused. He pulled me into the bathroom and passionately kissed me. *What the heck is Keith doing on this plane,* I thought, *and what happened to all of his clothes? And holy moly, I totally forgot what a good kisser he is, but this is way too much, and it's way too fast, and it's totally and completely weird,* so I pushed him back and found myself standing right before Meri! Oh my God, oh my God, oh my God. She was naked too. And she was smirking.

5

"Uh-huh. So this is what you want," she sneered. "I should have known."

She yanked me into an embrace. Meri was making out with me. Ahhhhhhhhhhh! She wouldn't let go, I couldn't push her away. Voices swirled. *Cindy's my little bow-wow. Bow-wow. Woof woof.* I struggled with all my might. *Oomph!* I pushed her back. Now I was standing before Lisa. My sister. Naked!

"*Playboy* made me an offer," she said, rolling her eyes. "And I'm like, dudes, I'm so not showing beaver this early in my career. Maybe later. When I'm desperate. Like Jenny McCarthy."

Then she tried to pull me into an embrace. Eeeow. I pushed her back and ran out of the bathroom. It was dark in the plane again, but I didn't care. *Run,* I thought, *run to the cockpit.* I couldn't see, but I kept going with my hands outstretched before me. I felt a door. It had to be the cockpit door. It had to be. I turned the knob, but it wouldn't open, so I stepped back and slammed it with my shoulder as hard as I could and—*bam!*—it flung open and I fell face-first to the floor. When I stood up, my eyes had to adjust. The cockpit was faintly illuminated by the overhead switch panels and communication consoles. I was alone. Completely alone. There was no pilot or first officer. I whirled around, and I saw it fall: a lit cigar. I saw it in slow motion, or at least it seemed that way. The cigar fell—slowly, slowly, right past my face, down, down— finally landing on the cockpit floor, where the tip suddenly hissed and sparked, and then the floor shuddered and cracked, breaking apart to create a sizzling line that started at the cigar, then circled up to the ceiling and back to the other end of the cigar. The plane trembled ominously.

That's when I heard the loudest crack of metal I've ever heard in my entire life. It happened so fast. The sizzling line fractured, the cockpit blasted apart from the plane, and I tumbled helplessly into the air, where I was sucked into the tornado. *This is definitely not good*, I thought as I felt myself spinning faster and faster. Broken shards of mirror twirled around me. I could see my horrified reflection. I brought my hands to my face in disbelief, and right as I did that, my face changed, growing younger and younger until I saw a wailing baby. I was a baby now (and a very unhappy one) (but definitely cute). Then I was sucked deeper into the tornado and—*whoosh!*—it spit me out. I fell herky-jerky through blackened storm clouds (which felt watery and tingly, kind of like a cool misty facial). A flock of ravens soared up past me, and I swear their *caw-caw*s sounded like "ha-ha's." I was falling faster, faster, and then, bounding up from a plump, dark cloud, it was Meri! She was on a broomstick, wearing a witch's black cape and hat, along with a stunning mauve-beaded St. John blazer and a flowing blood-red Michael Kors skirt. She was Fashion Witch! And she was coming right at me. I tried to scream, "No!" but nothing came out. Then I saw Meri lift up a gleaming double-sided ax. She hurled it right at me. And just as it made contact with my chest . . .

. . . I bolted up from my dream in my seat next to Mamacita on the plane, which came to a quick, jumpy stop on the landing strip at Corpus Christi International Airport.

"You hair looks like hell," she chuckled, handing me a hairbrush. I took it gratefully and tried to force a smile as I ran it through my scraggly hair (I really do need to get a better conditioner) (industrial-strength if I can find it). My dream was still playing in my head—but what the heck did it mean, anyway? Oh, where's Patty when you need her? Her psychological insights are so smart—not about herself, necessarily, but she's always sharp eyed when it comes to practically everyone around her. I wonder if that's the case with all psychiatrists. Are they good at diagnosing everyone's problems but their own? I mean, of course not all psychiatrists are addicted to crystal meth like Patty is, but then, getting addicted to crystal meth wasn't her fault. She was hoodwinked by Meri and

Wolfgang Rimmer. Still, getting off the drug will be her problem and hers alone. That sucks. Oh, why did she run away from Rumson's rehab center? She's still out there, somewhere.

When I followed Mamacita into the airport, I still had no idea where we were going. And jeez Louise, for someone who's so old and so tiny, she moves incredibly fast, kind of like a hummingbird. Earlier in the day, she magnanimously offered to help me find Lisa (she seemed dead certain about where she was). Mom's been hysterical, and Dad has been too. Lisa's never run away before. The only thing I had to go on was one of Lisa's e-mails that mentioned Los Lonely Boys, which I showed to Mamacita. I had a hunch, and it turns out I was right.

A rented town car was waiting for us outside the terminal entry, and after Mamacita gave the driver instructions, she sat back contentedly and folded her hands in her lap. "We'll be there in twenty minutes. Wanna play hangman? I always win."

"Where are we going?" I asked.

Mamacita's eyes narrowed. Then she told me where we were headed. And why. Mamacita, of course, isn't really what she seems to be—a supposedly frail and dutiful housemaid for the rich and pampered (including the Sugarman family). In fact, her covert lifestyle and fabulous wealth, as well as her many charities and foundations, have long been a legendary secret in the Latin community. Los Lonely Boys—or *"Mis buenos muchachos,"* as Mamacita sweetly calls them—benefited years ago from one of her foundations, Fundación de Santa Mamacita Para Los Artes. They were just teenagers when she bankrolled their first demo and their first tour throughout the Texas and Southeast circuit (where they found instant acclaim as "The Mexican Beatles"). But like all transactions with Mamacita, the Boys had to agree to keep her contribution a secret, thereby ensuring her ability to continue her role as a fragile, obedient maid (who slyly shaves a small, undetectable sum from each of her employers' bank accounts every month).

Her logic was simple: If Lisa was with Los Lonely Boys, then she was in Corpus. The boys frequently retreat to a secluded Corpus estate (with breathtaking views of the Bay) to create new music and lay down tracks at the nearby Hacienda Recording Studio. And when they do, they are not reachable, and they never answer their phones. For anyone.

"Then how do you know they're here?" I asked. Mamacita leaned in to me, glanced up to make sure the driver couldn't hear her, and whispered softly in my ear, "Last night, I appeared to them in a dream. As *La Pájaro Santa*, a black-billed robin with fine yellow plumage and a trumpet in her claw."

Whoa. I totally got goosebumps when she said that. Then she burst out laughing and elbowed me in the ribs. "I called them up, you ding-a-ling." All right, she got me there. And apparently, when "La Santa," or "The Saint," appears on your caller ID, you pick up, no matter who you are or where you may be, though for some reason, I don't doubt Mamacita's ability to transport herself into someone's dream. And apparently, I come equipped with some sort of sixth sense, because right at that moment, something told me to turn around. I did—and my jaw dropped. "We're being followed," I gasped.

Rocketing up only a few feet behind us was a shiny silver Lamborghini Diablo, and though I couldn't make out the face of the driver, I could see the contours of you-know-who's telltale raven hair. "It's Meri!" I shrieked. I was impaled by fear; I couldn't breathe. This was no dream. This was real.

"*¡Vaya más rápidamente! ¡Ahora!*" Mamacita bellowed to the driver, and he stepped on the gas. I braced myself as we blasted onward; we had to be going at least eighty miles an hour. I fumbled for my seat belt (and yes, I should have been wearing it all along, even though I was in the back). The driver made several quick, screeching swerves from lane to lane on the freeway, but Meri was still gaining—the Lamborghini was following our every move. How, I wondered, would our simple town car outrun Meri's flashy sports car? And what would she do to us once she caught up with us? Run us off the road? Smash into us? Where the heck's a cop when you need one?

"¡*Conduciré el coche!*" screamed Mamacita at the driver. "¡*Ahora consiga de la carretera!*" The driver jerked the wheel and whipped across three lanes of traffic to a freeway exit that was just yards before us. Car horns blasted (and I'll admit, I shut my eyes). When we came to an abrupt stop off the exit ramp, doors flung open. Mamacita leaped out and switched places with the driver, who sat next to me in back, smiling nervously. A car engine revved up behind us. Meri was blasting down the exit ramp.

"She's coming!" I cried.

"Hold tight, *mi querida*." Mamacita chuckled. I should take a moment here to say that Mamacita is so tiny that her head barely cleared the steering wheel, much less the front windshield. I screamed in horror when she hit the gas, because as fast as I thought the driver had gone before, Mamacita went faster—much faster. And yet I wasn't the only one screaming. As we raced down a street and flew right toward a railway crossing with its gate arm down and its signal light flashing red—and a high-speed commuter train whizzing forth—my eardrums nearly shattered when the driver (who had seemed like such a manly man) shrieked like a schoolgirl and clutched my arm. "Aaaaaiiiiyyyaaaaa!" he squealed (and it was really high-pitched).

"Mamacita, no!" I wailed.

Too late. *Ka-pow!* We flew right into the signal arm, shattering it, and soared over the railroad track. In my head, the two seconds or so that we were airborne and over the track seemed like eternity;

I turned my head, glanced (somewhat casually) out the passenger window, and saw the front of the high-speed commuter train hurtling right at me. *This is such a bummer,* I thought. *Close but no tomato, and all because we're not in a car that's as fast as Meri's Lamborghini.* The train rushed closer. I shut my eyes tight. I really didn't want to see (or feel) the inevitable. *Maybe,* I thought, *I can will my spirit or soul to leave my body. That way I won't feel a thing.* It seemed like a good idea. I mean, who wants to feel a train smashing into their body? Not me. Unfortunately, there were practical issues to consider, and in that hairbreadth of a millisecond, my mind hungrily scanned all the literature I'd read on the subject. Visions of the soul leaving the body are especially common in prose from the Middle Ages. Pope St. Gregory I, who reigned from 590 to 604, had once stated that angels, sweet fragrance, and lovely music from Heaven accompany such an event, and while I thought I could do without the perfume and especially the music, because I feared it might be Enya (just a hunch), the angels sounded nice. And yet, for the life of me (pun sort of intended), I couldn't recall anything I'd read that actually gave hands-on instructions on how to begin the process; it just sort of happens. *I should have read more,* I thought forlornly. *This is what I get for skimming sometimes.* And then *ker-runch!* I heard the sound of metal bashing, but I didn't feel a thing. *Eureka,* I thought, *my soul has left my body automatically,* and then I thought, somewhat perturbed, *But where are all the pretty angels? This is such a rip-off.* And then I opened my eyes and I was flat-out stunned to realize that we'd made it over the track—we'd really and truly made it. And obviously not a moment too soon. The train was blazing past behind us, and Mamacita was gripping the wheel, her eyes ablaze, a cigar dangling from her lower lip (when did she have time to light it?). She pumped her fist, triumphantly calling out, *"Pinche, soy el jefe!"*

Twisting around, I saw the end of the train zoom past—and

Meri's Lamborghini at least six cars behind in a line waiting to cross. "She's still on us," I exclaimed. Mamacita barely batted an eyelash. She was already hightailing it across the Corpus Christi Harbor Bridge. There was no way Meri would catch up with us now. As I gazed out at the impressive views of the harbor and the tall ships entering port, I heard soft whimpering and sniffling. The driver, poor thing, was curled up shivering on the floor of the car. Luckily, we made it off the bridge without incident and Mamacita, who saw no reason to slow down, floored it and (just for fun) (I assume) ran a red light.

"Mamacita," I scolded. "You'll get us in trouble."

"Oh, don't be so boring," she tittered.

Uh-oh. A police siren whirred behind us. I was about to say, "I told you so," but that would have been pretty rude, especially, I realized, since she was about to get a whopping ticket—and all because she was doing her best to help me find my bratty little sister and escape from Meri. We swerved to the side of the road, and two Mexican-American cops (one of them was seriously handsome) stepped up to the driver's-side window. Mamacita gave them a little wave and a bawdy wink, which seemed dangerously informal to me. Most cops don't have a sense of humor, especially when they're pulling you over, but silly me, when one of them gasped, "La Santa!" and the three of them began to chatter away in Spanish like old chums, it suddenly dawned on me that there were probably very few stoplights that Mamacita couldn't run through in Corpus Christi (should she happen to feel the urge).

I heard the *vroom* of a car motor behind us. Oh, darn it. Meri's Lamborghini had pulled over to the shoulder just a few feet behind us. She was lying in wait. Mamacita saw it too. She leaned over to the cop (the handsome one) and said something in Spanish. The cop gave her a wink and a thumbs-up. Jeez, what can't Mamacita do? As we drove off (our driver was up off the floor and sitting next to me by now), I could see the cops turning around and pulling up to Meri's Lamborghini. Ha. *Tough luck, Meri, I thought, you can't always win.*

But from one "problem girl" to another. When we arrived at Los Lonely Boys' rambling bayside estate, the *"buenos muchachos"* were long gone. They'd already been instructed by Mamacita to make themselves scarce. But Lisa was there. She was in the backyard, sunning herself by the pool in the late afternoon sun, wearing a hot-pink string bikini and Pucci-print marabou mules with big, poofy flower-print puffs on the toes. She wasn't the least bit surprised to see us.

"Hi, guys. I made pigs in a blanket. Want some?"

"Get up," I commanded. I was in no mood for Lisa's games. "Do you know how worried Mom is?"

"Worried about what?' she said, lazily spritzing herself with suntan oil. "Me and LLB have been laying some tracks. They're s-o-o-o-o into my music. Oh, and Ringo thinks I'm cute. How sick is that?"

I grabbed her arm and forcefully yanked her up.

"Fer shizzle, Sis!" she cried, jerking her arm back. "Like, what the fuck are you doing? You're bruising my arm."

I was about to tell her that you can't just run away from your parents when you're only fourteen years old and hightail it to Corpus to "lay some tracks," but really, would she have listened? Her two trashy singles, "Tune My Motor Up" and "Touch My Daisy," were already big dance club hits, so in her mind she was an untouchable star. But she was still my baby sister. And she was being a brat. I seized her arm again and steered her to the house. "Get dressed and meet us out front," I scolded. "Or I'll call the police. I can do that, you know. You're underage. Do you want to go home in handcuffs? Well? Do you?"

"Call *Entertainment Tonight*," she smirked. "'Lisa in chains.' You know I'll work it. Then I'll have a sob session with Mary Hart. 'Boo-hoo, Mary. I'm so naughty.'"

"I can't believe you," I said. "I'd never in a million years treat Mom this way."

"No, you wouldn't. And you wanna know why? 'Cause you're a wuss. You're a doormat." That threw me for a moment. Am I a doormat? Do I have, as they say, the "disease to please"? I'd read about that in *Elle* once and it definitely hit home, in a cheap shot sort of way, but then Lisa is all about cheap shots, I realized, so I once again ordered her inside, and despite her big talk, she obeyed me. I strode to the front of the house with Mamacita, who smiled wryly. "Lots of spirit in that one."

"Yeah, and someone ought to shake it out of her," I retorted. I was so angry. A few minutes later the front door opened, and Lisa haughtily swept down the porch steps in a bright yellow princess dress with a knapsack slung over her shoulder. "Well?" she sniffed. "I hope you have a good driver. Paparazzi crawl up my asshole twenty-four seven."

I was about to respond, but then I froze. I heard the whirring of a car motor. Meri's Lamborghini screeched into the driveway! Oh my God, oh my God, oh my God. The door flew open, and all I could see was hair—thick raven hair. Then I blinked. What was I looking at? This wasn't Meri at all. She was shorter than Meri, a bit older, too—maybe in her thirties—but somehow more beautiful, and, oh my God, more scarily assured (if that's even possible). It all happened in a flash. She made a beeline toward Lisa, and in one swift move sat on the porch steps, flung Lisa over her knees . . . and began spanking her! I couldn't believe what I was witnessing. She spoke, too, and in perfect rhythm with her spanking. *Spank-spank-spank!*

"You. Will. Never. Ever. Run. A-way. From. Your. Par-ents. Again." Lisa burst into tears, but the spanking didn't stop. "Never. Ever. Ever . . ."

"Okay," Lisa wailed. "I promise."

"Ever. Ever. Again." The spanking stopped. She pulled Lisa into her arms, gave her a quick but warm hug, helped her up, brusquely wiped the tears from her eyes, and curtly instructed, "Tell me you're sorry. And I want you to mean it." Lisa whimpered. She was actually shaking.

"I'm sorry, Jennifer."

Finally taking notice of me and Mamacita, she extended her hand. Her grip was strong. "Hi. I'm Jennifer. Lisa's agent."

"Nice car," said Mamacita, casting an admiring glance at her Lamborghini.

"Wait a minute. I thought Frederick was her agent," I asked. I was pretty confused at this point.

"No. Frederick's her manager," she said. "He's based in L.A. I'm her agent. I'm based in New York."

Why Lisa needs so many representatives is beyond me (she needs a babysitter more than anything else) (or maybe a jailer), but everything else was starting to make sense. In her efforts to find Lisa on behalf of Mom and Dad, Jennifer had tracked my movements. I was about to apologize for trying to ditch her—and okay, I was secretly hoping for a repeat performance of the spanking, too—but Jennifer had already turned her back on me. She took Lisa's hand and bent down toward her. "You. Time to grow up. Do you understand me?" Lisa sighed heavily.

"Whatever."

"No 'whatever.' It's time to grow up. You have a career—and a pending lawsuit from Lindsay Lohan. Remember?" That made Lisa pout. She's being sued for stalking Lindsay Lohan during her visit to Hollywood, even though she still insists that she and "L. Lo" are "megatight" best girlfriends. "Say good-bye," continued Jennifer. "We're going. I'm taking you back to Ohio." Lisa screamed bloody murder: "N-o-o-o-o-o-o!" Poor Lisa. Off she went with Jennifer. Mamacita rolled her eyes. "Are we done now?"

We were. Thank God. On our ride back to the airport, I chuckled at the notion of Jennifer telling Lisa to grow up. Fat chance of that ever happening. Then I thought, *What about me? Am I grown up? Finally?* I decided that I was, and to be honest, it sort of bummed me out. I mean, I've definitely had to keep my wits about me with Meri in my life, and you have to be grown up (i.e., sort of cold and steely eyed) to do that. *But where,* I thought, *does that leave me? Has Meri taken something away from me? My innocence, perhaps?* I used to be so openhearted and really nice (and I'm not saying that to brag). I'll change that, I assured myself. When I stop Meri once and for all, I'll be able to relax and be myself again; innocent and happy and ready to live life the way I always have (and should). I gazed out the window as we drove over the harbor bridge. "Penny for your thoughts," Mamacita said gently.

In that moment I was thinking about the dream I had on the plane, and I tentatively outlined it for her. "What do you think it means?" I asked. She shrugged.

"Means you're nuts? How the hell should I know? Maybe you had gas. I tell you, if I eat cucumbers before bed, my dreams are loco."

I laughed. Mamacita's so plain-spoken (but not plain), and yet I also felt sad. Where the heck was Patty? She'd be able to decipher my dream in a snap. Oh God, I still have so much to do. I have to find Patty and get her off crystal meth (an addiction created by Meri), and I have to find some way to help dear, sweet Lindsay, who's been in the throes of torment ever since her boyfriend, Bud Finger, was arrested by the FBI for illegally downloading, copying, and selling DVD movies (thanks to Meri, who treacherously snitched on him). Oh, and poor Shanna-Francine. Her self-esteem is shot. She tried to be a good president for Alpha Beta Delta once Meri was gone, but all of her "politically appropriate" house events and fund-raisers backfired (badly) (again, thanks to Meri). And I can't forget Professor Scott. Sure, he's skeevy and all, and he tried to bust a move on me (eeeow!), but he's also brilliant, and in my fervor to destroy Meri, I inadvertently caused him to be fired from RU.

Even worse, there's a looming deadline for all the girls at Alpha Beta Delta. December 15. That's when we're scheduled to appear before the National Intersorority Governing Council in Vero Beach, Florida. Given all the bad publicity that the house generated when I first exposed Meri, the council curtly informed us that we have until December 15 to prove we're worthy of keeping our membership. And without membership and recognition from the council, that's it—*poof!*—Rumson U. will disband Alpha Beta Delta. The save haven for all the "different" girls on campus will be gone. At this point, I don't see how we'll prove ourselves, but there must be a way (there has to be!). My heart sinks when I think about everything I have to do. And it's definitely not fair that my friends have had to pay such a horrible price for being my friend—and all because Meri is out to get me.

"Why is this sorority thing so important to you?" asked Mamacita as we turned onto the freeway and headed to the Corpus airport. I didn't have to think about my answer. Growing up in Marietta, Ohio, I told her, I was a complete loser—the "butt-ugly" nobody with books in my hands, pimples on my face, and one desperate dream: I wanted to fit in. I did not want to be different. I even sought help from Lisa. Sure, she was four years younger than me, but she was already popular and beautiful and all too happy to give me her sage advice.

"Start using these," she instructed, handing me Stri-Dex Pads and Clearasil ointment one morning in the bathroom. Then she roughly turned my head to the mirror. "Look. Glassy. You throw off glare. Gross. And look at your forehead. See that big honking goober? See the puss? So gross. Yuck. Now pop it." I tried my best, but Lisa wouldn't even let me pop a pimple without criticizing. "No, no, no! Fingertips, not fingernails. Otherwise you'll pock. Jeez. Don't you know anything?"

I was beginning to get a little tired of Lisa's lessons. One morning in the bathroom, she tweezed my eyebrows, and when I looked in the mirror, I screamed. To say that she overdid it would be an understatement. I no longer even had eyebrows. I had two faded ridges above my eyes; I had Frankenstein's forehead. I was so angry that I slammed the bathroom door, cornered her, and held two fingers around a huge, oily pimple on my chin.

"I'm a dumb bimbo. Say it, Lisa. I'm a dumb bimbo. Say it or this pimple goes pop. Right in your face."

"You wouldn't!" she seethed.

Pop! She ran screaming out of the bathroom. "Ahhhhhhh! You're a mutant! You're a pig person!"

Okay, so I wasn't able to fit in with anyone at school. That much was clear. I was too much of a goofball. I was too easy a target. I only had one option left, and I took it. I vanished. Completely. I held my head low, kept my mouth shut, hunched up my shoulders, and blended into the background. I was Nadaville. Cindy Bixby didn't exist, so therefore no one could pick on her. It worked. At night I cried myself to sleep and dreamed of a better world. And at Alpha Beta Delta I actually found it. Hooray! All my friends—Lindsay, Patty, Shanna-Francine, everyone—helped me to realize that it was okay to be different. In fact, it was more than okay, it was something to celebrate. I didn't get it at first—I was skeptical of happiness, even fearful. Patty finally helped me see the light once when she played me this old song, "Different," by Mama Cass:

Different is hard, different is lonely
Different is trouble for you only . . .
But I'd rather be different than be the same!

And yet my happiness was short-lived. The fly in the ointment was Meri. Perfect Meri. She was the president of Alpha Beta Delta. She tried to destroy me. Why? Because I represented everything she loathed: I wasn't perfect (far from it), I wasn't "pretty" (not by a long shot), and God forbid, I took my studies seriously. Even more threatening (and mysterious to her, perhaps?) was the devotion and unconditional support I shared with my new friends. She tried to being me down, but the "doormat" fought back. With help from my friends at Alpha Beta Delta, I triumphantly exposed her as a diabolical psycho—one who used illegal wiretapping, blackmail, and deceit (among other things) in order to squash her enemies and get her way. Because of me, she was publicly booted from Alpha Beta Delta and banished from RU. She even faced criminal charges. Unfortunately, she struck back. And, boy, Meri knew just where to strike: She knew how important my friends were to me, so she systematically brought each of them down, and with a final flourish that must have seemed like icing on the cake, she made it appear as if I was the crazy one, not her. Cleverly sidestepping all the legal charges against her, she triumphantly reemerged as a "reformed" bad girl who now promised to "do good." A surprising number of people bought into her charade. She also pulled just the right strings to gain readmittance to RU, though not, thank God, to Alpha Beta Delta. She's at RU now (plotting her next move, no doubt). I can't relax. I have to stay one step ahead of her; I've got to help my friends.

"Fight fire with fire," advised Mamacita as we pulled into the airport parking lot. "You want to fight a snake, you become a snake. Battle with a tiger, bite like a tiger. There's no other way."

I took her words in, nodding my head in agreement, but my insides were screaming, "No!" Become like Meri to fight Meri? Forget it! Why can't I be myself? I mean, isn't that part of being a grown-up (which presumably I am)? And if were to actually "become Meri," wouldn't that make it hard—if not impossible—to be the happy, nice girl I used to be once Meri's finally out of my life?

I'm sitting in the airport terminal café now. I've been here writing for an hour. Mamacita's at the bar smoking a cigar and playing shot chess with a handsome businessman (the chess pieces are replaced by shot glasses filled with Jägermeister; when your opponent captures a piece, or shot glass, you have to down it) (Mamacita's winning). See, she didn't tell the pilot when we would be departing (we didn't know how long it would take to deal with Lisa), so now we have to wait for both the plane to be refueled and a scheduled departure time, which will hopefully be soon. I really want to get back to Alpha Beta Delta. In my gut I know everything will be okay. Or maybe I just want to be happy again. And why shouldn't I be? I'll start now. Woo-hoo! There's an old Scottish proverb that goes, "Be happy while you're living, for you're a longer time dead." And okay, that's kind of grim, but the point is, why can't I be happy now? I'm going to "own that feeling" (as they say on *Oprah*). Meri Sugarman cannot take my happiness away, no matter what she does. So that's it, Diary, it's decided. I'm maxin' and relaxin', as Bud Finger says (which is just about the only thing he says that isn't dirty). I'm going to be okay. Really. This is how grown-ups adjust their moods. Just say it. Just be it. I'm happy. *Phew!* It feels good to write that down.

November 4

Dear Diary:

Am I happy? Not yet. Am I behaving like a grown-up? I can't tell anymore. The day is over. I'm back at Alpha Beta Delta. Lindsay just left my room—and she told me something so outrageous, and so insane, that I can barely hold this pen in my hand. At first her appearance distracted me. She's no longer wearing her Aunt Christiana's tiara; it was a fake, she discovered, and was never once worn by her aunt. It also had a tiny mic implanted within its jewels by Meri. When Lindsay discovered this, she was grief-stricken, so she pleaded with her mother to send her something real—anything—from her aunt's royal garment collection. Her mother Fedexed an article of clothing the very next day. Lindsay hasn't stopped wearing it since. It's a royal hennin hat that was handed down to her aunt from the fourteenth century. It's lilac, and it's kind of shaped like a very long, stretched-out coffee filter. The wide-open bottom of the hat crowns Lindsay's head and extends up—way-way up—to a sharp point, where an attached piece of flowing lilac georgette crepe chiffon falls down past her shoulders. I shouldn't say this, but it looks kind of ridiculous. "In the fourteenth century, noble women shaved their heads when they wore hennin hats," explained Lindsay. "They thought high foreheads were glamorous." I gasped, noticing for the first time that she seemingly had no hair.

21

"You didn't . . ."

"Of course not," she giggled. "I just pulled it up." Then she twirled and posed. "Auntie had it in her private collection. Isn't it beautiful?"

"It is," I said, and yes, that was a lie, but Lindsay was beaming with such joy that it seemed like the right thing to tell her (I really don't want to be known as a spoilsport when it come to my friends' happiness). Lindsay adores her aunt, who, like Lindsay, was born of Canadian royalty. She was known the world over as the Princess Christiana of Northumberland. She worshipped the sun, too, and after many decades spent smoking crème-de-menthe-flavored cigarettes and sunning topless on her yacht with her international jet-set friends (Princess Margaret! Mick Jagger!), she sadly succumbed to melanoma and died. Because of this, Lindsay is never without an umbrella—she prefers her Anna Sui limited-edition dragon-bird-and-pagoda "chinoise fantasy" patterned umbrella these days—which she uses obsessively to shield herself from the sun's damaging rays (even indoors on occasion). When Lindsay sat on the edge of my bed, she whispered, "I have to tell you about Bud."

I gulped. Was I ready to hear about Bud Finger? After everything I've been through? After all, I saw Meri tonight. Yikes! And yesterday, at the airport, Mamacita and I found ourselves victimized by Meri's latest curveball. Oh, why didn't I see it coming? We were both waiting for the plane to be refueled—and then I heard Mamacita scream. I rushed to her side at the departure gate window, where she gestured fiercely. Outside I could see the Sugarman private plane turning onto the runway for takeoff. It was leaving without us. Oh my God, oh my God, oh my God. And Gloria Daily (or was it her twin sister, Gilda?) was in the passenger window. She was waving at us! My phone abruptly vibrated in my pocket. I whipped it out. I had a text message. It read:

TEXT MESSAGE
It's not nice to steal other people's planes. Kiss-kiss. :)
FR: M. Sugarman
NOV. 3, 05:36 p.m.

A mariachi band jingle prompted Mamacita to yank out her cell phone. She had a text message too.

TEXT MESSAGE
You're fired!
FR: M. Sugarman
NOV. 3, 05:37 p.m.

Surprisingly, Mamacita wasn't all that concerned about losing her job as a maid for the Sugarmans. She had clients far and wide, she calmly informed me, and the loss of the Sugarman job—along with the money she accumulated for her charities and foundations by dipping into several Sugarman accounts—would hardly be felt. She was, however, completely outraged by the fact that we had to fly "commercial" back to Rumson. I didn't have any cash on me, and I insisted we ride coach. I didn't want her to spend too much, or be in debt to her for too large an amount, but Mamacita wouldn't hear of it. We flew back on a Delta jet in first class (I've never ridden in first class before!) (they offer you free drinks and a moistened towlette before takeoff!) (the seats are supposed to spread out like a bed, but they felt more like high-class La-Z-Boys to me) (but they were still nice). After take off, Mamacita stepped away to use the bathroom and I began reading Delta's in-flight magazine. A sudden high-pitched alarm made everyone sit up. Luckily, it wasn't an emergency. An angry steward was yanking Mamacita out of the bathroom and grabbing her lit cigar, which apparently tripped the bathroom's smoke alarm.

"All right, all right," Mamacita sneered at the steward. "Jesus, I bet you live for this." Then she plopped down next to me and furiously blurted out, "Meri will crawl over baby skulls to get what she wants! You remember that." Then she took a breath and added (a little more calmly), "You want to know what that girl is up to? And how she's doing it? Follow the money. That's all there is to it."

We continued in silence back to Rumson, and more silence still when she drove me back to Alpha Beta Delta in her vintage 1956 Ferrari 860 Monza. After we pulled up, I couldn't help myself. I thanked her profusely for everything she had done. She took my hand and gripped it tightly. "Fight a bee, sting like a bee. Fight an elephant, kill with an elephant's tusks." I nodded, but I still didn't think I had to "become Meri" to fight Meri. I still don't.

"You're back!" screamed Shanna-Francine when I stepped into the house. *Ka-boom!* She practically crashed into me. Oh, I adore Shanna-Francine. She pulled me into such a warm hug, and then she led me into the kitchen. I couldn't believe my eyes. Dinner was served—and what a dinner! Bobbie Sugar, Lindsay Cunningham, and the rest of the girls had prepared a special "politically inappropriate" dinner for my return. Real chicken, not tofu "chicken," and Coca-Cola and white rice, not brown, and a delicious baby-leek-and-tomato confit. I almost cried. I knew how hard it must have been for Shanna-Francine to sanction the preparation of a nonvegan cruelty-free meal, but she did it just for me. So sweet.

"I'm still president of Alpha Beta Delta," she said smiling, but obviously wearied. "I'm still here. We all are."

"I think we owe Cindy an apology," hollered Bobbie gruffly, but sweetly. She was sitting right next to Shanna-Francine, and I suddenly noticed that they were wearing matching blue-and-red-plaid hunting shirts. It seemed a little odd. I was at least relieved that Shanna-Francine hadn't decided to imitate Bobbie's dyed black Mohawk. Bobbie's a really big girl (her hands are huge!), and she has several nose and lower lip piercings—and a silver tongue stud too—and though she's the first and only lesbian I've come to know so well, I know for a fact that not all lesbians dress or look like her. They probably aren't as devoted to Barbara Cartland romance novels, either, and despite her scary appearance (scary to me at least), she's a really nice girl, so I figured that she and Shanna-Francine were dressed alike because they're such good girlfriends. A few other thoughts skipped through my head, but I batted them away because they kind of grossed me out and I know they're not true. I don't even want to write them down. Besides, what's important is that Bobbie said what I'd longed to hear from all the girls at Alpha Beta Delta.

"We should have believed you, Cindy," she announced huskily. "You were right about Meri. All along."

"It's true, you were," blurted Shanna-Francine. Then she covered her face in shame. "And I wanted to kick you out of the house. Oh God, you must hate me."

My eyes welled with tears. Finally Shanna-Francine, Bobbie, and all the other girls knew that Meri was the crazy one, not me. Lindsay held my hand under the table. Lindsay believed me all along, and I doubt I could have made it this far without her unconditional faith and friendship (and her strength). Of course I forgave everyone, but I knew we weren't out of the woods with Meri yet.

"Has anyone heard from Patty?" I asked. Shanna-Francine shook her head. I turned to Lindsay. "And what about Bud?"

"He has a preliminary hearing this coming Thursday," she gulped. "I talked to Daddy. He said he'd get one of his lawyers to help. He promised. He swore. He said he's doing it for me. But he won't pay Bud's bail. And Bud's parents can't afford it." Then she became short of breath, clumsily excused herself from the table, and ran upstairs to her room. We all sat frozen for a moment. Finally Bobbie said what we were all afraid to even think.

"This doesn't look good, does it?" she asked. "I mean, he down-loaded Hollywood movies and sold them on DVD, right? That's against the law, isn't it?"

She was right, of course. And all of this is happening because Meri snitched on Bud. Yes, what Bud did was illegal, but Meri only knew about Bud's activities because Lindsay was always wearing that bogus tiara (no one knew it had a hidden mic). Meri recorded every conversation between Bud and Lindsay about the DVDs, then handed the tapes over to the FBI, who promptly arrested Bud. Meri wanted to hurt Lindsay by hurting her boyfriend, because Lindsay is my best friend. And it worked. Lindsay is beyond devastated. She's crushed. My cell phone trilled. I looked at the caller ID. It was Mom. Excusing myself from the table, I strolled into the living room.

"Hi, Mom."

"Cindy, thank you," she said firmly, and I knew what she was talking about. She and Dad were back in Ohio, and Lisa was safely under their watch. "Oh, and I have some news. About Dean Pointer." I stood very still. Meri had pulled strings and used the awesome influence of her moneyed and "connected" family to have me booted from RU, and Mom and Dad were supposed to have a conference call about it with the dean today. Mom had promised she'd work everything out. "I'm sorry, but in all the con-fusion with your sister, your father and I had to reschedule our call with the dean until Tuesday afternoon. Don't worry, dear. Everything will be fine. You're not leaving Rumson." Then she chattered amiably about her hairdresser, Billy Sandwich, who gave her a new shag cut, and told me how she'd "saved" her pre-cious African violets by whisking them inside to shield them from an early November frost. Then she hung up. I stood there in shock. I couldn't move. I could still be kicked out of RU, I thought, Meri could still win.

"Meri went to church today," blurted Shanna-Francine, who had stepped in behind me. I nearly leaped out of my skin. "She went with the Campus Evangelical Crusade. They had a special Saturday service honoring Saint Clarus."

"Who's that?" I asked numbly.

"He was some sort of Benedictine monk. One of the Evangelical girls told me about him. Apparently, he rejected the advances of this beautiful noblewoman who wanted to have sex with him—'cause, you know, monks don't have sex—and I guess that really pissed her off."

"Why? What did she do?"

"She had him beheaded. Bam. Chopped his head off. On November fourth. Harsh, huh? Today was his feast day."

"So who was Meri celebrating?" I asked suspiciously. "The saint or the noblewoman?" Meri was up to something. Already. There had to be a reason, I thought, for her to align herself so closely with the Campus Evangelical Crusade (or CEC). I can't imagine she actually enjoys their daily prayer breakfasts and hymnal sing-alongs, and if it turns out that Meri really is born-again, then I swear I'll walk to the nearest church and eat ten candles. I really will. I don't even care if they're lit. Meri doesn't believe in God; Meri believes in Meri.

"You look like you could use a cocktail," said Shanna-Francine, and, truth be told, I did. I hadn't had a beer or a glass of wine or anything for ages. While Bobbie and the rest of the girls did the dinner dishes—with Lindsay still up in her room with her door closed (and probably crying out for Bud)—Shanna-Francine and I strolled to Cahoots, a small off-campus bar with a nice jukebox and a pool table. The air was nippy, so I was glad Mom had sent me a new faux-lamb leather winter coat.

"Do you like my new shirt?" asked Shanna-Francine shyly. "Bobbie bought it for me."

Think fast, I thought, *and don't say what you're really thinking (and don't even want to think).* "It fits you so well," I said. "And I like the patches on the elbows."

"Thanks," she said, then she cleared her throat. "Um, there's something I've been meaning to tell you. About me. About Bobbie and me."

My eyes widened. Did I really want to hear this? And if it was true (I can't even write it), was it catching? Would I become "that way" too? Oh my God, I really do not want to wear manly plaid shirts.

"Hey, Bixby!" a voice screeched, interrupting Shanna-Francine. Saved by the bell, as they say, or in this case, by Doreen Buchnar, aka Bitch Kitty, who even in cold weather was wearing a skintight T-shirt with "Pink in the Middle" scrawled across her ample bosom in red cursive appliqué. She strode right up to me and slapped me across the face. Oh my God. I was too stunned to react. Her face was streaked with tears. She cried out, "I hope you're satisfied. You sleaze! You slagheap! You're nothing but a hobag. Uh-huh. That's it. That's what you are. A big ol' nasty hobag! Yeah. I can smell you from here—and it's raunchy. You're so easy you're remedial!"

Honest, I had no idea what she was talking about (and I'm so not a hobag) (the fact that anyone would even think I am gave me my first good laugh of the day). Shanna-Francine had leaped in between us, and when Doreen tried to take another swing at me, she blocked her with her outstretched arm (which was awfully brave of her) (even manly).

"Doreen, stop it," I wailed. "I didn't do anything. I swear."

"Oh, right. You stand there and lie. Like a hobag. And Keith dumps me for you. You! What did you do? Huh?"

"Doreen, I didn't—"

"It couldn't have been sex, 'cause everyone knows you're a lousy lay!"

Several questions were suddenly buzzing inside my head. Am I a lousy lay? I honestly don't believe that I am (or was). Okay, so I don't know about all the latest slinky sex positions (*Cosmo* seems to "discover" a new one every other week), and yes, occasionally I gagged when I went down on Keith, but jeez, he never went down on me, and what, I'm supposed to be "Miss Pro" or something? We can't all be Jenna Jameson (and, yuck, do we even want to be?). And then I thought, *Wait a minute, Keith dumped Doreen? For me?* That made no sense. I mean, Doreen's head cheerleader at RU, she has a truly astounding rack (I can admit that now) (though I still wish she would wear a bra), and yes, it's true, Keith used to be my boyfriend (I wasn't dreaming), but he dumped me for Doreen. And now, hold on, he's actually dumped Doreen and wants me back? What?

"Doreen, I haven't talked to Keith since the Harvest Ball," I told her as calmly as I knew how. "We talked. That's all."

"About what?" she demanded.

I've always believed that honesty is the best policy. Why should I lie to Doreen? So I told her the truth. Keith wanted to get back together with me. And I said no. That was it.

"You?!" she exclaimed, her eyes popping wide with disbelief. "You said no to Keith?" Then she burst out laughing. She could barely contain herself. "Oh, that's good. That's rich. I'll put that one in the bank. No, no, I know—we'll put it on your tombstone. 'I dumped Keith.' Yeah, right. And Gwyneth Paltrow doesn't sound like a duck. Quack-quack-quack. Hey, have you seen *Shakespeare in Love*? I couldn't understand a fucking word she said. 'I'm s-o-o-o in love . . . quack-quack-quack.' And what's up with her kid? Her name's Apple, right? But I swear, she looks like a cow patty. Hahahahaha. Oh, Cindy. Oh God. You're good. Whoa. Thank you. Phew. Now I know everything's okay." And off she went. She was holding her sides, she was laughing so hard. Shanna-Francine was a bit confused. And who could blame her?

"Do you think Apple looks like a cow patty?" she asked with total sincerity.

"I haven't given it much thought," I said.

At Cahoots, Shanna-Francine and I ordered lemon-drop martinis. They were really good. So good, in fact, that we ordered two more. And jeez, for something as innocent sounding as a lemon-drop martini, they sure packed a punch. I was tipsy. Real tipsy. And for some reason, by the time we moved on to key lime pie martinis (even better than the lemon drops!), we couldn't stop laughing.

"Too much vodka makes me sing," Shanna-Francine squealed. Uh-oh. She started singing along to Madonna on the jukebox. Loudly.

> *Every little thing that you say or do*
> *I'm hung up*
> *I'm hung up on you*

But after a minute or so, I could barely hear her. I went into some sort of warm and plushy trance. I took another sip from my martini. Mmm. Watermelon. When did that happen? I felt myself swaying. I was happy. My body was fluid. Ahhh. I should definitely drink more often. At least on occasion.

I closed my eyes. Keith dumped Doreen. Keith! My love, my sweet, my everything! *Oh, Keith, I'm a big hobag.* That made me smile. I opened my eyes wide. *I am a camera. I can see everything.*

I leisurely scanned right to left; from the far corner, where a bunch of gay-seeming guys were crowded around the jukebox—*ohhh, that explains all the Madonna music*—to the dartboard area, where a guy was pressed up behind a girl and guiding her arm as she attempted to throw a dart—*gosh, I wish I had naturally curly hair like hers (but then who knows if it's actually natural?)*—to the back seating area, where a guy was majorly making out with a girl—*it's so not fair, everyone in this bar has a guy except me, and I only have Shanna-Francine and she's turned into a . . . oh, no . . . no, no, no . . . but she did ask me out for a drink . . . oh, no . . . no, no, no*—to the pool table, where I could barely see anything at all because a girl in spiked brown leather thigh boots and a huge fur coat was blocking my view. She was gracefully curving her body, taking aim with her stick. *Jeez, who wears fur anymore? That's one heck of a floor-length coat. It looks like real sable.* I took another sip from my martini. Then I heard gales of breathy laughter.

"A perfect topspin," cooed a shockingly familiar voice. "And not one scratch the whole game. Aren't I the cutest?"

"Mmm, yer fine," lip-smacked the guy she was playing with. "I could eat you up."

"Munch-munch," she teased. "Don't 'cha know? You can eat all you want and you won't get fat." Then she laughed and laughed. My head was frozen. I couldn't look up from my martini. All I saw was my face fuzzily reflected in the light pinkish liquid. I had the same traumatized expression that soldiers have in old WWII movies—right after they've been shot. *Bam!* Gotcha! My mouth was hanging open, but I couldn't scream. My eyes were wide, but all I could see was my own naked fear. *Meri Sugarman! She's right there in front of you!*

"Anybody got a light?" she inquired in a delicate, whispery voice. *Don't move,* I thought, *don't say a word.* "You? How 'bout you?" My spine thickened like a cold steel rod. *Not much longer now, it'll all be over soon.* "Maybe you?" A hush of a breeze swept over me; it was very cool, infused with the tingly scent of sable and Fleurissimo, Jackie O.'s favorite perfume. "Well, how about it?" she whispered, barely masking a snicker. Her face was mere inches from mine. "Do you have a light?"

I don't know where I got the courage. My head snapped up and I said, all cool and calm, "Do I look like I'm on fire?"

I heard gasps and a few muffled chuckles around me. Only then did I realize that everyone in the bar had stopped what they were doing. All eyes were on Meri and me. They were waiting, hanging on our every word and gesture. Meri moved to speak, but I cut her off. "You can't smoke in this bar," I proclaimed. "It's against the law." That got a smile out of Meri—a slight one—then she moved even closer. Her lips met my ear. She murmured softly, "Then why don't you and I take this outside."

Holy crap! What possessed me? Why did I follow her outside to the narrow dead-end alley behind Cahoots? I closed the bar back door and—*whoosh!*—she was right in my face. "Well?" she snapped impatiently. She was holding out a thickly rolled joint. Lucky for Meri (and me too, probably) I did have a light. I had a book of matches from the coffee shop at the Corpus Christi International Airport ("Freedom lights the way!" it said on the cover, with an American flag beneath it). I nervously lit a match and brought it up to the joint. She took a deep toke and stepped back. She was smiling again—just slightly—and in some odd way, it felt like we were best girlfriends who'd stepped outside to share a doobie (although I'm definitely not the doobie type). She looked me up and down. I looked her up and down too. Who on earth but Meri would wear a floor-length sable coat? It was unbuttoned at the top, revealing a ruby-bejeweled three-tiered necklace, a white strapless La Perla bra, and a peek of her ample bosom (she obviously wasn't wearing a blouse). She took another toke, exhaled luxuriantly, and ran a hand through her thick raven hair. "Here," she said, extending the joint to me. "It's Creeper Weed. The high comes on slowly."

"You know I don't smoke pot."

"Oh, that's right. I forgot." She took another toke and exhaled slowly. "By the way. Did you know? Louis Armstrong smoked pot every day. And John Tesh doesn't." She chuckled. "Good old Satchmo. He smoked it on his porch in Queens. Every morning."

I gasped abruptly. Fear shook through me. It all came flooding back to me in a rush. Patty's hooked on Skinny, Bud Finger's in jail, Lindsay's a wreck, Shanna-Francine's presidency is on thin ice (to say the least), Alpha Beta Delta might be shuttered forever, and I might be kicked out of Rumson—and the cause of it all was standing right in front of me.

"Aw. What's wrong, little bow-wow? You look short of breath. Are you worried about Tuesday? Big day for you, isn't it? Will you stay or will you go? What a question."

"I'm not leaving Rumson, Meri."

She didn't hear me (or didn't care to). She was indulgently brushing her fingertips against her sable collar. "Mmm. I love it when animals die for me. Just think, nearly forty little sables were killed to make this coat. They catch them in steel traps. Isn't that fun? Some of them actually chew off their legs to get loose, but most of them can't move. It takes three days for them to die. Three whole days. After that, if they're still alive, furriers shoot them point-blank in the head, or crack their little skulls with steel clubs. Crack-crack-crack! Now, of course, a lot of furriers do it quicker. Some of them gas the little sables—ten at once, to save time—or they'll just break their little necks. Snap-snap-snap! Or they'll inject insecticide into their hearts. Pop! That makes their little hearts explode. I don't like that method at all. It's too quick. It's too efficient. They haven't suffered enough for me. Once they're dead, they're ready to be skinned. And made into coats. For me. Isn't that a wonderful thing to know?" She took another toke, held it, and her eyes lit up, as if the thrill of dead little sables had suddenly overwhelmed her (or maybe the Creeper Weed had finally creeped). Then she strode up to me, leaned into my face, and said, "Pop! Maybe it'll be that quick for you on Tuesday. I mean, you have suffered enough, haven't you? Or should I use a steel club?"

"I told you, I'm not leaving Rumson." I was determined to stand up for myself. *This time*, I thought, *there's no backing down*. And yet she threw me for a loop when she took another toke and said, "By the way, I sent the bill to your father."

"What bill?" I asked. What was she talking about?

"For the fuel and maintenance. For the plane to Corpus. Count yourself lucky that I'm not pressing charges—I mean, you did steal a plane. It's twenty-five hundred an hour and your bill is around, let's see, twelve thousand, five hundred, before taxes and airport landing fees, of course. But then you can't put a price on your sister's safety, can you? Or your mother's. Or your father's. They're all back in Marietta now. Aw, I bet they miss you. You'll be joining them soon. You'll be home, and I'll be here. And that'll be that. It'll all be over. Finally. Won't that be a relief?"

Don't say a word, I thought, *make her think she's won*. Thinking quick, I deliberately let my shoulders slump. "My suitcases are already packed," I murmured. "Just so you know."

"Are they?" she responded with a eerie, cheerful lilt. "Now, don't you forget to buy a nice Rumson sweatshirt before you go. Oh, and a coffee mug. Cute little mementos to help you remember all our good times."

"Our . . . our what?" I couldn't help myself. And maybe that was a big mistake, but jeez, our good times?

"C'mon. It's been fun. Don't you think?"

"I . . . I . . ." I was tongue-tied. I really didn't know what to say.

"This spring I'm flying to Capistrano," she continued breezily. "I didn't have time last year." Then she gasped and cried out, "Oh! Why didn't I think of it before? You've got to come. Oh, Cindy, you've got to. We'll go together, just you and me. You'll see, there's nothing in the world like watching the swallows return to Capistrano. Will you? Please? Oh, you've got to!"

"I . . . I . . ."

"Promise? Oh, we'll have such a good time. We'll reminisce, and we'll watch the swallows." Before I could answer—and good Lord, what could I have said?—the back door was kicked open, and out stepped the guy she'd been playing pool with. He was definitely the tall, dark, and handsome type (he was at least 6'1", and he had the most gorgeous green eyes), but what I noticed most of all was Meri's complete change of demeanor. She scrunched her face up in a girly manner (I don't think I've ever seen her do that before), then purred, "Hey."

"'Sup," he growled back. Obviously this wasn't going to be a profound conversation. "Gonna go get my truck. You ready?"

"Yeah."

"Cool."

"Awesome."

He sauntered off. Meri gazed after and I followed her eye line right to his butt (or "fascinating fanny" as my grandma used to say) (usually in reference to Paul Newman or Tom Jones). Once he turned the corner, Meri's girly demeanor dropped like a ton of bricks. She flicked her roach to the ground and decisively stubbed it out.

"Don't fuck me over, little bow-wow. If you're not gone first thing Wednesday morning, then I bring out the big guns."

"Wha—what big guns?" I stammered.

"Tsk, Cindy," she chuckled. "You think so deep, yet you miss the obvious." She held up her hand. "Look at my hand. Think of it as a big gun. Ready?" *Kapow!* She smacked me across the face. Really hard. "Get it?" she asked. "It hurts, doesn't it? And that's just a sample."

Jeez, that was the second time in a row I'd been slapped tonight. First Doreen, then Meri, and I guess I just sort of freaked out or something, because without even thinking about it, I slapped her right back. *Bam!* Right in the kisser. Then her leg kicked out and—oh my God—I found myself flat on my back on the ground. Meri was on top of me and, holy crap, her hands were batting and slapping me in the face, in the chest. Ahhhhhh! I brought my arms up defensively. *This can't be happening*, I thought, *it's just too tacky*, and then I thought, *To heck with defensive.* I fought back. I jerked my knees up—*oomph!*—elbowed her neck—*biff!*—and got in a few good cuffs and slaps. Ouch! She pulled my hair, so I pulled back at hers, yanking it with all my might. *So this is what it's come down to*, I thought, *me and Meri brawling in an alley like two roller-derby queens; I have to stop this, it's so not me (I never thought it would be Meri, either, to be quite frank).* But then I heard Mamacita's voice roaring in my head:

"Meri will crawl over baby skulls to get what she wants!" and "Fight a bee, sting like a bee!"

Adrenaline blasted through my body. I fought like Meri. I became Meri. Every strike she made, I struck back twice as hard. She screamed when I ripped a small tuft of raven hair from her head. I had the advantage. I flipped my body up. I was on top of her. I pinned her shoulders down with my hands, leaned in, and wailed at the top of my lungs, "Do you have any idea how tacky this is?"

I was overconfident. I didn't see it coming. Meri's hands slammed the back of my head and forced me down. My lips crushed against hers. And she kissed me! Oh my God, oh my God, oh my God! *This is my nightmare*, I thought, *and it's coming true, and any second now Meri will turn into Fashion Witch and kill me with her double-sided ax.* Ahhhhhhhh! She wouldn't let go, I couldn't push her away. Then I heard gasping laughter and snickers. Meri leaned back. How did I end up with her on top of me again? I craned my neck. The bar back door was swung wide, and a group of guys and girls were hooting and laughing (one guy was grabbing his package) (gross!). They were all turned on by our super-icky lovelock, or maybe they thought we were joking (I hope), or God forbid, so drunk that we had no idea what we were doing.

"Need a third?" one guy cried out. A few others bellowed, "Woo-hoo! Showtime!" and "Pour your beer on 'em!" and I heard a cluster of girls giggling, "Eeeow, her hair's tragic," and "I wouldn't make out with her, would you?" and I knew which one of us they were talking about. Meri leaned into me—oh God, please don't kiss me again—and whispered into my ear.

"Wednesday morning. Pop! You're gone. Get it?" Then she seemed to float up into the air. It took me a sec to realize that the guy she'd played pool with was back, and he was lifting her up with his strong arms. She looked down at me, stifled a smirk. I couldn't move; I didn't dare. When I gazed into her hard blue eyes, I realized that Mamacita was wrong. Dead wrong. Yes, I had become Meri—okay, only briefly—and look where it got me. I was sprawled flat on my back in a filthy back alley next to the Dumpster. This was adult behavior? This was the way to defeat Meri? I don't think so. And how come Meri didn't have the slightest smudge on her face? It was so unfair. Her makeup was absolutely flawless. Her hair was gently fluttering, as if an enchanted ocean breeze had just whipped past (and only for her). Her boyfriend (or boyfriend-for-the-night) put his arm around her waist, and Meri put her own hand in his back pocket (cupping his "fascinating fanny"), and off they went, leaving me shamed and defeated. I felt like crying. Luckily, I was saved from further public humiliation by Shanna-Francine, who picked me up, put her arm protectively around me, and whisked me to the street.

"Are you okay? Did she tongue you?" she squealed, or at least that's what I think she said. I was still so drunk, and so shell-shocked, that I couldn't be sure what I was hearing. As she led me down the street, cold air gripped my body, then—*poof!*—it blew up into the sky, leaving behind slightly warmer air. I felt a rush of panic. What was happening? My face was stung with tiny drops of fluffy moisture. I blinked twice and gazed up at the heavens. A light snow was falling. I laughed involuntarily. It was so beautiful. It was cleansing. *Meri is getting desperate,* I thought. *She has to be. I mean, why else would Meri, who prides herself on the elegant kill, lower herself to a common street brawl in the back alley of an off-campus bar? It's so not her.* At first I didn't realize that I was laughing and twirling around with my arms thrust skyward. Meri is getting desperate!

"Are you okay?" exclaimed Shanna-Francine. I was more than okay. I was thrilled. For some reason, Meri is now scared of me. She's the one who's freaking. Or at least she realizes that we're on common ground now; we're an even match.

Back at Alpha Beta Delta, I straightened myself up with two aspirin and a strong cup of coffee (I knew the coffee wouldn't keep me up all night) (mom's the same way). I needed a plan of action, one far-reaching enough to anticipate Meri's every move, and not just for the next few days. I know come Tuesday morning that I'll still be at Alpha Beta Delta and RU—that's a given—but that's not enough. I have to formulate a definitive plan to permanently barricade Meri from my life and the lives of my friends (who still need my help to escape from all the horrible traps Meri's set) (it's the least I can do!).

I stepped into the bathroom—and laughed bitterly. Reflected back at me was my hair, frizzy like a fright wig, with clumps of mud and God knows what from the back alley Dumpster. I wondered, Was my hair a tragic, outward expression of huge denial, or a devil-may-care symbol of my newfound confidence? (Meri is getting desperate! Woo-hoo!) I decided it was neither and stepped into the shower and used huge dollops of Bobbie's vegan-certified Rice Protein shampoo and conditioner. I rinsed. And I recalled that nasty girl who'd snickered, "I wouldn't make out with her, would you?" Should I be insulted by that, I wondered (as if I would ever make out with her!) (please!), or should I just dismiss it as yet another free-floating insult (I'm certainly used to those)? I looked at my body as the conditioner rinsed down to my toes, my smallish breasts, my too-big hips, my cottage-cheese thighs (that no amount of "miracle" anticellulite cream can get rid of), my flat pancake knees, my clunky, wide feet (they never feel comfortable in heels).

"Oh, stop it!" I said out loud. There's no way I'll ever look like Jessica Alba, so I should just be happy with the way my body is now. Ha. Easier said than done. I felt better when I dried off and wrapped my hair in a turban towel. The bathroom was steamy, and when I stepped into the hallway, I felt a whisper of fresh, tingly air. Ahhh. When I stepped into my room, Lindsay was lying in wait.

"Shanna-Francine told me everything," she yelped, closing the door and jumping onto my bed. "Did she tongue you? Oh my God, I hope not."

"I don't remember," I responded. Just thinking about it again was making me ill.

"Sorry. Sorry. Oh, I hate Meri Sugarman! She's a bitch. She's a scum-sucking pig fucker!"

"Lindsay!" I cried. I've never heard Lindsay use language like that before. Not once.

"Sorry. Sorry. I just . . . I just . . ." Then she cried out for Bud, which is probably what she'd been doing in her room all night. I did my best to calm her down. We talked about her Auntie Christiana's fourteenth-century hennin hat (it probably hasn't left Lindsay's head all night) (she's already developed a nervous habit of covering her mouth with the georgette chiffon during moments of high stress) (and oddly enough, this makes her look even more glamorous than she already is). Then, without warning, she dropped a big bomb. "I have to tell you about Bud." Oh, no. I braced myself. What about Bud? What could Bud Finger—her disgusting, snot-dribbling, übergeek, sex maniac boyfriend, who's lately taken to wearing Capri pants that show off his icky, scrawny legs—have done or said to dear, sweet, innocent Lindsay? She leaned in closer. Just after she and Bud reunited, she told me, and just before the FBI crashed the house and arrested him, he asked her a question that brought her to tears. "He . . . oh my god, you'll never believe," she exclaimed. "He asked me to marry him!" Whoa. Did I just hear what I thought I heard?

"Of course you said no," I snapped without thinking.

Lindsay pouted. "You're being mean."

"I'm sorry. Did you answer him? Did you have time?"

She shrieked joyfully, "I said yes."

"Lindsay!"

"What? Oh, I love Bud Finger. I love him, I love him, I love him."

"Lindsay, you're too young to get married. You both are. You guys are freshmen." I needed any excuse to bring her to her senses, and that one seemed as good as any.

"But what about Reese Witherspoon and Ryan Phillippe?" she protested. "They got married when they were around our age. And Reese is so happy."

I sighed impatiently. I'm not big on referring to celebrities in intimate terms as if they live just down the block or something, but in this instance I decided to follow her lead by saying, "But Ryan is hot. And he's really good with kids. I mean, do you really want to be known as Mrs. Lindsay Finger? And have little baby Fingers with him?"

"Kids," she swooned. "We haven't even talked about kids yet. I hope he wants them. Oh, I know he does."

There was nothing I could say. Obviously, this was a train that had already left the station. But I figured that if anything could stop it, it wouldn't be me, but Lindsay's wealthy, royal Canadian parents, who weren't likely to approve of their royal-born daughter's impending nuptials to one Bud Finger of Marietta, Ohio. "Have you told your parents?" I asked.

"Not yet. Daddy's lawyers are busy helping Bud get out of jail.

Once they do, we'll tell them, and then we'll all celebrate." She blushed. "You know what he gave me?"

"An engagement ring?" I stammered.

"No, no, not yet. We're going to pick that out together. Look, he gave me this. You promise not to make fun of me? Or Bud?"

"I promise," I said, and then she held out a black iPod nano. "He gave you an iPod?" I asked. That didn't seem very exciting.

"It's not just any iPod," she enthused. "It's filled with all the songs he listens to when he thinks about me. There're hundreds of them." Actually, that did seem kind of sweet, but given that this was Bud, there was more. Much more. She pulled out what looked like another iPod; it had a thin wire connecting the two. But it wasn't another iPod. It was an iBuzz. The iBuzz had its own wire with two small, plastic, ribbed balls dangling from it. She placed the ribbed ball thingies in my hand, put the earbuds in my ears, and played Goldfrapp's "Lovely Head." She played it softly at first, then turned up the volume. The rubber thingies started vibrating in my hands in perfect time to the music, and all I could think was, *Good God! I hope she washed these thingies off before putting them in my hands!* I nervously let them drop to the bed.

"You think it's dirty, don't you?" she asked petulantly. Oh, brother. I didn't think it was necessarily "dirty" (which just goes to show how far along I've come these days) (not that I was a prude before, though I was maybe unexposed to a certain degree) (and come to think of it, that wasn't such a bad thing). At worst, I thought it was the most unromantic gift a guy could give to his girlfriend. Ever. Period. Vagina balls that vibrate in sync with your iPod? Yuck. But who am I kidding? Lindsay and Bud are so ridiculously in love they could give each other gift-wrapped rocks and they'd still shriek with delight.

"I think it's nice that he makes you so happy," I said, and I really and truly meant that.

41

"Will you be my bridesmaid?" she asked. That almost brought me to tears. I said I'd be honored—and I would be, or I will be, when she gets married to someone other than Bud Finger, because I don't believe that'll ever happen (but I didn't tell her that). She gave me a sweet kiss on the cheek and swept into the hall to her room, her georgette chiffon trailing after her (and almost seeming to wave at me). My cell phone trilled. I had a text message:

TEXT MESSAGE
I hate you!

This surprised me. It was so blunt. Why would Meri send me such a simpleminded text? Then I saw who it was from:

FR: L. Bixby
NOV. 4, 11:24 p.m.

Okay, so now Lisa hates me. Fine. I suddenly realized how tired I was, but before climbing into bed, I checked my e-mail.

From: <lissa@lissabixby.com>
Date: 4 November
To: <cindybixby@yahoo.com>
Subject: Hate You!

Dear Sis:

How do I hate thee? Ohhhhh, let me count the ways. Like, how dare you interfere with MY career! Don't you know how totally important I am? Don't you know my fans totally depend on me? I bring sunshine and happiness into their blah lives . . . and you dare to interfere? You?!

Dark Cindy

Because of you, dear Sis, I'm back home in Ohio. Ahhhhhhh! I heard my second single, "Touch My Daisy," playing in Chesterfield Mall yesterday, and of course I was mobbed by fans. Everyone wanted my autograph–which I refused to give them unless they bought my CD, and some of them were kinda pissed by that, but yo, there was a Virgin Megastore, like, two feet away from us, and besides, my autographed CD will be worth a whole lot more someday than just my autograph (I'm always thinking of my fans!).

Anyhoo, they also wanted to know WTF I was doing in back in Ohio. I almost told them, "Because my sister is a such a doormat, and she's so jealous of me." But I didn't. Why? Because I'm s-o-o-o-o not a hater. And of course they wanted to know about me and L. Lo (everyone does), and I tried to them explain to them that it's just a silly misunderstanding between me and her security people. "People, listen to me. Fame is, like, hard," I said, but they so didn't get it (how could they?).

After about twenty minutes, Dad grabbed my arm and dragged me to the car. And I'm, like, oh my God, my fans–I s-o-o-o-o-o didn't spend enough time with them (and I bet I could have sold a whole lot more CDs, too). This is all your fault, Sis. Mom and Dad actually want me to take a break from show biz and go back to school for a few months. Can you believe?? Me?? At school?? With ORDINARY people?? You can't just "take a break" from being a star. That's like saying, I think I'll stop being Cleopatra or the Queen of England. Doesn't happen.

This is where you come in. Yes, you can help . . . AND get back into my good graces (and you want that, trust me). You

need to call Mom and Dad now. You must tell them that I've
GOT to go back to Corpus. I laid down my tracks with LLB
for our new single, but they haven't laid down theirs yet,
and I so need to be there when they do. And I've GOT to get
back to Hollywood. I don't belong in Marietta anymore! I'm
not Lisa anymore . . . I'm Lissa! Love me or hate me, Sis,
that's who I am. I can only be m-e-e-e-e-e. And I'm never
gonna stop!

Peace up,
Lissa

From: <cindybixby@yahoo.com>
Date: 4 November
To: <lissa@lissabixby.com>
Subject: RE: Hate You!

Lisa:

First off, I sincerely hope that you'll always be "you,"
because you will always be "Lisa" to me, Mom, and Dad (not
"Lissa"). And that's a good thing.

Second, if Mom and Dad think it's best for you to go back
to school for a while, then do it. Education is important.
Did you know that Claire Danes went to Yale? It's true. And
Julia Stiles went to Columbia. Think how much better your
songs might be if you actually studied music and writing.

Third, I have my own problems, so stop trying to guilt me
into solving yours. I do not need to get back into your
"good graces." I am your SISTER. I am NOT one of your fans.

Listen to your agent. Remember what she said to you in
Corpus? "Time to grow up." That's good advice. Listen to
her, and listen to Mom and Dad from now on too.

Love,
Cindy

When I hit send on my e-mail, I could almost hear Lisa's
screams of fury—how dare I not do what she wants!—but honestly, there's only so much I can do for her from here (and not
much I could do for her even if I was there).

I'm in bed now, and I've just noticed a long scratch down my
right forearm from Meri's back alley attack. It kind of makes me
smile. The scratch is a sign of Meri's desperation. I'm not afraid of
her anymore. Yes, I need to help my friends, and I'm still a little
nervous about Tuesday, but as far as me and Meri go, I think I've
already won. In fact, I know I have.

November 5

Dear Diary:

Sundays are usually a time to unwind at Alpha Beta Delta. But not this Sunday. Since Shanna-Francine is so desperate to prove herself as a worthy president, given all the horrible criticism she's endured from both the campus administration and the campus newspaper (all of it orchestrated by Meri) (of course), nobody in the house was allowed to relax. We had an exhausting, nearly seven-hour emergency meeting. When we sat down in the living room, I noticed that Shanna-Francine and Bobbie were wearing matching houndstooth culottes, Lindsay was wearing her hennin hat, and I was wearing a particularly drab Gap blouse (the only clean one I could find) (I've got to do my laundry this week!), while the rest of the girls looked all too "played out" (a phrase Lisa likes to use) (in reference to me) (obviously). I'm definitely not the sort to put a lot of stock in having the "right look," but I have to say that all the girls of Alpha Beta Delta, myself included, looked pretty darn unfortunate. We were all exhausted, and boy, we sure didn't expect to have to wake up on a Sunday morning and come up with "new ideas" for a "great fund-raiser" to make our house "look good again," but Shanna-Francine was insistent.

"It has to be freakin' out of this world!" she screeched. "We have to blow away what any sorority has ever done." Her hands were shaking, and at one point, Bobbie gently put her hand on her knee, which seemed to calm her down (or at least temporarily). I tried to tell Shanna-Francine that our real goal should be to block Meri from making any more hostile moves against us—that's why we're in this predicament, after all—but she strongly disagreed. So did Bobbie.

"Meri ain't worth a bucket of warm spit," she cried. "When we go in front of that Intersorority Council thingie in December, you think they're gonna give a rat's ass about Meri? Please. Meri who? They're going to be looking at us, and what we've done. We need a hook, damn it. We need big-time ideas!"

"November fifteenth is America Recycles Day," said Lindsay, who was helpfully thumbing through a calendar.

"Not good enough," snapped Shanna-Francine. "What are we going to do, have people dump Coke cans and garbage on our front lawn?"

"Shh, sweetie, calm down," said Bobbie, who again placed her hand on Shanna-Francine's knee.

"Um, November twelfth is National Pizza-with-the-Works-Except-Anchovies Day," said another sister meekly. "I'm totally not kidding."

The other girls, however, were intrigued by Veterans Day on November 11. The holiday could conceivably be combined with another, larger event, which seemed feasible, but nothing satisfied Shanna-Francine. I zoned out after four hours or so. It was noon, and bright light was streaming in through the large picture window. Tamari and Pumpkin Seed were delighted. They were sprawled flat on their backs, paws up, exposing their cute little cat bellies to the sun. *Now that's the life,* I thought. I smiled, and I caught Lindsay watching them and smiling as well. Then her lower lip trembled. She was thinking about Bud again. I began thinking about Patty. Poor Patty. I called her cell phone this morning before breakfast, but all I heard was her unsettling new outgoing message: "Hi. Got a bump? You do? Be right over. Hahahahaha. Who's your biatch!" Then she laughed maniacally before being cut off by a beep. I left her a message, begging her to call me or come see me or anything. I haven't heard a thing from her since.

At dinnertime Lindsay and I strolled across campus toward Long John Silver's. I needed hush puppies bad, and I really didn't care when Lindsay kidded me by saying that they're basically fried fat (I still don't care) (because they're so good!).

"Do you think Bud is thinking about me?" she asked timidly.

"I know he is," I said, and I believed that, because no matter what kind of holding cell Bud is in, I'm sure he's thinking dirty thoughts, and these days Bud's dirty thoughts lead right to Lindsay's doorstep. When he was little, and we were in sixth grade together in Marietta, his thoughts were already gross, though not quite as developed sexually. One day while we were taking a spelling test, he leaned forward from the desk behind me and whispered singsongy into my ear, "Everybody's doin' it, doin' it, doin' it, pickin' their nose and chewin' it, chewin' it, chewin' it." I turned around and yanked on his ear. Surprisingly, he burst into tears. Not so surprisingly, I was the one who had to spend the rest of the afternoon in detention ("She's violent!" he wailed as I was led out of the classroom).

"His preliminary hearing is Thursday," said Lindsay tentatively, and I knew what she was going to ask. She choked back a sob and used the georgette chiffon from her hennin hat to wipe her abruptly tearstained cheeks. "Will you come with me? Please? I can't go alone."

I assured her I would. We continued walking in silence, and after a moment, she retrieved earbuds from beneath her jacket and put them in her ears. I used to think it was strange when I saw people do this, but these days it seems like everyone walks around listening to their iPods; in the grocery store, in classes, even in the ladies' room. I once saw a guy listening to his iPod at a club. He was all by himself in the center of the dance floor—literally dancing to his own beat.

"Oh my God," I yelped, suddenly realizing that Lindsay was doing something else to her own beat. I tugged at her jacket, and when she whipped around, she let out a terrified scream. Purrfect, Meri's humongous Savannah cat, was leaping through the air right at us. In a flash Lindsay was down, and Purrfect was chomping down on the fluttery chiffon from her hennin hat and becoming entangled in her iPod wires. At first I was too stunned to react. Then I decided to reach out and pull the cat off her, but before I could, Purrfect whipped around and let out a fearsome roar, as if he was protecting his kill. I leaped back—and heard gales of laughter.

Breezing forth was Meri, who wore a floral-and-butterfly-patterned Dior jacket, a short black Dior skirt, and brown leather Dior boots with wool lining that peeked through the knee-high laces (obviously, today was some sort of "Dior Day" for Meri, and I fleetingly speculated that her bra and panties were Dior as well). At Meri's side, and laughing right along with her, was a face I recognized all too well. I was instantly chilled to the bone.

It was Nancy Forbes, a twinkly-eyed old lady that Meri met last month while delivering food to the elderly as part of her community service. It was strange. She didn't look so old standing there in front of me—she looked mid-sixties, at the most—and I suddenly realized that I had only seen her once, from a distance, when I was spying on Meri during her banishment to Chappaqua. Still, this was no regular "little old lady." Nancy, I found out, had been convicted of murder. Decades ago a criminal court found her guilty of murdering her fourth husband, the wealthy Benjamin "Binks" Von Huffling. At the time, speculation ran wild that she may have killed all of her former husbands (they were all quite rich and left her their fortunes), but incredibly, her conviction was

later overturned on a technicality. Presently Nancy lives a seemingly quiet life in Ronkonkomo County, where she takes care of her
granddaughter, none other than Eileen Forbes, a psycho ten-year-
old Catholic school girl with pale skin, whiter-than-white hair and
supercreepy pink eyes (she's albino!). Eileen was once charged with
setting off explosives at her former elementary school, and now she
leads a group of treacherous skateboard-riding Catholic school
girls who've become Meri's informal posse (and okay, they use
squirt guns, but they're Super Shooter Aquapack squirt guns that
can blast up to thirty-five feet, and they really hurt) (especially
when you're shot in the head).

"So you're Cindy," said Nancy with a surprisingly frail voice.
"How lovely to finally meet you."

"Get your cat off Lindsay!" I wailed.

Meri smirked. Then, in a deliberately soft, monotone voice, she
said, "Purrfect. No. Bad. Stop." That got a big laugh out of Nancy,
but I didn't think it was funny at all. Lindsay was still screaming in
horror. I insisted again, and Meri finally brought her fingers to her
lips and let loose with a piercing horse whistle. Purrfect leaped up
into the air, and when he did, his claws unwittingly slashed
through Lindsay's hennin hat, and wires ripped loose from her now
torn open coat. *Ka-boink!* Two ribbed vibrating ball thingies
plopped to the ground. Purrfect was thrilled. He pounced on them
and bat them about with his paws. Even Meri's jaw dropped.

"My, my. There are some things I really don't want to know about,"
she said. I ignored her. I was helping Lindsay up. She was in tears,
holding out the tattered remains of her beloved aunt's hennin hat.

"This was from the fourteenth century," she screeched. Then
she fiercely proclaimed her intent to sue Meri for damages.

"Really? Should you? I hear your father's lawyers are already
quite busy," said Meri with a wink. "By the way, what are you guys
doing tonight? Nancy and I are watching a DVD. We bought it.

From the store. Legally." I had to hold Lindsay back from jumping her. Violence against Meri, I already knew, would lead nowhere.

"Golly, you girls need to get ahold of yourselves," added Nancy. She then proceeded to tell us that she had once attended college right here at Rumson U., though she wasn't a sorority girl. "I was on the Rumson Rifle Squad," she said in chirpy voice that bordered on bloodcurdling. "I was on the Double Shot Team. I had me a twelve-gauge shotgun that I aimed at clay targets. They shot up four at a time, and Lord, I tell you, I never missed. Pow-pow-pow-pow! Not once. And don't you know, I still have the gun. It's a beautiful Beretta 682 with a lovely mother-of-pearl handle. I've got bullets for it too. Isn't that nice?" Then she gazed directly at me. "I've been just itchin' to shoot it again. Pop! Isn't that right, Meri? Isn't that how it goes? Pop!"

They both tittered, then strolled arm in arm into the chilly night, winsomely exchanging giggly exclamations: "Pop! Pop!" I shuddered, remembering that Meri had used the word "pop!" to scare me just last night, and yes, to be completely accurate, she was referring to an injection that causes your heart to explode, and not gunfire (like Nancy had), but really, arguing over the difference in my head was only making me more terrified, and more frantic. Why is Meri still hanging out with Nancy?

At Long John's, the hush puppies landed like rocks at the bottom of my stomach. Meri has ruined my comfort food. Lindsay ordered a small salad, but she barely picked at it. Instead, she gazed brokenhearted at her tattered hennin hat, which was plopped like roadkill on the seat cushion next to her. "I'm sure your aunt has other clothes you can wear," I said, breaking the silence. She didn't seem to hear me. She was still looking at the tattered hat. Her face toughened, and when she spoke, her tone was frighteningly severe.

"This time she's gone too far," she said. "This time she'll really pay." Uh-oh. Now I'm actually frightened for Meri (in a good way). By attacking Lindsay's hennin hat—which Lindsay obviously regards as a direct attack on her aunt—Meri had crossed a line. Big mistake, Meri.

When I returned to Alpha Beta Delta, I left another message for Patty on her cell phone. I'm really getting worried. If only I could convince her to go back to rehab. The college has already alerted her parents, but no one can do anything (like file a missing persons report) (she hasn't been gone long enough for that). Before climbing into bed and shutting down my computer, I saw that I had an e-mail waiting for me. I didn't even bother to look at the address. I knew it was from Lisa. I clicked it open.

From: <msugarman@versalinkindustries.com>
Date: 5 November
To: <cindybixby@yahoo.com>
Subject: Hi

Dearest:

It was such a pleasure to run into you tonight, though I am sorry that Purrfect created a bit of a commotion. He's such a rambunctious little thing, and he loves to play! :) But I do feel bad about Lindsay's hat thing (or whatever it was), and I'm of course willing to compensate her.

To that end, I'll speak to Father first thing in the morning and have him waive your plane fees. That way, you'll free up twelve thousand, five hundred dollars in your account (which is what you owed), and you can give it to Lindsay. That should buy her lots of new hats, and hopefully more fashionable ones.

By the way, Nancy was overjoyed to meet you, and guess what? She wants to join us on our trip to Capistrano! Isn't that wonderful? She's never seen the swallows, poor thing. Oh, and more good news, she found her gun. It really does have a mother-of-pearl handle. Sweet. We found her bullets, too, and just to make sure everything was in good working condition, she loaded it and gave it a shot.

I wish you had been there to see it. See, there's this pesky little raccoon who's always sticking its grubby paws in her garbage when she sets it outside to be picked up. She named him Harold. Anyway, she's been battling Harold the Raccoon for the past six months or so, but nothing seems to stop him; she sets traps, she swats with her broom, and yet Harold keeps coming back.

But thanks to you, she remembered her stint with the Rumson Rifle Squad, which compelled her to find her gun tonight and shoot Harold dead. Right between the eyes. Literally. I looked. And in one shot! It was so wonderful to see Nancy relive the joys and accomplishments of her youth, and you should be so proud to know that you alone are responsible for helping her do this.

By the way, I hope you enjoy your last few days at Rumson. And please, if you need any help moving out Wednesday morning— any help at all—please feel free to contact me.

Sincerely,
Meri

P.S. Give my best to all of your friends!

November 6

Dear Diary:

Mom almost hung up on me today! I was really concerned about her upcoming conversation with Dean Pointer tomorrow—my future at Alpha Beta Delta completely depends on it—and yet, she got so snippy with me when I asked her if she was prepared. "Cindy," she admonished. "I'm a former president of Alpha Beta Delta—remember?—and an alumna in good standing. I just wish you'd concentrate on your studies." When I reminded her about Meri, she cut me off. "I've already had a conversation with Mr. Sugarman. So please, Cindy. Enough." That surprised me, and it also made me unbelievably happy (Mom is being proactive on my behalf!), though when I pressed her for details, she cut me off again. "You girls. You both have to stop it. Just stop. Your father and I are up to our eyeballs in your shenanigans. I spent two whole hours on a conference call this morning with a lawyer and both of your sister's representatives. Now, I don't know who the heck this 'L. Lo' person is, but she's working my last nerve with this ridiculous lawsuit."

I almost started laughing, and crying, too. I love Mom. And no, Mom and I are not alike (to say the least), and though some people think she's cold and uncaring (I used to be one of those people), I've since learned that she simply handles things her own way. Everything in her life has to be perfect, and yes, that includes her hair. Especially her hair. "I saw my first gray strand yesterday," she snapped accusingly. "Now that's a fine how-dee-do for a Sunday morning. You girls are turning me gray!" In Mom's world this is a deadly serious issue. She was, after all, a much-sought-after beauty when she was my age, something I cannot relate to, no matter how hard I try (and she's still very beautiful) (by any-one's standard, young or old).

And boy, Lisa's always known how to work it to her own advantage. A few years ago we were all riding in the car, and Mom was chastising Lisa for her bad report card. She took off her sun-glasses, and she was just about to lay down the law when Lisa bolted upright, pointed at Mom's eyes, and screamed at the top of her lungs, "Mom! Oh my God! Fine lines! Fine lines!"

I'd never seen Mom pull a U-ie before, but in what seemed like a flash, she whipped the steering wheel and the whole car spun around violently. Then she gunned it and we flew to Plaza Frontenac (a Mom-preferred shopping mall) (because it has both a Neiman's and a Saks). She ran like a woman possessed (which she was) from one store to the next, pestering every saleswoman to sell her only the finest and most effective eye creams (cost be damned!) (of course). By the time we hit the sixth store, Lisa couldn't take it anymore. She doubled over laughing. When we left, Mom had spent over two thousand dollars (easily). And yes, she had forgotten all about Lisa's bad report card. Back home, I angrily confronted Lisa in her room.

"That was a terrible thing to do," I said. "And by the way, I hope you know you can only pull that once."

"True." She sighed. Then she grinned mischievously. "But guess what? I hear Restyline does wonders for all those gashy little creases around the mouth." She doubled over laughing again. "Oh! Oh, it's just too easy." When Mom got Lisa's next report card, well, let's just say that Mom's mouth looks absolutely flawless.

"Have you called Billy?" I asked Mom on the phone, referring to Billy Sandwich, her trusted hairdresser. If anyone could take care of her single strand of gray hair, it would be Billy. She assured me that she had (he could "squeeze her in" tomorrow) and she thanked me sweetly for suggesting it, then merrily prattled on and on about her garden—her Moroccan sage and hollyberry plants are both doing "quite well." Then she hung up.

I'm so glad I have a mom like Mom! She's so take-charge, and she confronts problems head-on. I'll sleep well tonight. she'll talk to Dean Pointer tomorrow, and then that's it, one (big) problem solved. I'm glad I didn't listen to Mamacita. I'm battling Meri my way.

I tried calling Patty on her cell again (no answer, but I left another message), then I decided to do what Mom told me: concentrate on my studies. I had a report to finish for my Modern Masters class on *Still Life with Woodpecker* by Tom Robbins (I hadn't read Robbins before, but any book that has the nerve to take place inside a pack of Camel cigarettes—really, no joke—is okay by me) (plus the lovemaking scenes are amazing!). I felt sad as I finished up the report. I miss Professor Scott. I finished the report, and I was in the midst of spell-checking when I received an IM. I had forgotten my iChat was on. A cupcake popped up with this message:

 Yer SUCH a meanie! Meanie-meanie-meanie!

I sighed heavily. I really wasn't in the mood.

Lisa, go away.

 Why won't you help me?! Marietta is DUNZO! Get. Me. Out. Of. Here. NOW!!

Lisa, I don't have time.

 Right, cuz yer s-o-o-o-o busy. ROTFL!!

 I'm logging off. Bye.

 Wait!!!

 What? Hurry. And it better be good.

 Oh, it is. Get this. Mom just junked all ur stuff and turned ur room into a sewing room!! Hahahahaha. It's like you never even existed!! Hahahahaha. Cindy who?

** CindyB has logged off and ended this session. **

I hate when Lisa makes me feel bad about myself. I spent the next twenty minutes or so pondering the significance of Mom's actions (where will I sleep when I go home for Christmas?) (I hope she didn't throw any of my books away!). But then I consoled myself with the true and wonderful notion that tomorrow afternoon, Mom will save me. I'm not going anywhere. Which means good ol' Meri will just have to get used to me hanging around (whether she likes it or not).

November 7

Dear Diary:

Oh my God, oh my God, oh my God, oh my God! I've been crying for hours. I just got off the phone with Mom. I can't even write. I don't have time. I have to start packing!

November 8

Dear Diary:

"Today is National Bittersweet Chocolate with Almonds Day," said Meri in a breathy, menacing whisper. "It's also World Kindness Week. Isn't that nice? Now, why don't we all give it a try? Let's be kind."

"Kind?" asked a confused Eileen Forbes, aka Albino Girl, who really did seem to be completely mystified by the word. Meri and Albino Girl were at the front doorstep of Alpha Beta Delta, along with several girls from the St. Eulalia posse who'd just swept up on their Hello Kitty skateboards. Their act of kindness? They decided to help me carry my packed bags and belongings from my room to a gleaming Lexus SUV that Lindsay had rented for the occasion (when I had suggested a small U-Haul, she gasped in horror) (God bless Lindsay). For the life of me, I still don't fully understand what happened on the phone yesterday with Mom and Dean Pointer. He was apparently in no mood to negotiate or even discuss the matter. All he told her was that I had proven to be an ongoing nuisance, as well as a potential danger, to the students and faculty of Rumson. He even mentioned the toilet explosion and the cherry bomb. The only deal he offered Mom, if you can call it that, was this: If I immediately vacated RU, my college record would simply state that I had left of my own accord. At first Mom was "quite put off"—she had been assured by

Mr. Sugarman that his family would not be advocating my dismissal—and yet, when she called Mr. Sugarman after speaking with Dean Pointer, he wouldn't take her calls.

"I can't leave here!" I wailed to Mom on the phone. I was beyond tears. I couldn't believe Meri had won (I still can't).

"Cindy, stop crying and do what Mommy does when she doesn't get her way."

"What's that?"

"Suck it back and think of yourself. Right now you need to continue your education. I've already spoken with Ohio University and Marietta College. I sent them your transcripts, too, and they both—"

This time it was my turn to cut Mom off. Out of nowhere, a brilliant idea popped into my head. Oh my God, it was genius (okay, not "genius," exactly, but considering that I was in total shock, I really do give myself big points for coming up with it). I knew exactly where I wanted to go. It was the only solution. Unfortunately, Mom was not supportive.

"Cindy," she tsked. "Meri Sugarman is not the be-all and end-all. Frankly, I think it's time for you to toddle off and get on with your own life. All right? That's what I think you should do. Period."

"Period?" I shrieked. "There's no period here. Who put it there?"

"Cindy—"

"Toddle off? If you were in my shoes when you were at Alpha Beta Delta, is that what you would have done? You would have just 'toddled off'?"

"Cindy, we're not talking about—"

"You? No, we're not. Because you were beautiful and you were popular and you never once had to—"

"Cindy—"

"You know what it's like to be . . . ." I couldn't speak anymore. I started weeping. How could I make Mom understand? I couldn't let Meri win without a fight. And I couldn't just "think of myself," as Mom had advised. What about dear, sweet Lindsay (and okay, Bud)? And Patty? And Shanna-Francine? And poor Professor Scott? What am I supposed to do? Just "toddle off" and let them deal with all the wreckage that I'm (at least partially) responsible for? Is that the kind of person I should be? Is that what it means to be an adult? Look out for numero uno! Coldhearted Cindy! Feel my thick skin! Ice cubes won't melt in my mouth!

"Cindy, please," said Mom gently. "You know your father thinks you're very beautiful."

"Oh, Mother!" I cried angrily. Couldn't she at least go out on a limb and say she thought I was beautiful too (couldn't she stretch the truth?) (just a bit?) (just once?)? But my anger vanished when I thought, *Okay, you want to be an adult? Fine, then act like one.*

"Mother," I announced firmly, "I've made up my mind. And we're not going to discuss it anymore." I hesitated, and then I added, "Period!" There was dead silence on the other end of the phone. Then I heard soft giggling. "What's so funny?" I demanded.

"Nothing, dear," she said, obviously amused (but by what?) (will people always laugh at me when I try to be adult?). "I guess if you're putting a period on it, then the decision is made. I'll make some calls and arrange everything for tomorrow." Then she prattled on and on about Billy Sandwich, who'd spent more than thirty minutes mixing just the right custom color to use on her single strand of gray hair. Then she hung up.

My "Last Supper" at Alpha Beta Delta was dreary and vegan. Shanna-Francine couldn't stop crying. Lindsay was spitting mad, and also quick to tell me that her father's lawyers were happy to take all the time in the world to sue Meri for destroying her beloved auntie's hennin hat, which is worth "way more than twelve thousand dollars." After dinner I left another message for

Patty on her cell phone and told her where she could find me the next day in case she wanted to visit. Then I began the emotionally difficult task of packing my belongings. Shanna-Francine was too upset to help, but Bobbie did. Thank goodness. She's so strong. She had no problem pulling my half-filled trunk from the top shelf of my closet, and when I wanted to look under my bed, she lifted it right up (perpendicular) (with one hand). She also gave me *A Hazard of Hearts* by Barbara Cartland, which she felt would have special significance for me because the pure and beautiful heroine becomes the property of an evil lord when she's lost in a dice game.

"But guess what?" roared Bobbie. "She triumphs. Just like you will."

That was sweet, and by the time everything was laid out, I told her she could go; I could finish the rest. That's when Lindsay stepped in with a basket of my laundry from the dryer. She wanted to know if I knew yet where I'd be attending college, and when I started to tell her, she clamped her hand over my mouth.

"Write it down," she whispered.

"Lindsay, we're not bugged."

"Says who?"

What a world I live in. I'm 99.9 percent sure that Alpha Beta Delta is not bugged anymore, but just to keep Lindsay calm, I pulled out a blank piece of paper from my official pink-embossed Alpha Beta Delta notebook and wrote down the name of the college. Lindsay's eyes widened in shock.

"Good, huh?" I asked. I knew she'd be proud of me.

"It's perfect," she gasped. Ever paranoid, she leaned over and whispered in my ear, "Don't tell anyone else. No one." Then she swiped the paper from my hand, ripped it into three pieces, and clumsily stuffed it in her mouth.

"Lindsay, I really don't think that's necessary." Poor Lindsay. She had trouble swallowing. Then she began choking. She couldn't breathe. Holy crap! But Lindsay's smart. She ran to the window, flung it open, stuck a finger down her throat, and tossed her tacos, as they say. Gross. Double-gross. A light rain was falling, and when I gazed out the window, I could see Lindsay's gooey little whoopsie pile splashed on the ground two stories down.

"Ha: Let Meri pick through that," cried Lindsay triumphantly. Wow. Lindsay's such a good friend.

Later that night, I sat in my room all alone. My closet was empty, my bags and boxes were packed, my computer was shut down. I left one box of books open so I could put my diary in it before taping it shut in the morning, and when I glanced over at it, the pink book on top caught my eye: *Alpha Beta Delta: Pledge Book. I don't deserve it anymore*, I thought. The bylaws clearly state that you have to return your pledge book to the president of the sorority if you're ever asked to leave the house. *Don't cry*, I thought, *just do what's right*. I picked up the pledge book, strode to Shanna-Francine's room, pushed the door open—and nearly screamed! Holy mackerel! I couldn't believe what I saw. Shanna-Francine was reclining on her bed with Bobbie, and for a split second I was hoping against hope that Bobbie was just giving her mouth-to-mouth resuscitation, but in the next split second I realized that they were way too cozy for that (in their matching rainbow-patterned muscle Ts!).

Sensing my presence, they gasped, swiftly separated, and lunged for textbooks as if they were studying. I jerked my head down. *Look at the nice shag carpeting*, I thought, *don't look at them*. Trembling, I placed the book on Shanna-Francine's dresser and said, "Um, my pledge book. Because I'm leaving." Then I raced down the hall, flew down the stairs, and ran into the kitchen. I needed water. Then I thought, *Okay, why am I so freaked?* It's not like I didn't know, and yet there's a world of difference between "thinking you know" and really and truly knowing. Of course I was shocked. I've never actually seen two girls make out before (yes, of course on TV, but it's not quite the same as seeing it right in front of you with your own two eyes). I don't think I've even read that much about girls making out (or liking each other "that way"), though once in my high school library I flipped through *The Poems and Fragments of Sappho* because I'd heard that Sappho, an ancient Greek poet who lived on the isle of Lesbos in 630 B.C., invented the "literate lyric." I guess I glossed over the fact that many of her poems were about loving and appreciating the beauty of women (though there were poems and fragments about loving men, too), because the language was so striking and heartbreaking and pure. I later learned that "the Sapphic stanza," as it's called, was a major stylistic influence on poets throughout the ages, including Homer, though sadly, a lot of Sappho's work was destroyed by the Catholic Church (they thought she was "whorish"). Pope Gregory VII, who must have been terribly small-minded when it came to literature, even went so far as to burn her poems publicly. So that's as close as I've come to learning anything about real-life lesbians making out or loving each other—which isn't much at all.

"Cindy . . ."

I whirled around, nearly dropping my glass of water. Shanna-Francine was standing meekly in the doorway. Words came speeding out of my mouth: "Oh my God, I'm so sorry. I should have knocked. I'm so rude. I'm so sorry. I was so . . ."

"Grossed out?"

"Um, er . . ." Come to think of it, I had been grossed out. But was there a nice way to say that?

"I tried to tell you," she said shyly. Her chubby cheeks were flush with embarrassment, and her wild, frizzy hair, which always seems to be happily gesturing this way and that (what a prop!), now hung limp, like it, too, was caught with its pants down (so to speak). Shanna-Francine was very brave, and she really did try to take my mind away from the physical aspects of her relationship with Bobbie—or the notion of her and Bobbie making out (yuck!)—and instead talked in very simple terms about love. "We're just like anyone else," she explained. "You know, like, uh, let's see. Oh, I know, like Bud and Lindsay." She must have seen me gape, because she promptly corrected, "Right, okay. Just Lindsay. But you know what—"

"I know what you mean," I said. She smiled, then she gave me back the pledge book.

"You're not leaving," she insisted. "This whole thing, it's just temporary."

"Damn right it's temporary!" hollered Bobbie, who strode manfully up to Shanna-Francine's side. "You're gonna win this one, Cindy. You hear me? You're a winner. You're shit in high cotton."

"I'm what?"

"You'll blow the crap out of that Sugarman bitch and lay her flat—and we're here to help you."

I nearly fell over from the force of Bobbie's enthusiasm. I still don't understand what Shanna-Francine sees in Bobbie physically (or any girl for that matter), but let's face it, if Bobbie were a guy, she'd make one heck of a supportive boyfriend, and that made me happy for both of them.

I cried softly in bed that night, and when I woke up this morning, I was drained of emotion. *Just move and it'll all be over*, I thought. I didn't even blink (too much) when Meri, Albino Girl and the St. Eulalia posse showed up to "kindly" help me transport my belongings to Lindsay's rented Lexus. Shanna-Francine stayed in her room with her door shut because, as Bobbie loudly explained, "She's just so damn sensitive."

"Everything's packed," said Lindsay, who gently took my hand, opened the front door, popped open her Anna Sui dragon-bird-and-pagoda "chinoise fantasy" patterned umbrella, and led me outside. That's when it hit me. And how could it not? Everyone was there. A large crowd of RU students had gathered to witness my forced departure from Alpha Beta Delta. I barely took one step forward when Nester Damon leaped forth—flash!—and took my picture. Then Randy O. Templeton peppered me with questions.

"Do you feel like a total loser? Is this, like, the biggest bummer of your life or what? Are you really going to Capistrano with Meri?"

Thank goodness for Lindsay. She snap-closed her umbrella and poked him hard in the tummy, causing him to stumble back and wail like a baby. I kept moving forward to the Lexus, and I tried to keep my eyes on the ground but I couldn't help it, I looked up, and I saw Dean Pointer standing at the curb, his mouth curled in a sneer, and Bitch Kitty, who was bobbing up and down above the crowd to get a better look, and as a concession to the cold (I'm guessing), she wore a pink Spencer jacket that was nevertheless open enough to reveal her tight T with "It's Not Because of the Cold!" scrawled in red appliqué across her bouncing braless bosom. Significantly, Keith was not at her side (did they really break up?). Tears welled in my eyes when I finally did see him. He was shivering and clutching Rags close to his side, and he looked so upset, which only made my situation hit home even more—like a punch in the gut. *I'm actually being kicked to the curb*, I thought. *This is really happening.*

A high-pitched voice abruptly cried out, "This is a lousy crock!" It was Sebastian, who began loudly singing "Don't Cry for Me, Argentina" from *Evita* with his Drama Club friends, though they changed the words:

> *Don't cry for us, Cindy Bixby!*
> *The truth is we'll always love you!*
> *And we'll hate Meri, cause she's a cheap whore*
> *Don't keep your distance, we think you're top-drawer!*

As I neared the Lexus, I smelled Aquanet. A gentle voice intoned, "Shh. Whisper thy name." I nearly gasped. Rushing to my side was none other than Sheila Farr, who looked lovelier than ever in a musket-colored velveteen walking coat with ermine trim, which matched the trim on her oversize black garrison cap, black gloves, and faux-mink muff.

"Miss Farr . . ."

"Sheila to you, my dear. And remember, when they cast me from the studio after calling me 'box-office poison,' I had my revenge, I had my triumph."

"Thank you, Sheila."

Dean Pointer suddenly elbowed his way forth and sneered, "Mizzz Bixby. Your Mother still hasn't told us where to forward your academic records. Perhaps you could enlighten me." In a flash Meri appeared at his side, and she seemed all too eager to hear my answer. But Lindsay jumped in for me.

"Speak to her mom. And move the crowd back, would you? What is this, a clambake? How are we supposed to drive out of here when the road's blocked by all this riffraff?"

Dean Pointer is not a man who likes to be told what to do, and he bristled at Lindsay's firm tone, but jeez, she had a point. The gawking crowd was growing so large and out of control that some people were actually standing on the second-story ledge of the house next door in order to get a better view. Even the Campus Evangelical Crusade was getting jostled (they were on their knees praying for my damned soul). I felt so small, so vulnerable—I was shrinking beneath Lindsay's umbrella—so I barely heard Dean Pointer's booming voice when he ordered the throng to clear the street. All I knew was that Lindsay and I now had a clear path to the Lexus. *Run*, I thought. But then a hand gripped my arm. It was Meri, who leaned in close and whispered delicately in my ear, "Don't worry. I'll find out everything." Then she slipped something into my hands. It was a Lindt Surfin Bittersweet Bar with Almonds. "The Swiss make the best chocolate," she cooed.

The next thing I knew, I was in the Lexus. Lindsay hit the gas and we were off. I turned around, and the last thing I saw was Meri. She was standing in the center of the road, smiling complacently and using her entire arm to broadly wave good-bye—like a queen perched atop her castle and benignly gesturing to a gathered crowd of lowly serfs and dirty peasants—while Albino Girl and the St. Eulalia posse whirled around her on their Hello Kitty skateboards.

"You can cry now," said Lindsay gently. "It's okay. Meri will never know."

Oddly enough, I didn't feel like crying. I didn't feel anything. I was in shock. All my dreams seemed to be vanishing; my hopes of graduating from RU and from the same sorority as Mom, and all my pie-in-the-sky dreams of finding true love. *Oh, please, don't take that away!* Wasn't my future supposed to be brighter than my loser-ish past? I glanced at the Swiss chocolate bar in my hands, then set it on the dashboard and angrily pounded it with my fist (which was pretty dumb on my part, because I bet it would have tasted good).

"Hold on!" screamed Lindsay, startling me out of my reverie. She whipped the wheel, veered into the next lane, then took a hard left. I had no idea what was going on until I looked in the rearview mirror. Oh my God. We were being followed by Albino Girl and the Saint Eulalia posse, who were getting dangerously close to the Lexus on their skateboards.

"Lindsay, be careful," I shouted. "They're little girls." The last thing I needed, I thought, were parents crying foul because of their daughters' scraped knees or sprained ankles. But Lindsay wouldn't listen—the girls, she cried, had probably been ordered to follow us by Meri. Luckily, when she hightailed it around the next street corner, we were safe. I looked in the rearview mirror again, and nothing—*poof!*—they were gone. We both laughed with relief; what a day it had been so far.

Lindsay sped onto the freeway and right over to the fast lane, and jeez, I know the fast lane means going faster than fifty-five miles an hour, but Lindsay had to have been going at least seventy-five or eighty (which I didn't think was very safe) (but I didn't say anything) (and I had my seat belt on) (thank goodness). We were both confused when we suddenly heard cars honking frantically. I turned around. The nearest car in our lane was a good two or three car lengths away, so we weren't going too slow in the fast lane, and yet the car honks kept blasting. I sort of freaked out.

"Maybe we're leaking gas," I shrieked. "Oh my God, we're going to explode." Okay, that was silly on my part, I was hysterical, but given the day, and my paranoid state, I really thought it might be possible. I so didn't want to explode, and I thought, *Who knows what Meri or her posse might have done to the Lexus (or the gas tank)*. Lindsay ignored my outbursts, but with the car honks still blasting, I begged her to please-oh-please pull out of the fast lane. She veered quickly to her right, and when I looked behind, my heart fell to my stomach. *I do not believe what I am seeing.* The Lexus SUV is elevated, so when I glanced around before, I couldn't see what was directly behind us, or more to the point, directly below, but now that we were turning so quickly at an angle, the rope attached to the SUV's bumper was at an angle too, and it strung out taut to Albino Girl, who clutched it maniacally while riding her skateboard on the freeway! Lindsay must have seen it at the same time I did, because without missing a beat, we both screamed, "Ahhhhhhhhh!"

"Slow down," I wailed. But she couldn't. We now had so many fast-moving cars crowded around us that we were boxed in. If we slowed down, we'd put Albino Girl at risk of being smashed from behind. If we went even faster, or tried to change lanes, she might lose her grip on the rope. I knew what I had to do, and I still can't believe I did it—but I just couldn't have a dead Albino Girl on my conscience. I flung off my seat belt and crawled clumsily over the seat and into the back cab. Then I gathered my courage—*please God, oh, please*—clicked open the back cab door, which flung open violently from the force of the wind, laid myself flat, and hoped against hope that I wouldn't tumble out of the Lexus. I reached down to the bumper and grabbed hold of the rope. I looked up, and I could see Albino Girl; her jaw was dropping in horror. Oh, no, I realized, she thinks I'm going to untie the rope or cut her loose and let her fend for herself. But I held her eye, trying to reassure her, as I very slowly pulled the rope closer to the SUV. Slowly, slowly; closer, closer. In less than a minute—one of the scariest minutes of my life—she was right below me, right near the bumper, and she was wailing and shaking uncontrollably, and I think I was too. "Don't let go!" I screeched, but who knows if she heard me. *Please God*, I thought, *give me as much upper body strength as a guy, or at least as much as Bobbie*, and then my adrenaline burst like a dam and I yanked with all my might, screaming at the top of my lungs as I fell backward into the van. When I opened my eyes, I bore witness to a horrifying sight: Albino Girl's Hello Kitty skateboard flipped up ten feet in the air, then slapped onto the freeway, where it was run over by an oncoming car. Then it shot up from behind the car, smashed against the guardrail, and tumbled into an adjoining ditch. I screamed again. *What have I done?* I thought. Then I heard the flick of a lighter. Huh? I jerked around. Albino Girl was right next to me, cool as a lead pipe, lighting a Kool menthol cigarette.

"'Sup," she said. "Now that I'm here, where are you guys going? You might as well tell me." I acted on instinct. I slapped the cigarette out of her mouth. She's just a little girl, and everyone knows that cigarettes stunt your growth (and who knows what they might do to you if you're an albino). Then I reached past her and slammed the cab door shut.

"You could have been killed out there," I scolded. She faux-gasped.

"No. Really? Oh my God, is the Pope Catholic? Do bears shit in the woods?"

"Listen to me—"

"Is the bear Catholic? Does the Pope shit in the woods?"

"Hey—"

"Tell me, do they really grow corn in Iowa?" She snickered. I peered at her closely. When did little girls become so coarse?

"Meri made you do this, didn't she?" I asked.

"Gee, you're sharp as a tack, aren't you?" she snorted. "So c'mon, where are we going? I've got T-ball practice today and s-o-o-o-o many other things to do before that." Not only was she coarse, she was impatient. And I had no intention of telling her, or rather Meri, where I was going. Why the heck should I? I told Lindsay to turn off the freeway and pull over to the nearest bus stop, where I ordered Albino Girl to give me her cell phone; either that or we would abandon her. She reluctantly handed it over, and after searching through her contacts and finding the right number, I hit speed-dial.

"Where is she?" a familiar, breathy voice asked urgently.

"Hi, Meri, it's Cindy." There was the merest pause after I said that, and then:

"Why, hello there, Cindy, I was just thinking about you. Guess what? I locked in the tickets for Capistrano—just ten minutes ago. Isn't that wonderful? Where should I send yours?" Nice try, Meri, but no tomato. I told her exactly where I'd be leaving Albino Girl and made her promise to come pick her up.

"What a nuisance for you," she tsked. "Wait, I know, why don't

71

you continue driving to your destination and I'll pick her up from there. Then we can all get lunch. A nice spa lunch. Wouldn't that be nice? I have MapQuest on my phone. What's the address?"

"Meri, your little friend is at the corner of Thornhill Drive and Timber Lane, just off the 10. She'll be waiting for you at the bus stop."

"Cindy, wait!"

I clicked off, handed the phone to Albino Girl, and told her she could call my cell phone if Meri didn't show up within thirty minutes. To my surprise, she burst into tears. "Are you guys serious? You're leaving me here?" she wailed. My heart sank.

"Faker," scoffed Lindsay. Albino Girl abruptly stopped the blubbering, whipped out a Kool, and torched it with her lighter.

"Some people fall for it." She shrugged. I'd had enough. I once more slapped the cigarette out of her mouth, then grabbed her pack. "What are you doing?!" she shrieked. I threw the pack to the ground and stomped on it (several times).

"Smoking is bad for you," I told her.

"Yeah?" she seethed. "Well, so is sunshine." Then she flew through the air and made a fierce swipe for Lindsay's Anna Sui umbrella. Lindsay gasped and leaped back, but too late. Albino Girl had already mangled one of the umbrella's metal ribs before I could grab her and hold her back.

"Stop it," I demanded. She wriggled ferociously to get loose, and honest, I've never heard such gutter language in my entire life (not even on late-night cable) (not that I watch much, but still). As Lindsay and I drove off, and Albino Girl kept shouting and swearing, I wondered what kind of home life she had, and if there was anything anyone could do to help her. I mean, she's so young, so she can't be a total lost cause (though maybe she will be if she keeps hanging out with Meri). I've always believed in the inherent goodness of everyone around me (especially children), though a lot of philosophers would probably disagree with me, like Jean-Jacques Rousseau, a French philosopher from the 1700s who I absolutely loved reading at first because he wrote "man is good by nature," "a noble savage," but then I kept reading and was shocked when he concluded his thoughts by declaring that man's goodness doesn't stand a chance in the long run; we're all corrupted by society. "Man was born free, but everywhere he is in chains," he said, which isn't a terribly optimistic sentiment, but then the French can be such killjoys sometimes (though maybe it wasn't all Rousseau's fault, because a lot of people didn't like his books so they kept stoning his house) (which is bound to make anyone a killjoy).

"It was limited edition," Lindsay sniffled, placing her hand gently on her mangled Anna Sui umbrella. I didn't know what to say, but I instinctively put my hand on the umbrella too (and hoped she wouldn't want to bury it or anything like that). Then she turned the wheel and we pulled onto the grounds of the campus and right up to my blocky nondescript dorm building. My body tightened—I think I was even sweating—but I knew I was making the right decision (even if Mom still has her doubts).

"Do you want me to come inside with you?" asked Lindsay. I knew she would if asked her to, but the noonday sun was shining so brightly, and I could already see that her anxiety was rising at the thought of stepping out of the Lexus. I assured her I'd be fine, and I promised that I'd call her once I was settled in. *Be brave,* I thought, as I pulled my belongings from the Lexus and stepped into the glaring sunlight. The air was bone dry, and when Lindsay pulled away, a puff of gritty dust blew up around me. I coughed several times, and though I could say that the dust in my eyes is what made tears streak down my cheeks, that would be a lie.

I'm in bed now. I'm having trouble get a signal on my cell phone out here, but I did manage to reach Mom and have her go ahead and forward my records from Rumson. I checked in with the administration office too. Everything's squared away. I start classes tomorrow. The lone dorm building here is very small. Most students commute from home.

I'm cold. There's not much heat in my room, which looks like a jail cell with its concrete walls, metal sink, and single bed. There's not even a desk, much less a cord to hook up to the Internet. There's no TV, either, though I guess I could get one of those little tummy TVs (even though there's nothing I really want to watch) (except for *Project Runway*). I'm starting to get depressed, but one thing cheers me up. When I told Lindsay where I was going last night, she gasped, "It's perfect." And it is. Because in order to bring down Meri, I need to be near Meri—and near Rumson and Alpha Beta Delta, too. Dean Pointer's probably told her where I am by now. Fine. Maybe she'll have a good laugh. But maybe not. Because I'm exactly where Meri was when she was banished from Rumson. I'm at Chappaqua Community College in Ronkonkomo County.

Oh my God, oh my God, oh my God. I was asleep for only a few hours when my cell phone rang. I was barely awake, but when I heard who was on the other end of the line, my brain snapped to attention.

"Axis I delirium caused by substance abuse leads to a reduced level of consciousness and a fractured psychomotor."

"Patty?" I yelped. "Where are you?" There was no answer, but I could tell she was outside; I could hear the hum of traffic, and her own scary, rapid breathing. "Patty?" I insisted. "Oh, please answer me."

Then she spoke rat-a-tat fast: "Dyskinesia causes involuntary muscle activity, which is different from dystonia, which leads to seizures, heart failure, even death." For some reason, this made her burst out laughing. Then I heard a loud clunk. She must have dropped the phone. I could still hear her high-pitched squeals and chuckles. I screamed, "Patty, pick up the phone. Please!" I started to panic. I had no idea where she was—maybe she was in a dangerous back alley, or strolling alongside a busy highway. I kept crying out her name, hoping she'd hear my voice. Then I heard another rustling sound. She'd grabbed the phone (thank God) (my screaming must have worked) and she was whispering intently and very fast, "Methamphetamine addiction causes the patient to feel insanely happy, tireless, powerful—mimicking, and commonly inducing, bipolar I disorder, auditory hallucinations, and persistent schizotypal psychosis not otherwise specified."

A chill ran up my spine. Patty was diagnosing herself. I covered my mouth in shock. I felt a lump in my throat. Despite her affliction, she was bravely fighting to gain control—to analyze herself, to help herself. But could she? "Where are you?" I asked softly. I didn't want her to hang up. I had to be careful.

"Never turn your back on a drug," she whispered. "Especially when it's waving a razor-sharp hunting knife in your eye." I gasped. I recognized her words immediately. She was quoting from *Fear and Loathing in Las Vegas* by Hunter S. Thompson. She was trying to speak to me—in my language, the language of books and literature—and I realized I had to respond in a way that would give her real hope (and real strength) for the future. The words rushed out of my mouth. I quoted Maya Angelou: "History, despite its wrenching pain, cannot be unlived, but if faced with courage, need not be lived again."

Unfortunately, she didn't seem to get it. She tittered and blurted out yet another quote from Hunter S. Thompson: "I hate to advocate drugs, but frankly, they've always worked for me!" That sent her into another spastic fit of giggles.

"Patty, where are you?" I pleaded.

"Suffering knocks at your door," she sputtered between chuckles.

"What? What does that mean?"

"Door-door-door," she said in a singsongy fashion. "When suffering knocks at your door and you say there is no seat for him, he tells you not to worry because he has brought his own stool."

I was astounded. Again, Patty was trying to communicate with me in the language of literature. She was quoting from novelist Chinua Achebe, whose 1958 masterpiece, *Things Fall Apart*, is regarded by many as the Nigerian *Heart of Darkness* (which is a valid comparison, I guess, though I really do prefer Achebe, given his darkly elegant and deceptively simple prose)—and yet, why was Patty using this particular quote? It just didn't make sense. I was startled by a sudden *boom-boom-boom!* From the door. My door. Ugh. Okay, sometimes I really am a birdbrain (and slow on the uptake, too) (needless to say). I raced for the door, swung it open—and tried not to scream. Patty was a wreck. There's no nicer way to put it. She practically fell into my arms. I guided her gently to the bed (there's nowhere else to sit in here). Her weight loss was alarming. She was still a bit overweight (by *Maxim* standards), but she had definitely slimmed down, and it looked creepy and unnatural. Her eyes were hollowed out too, and her teeth were crusty and brown, and she kept snapping them together and grinding them. *Snap-grind, snap-grind.* If ever I needed a warning not to do hard drugs like crystal meth (though I don't), this was it. Suffering had indeed knocked at my door. I forced a smile.

"Gosh, who knew you were so well-read," I murmured like a dimbo. Then she bolted up, whirled around in a circle, and raced for the door.

"Gotta go, gotta go, gotta go," she tittered. *Holy moly*, I thought, *I can't let her out of this room, I've got to think of something—quick, hurry*—then, bingo, I had the answer, because no matter how disturbed Patty may be, there's one part of her brain that will always be active and responsive.

"Patty, wait," I cried. "I had a dream last week. On an airplane. And I have no idea what it means. And it was so scary. Really scary." She stopped cold; her hand was just reaching for the doorknob. She whispered in the darkness, "Dreams are the royal road to the unconscious."

"That's right. They are. And, oh, boy, I had a doozy. Phew. Wait till you hear it."

"In order to properly analyze dreams, a psychotherapist must be well versed in literature and art and religion and music, in addition to traditional psychological schooling."

"Oh, I'm sure. No wonder you're so well-read. And gosh, wait till you hear my dream. Wow. It's really nutty." Slowly she turned back around—hooray!—and her eyes were lit up. She was more than curious, she was glowing with unholy delight. She had taken the bait. She sat on the bed and eagerly instructed me to start at the beginning. So I told her about being on a plane, and that awful tornado that was headed right toward me just outside my window.

"Common, very common," she tsked. "The tornado symbolizes all of your emotions spinning out of control—your unresolved obstacles. But the fact that you're on a plane indicates a strong desire to overcome these obstacles and 'fly up,' so to speak, to a new level. Mmm. Good, good. Go on." When I told her about the raccoon that ran between my legs, she said, "Oh, yes. Interesting. Down through the ages, the raccoon has stood for deception, a warning that people are presenting false faces to you."

"Like Meri?" I gasped.

"Possibly, but let's not go there yet. Continue." Next I told her about seeing a dead baby at my feet (that part of the dream really did freak me out). "Ah," she said, her eyes narrowing. "A wonderful old chestnut. Very archetypal. The baby is you. Or a part of you. Loss of innocence. The death of childhood. The entry to adulthood. Yes. Mmm-hmm. Very clear." I was speech-less. I never would have looked at the dead baby that way, but it made sense (a lot of sense). Patty's so smart!

"After that," I said, "I saw a bunch of aerosol cans spinning around and spraying all on their own." She stifled a snicker. "What?" I asked. I really didn't see what was so funny.

"Oh, come on, Cindy. They're long, they're hard."

"You mean . . . ?"

"Yes, Cindy. They're penises. Of course. Perfectly normal, free-floating, erotic dream imagery. And the fact that they were 'spray-ing' . . ."

"Okay. Fine. I get it." Gross. I sure as heck didn't want that one spelled out any closer. "After that I saw a golf club."

"Right," she chuckled. "Penis. Go on." I was stymied for a moment. Was my dream really so obvious (and so smutty)?

"I also saw a fishing pole."

"Penis," she said, stifling a yawn.

"Um, then I saw a screwdriver, a telescope, a wrench . . ."

"Penis, penis, penis."

"And a long toy train." She rolled her eyes.

"Mmm-hmm."

"Then a syringe, a necktie, a drill."

"Oh, man. Your dream's throwing the book at you."

"There was also a cluster of French bread loaves."

"Well, well," she tittered. "Many penises at once. And they're French. Oooh la la!" She doubled over laughing, then quickly composed herself. "Sorry. Totally unprofessional. Go on."

"I saw a large spinning globe, too. Now I know that's not a penis."

"No, it's not. It's your world spinning out of control. Obvious. Go on."

"After that, I went to the bathroom. . . ."

"Of course. A place to purify, to cleanse."

"And Keith was there. He was naked. He kissed me."

"Tsk. Poor Cindy. Still not over Keith."

I hesitated.

"Keep going," she said. "You won't shock me."

"Keith wasn't there anymore. It was Meri. She was naked. She was kissing me. I couldn't get away."

"Interesting. The 'kiss of death,' as they say. A warning to be vigilant around a person who intends to harm you. But you already knew that."

I hesitated again. I just couldn't bring myself to tell her the next part, so instead I said, "You know, she really did kiss me. Later. In a back alley. To scare me."

"Okay." She shrugged. "And I'm sure that was very unpleasant for you. But dreams aren't prophetic, Cindy, if that's what you're thinking."

"Yeah, but . . ."

"Dreams are not prophetic. Okay? That's magical thinking. We've talked about this. Magical thinking is a belief that your own words or thoughts can 'magically' produce a specific outcome. Ergo, you dream something, it happens, so you think you've caused it. But you know that's not true."

"Right, but . . ."

"Shh. Absorb. Process. Now, hands on your knees, back straight. Ready? Inhale. Hold. Now exhale. Ahhh. Feel better? Good. Now, we've strayed off topic. I sense evasiveness. Please don't be afraid, Cindy. We're in a safe space. What happened next?"

I gulped. The only way to get it out was to blurt it out: After Meri kissed me, I said, I dreamed that Lisa kissed me. "Oh, I see," she said, gently taking my hand. "Listen to me. Your sister in your dream is not, I repeat not, your real sister. But the vision you had of her does represent a conscious or unconscious belief that you have." I didn't get what she was saying, and she could tell. "All right, try this. How do you feel about Lisa? Normally?"

"Normally? Um, I guess I feel ridiculed by her," I said (which is so true). "And, I don't know, responsible for her too." She let my words hang in the air, then she smiled and said, "There you go."

"What? That's it?"

"Mmm-hmm, that's it. Your dream is putting her right in your face—literally—and your mind is saying, whoa, hold on. I'm not responsible, and I don't deserve to be ridiculed, either. Pretty straightforward stuff." That was a relief. I was so happy to know that it wasn't anything icky. I told her about the rest of my dream too—the plane exploding, the cigar (and yes, that was a you-know-what again), being sucked into the tornado, and trying to get away from Meri, and how I grew younger and younger until I was a baby. "Oh, wonderful!" she enthused, catching me off guard. "The birth of a new self. The adult self. Free of innocence and ready to confront life's obstacles anew. This is very good, Cindy. Your dream may be traumatic, but it's also telling you that you're ready to take brave new initiative in your conscious life."

"But I don't want to lose my innocence," I exclaimed without thinking.

"Mmm. Let's examine that. Let's look at your associations with innocence. What does innocence really mean to you?"

"It means, I don't know . . ." I grappled with my thoughts. "It means . . ."

"Hold on, hold on," she commanded. Then something strange happened. Her shoulders dropped abruptly, her body quivered. Then she murmured hazily, "I'm afraid that's all we have time for today. . . ."

Boom. She fell backward flat across the bed. Vertically. She was out. *She needs sleep*, I thought, *and tomorrow morning I'll take her back to RU's rehab center and she'll get better. Finally.* Just thinking about that made me so happy. I was pretty zonked myself, so I stretched out on the bed (not too much, though, because I didn't want to hit her), and I was just about to fall asleep when I heard her mumble, "So tell me, is your insurance an HMO or a PPO? Substance abuse sometimes leads to pulmonary disease." She was diagnosing herself again. Or that's what it sounded like. I slept for a few hours (not very well). A cold, shuddering breeze woke me up. My door was swinging wide. Patty was gone. I blinked twice to make sure I wasn't dreaming. Was she even here before? Oh God, I don't know how I'm going to get back to sleep.

November 9

Dear Diary:

I had casual sex tonight with a guy I don't even know, and I'll probably never see him again. Ha! And it was great! I really and truly enjoyed myself (if Mom and Dad ever read this diary I'm dead). It's definitely not something I'll ever do again (I don't think) (and despite what Bitch Kitty may think, I am so not a hobag) (though I was tonight) (technically), but given the day I had today, I think I deserved a little reward. Things started off with a bang, so to speak, and not in a good way. I took two steps into my first class, Literature 101 (an elemental lit class, but it's the only one they offer here), and froze in horror. I felt physically pained, as if someone had just thrown a pot of coffee right in my face, because standing at the head of the class was none other than Professor Scott. *Oh no*, I thought, *so this is where he went after I caused him to get booted from Rumson.*

I tried to be inconspicuous. I tried to spare him (and myself) by lowering my head and discreetly slinking to a seat in the very last row, which I would normally never do (I'm always in the front row, and I really don't give a flip when people say that makes me a suck-up; I want to be able to hear the instructor and have a clear, unobstructed view of the chalkboard). But darn it, right when I sat down, I looked up just as Professor Scott looked up, and we both squelched a gasp. I knew what he was thinking. "There's the dirty little double-dealer. There sits Judas." Oh God, I felt so horrible, and yes, completely bored by his "beginners" lecture on *The Scarlet Letter* (tailored for the class) (of course).

"Hester Prynne wore the letter *A*," he droned. "Can anyone tell me what the *A* stood for?" Unfortunately, this didn't quite get the response he had hoped for. A dopey-looking jock type called out, "Action! Heh-heh."

Another said, "Alfalfa? Alimony?" while yet another screamed, "Athletic supporter!" That elicited a blast of snot-filled snorts and chuckles. The class was out of control. I felt so bad for Professor Scott. I had to help. I raised my hand.

"You there," said Professor Scott, "way in the back with your head bowed down. Do you know the answer?"

I gulped and mumbled, "Um, the *A* stands for adulteress."

"That is correct," he responded with a cold snap. "Adulteress."

Thwack! I was beaned in the head by something hard and sticky. I discreetly reached into my hair and tore it out. Gross. It was a gooey chewed-up Tootsie Roll. Professor Scott stalked toward the back, directing his words at me frostily.

"*The Scarlet Letter* is a novel of betrayal," he continued. "In Chapter Fifteen, Hester believes Chillingworth's betrayal is greater than hers. Agree or disagree?"

And on he went, putting special emphasis on the word "betrayal" and fixing me with a bitter scowl whenever he did. The class, however, was more interested in discussing the Demi Moore version of *The Scarlet Letter* and the fact that Demi once posed for a *Oui* magazine spread in the early 1980s.

"She shows bush!" exclaimed one girl. "She's totally untrimmed."

"Does Ashton know about this?" another responded.

I felt so low. Each glare from Professor Scott felt like a dagger. I almost felt like crying, and I wanted so desperately to explain, but what could I say? It didn't help that all the students now regarded me as a total dweeb, and I don't want to judge or anything, but there's a reason these kids aren't in regular college. There was one guy, though, who looked at me sympathetically, and it kind of threw me off. He looked like Kurt Cobain mixed with Mark Ruffalo, but scragglier and a bit skinnier, and he had paint smears on his jeans and T-shirt and small gold earrings in both of his ears (and a smaller one in his left eyebrow). I guess he paints houses or something when he's not at class, but who cares, his "simpatico" gaze made me feel uncomfortable and even dweebier (if that's possible).

I've got to get out of here, I thought. I chose Chappaqua because it's the closest college to Rumson, which will make my return to Rumson easier—but how the heck am I supposed to pull that off, I wondered, and how, exactly, am I going to bring down Meri and save my friends? As if on cue, my cell phone vibrated. I had a text message. I discreetly flipped it open.

```
TEXT MESSAGE
The Chappaqua cafeteria has delicious mystery meat on
Thursdays! Enjoy! :)
FR: M. Sugarman
NOV. 9, 11:52 a.m.
```

Ha-ha. Very funny. After class, I tried to speak to Professor Scott, but he was gone in a flash, leaving me to ponder the word "betrayal," which he had written in large letters on the chalkboard. My phone vibrated again. It was a call, not a text, and I angrily flipped it open without looking at the caller ID. *I can handle Meri's calls*, I thought.

"You didn't answer my e-mails," exclaimed Lindsay. "Bud's prelim is in less than an hour. You're coming with me, aren't you?" Oh, jeez. I had forgotten all about Bud. I explained to Lindsay that my little Chappaqua jail cell doesn't have Internet access (and my phone reception's crappy out here too). She expressed her sympathy—she'd be lost without e-mail, she said—and we agreed to meet out front in about thirty minutes. That gave me time to grab a quick lunch.

And yes, just as Meri had said, the Chappaqua cafeteria does indeed serve mystery meat on Thursdays. I passed on that and instead allowed Lenora, an aging cafeteria server with a slight mustache, to ladle a soupy, chunky mass onto my plate.

"What is it?" I asked.

"I was hoping you'd tell me," she said with a wink. "It's frank 'n' beans, okay?"

"Gross," I gasped involuntarily.

"Government food. Get used to it. Here. Butter's free. Take all you want." Even though it was a bit chilly, I sat outside at a ratty picnic table so I could be alone.

"Are you really gonna eat that?" Startled, I looked up. The Kurt Cobain/Mark Ruffalo-ish guy had sat down across from me.

"No, it's for the flies," I murmured, attempting to be sarcastic. *That oughta scare him off,* I thought.

"Here, have one of these." He offered me a thick stick of beef jerky. "Good source of protein."

"Gee. No thanks."

"I'm Cliff," he said, offering his hand. "Cliff Haven." I let his paint-spattered hand hang there. Then I glanced at my watch.

"I've really gotta go."

"Wait. What are you doing tonight?"

"Tonight? Sorry. Busy."

"Aw, c'mon. Doing what?"

I sighed heavily. "I'm cutting up my party dresses and making pillows. Okay? It'll take all night." Then I slung my book bag over my shoulder and strolled off. To my annoyance, he actually followed me.

"Need any help?"

"Don't be weird."

"You're weird. Which is cool." An insult and a compliment, all at once. Who did this guy think he was? "We should hang out," he said.

"Look, uh, Kurt . . ."

"Cliff."

"Cliff. Right. I'm busy, okay?"

"Aw. Bet you're not."

"Hey," I sputtered. "I'm—I'm trying to be nice here."

"Naw. Don't. Be yourself."

"Fine, then Kurt, listen carefully."

"Cliff."

"I really don't have time to hang out and eat your beef jerky, and normally I'm so not this rude, I swear, but you're being kind of . . ." A car horn blasted. Lindsay pulled up to the curb in her Porsche. Thank God. I swung open the door, stepped inside.

"See you later," Kurt called out. Lindsay hit the gas.

"Oooh, he's cute," she said. My eyes popped out of my head. Cute? I needed to change the subject. Fast. But Lindsay was one step ahead of me. "Meri knows you're here. Oh, and she's starting her own clothing line."

"Whatever."

"Oh my God, how'd you know that?"

"Huh?"

"Whatever!"

"Whatever what?"

"That's the name of her clothing line. 'Whatever.' The national rollout's the day after Thanksgiving. She's already filming a commercial. I read the script. A girl goes up to this other girl and says, 'Love your outfit,' and the other girl just shrugs and says, 'Whatever.' Oh, and you have to come to the house on

Saturday—you're formally invited, so Dean Pointer can't stop you. We're throwing a charity luncheon and ball. Viva Veterans Day. It was Shanna-Francine's idea. We'll be honoring the wartime contributions of our Latin American veterans. Isn't that great?"

It wasn't bad, I thought. Good for Shanna-Francine. She wanted a hook and she got it. And yes, it's "politically appropriate," but in a good way. I just hope Meri doesn't figure out a way to mess it up. The governing board is losing patience. One wrong move and Shanna-Francine's toast. Oh, just thinking about Alpha Beta Delta makes me homesick. Or make that heartsick. It reminded me of how I felt when I was in junior high doing homework in my bedroom and I'd hear laughter and lively conversation coming from Mom, Dad, and Lisa in the living room. *I'm not a part of this family,* I'd think. *I'm in a dark cave all by myself, and I'll never be happy because I'm here, I'm trapped, and if I try to crawl out, it'll somehow makes the cave bigger and bigger and even darker than before.* For the briefest moment I imagined I was back in the cave. It was dark. My hands fumbled. I found a lighter. I gave it a flick—and gasped. Meri was right before me, her face eerily underlit.

"Together forever," she whispered breathily, flipping back her thick raven hair. "You'll always be my little bow-wow. Woof woof."

The lighter singed my fingers. I dropped it, engulfed in darkness once again, and all around me Meri's echoey laughter grew louder, louder.

"I have to get out of here," I whispered. Lindsay squeezed my knee.

"You will. Something will come to us. Meri sent me a text message. Do they really have mystery meat on Thursdays?"

Bud's preliminary hearing was at the Rumson River Courthouse, and it was tense. Lindsay and I stood behind Bud and his well-dressed, smooth-talking lawyer, John Hadity, whose fee was being paid by Lindsay's father (lucky for Bud) (though maybe not so lucky for Lindsay's father once he finds out Bud's proposed). Bud looked terrified—openly terrified. And sure, he was outfitted in a very nice suit and tie (which kind of made him look like he was playing dress-up) (but better that than those awful capri pants he likes to wear), his scraggly hair was nicely greased back and flattened, but he couldn't stop shaking. His eyes were bugged out too, and his jaw hung open, and the tiniest bit of spittle was dripping from his lower lip. I'll admit, I felt sympathetic (honest).

Then I thought back to all the times I wanted to sock Bud a good one, like the time he pinched my still-developing breasts in sixth grade and shrieked, "Udder-udder-udder!" or the time in third grade when he cornered me on the playground, dropped his pants, and demanded I pay him a quarter for the privilege ("Down from the already low-low price of fifty cents!" he announced proudly) (though it was nothing to be proud of, I assure you), or the time in junior high when he did the morning announcements from the AV room, and after reading the day's lunch specials— including Salisbury steak with lima beans, and turkey-and-white-bean chili with cheese sauce—saw fit to add, "Cindy Bixby, please report to the men's bathroom on the second floor and remove your phone number from the wall. We know it's you. You cannot hide behind the name 'Ginchy Box.'" Naturally, I was called "Ginchy Box" for the rest of the day, which eventually morphed into "Stinky Box" by the time last period rolled around (Bud was kicked off the AV Club Announcement Squad, but still, the damage was done). Then there was the time in eighth grade when I innocently walked into the empty school band room and discovered Bud making out with Barbra Jiggergerinski, a notoriously slutty girl who would be moving to a new city soon. She actually allowed Bud to grind his scrawny pelvis against hers. She squealed, "Oh, yeah. Oh, Bud. I can feel it. Oh God! What am I going to do without you?"

"Mmm, don't worry, babe, I'll make you a mold," he responded greasily. Then he saw me. "Cindy-boo," he leered. "You want a mold too?"

Eeeow! I don't think I've ever run out of a room as fast as that (and Bud, I heard, did actually try to make a mold, though the liquid rubber stuff he used was unfortunately way too adhesive, which made him the butt of jokes for many weeks after in the gym shower because of all the crusty, gooey gunk that stuck to his thingamajig) (yuck!).

At the hearing, Lindsay and Bud were hoping that the judicial officer would find there was insufficient evidence to proceed, and if that was the case, Bud would be released. For my part, I couldn't stop thinking about Kurt, and especially Lindsay's comment, "Oooh, he's cute." Cute? Had I missed something? I mean, maybe he was (in his own way), but I could never in a million years date a guy like that. What would Mom say if I started seeing a guy who wears nicer earrings than I do (and I really don't care how conservative that sounds)? And besides, I thought, he was rude. He made the assumption that I had no plans tonight, which is pretty annoying when you think about it. *He's a player*, I thought, *a player with earrings*. That made me angry. And it made me think of that song "He's a Dream," by Deep Dish.

> *Just another pretty face to see*
> *He's all over town, he's knocking 'em down*
> *Oh, honey, I'd never let him next to me*

Lindsay's wail of anguish snapped me out of it. Bud's case was not dismissed by the judicial officer. So horrible. Bud gave Lindsay a quick, desperate hug and a sloppy tongue-plunging kiss before they were separated by the court guard. Rain was falling in torrents when we stepped onto the courthouse steps. Lindsay opened up her new limited-edition indigo lace-patterned Stella McCartney umbrella and led us to her car—and my eyes widened in shock. Did I see what I just thought I saw? From the corner of my eye? Dashing past on the courthouse steps? I didn't see her face because she was using a windbreaker to protect herself from the heavy rain, but the little tartan uniform gave her away. It was one of the St. Eulalia girls—possibly Albino Girl, or one of the others—no doubt monitoring the hearing for Meri. I was about to say something to Lindsay as we drove off in silence, but she was so shell-shocked. She just drove; her eyes were staring straight ahead, her breathing was oddly irregular. My phone vibrated. I flipped it open. I had a text message.

TEXT MESSAGE
Aw. So sad. And just think. It's all your fault. :(
FR: M. Sugarman
NOV. 9, 3:55 p.m.

"Who's it from?" asked Lindsay halfheartedly.

"No one. My sister," I lied. "It's nothing." We continued riding in silence, and I wondered, Why are all those nasty little St. Eulalia girls doing everything Meri tells them to do? Then I remembered what Mamacita had said to me on the plane: "You want to know what she's up to? And how she's doing it? Follow the money. That's all there is to it."

Yes, Meri was paying them. Of course. But is she paying anyone else? And if I were able to find out who, exactly, could I use this information to my advantage in order to return to Rumson and Alpha Beta Delta? It was worth mulling over. The rain had stopped by the time Lindsay pulled up to Chappaqua. I invited her to my dorm room, or my jail cell as I like to call it, but she wanted to get back to the house.

"I want to go to my room," she sniffled, "and close the door and . . . and . . ."

"And what?" I asked.

Lindsay tells me everything. But that doesn't mean I have to write it all down in my diary. Let's just say that Bud has apparently perfected the problems he once had with adhesive liquid rubber.

I didn't have a late-afternoon class, so I decided to head to my jail cell and reread *The Scarlet Letter* in case Professor Scott decided to (spitefully) (and I wouldn't blame him) call on me in class with some detail I'd forgotten about.

"Hey. Wanna get toasted?"

Oh, no. It was Kurt. He had bounded up alongside me like we were best friends or something. Please.

"I have studying to do."

"C'mon. You don't need to study. Not you." He grinned. Oh, brother. He was complimenting me on my intellect? How desperate can you get?

"Have you met Mark?"

I hadn't noticed, but there was another guy who'd just stepped up. "Sorry, no," I said. I shook his hand, though I was barely looking at him. I really did want to go back to my jail cell and read.

"'Sup," he said. "I'm Mark Sugarman."

Seconds can seem like an eternity. In that very first and very brief second after I heard the name "Mark Sugarman," the air collapsed to the ground—*ka-boom!*—as if its jaw had dropped in shock. I suddenly felt cold and powerless and totally exposed. *Impossible,* I thought, *this can't be real.* Then I screamed to myself, *Pull it together. Look. Make sure.* My eyes scanned his face hungrily. His eyes? Check. Identical shade of icy blue. His hair? Check. Lustrous, raven. But different jawline. Fuller lips. A warmer smile. And certainly not the fashion plate in his weathered down jacket, raggy Lee jeans, studded belt, and black creeper boots. He kind of looks like a modified hippie or a punk boy, but one who's well fed and probably carrying at least three credit cards.

"Are you okay?" asked Kurt. Then he turned to Mark with a rakish laugh. "Yo, I'm the jerk. I don't even know her name."

"Sheila Farr," I blurted. "Nice to meet you, Mark. Um, have you been studying at Chappaqua long?" That got a laugh. Mark, it seems, is the black sheep of the Sugarman family. College just isn't his "thing," he said, and though he was accepted to Amherst College last August (a rich kid school that'll take just about anyone), he's spent the months since then traveling across the United States with only his backpack.

"It's been awesome," he said. "I've been exploring the self-expanding global consciousness of humanity. And communing with sacred shamans. They're everywhere."

"Dude, that's sick," added Kurt approvingly.

"Dude, I'm telling you. Free your soul. Travel the cosmos. Your mileage may vary."

I had no idea what they were talking about (and what were the "sacramental substances" that Mark kept referring to, anyway?). They kept on chattering—so many "whoas" and "dudes" and "all rights"—and then they made a sly little exchange. A bit of rolled-up cash from Kurt to Mark, and a small baggie from Mark to Kurt. Marijuana. *Say something*, I thought, *because this is too good an opportunity, and it may never come again.*

"Does your family know you're at Chappaqua?" I asked innocently.

"Naw, not my dad," he said. "But my sister does. Or did." *Hold tight*, I thought, *and ask clear questions that can give you usable answers.* As we continued chatting, I learned what I needed to know: During his travels, Mark had deliberately come to Chappaqua to "hang" with his sister upon learning that she was here, and once she was able to leave, he had planned to move on as well. But he didn't.

He stayed in order to sell some "doobie" and shore up his funds.

"So she knows you're still here?" I asked maybe a little too insistently.

"Naw. Please, my sister's so into herself she's crawling up her own butthole," he chuckled. "Why would she care what I'm doing?"

Tread carefully, I told myself, *and be shrewd*. I think I was. In fact, I know I was. I talked about Lisa—deliberately leaving out the part that she was a (hopefully) two-hit wonder. "My sister is such a pain in the wazoo," I said, craftily creating a momentary bond between us. And then he let the bomb drop. A big bomb. Huge.

"Dude, my sister's so into herself that she keeps an online diary. Like, she's been adding to it every day since she was eight."

"So anyone can read it?" I gasped (actually, I practically shrieked, I was so excited).

"Uh-uh. Password-protected."

Oh, darn it, darn it, darn it, I thought. "Wow, major bummer," I said, attempting to sound "stoner-ish." Then I explained—ingeniously, I thought—that I was in the midst of creating a diary art installation, with scraps of diary entries fluttering from large moving mobiles (with the names of the diarists kept anonymous) (of course). I rightly figured that a blissed-out pothead in black creeper boots, such as Mark, would be interested in something as ridiculously "arty" and "meaningful" and "deep" as a diary mobile (Dad had once taken me to the Contemporary Arts Center in Cincinnati to see a pickled cow cut up into twelve pieces and a frozen horse head kept in several pints of the artist's own blood, and while I was definitely struck by the breathtaking crudeness of these displays—and the conflicted feelings about "what constitutes art" that they brought up—I was actually more intrigued by the organically and/or chemically altered crowd that surrounded me, and wondered if substance abuse was in fact a prerequisite to really "getting" what was going on) (and I am so not a fuddy-duddy, and I'm willing to "go there" and assume that maybe it is, because I was once really tipsy from some good merlot and flipped through an art book, and I swear I thought I "got" Picasso in a whole new way). I continued chattering, figuring that Meri's diary—which would have offered an invaluable peek into her mind, or her "disordered psyche" as Patty says—was an opportunity that had come and gone. Bummer, indeed.

"Dude, no worries," chimed Mark. "I have her password. I've had it for years. And she doesn't even know." I stuttered and gasped for air, I was so excited—it felt like my entire body was throbbing—and before I could even say anything, he asked, "What's your e-mail? I'll send you a few of her entries."

Oh my God, oh my God, oh my God, oh my God. I couldn't give him my e-mail, for obvious reasons, so I gave him misssheilafarr@yahoo.com, and hoped against hope that Sheila would give me access to her e-mail, or at least forward the e-mails to my account.

"'Miss'?" asked Kurt.

"Old family joke," I said, attempting to cover. Mark was off—he had a few more "transactions" to conduct—but he said he'd e-mail me some diary entries within the hour. *Oh, I hope they're useful,* I thought. The private musings of Meri were bound to be good ammunition. But then I realized that I had no access to my e-mail, I have no Internet connection in my jail cell, and I must have said this out loud because Kurt told me "no prob." But first he had to make a quick detour to the cafeteria, because his pipe was "totaled." I wasn't sure what was going on—what did his drug pipe have to do with getting a bite at the cafeteria? I was even more mystified when he asked Lenora for a potato. Uncooked. Raw.

"Knock yourself out, kid," she said, handing one over, apparently as bewildered as I was.

Back at Kurt's jail cell—which was as dreary as mine, save for a few nice tie-dye wall hangings—he used a pen knife to cut into the potato vertically, and then diagonally, so that the two ends met in the middle. At the same time I thought, *I've got to call Sheila*, so I quickly ducked outside while Kurt played with his potato, gave her a call on my cell phone, and breathed a sigh of relief when I got a signal and she said, "Darling, of course. My password is 'Ars Gratis Artis,' no spaces, which is 'Art for Art's Sake,' the not entirely accurate and some might say wishful-thinking trademark quote on the MGM logo. Ah-ha-ha."

"Thank you, Sheila."

"Remember? The one with that awful roaring lion? Which reminds me. Did I ever tell you about the time I made my first dessert? It was pound cake. Hard as a brick. Fell off the counter and killed the cat. Tsk. Poor little Jinx. Never saw it coming. Then there was the time I served cordials with Bromo-Seltzer. . . ."

"Sheila, I really have to go." I hated to cut her off, but I had to get back to Kurt to access the e-mail. I mean, I don't have a car (and the campus is so isolated and far from town). When I stepped back into Kurt's jail cell, I was enveloped by curling smoke and soft Brazilian-influenced music. The smoke was marijuana, and it was being puffed—no joke—through the uncooked potato. The marijuana was stuffed and lit in the penknife hole at the top of the potato, and Kurt was sucking a "hit," as drug addicts say, through the adjoining hole on the side. I didn't know whether to applaud his resourcefulness or what, so I just said, "Gee, I guess you can't do that with an avocado." I was trying to be funny, and he actually laughed (he has a nice, manly laugh). I glanced at his little iPod Bose setup. We were listening to Thievery Corporation's "Revolution Solution," which had a pleasant, swaying beat and a dreamy vocal (drug addicts, I've noticed, frequently have good taste in music). He invited me to take a hit, and though I'm not a marijuana smoker by any stretch of the imagination, I thought, *How high can a potato get me?* So I pressed the potato to my lips and sucked in a really huge puff of smoke.

"Hold it," Kurt advised gently. I did as he said, and when I exhaled, very little smoke came out, so I figured that was that; potato smoking is dumb. Then I sat there listening to the music. And listening. And listening.

"Wanna see my studio?" he asked. He didn't wait for a response. He gently took my hand and lifted me up. Holy moly! *Don't fall*, I told myself. Uh-oh. It was official. I was high. And I don't mean just kind of high, I mean full-out-can't-stop-giggling-does-anyone-have-any-Cheetos-gimmie-gimmie-gimmie high (something I've only witnessed, not experienced). Cheetos. Yes. Mmm. Sounded so good.

"They're dangerously cheesy," I tittered errantly. Kurt had no idea what I was talking about, but he chuckled along with me, led me out of his jail cell, and used a key to unlock an adjoining jail cell. "Shouldn't we knock first?" I asked. "Suppose someone's doing stretching exercises in their undies? Or . . . or . . ." I couldn't complete my thought. And who knows what it was. But it must have been terribly funny, because I fell into his arms, I was laughing so hard (he smelled like a man, I noticed fleetingly noticed, and not all overcologned like Keith). Then I allowed him to sweep me inside, where I was abruptly engulfed in lush colors and abstract images and nude figures and the strong smell of turpentine.

"Hardly anyone stays in these dorms," he said. "So I kinda took this one over."

"W-o-o-o-o-o-w!" I exclaimed, making the word stretch out to at least four syllables, and realizing, to my astonishment, that this was exactly how the organically and/or chemically altered crowd sounded at the Contemporary Arts Center. *Kurt's an artist*, I squealed to myself, and I was even more thrilled to see that he was good. No, not good, wonderful! His paintings were alive with bold splashes of abstract colors and sensuously rounded shapes, and his more formal portraits, all of them nudes of both men and women, had a courageous effrontery that seemed to be saying, "Look, enjoy, be free!"

"What do you think?" he asked.

"They make me feel like this," I shrieked, then I threw my arms up over my head and twirled around in circles. "F-r-e-e-e-e!" I stretched that word out to eight or nine syllables (at least), and I could have stretched it out even further, I'm sure, but I tripped on a canvas stretcher, fell backward, whacked my head against the wall, and dropped like a rag doll—*plop!*—into an orange beanbag. Was I hurt? I wasn't sure. Ha. Kurt was sweet. He rushed to my side, asked me if I was okay.

"I feel all reet," I said between giggles. My mouth was barely functioning. And dry. Water? Huh. Could help. I looked into his eyes. Blue. Very kind. And I was. Such. A stinker. To him. Before. Cheetos? Huh. Could help. Ah. Look. Stubbly-ish blond chin. Intentional? Or missed a spot? I reached out and touched it with my forefinger. "What's . . ." I couldn't finish my sentence, but he told me.

"Love patch," he whispered.

I gasped. I felt a sudden electrical buzz travel from his love patch right through my finger and right into my chest. Magic love patch? Huh. Could be. Cheetos? Mmm. Could help.

"Wanna do something fun?" he asked.

"All reet."

"Do you like to cuddle?"

Gosh, of course I do, I thought, and it sounded like such a nice idea, and I said yes, and then—huh? wha?—he lifted me up and we were outside (brrr!), zipping down the street in his teeny-weeny two-seater Global Electric Motorcar. Wheee! After we parked, he led me to a scary-looking warehouse building, and once we were inside we were separated—*no, Kurt, don't leave me!* Then I found myself in a clean locker room where women of all ages were changing into snuggly robes and fluffy footsies and comfy jammies. When in Rome, I thought (Cheetos, I thought too). I chose pink jammies with matching comfort socks, and followed the jammie-clad crowd into a large, softly lit auditorium strewn with countless pillows and beds and blankies, and everywhere—and I mean everywhere—people were lying down and cuddling. *Orgy*, I thought, and I was immediately panic-stricken; this is what you get for smoking a potato.

"Are you okay?" a nice middle-aged woman asked. "Is this your first Cuddle Party?" I must have looked pretty confused, because she took my hand, and suddenly we were laying down on the cushiest mattress ever with a warm down comforter and pillows. She held me in her arms. We were cuddling! Literally. Oh my God. She told me her name was Sherry Sadoff. Cuddle Parties, she said, are safe-play events for adults where you can enjoy nurturing, nonsexual touch and communication. And there are rules: no alcohol, no drugs, and you can say yes or no to people who would like to cuddle with you. There are even Cuddle Lifeguards on hand to make sure that all the rules are followed.

"Touch is necessary for healthy immune systems," Sherry told me. "It helps injured people heal and reduces stress." That made sense. I once read about an orphanage where one group of babies were held and touched every day by nurses, while another group of babies were merely fed—and that's it. Sadly, the babies who weren't held developed diseases (some of them even died). I have to say, I enjoyed cuddling with Sherry. It kind of felt like I was cuddling with Mom (even though we haven't done that since I was a kid). As the party wore on, I got to cuddle with a lot of people, and they were from all walks of life: I cuddled with a very kind lawyer whose wife had died two years ago; a girl who's getting her doctorate in veterinary medicine; and another guy who was just laid off at his accountancy firm (along with eight others) (I assured him he would find work). Some people were chatting, some were silent, there were even a few people crying. And all the while I kept thinking, I want to cuddle with Kurt, and that alarmed me (just a bit), because I wasn't high anymore—the potato had worn off—which meant that I was really thinking what I was feeling. Why, I wondered, do I want to be so close to Kurt?

"Will you cuddle with me?" he asked, startling me as I stepped past a group of mattresses.

"Um, sure," I stuttered. We lay down on a cozy pillowtop mattress and wrapped ourselves in a chenille blanket. Then he spooned me and I could feel his breath against my neck and his arms wrapped around my waist and his knees bending into mine, and my heart was going *boom-boom-boom-boom-boom*.

"This is nice," murmured Kurt. It was nice. After that, neither of us said anything. I relaxed. My heart stopped beating so fast, and honest, I might have fallen asleep in his arms if he hadn't whispered, "By the way, my name's Cliff." *Okay*, I thought, *it's official: I'm a dope. What the heck is wrong with me? I can't even remember this guy's name? This nice guy who shared his potato with me? And showed me his art? And brought me to an immune-system-enhancing Cuddle Party?*

"Sorry," I said. I felt so ashamed. "Cliff."

I allowed him to hold me closer. And we confided in each other. Cliff's had a rougher ride than I have, that's for sure. Growing up in Winfield, Tennessee, a rural town near the Appalachian Mountains, he always knew he wanted to be an artist. His first drawing of any note, he said, was his childhood home, which burned to the ground when he was just six years old after his alcoholic father (who hid his rum in small bottles of Yoo-hoo) dropped his lit cigarette to the floor, igniting the family room drapes and within seconds, it seemed, the house itself.

After that the family moved to a derelict trailer home, and Cliff kept drawing the house over and over and over, trying, he now realizes, to will it back into being. When high school rolled around, Cliff sent his portfolio to some of the best art colleges in the nation, and he was accepted by the undergraduate Department of Art & Art History at Duke University in Durham. Tragically, his father flat-out refused to allow his son to go to any "fag art school," so Cliff formulated a plan. He decided to go to the least expensive college he could find that was closest to Duke, none other than Chappaqua (which his oblivious father helps pay for). Cliff works two jobs, and he's hoping to save enough money for at least his first semester at Duke next year, and he's also applying for scholarships and loans.

"What about you?" he asked wryly. "You're not at Chappaqua because you want to be." Ha. My suffering? Is that what he was asking? Well, you see, Cliff, there's this psycho sorority girl who's out to destroy my life, and, oh yeah, she's booked a vacation for the two of us to see the swallows return to Capistrano. That ought to go over big. Then I thought, *Holy moly, I've got to check Sheila's e-mail, I've got to look for Patty, I've got to start thinking about Mamacita's words, "Follow the money," and I've got to keep my eye on the prize: my return to Alpha Beta Delta and the destruction of Meri.*

"Where'd you go just now?" he asked. He could tell my thoughts had taken flight. I'm not sure why, but I said, "I was in a dark cave. I was all by myself. I was trapped."

He kissed the back of my neck. Wow. Before, my heart was going *boom-boom-boom-boom*, but now it was going *boom-chick-a-boom-chick-a-boom*. That's when a Cuddle Lifeguard cried out, "Puppy pile!"

A puppy pile, it turns out, is exactly what it sounds like, and a sort of grand finale to the party. Everyone, including me and Cliff, flung ourselves toward the center of the room until we were all stacked on top of each other. People were screaming and laughing. I was too (it didn't help that Cliff was tickling my feet). I also couldn't help thinking, *Cindy, you ding-dong, how dare you have a such good time when you have so much to do! Cuddle parties? Puppie piles? What would Mom say? What the heck are you doing? Knock it off!* Then I heard it. It was just one person at first: "Woof woof!"

I froze. Was that Meri? Was she under me? Above me? I heard it again: "Woof woof!"

My throat dried up. I panicked. I couldn't breathe. It seemed like everyone was saying the same thing—chanting "Woof woof! Woof woof!" One part of my brain told me, *Cindy, it's a puppy pile, and puppies go "woof,"* but the other part of my brain screamed: *Meri is everywhere! She's over you, she's on top of you, she's going to smother you to death because you're a small, defenseless puppy, and then she'll make you into a coat.* The woofing grew louder, louder. A hand reached out. It was Meri's hand. She was aiming right for my face; I could smell her Kiehl's Satin-Soft body moisturizer, and her nails were glistening and freshly manicured. Woof woof! I screamed hysterically, wriggled through the mass of arms and legs and squirming bodies, and tossed myself to the outer edge of the auditorium floor where I was safe from the large stack of Meris still calling out, "Wow wow! Woof woof!"

We drove back to Chappaqua in silence. *Great,* I thought, *Cliff now thinks I'm a total nut job.* It had taken two Cuddle Lifeguards to calm me down, and I had to put them at ease too by assuring them that no one had touched me "inappropriately." Cliff had one hand on the wheel. After a moment, he put his other hand on my knee and gave it a squeeze. It was a reassuring squeeze. Or at least I thought it was. But then I thought, *Oh, no, what have I gotten myself into? What am I going to do now? Will he be, like, you know, expecting something? Am I expecting something?*

"Can I check my e-mail when we get back to your place?" I asked.

"Sure," he said. At his jail cell, he opened his laptop and grinned sheepishly. "I steal access from the college's cable line." He stepped away and I decided to forget about my e-mail for now and just log on to Sheila's. I was hoping against hope that Mark had forwarded some of Meri's diary entries. After typing Sheila's password, I hit return and her in-box loaded. So far, so good. I scanned the many e-mails listed, most of them already read. There were several from singoutlouise@gmail.com, which is Sebastian's e-mail. One had the header "I've Got a Hot New CSP!" CSP, as I've heard around RU, means Casual Sex Partner. I think I'm the only one who doesn't have one, or "get any," which is just as well because the more CSP's you have, the better your chances of getting crabs or something equally icky (Lindsay says that just looking at Doreen, aka Bitch Kitty, is enough to give you crabs). My heart choked abruptly. There it was. One e-mail from sugarrush@aol.com. It had to be Mark. I clicked it open.

From: <sugarrush@aol.com>
Date: 9 November
To: <misssheilafarr@yahoo.com>
Subject: (no subject)

Hi, Sheila:

Here's a few diary entries I downloaded from my sister's
site. Hope they help your project. And, hey, I shouldn't say
anything, but Cliff's majorly into you. :)

It was great meeting you, by the way. I'm going be at
Burning Dude around Thanksgiving. Cliff's coming too. Maybe
you'll be with him . . . ?

Death to the fascist insect!
Mark
HTML Attachment (MSWord Document) [*Download File*]

Cliff said I could download and print the document Mark had attached, and once I had the pages in my hands, all I wanted to do was race back to my jail cell and devour them whole and hope that they gave me something to use against Meri, so I strode to the door—*hurry*, I thought, *get going*—and there was Cliff, reaching for the doorknob, and I thought, *Hold on, if he's so "majorly" into me, as Mark said, why isn't he making a move? All he wants is a little action from a CSP, right? So then why is he reaching for the doorknob?* I felt insulted. He probably changed his mind and was thinking, "Word, I am so not sexing up Miss Thunder Thighs," and okay, he probably wasn't thinking those words exactly, but I suddenly felt a lot more hiddy then I usually do, and God only knows what my hair was looking like after my freak-out at the Puppy Pile, but I was right in front of him and I couldn't help it, I could hear Mark's words—"Free your soul! Travel the cosmos!"—and my lips traveled right to Cliff's. I. Made. The. First. Move. Oh my God. And he responded. We kissed. It was so sweet. And so gentle (and so easy). Then he led me down to his (messy, unmade) futon. I was pretty nervous, because I knew what was going to happen: I was about to have sex with a guy I'll never see again. He lit a candle, turned on his iPod—and then we really made out. He moved on top of me. He slowly unbuttoned my blouse, unhooked my bra. I could feel his mouth on the nape of my neck, his hands caressing my breasts. Then I felt his tongue lightly circling my nipples. I held back a gasp. From the iPod, I could hear the throbbing beat of "Heaven's Dead" by Audioslave:

> *Shipwreck the sun, I'm on your side*
> *An army of one, onward we'll ride*

I pulled off his shirt. I ran my hands across his chest. I felt metal. Cliff has small gold nipple rings. It kind of excited me—and I'm definitely not into body piercing or anything (semi-strange) like that. But it made me think, *Wow, this guy is really experienced, this is going to be fun, this guy knows what he's doing*, but in the next second, I thought, *Crap! Crap! Crap! I'm not experienced*. Yes, I slept with Keith on a regular basis, but it was pretty standard stuff, or at least I think it was from the way everyone at RU is always bragging about all the "hawt" sex they have, and the way it's written about in *Cosmo*.

"You're beautiful," whispered Cliff.

Ha. I bet you say that to all your CSPs, I thought (someday a guy will say that to me and mean it) (I hope). And yet I didn't have time to think about anything else because Cliff's tongue was suddenly flickering down to my nether regions, where Keith's tongue had never been and—oh my God—okay, I get it. I really do (and what the heck was Keith's problem with going down on me anyway?) (*note to self*, I thought, *my next boyfriend must do everything that Cliff is doing to me now*) (*and just as well!*). When I let Cliff inside me, I let go. Completely. We were so close and so intimate. I could feel his nipple rings against my breasts, his lips against mine. Then his heart burst right through mine. It was beating inside my body.

We finished at exactly the same time (I think) (either that or he was being very polite). I had no idea what to do next. I mean, I was still buzzing with pleasure, but I didn't know the protocol. As a CSP, was I supposed to be all chill and just go, "Yo, thanks.

Later"? Or "Dude, if you're up for a do-over, gimmie a jingle. Ciao." Or was I supposed to be Miss Super Coolio, kiss him on the cheek, and just stroll out? I didn't get any cues from Cliff. After he pulled off his rubber, he held me in his arms, and I could feel his breath against my neck, which was nice, but I was torn. One part of me wanted to run from the room—it's over, I did it, I had a one-night stand, now scram!—but another part of me wanted to fall asleep in his arms forever. I closed my eyes, and for the briefest second, I was at our wedding on a beach. It was a beautiful, sunny day and everyone was there, even Lisa, who was so jealous, and Patty was there too. She whispered to Lindsay, "Aw. Isn't it sweet? Cindy's finally resolved her Electra complex. Cliff looks nothing like her dad." A gust of wind abruptly blew off my veil. I shrieked. Whipping around, I saw Dad and Mom charging down the beach, both of them screaming furiously. Dad had a shotgun, Mom had a brick-thick copy of *Modern Bride*, and she threw it—*bam!*—hitting Cliff in the head. Then *poof*, I was in a shabby, paint-spattered, canvas-filled trailer five years later with Cliff and our flabby four-year-old twin boys, Bubba and Buford, both of them shirtless, and—eeeow! gross!—they both had matching nipple rings.

"I have to go," I gasped, quickly disentangling myself from Cliff and putting my clothes on. *I just had a one-night stand with an artist*, I thought, *and yes, it was dark and cool and edgy (and dirty) (and he went down on me), but it's time to go. Right now!*

"See you tomorrow?" asked Cliff. I didn't even turn around. I babbled nervously, "Sure. Thanks. Later."

I'll never see him again, I thought. I swiped Meri's pages, rushed outside, turned the corner, held my head down, and walked/ran through the outside hallway, where I passed a group of students who snickered and whispered, "Oooh, yeah, doin' the Walk of Shame," and "Is that a hickey on her neck?" and "Her hair is tragic." Thank God this didn't happen to me at RU. It's not called the Walk of Shame there, it's called the Pig Walk, and people actually oink at you when they see you scurrying off from a one-night stand back to your car or your dorm.

I stepped into my jail cell—and stifled a gasp. There was a sealed envelope on the floor. On the front, it said simply, "For Cindy," and I know of only one person whose cursive writing is so rife with curlicues (not to mention ridiculous little daisies instead of dots above the *i*'s.). I boldly ripped it open. Inside was a first-class round-trip ticket to the John Wayne Airport in Orange County, and a note.

From the Desk of Meri Sugarman

Dear Cindy:

I hope you're enjoying your stay at Chappaqua. Have you joined the Polo Flat-Racing Team? It's quite popular there. Large or big-boned girls are the ponies—down on their hands and knees—while boys of lighter weight mount them and use walking sticks to drive tennis balls through goals. It sounds like a terrific way for you to meet new friends (and I'm sure you'd make an adorable pony!). In the meantime, as discussed, here is your ticket to Capistrano.

Warmly,
Meri

I angrily tore up the note and ticket, turned to the sink, splashed cold water on my face, then gazed at myself in the mirror—and screamed. On the right side of my neck was a whopping big hickey. It was red and purple, and you could even see the indentation of two front teeth at the top of it.

That made it official. I had become, as Grandma used to say, a "Sidewalk Susie." I felt so ashamed, and so unclean (I still do).

I'm in bed now. I should start reading Meri's diary entries, but I'm just too exhausted. I can't lose my focus. No more screwing around (figuratively speaking) with boys or anyone else at Chappaqua. I can't stay here. I belong at RU. I belong at Alpha Beta Delta. And, okay, I admit it, I can still feel Cliff's strong yet gentle hands caressing my body, and I really did have a wonderful time tonight, and he's definitely a sweet guy, but a one-night stand is a one-night stand. *C'est la vie*, as they say, something actors in French movies say a lot. They usually say it with a bored shrug, as if they're really saying, "Eh, whatever." That's exactly what I've got to do about Cliff. Eh. Whatever. That should be easy. It already is. I'm totally over him. Cliff who?

November 10

Dear Diary:

I woke up this morning completely disoriented. Where am I? And why the heck is there a half-empty bag of BBQ chips next to me? Was Meri here? I bolted up, petrified—and saw a scribbled note on a ripped piece of paper sticking out from under the comforter that read: "You snore!" My eyes widened. In an instant, I knew. It was Patty. It had to have been. In my "Sidewalk Susie" stupor back from Cliff's last night, I must have forgotten to lock my door, and in a way, thank goodness, because at least she had some place to crash. But it's got to stop. She can't go on this way. She has to get help (and I don't snore) (I don't think).

I whipped my covers aside, stood up to face the day—and found myself directly across from the mirror, where I learned the hard way that hickeys do not always lessen or go away overnight. Oh, cripes! I stepped closer, turned my head to the side, and gave it a good, hard look. If anything, it was even more gruesomely purple then before (it even seemed to throb a bit). But I was proud of myself; instead of getting upset, which I would normally do, I decided to be practical. Makeup wouldn't cover it, that I knew for sure, and I don't own any scarves, but I do have several blouses and dresses that I don't wear that much anymore, and a pair of scissors. Rummaging through my suitcase, I pulled out my Trina Turk paisley gauze dress and got to work on it. I've always liked the dress, the colors are so bright and happy, but I didn't wear it all that often, and besides, this was an emergency. I cut horizontally about four inches from the bottom until I had one long paisley strip. It was frayed on the end where I had cut it, of course, but it would have to do. I doubled one end through the neck, tied it like a bow, and voilà, a nice paisley oblong scarf knot. I glanced in the mirror. Hmm. *Not bad*, I thought, *but not great, either—I'm certainly not going to start any fashion trends (ha!)—but not bad. Problem solved.*

It was eight a.m. My first class wasn't until eleven, so I had plenty of time to look over the e-mail printouts from Mark. As I reached for the pages, I saw that my hand was shaking. Oh my God, I was excited, I was nervous—everything all at once. I propped up my pillow and began reading intently. There were three entries altogether, and from different time periods in Meri's life. In her first entry, Meri is eight. My mind boggled. *Here I am*, I thought, *reading something that Meri wrote when she was just a little girl.*

Apostolina

Bonjour:

My name is Merial Sugarman. My hair is pretty. Father calls me Meri. I'm eight and three-quarters years old. I live in Newport, Rhode Island. Jackie Kennedy Onassis grew up in Newport too. Father says she was an important pretty lady. I am much prettier than her. She had a pony named Danseuse. That's the name of my blog. I want a pony. I know I can make Father buy me one. And he should. Father should always do what I say.

My blog is private. I will never-never-never-never-never-never-never-never give the password to anyone—except when I've gone to Heaven, then everyone can read it. Then they'll learn everything about me, and they'll see how special I was, and they'll wish they had been much nicer to me. Some of them will pray to me, and I'll answer them. If I feel like it.

My brother is Mark. He is so incredibly dumb. My new mommy is named Marla. Marla's a stupid cow. Mark says she has "big boobulars," which she does, and she's much younger than our last mommy. She also has long blond hair, very white teeth, and seventy-eight pairs of flats and heels. Father just bought her a vintage Cartier Multicharm bracelet. The charms are pretty. There's a lion's head with diamond eyes and a ruby in its mouth, a trumpet player with a diamond-studded dinner jacket, and a sapphire-studded teapot with two cups. Marla doesn't deserve it. I should have it. Maybe I'll steal it from her.

I guess I could be angry at Marla, but I'm not. I barely pay attention to her. This morning, she came into my room and said, "Merial? Isn't it your turn to walk Precious?" Precious is the name of Marla's ugly Pekingese.

"Walk him yourself," I told her. "My nails are drying." Which they were. Marla tried to be strict.

"Watch yourself, young lady. Don't make me give your father a bad report." That made me laugh.

110

"Oh, please, Marla, watch yourself. And remember, I'm not the one who signed the prenup." Then I hopped off the bed and—*bam!*—slammed the door in her face. Marla's easy. She's like a turkey that falls over without being shot.

I bought a book about Jackie Kennedy Onassis. She says: "I separate my private life from my public life. I can drop this curtain in my mind." I'm going to do that from now on. But I don't think one curtain is enough. I'm going to have hundreds of curtains in my mind, so that if someone steps inside, I can let one curtain drop and pull another one up, just as three more are turning and two more are opening and closing sideways, and that way, if I want, I can trap them.

Which reminds me. Yesterday I stole Marla's favorite gold filigree cigarette lighter, flicked it, and set the living room curtains on fire. It was so funny. Mamacita ran in with a bucket full of water, threw it on the curtains, and yelled at me in Spanish.

The curtains in my mind will be fireproof. I am the only one who can set them on fire. If I want to.

Apostolina

Hi:

Father is being difficult. Again. He should know by now that I always win. My personal triumphs have been easy. I won with Trina (I barely blinked on that one), I won with Marla (there's a blast from the past!), and only recently, with Steffie. Poor Steffie. Hers was a rapid descent. Once I learned that she was a reformed alcoholic, it was simple. I started out small. A shot of vodka in her morning coffee, a little tequila in the Jell-O mold. By the time I was done with her, Steffie served everything flambé. And then the pièce de résistance. In her purse and in all her coat pockets, I placed matchbooks from the Commack Motor Inn, a happy-hotsheets hotel off the Jericho Turnpike. Father might have been able to deal with a cheap and common drunk, but not one who cheats (and at the Commack!).

I want Father to be happy—I really do—but not with bimbos. It's embarrassing. He's the chairman and chief operating officer of Versalink, we live in a mansion that hugs a coastline next to mansions originally built by the Astors, the Rockefellers, the Vanderbilts—and he dares to marry the likes of Steffie? A boozing (former) Vivid Video "star"? It's beyond gauche.

And Mark—well, I've given up on Mark. For example: I just turned twelve, and I'm on the honor roll at Miss Grayson's College Prep; Mark is eight, and he sucks on his bong twenty-four seven and goes to Newport Public Elementary School. Enough said.

And enough said about Miss Grayson's College Prep, too, and the town of Newport. It's time to move, and Father is being obstinate. But I can't go back to Miss Grayson's. Not after what happened to me this morning. I was strolling to my first class, and as usual, girls were crowding around me, seeking my opinion on this subject and that, soliciting my fashion advice. The school newspaper writes about my achievements constantly, and last June the *Newport Times* did a photo essay on my singular style choices. It's par for the course. Everyone knows me. Everyone envies me. Which is as it should be. Jackie O. once said, "I have become a piece of public property. It's really frightening to lose your anonymity." But I've never been frightened. Until today.

As I continued down the hall, the girls' chattering suddenly crushed to a strange silence. A few of the girls even giggled. I had no idea what was going on until I followed the gesturing hand of one girl . . . right to my lovely BCBG Max Azria inverted pleat white skirt. Only it wasn't all white anymore. At its center was an ever-enlarging blot of red blood. I had my first period—today, publicly, in front of everyone. But it got worse. Much worse. One of the girls cried out gleefully, "Bloody Meri!"

Horrified, I ran to the bathroom, and to my surprise, I successfully removed the blot. But not the shame. The impeccable reputation that I have so carefully cultivated over the years has been shattered. Forever. The rest of the day, cries of "Bloody Meri! Bloody Meri!" followed me from class to class. Having had enough by lunchtime, I called Dennis and demanded he bring the town car around to take me home.

On the way, we stopped at the Newport Pharmacy. I rushed inside, purchased formerly unnecessary supplies, and raced out to the car. But before Dennis could even swing open my door, a little boy strolling down the street with his mother pointed at me and shrieked, "Look, Mommy! There's Bloody Meri!" I gasped, dropping my pharmacy bag, and my supplies tumbled out. The mother stifled a laugh, then steered her son the other way. I whipped around to make sure that Dennis hadn't joined in. His face was stone. Good for Dennis. He can keep his job.

Obviously, word travels fast, which means that the sooner we move from Newport, the better. At dinner tonight—Cook served a delicious roast duck with caramelized red onion and juniper—I told Father that it was time to move. Greenwich, Connecticut, sounded nice to me, or perhaps Westport (though

Westport is a bit vulgar). I caught Mark's amused eye. He knew. But he also knew well enough not to say a word. Father was a different matter. He didn't understand why a move was necessary, and he flat-out refused. Wrong move, Father, dear.

Later this evening, Father retreated to the library for his usual brandy. I stepped in quietly, and after I dropped the document copies in front of him—the ones I was able to secure last week—I allowed him a few moments to glance at them. Predictably, his face turned white. He sputtered to speak. I could have allowed him to sit there and suffer, but I do love Father, so I was graciously quick and to the point:

"We're moving, Father. Tomorrow. And don't make a fuss. You know it makes no difference at all if you helicopter to work from here or from Greenwich. Greenwich is closer, in fact."

"Who else has these?" he managed to ask. For a moment I thought he was going to dry-heave.

"Just me. These are copies. The originals are in a safe place."

We stared at each other—and Father looked away first. By the time I stepped out of the library, Father was already on the phone with Cornelia, the bottle-blond real estate agent who found our wonderful summer retreat in Kennebunkport two years ago. Tomorrow will be a wonderful day. A fresh start. As I type, the diamond-eyed lion's head is clinking against the sapphire-studded teapot on my Cartier Multi-Charm bracelet. I need more jewelry. And a whole new wardrobe. In fact, there are so many things I need. I'm glad I found the documents. Now father will give me everything I ask for. Or else.

Dark Cindy

Hello:

I adore Palm Beach! We haven't yet found a home to suit my tastes—we've rented several suites at The Breakers until Cornelia finds something worthwhile—but already I'm heartened to see that most of the better mansions and estates here are well guarded and off-limits to mere mortals. Father amuses me. He actually slipped money to Dennis and ordered him to go through all my belongings during the move in order to find the original documents. Good-bye, Dennis. I know he'll be happy elsewhere. Why? Because after he fell to his knees pleading in front of me, I kindly agreed to have father write him a glowing recommendation. I'm fair, but firm. Father, on the other hand, is just plain stupid.

As for Pru, I wish I could do more to hurt her, but why continue to fight when a move—another fresh start—is so much easier? Still, Pru is on my list, and I will take care of her when the mood suits me. Maybe next year, when she begins applying to colleges, I'll make my move. Just when she's most hopeful about her future, I'll destroy her completely. And then there's Timothy. Did I really lose much? At best, he gave new meaning to the word "quick."

Father keeps asking me about college, but I haven't decided yet, and why should I? At sixteen, I have the time—and the grade point average—to pick and choose, and I don't see why on earth I have to rush matters. Besides, there are precious few, such as Yale, Harvard, the Sorbonne, that make my cut, so it's not like it will be a time-consuming situation. Jackie went to the Sorbonne. She lived with a French family of the old aristocracy and took vacations in Vienna, Salzburg, and Berchtesgaden (where Hitler lived).

Sometimes I like to imagine that Jackie is my mother. And yes, someday I'd like to meet my real mother, even though I can't for the life of me remember her face. I know that if I wanted, I could force Father's hand. He would tell me where she is if I really wanted to know. But it's fine for now. I enjoy the mystery, not to mention keeping Father on edge. I even like Edwina, whom I've allowed Father to keep (he was fearful she'd have to go after I told him that we were leaving Virginia). Edwina keeps Father happy, which is good, and she's smart enough to stay out of my way. Oh, she tried to cross the line once—she dared to suggest to Father that the move to Palm Beach was unnecessary—but I took care of that. I surprised her in the bathroom when she was taking a bubble bath and dangled a whirring hair dryer just above the water. She gasped, "Meri, please . . ."

"Want to play games, Wina? I'll wipe the floor with you."

"Meri . . ."

"You're getting a little long in the tooth, Wina. Wake up. For someone hustling for their keep, I doubt you'll do much better than this."

"You're right. I'm sorry."

"Just remember. One false move and you're out. And then what? Let's see. Hmm. I know. You'll be living with a construction worker. In Queens. And taking care of his incontinent dog and his grandmother, who you'll have to bathe. How does that sound?"

"I've actually grown very fond of the idea of Palm Beach."

"Aw. Good, Wina. Good."

Since then, Edwina's been a doll.

I have to go. I have an appointment to pick out a new polo pony. I already have a name—Buddy, the name of Jackie's most cherished horse—so it's just a matter of finding one that matches it perfectly.

I breezed through my classes today, and no one said a word about my scarf, which I now realize looked pretty darn ridiculous. I tried to use my cell phone to call Lindsay, but I still have trouble getting a signal out here. I needed to show her Meri's diary entries. Desperately.

But first, I stepped into Professor Scott's class—just as one of his classes was letting out. He was at the chalkboard erasing the book title *As I Lay Dying* (by William Faulkner), along with several questions. He was just about to erase the last question, "What does Vardaman do to help his mother breathe?" when I quietly answered, "He drills holes in her coffin." He still wasn't moving. I couldn't help it. I blurted out, "Oh, I'm so sorry, Professor." He turned around to gather his papers. Then he looked up at me. There was something flat and deadened in his eyes.

"I like Chappaqua. The students don't engage me, and that's freed me up to work on my book."

"The one about . . ."

"The girl, yes," he suddenly enthused, his eyes brightening. "The girl who's thirsty for real life, real experience . . ." *Oh no*, I thought, *that semi-porny thing he's been hacking away at for years*. "I finished it. I sent it out to publishers." Huh. I have to admit, that surprised me. But then I guess with so much time on his hands, why wouldn't he? "So you see? Chappaqua's actually been very good for me." He forced a smile. There were dark coffee stains on all his front teeth; the true mark (I've always thought) of either a real writer or a dedicated dreamer. As I walked back out into the sunlight I wondered, Which, exactly, is Professor Scott?

"I've been looking for you," said a voice behind me. And there he was—smiling, proud of himself, even—and all I wanted to do was smack him a good one. I grabbed his hand, yanked him behind a bus shelter, and pulled down my scarf.

"Look!" I seethed. "See? Look what you did!" He stumbled for words (big surprise). "It's huge!" I wailed. "It's turned four shades of purple since noon. It's practically its own continent!" Then I didn't know what I was saying, but I knew they weren't my words. "Want to play games?" I shrieked. "I'll wipe the floor with you. You're getting a little long in the tooth for someone . . . I mean . . ." I trailed off. I was shocked. And Cliff's eyes were wide with confusion.

"Are you okay?" he asked.

I ran. Oh, I'm such a cheeseball—and he looked so caring (and handsome) (in that rough-artist-trailer-park sort of way)—but I didn't care. I ran faster, faster. A female voice suddenly bellowed, "Heads up!"

I ducked, dropped to the ground. A tennis ball flew over my head. I was right in the middle of a Polo Flat-Racing game, and a really mean-looking big-boned girl on her hands and knees was huffing and puffing and charging right at me while a squirmy guy on top of her raised a walking stick, ready to strike.

"Move!" he hollered. I rolled to the side; my face was mashed to the ground. They galloped past—I could hear loud grunts from the big-boned girl—and a second later I heard triumphant screams. Obviously, someone had scored a goal. Catching my breath, I attempted to pick myself up. Standing before me was a twerpy little Vietnamese guy—short, skinny as a beanpole.

"Hi," he said, his nose congested. "Want to be my pony? I'll ride you hard."

Ahhhhhhhhh! I tore across the grassy knoll and finally caught my breath when I turned a corner and slammed myself against an outdoor student posting board. *You are not a pony*, I told myself, *you are not a pony*. Then I heard giggles. A group of girls strode past and they were tittering and pointing right at me.

"Oooh, nasty! That's not a hickey, that's Boise, Idaho. Jeez, why didn't he just carve his initials on her? Aw, it's like a doggie pissing on its own corner of the lawn."

I was mortified. In my flight from Cliff, I had lost my scarf. I was exposed! My cell phone vibrated. I flipped it open. "Hello?" I yelped, trying to hide the lump in my throat.

"I got through!" exclaimed Lindsay. "You really need a phone with better coverage."

Oh, thank goodness for Lindsay. She screeched up in her Porsche and—*whoosh!*—we were off. "Where are we going?" I asked.

"Long John's," she said with a wink, then she became all serious and whispered, "Look, we don't have to talk about it if you don't want to, but if concealer doesn't work, try turtlenecks or scarves. And take lots and lots of vitamin C. Oh, and water and ice don't work. Tried that. And neither does Retin-A."

"Maybe I should just hide in shady corners," I murmured. "Like a leper."

At Long John's, Lindsay was ready to give me more hickey advice when I thrust Meri's diary entries in front of her.

"What's this?" she asked.

"You'll see," I said, my anticipation building. I ate several Chicken Planks (which instantly made me feel better) as her eyes scanned the pages. She was spellbound, and every few seconds she exclaimed, "Oh my God. Shut up. Oh. My. God. Shut. The. Fuck. Up." She turned the last page and looked at me astounded. "Where'd you get these? Are they real?"

I told her everything. About Mark. About me being Sheila Farr. My supposed diary mobile.

"You've got to get more," she insisted. "You have to get the whole thing."

That would be a problem, I told her, since Mark had already left Chappaqua and was no doubt on his way to see his next shaman or exploring anthropological mystical transmissions.

"So? Shamans have e-mail, don't they? What's Sheila's password?" I told her. She whipped out her Treo 700w smartphone, logged on to Sheila's account, hit reply to Mark's e-mail, and typed this:

```
From: <misssheilafarr@yahoo.com>
Date: 10 November
To: <sugarrush@aol.com>
Subject: RE: (no subject)

Hi, Mark.


Thank you very much for the diary entries. My mobile project
is really shaping up, but of course I still need MORE diary
entries. So . . . if you want to send a whole bunch to me,
or maybe even the whole diary, that would be great!

Love 'n' 'shrooms!
Sheila
```

"Oh, c'mon. 'Love and 'shrooms'?" I asked.

"Don't worry," she assured me. "He'll laugh. People on drugs laugh at anything." Then she hit send. She was beside herself with excitement. "He's gonna send more, I know it," she squealed. "These are too good."

But were they? I mean, sure, maybe in the long term the blog entries will prove helpful (I hope), but in the short term? I'm still not sure. How, exactly, would they help me escape from Chappaqua and return to Alpha Beta Delta?

"News about the Big M," said Lindsay, suddenly lowering her voice. "She's consolidated her base with the Evangelicals. All proceeds from Whatever are going to their various charities."

"She's buying their loyalty?" I gasped. "Geez. Who knew Evangelicals could be bought?"

"Please, anyone can be bought. Buddha can be bought. Gets worse. She's in talks with the Intersorority Governing Council. She and the Evangelicals may be forming their own sorority house at RU."

"But that makes no sense at all," I said, and it really didn't. Meri wants what Meri can't have: Alpha Beta Delta. Why would she settle for being president at a newly formed Evangelical sorority?

"Um, well, she does have a God complex," added Lindsay, grasping at straws. "And, I don't know, they already have a president at the Muslim sorority house?"

"Since when is there a—"

"Since yesterday. It was just announced. Gamma Gamma Baba Ghanoush. They strive for the blessings of Allah through sisterhood. And they wear the prettiest headdresses. There're rumors that Homeland Security has them under surveillance, which is so wrong."

I almost wanted to cry (again), and not because of the Baba Ghanoush sisters (they sounded nice enough, and though I object to the idea of girls hiding themselves with headdresses and things—as if their faces and hair were cause for shame—it's their religion, not mine, and it's no stranger, I suppose, then all the Evangelical girls running around with the same stiff helmet hair and Liz Claiborne stretch slacks). No, I was upset because life goes on at RU and Alpha Beta Delta. My family, or what I considered my new family and friends at Alpha Beta Delta, was like a fast-moving train pulling out of the station.

"I'm picking you up at ten," Lindsay said, as she stepped back to her Porsche and drove off. "Viva Veterans Day. Remember? You're formally invited by Shanna-Francine, so Meri can't do anything."

I sighed. I had to get approval for tomorrow. How disgraceful.

"It'll be fun," she added, beaming brightly. I had to smile back. Lindsay's smile is so infectious, plus she was trying so hard to be upbeat about my situation, which is very nice considering her own problems.

"What's going on with Bud?" I asked.

"Everything's going great," she insisted, her voice shooting up at least two octaves. "Daddy's lawyer thinks he may have caught a break. I don't want to jinx it, but Bud could totally walk. Isn't that amazing?"

Bud walk? Given the charges against him? *Fat chance,* I thought, but I so didn't want to be a wet blanket. She was trying so hard to be positive. "Wow, that is amazing," I said.

"I visited him today, and, uh . . ." She struggled for words, and then: "Guess where he wants to take me when he gets out? First thing? It's so fun."

My mind went straight to the gutter (this was Bud, after all, and God knew what he wanted to do to poor, sweet Lindsay). "I have no idea," I said limply.

"He wants to take me to a strip club," she declared, forcing a grin. "What do you think? Pretty wild, huh? There's one near RU. Kristy's Bottoms-Up Lounge. Have you seen it? It has this neon thingie on top; you know, with the girl bending over at the stripper pole? And the flashing red stars around her boobs and her . . ." She cleared her throat. She was still trying to smile, though it was obvious she wasn't too thrilled by the idea. And jeez Louise, who would be? This was Bud's idea of romance? We drove silently for a moment, then she quietly asked, "Okay, is it weird? Tell me the truth." I didn't know what to say at first. Kristy's Bottoms-Up Lounge? This is where he wants to take the girl he just proposed to? His (supposed) fiancée?

"I hear they have awesome cocktails there," I offered, trying not to sound dorky. "Maybe he just wants to party with you. And celebrate."

"Right," she said, convincing herself. She even laughed. "Oh God, you're right. We're going to have so much fun." Then she abruptly hit the gas—flooring it. I was slammed back into my seat.

"What are you doing?" I yelped.

"We're being followed!" She was right. Albino Girl was racing up behind us on her Hello Kitty skateboard.

"Slow down," I said grimly. "Let her catch up. And drop me off at the end of the block."

"You sure?" You bet I was. I wasn't going to run. I wasn't afraid. Not of her.

"Call me if you need any help," said Lindsay nervously as she pulled up to the curb. "I mean, if you can get through. On your phone." I assured her I was fine, and off she went. And off I went too. I put one foot in front of the other, and I held my head high. I had (I thought) nothing to be afraid of. I could hear the skateboard swerving up behind me.

"Bow-wow. Woof woof," she hissed. Oooh, that made me angry (okay, pissed) (really pissed). It's one thing to be insulted by Meri—my true nemesis—but to be insulted by a little albino brat on a skateboard? I don't think so. I turned around and charged right up to her. She stopped short, clearly startled. And I let her have it.

"Hey! You have something to say to me? You say it to my face. And when you do, be prepared for the consequences. Get it?"

"Sure I get it," she smirked. "You're tough now. You're street."

"Go away."

"Uh-huh, that's it. You're C-Dawg." Then she laughed and laughed. Gosh, I wanted to slap her across the face, but I took the high ground. I ignored her. I turned around and continued walking. And she swerved up on her skateboard, circling around me. "So what are those papers in your hands?" she asked.

I stifled a gasp—and quickly folded them in half and stuffed them in my back pocket. If Albino Girl told Meri I had some of her diary entries, my God, disaster. "None of your beeswax," I snapped. "Oh, and how'd you get into my room last night? I got the ticket. And I'm having the locks changed. Just so you know."

"Ticket? What ticket? Is that what was in the envelope?" Then she mock-sighed. "Darn, nobody tells me anything."

"I asked you a question. How'd you get into my room?"

She whipped out a Swiss Army knife and proudly displayed the small blade, screwdriver tip, and nail file. "Nice, huh? It was a gift. From Meri."

She suddenly wailed at the top of her lungs—because I had leaped forth and grabbed her wrist. Then I banged her hand against a streetlamp post, swiped the knife, and threw it down a sewage drain.

"You bitch!" she shrieked.

"Little girls should not have knives," I scolded. Then I turned around and continued walking. *Oh God, I can't believe I just did that*, I thought. *Keep walking, keep moving, and hope she doesn't attack from behind.*

"You're dead," she seethed, swerving up on her skateboard.

"Yeah? Well, guess what, Eileen? It takes a lot to make me shiver. And you? Please. All you do is make me laugh. Ha, ha, ha." Holy moly, I wondered, where the heck was this tough-girl talk coming from? I honestly don't know, but I do know that I was sick and tired of Albino Girl's games. "You think you're so cool," I continued. "On your dumb little skateboard."

"Get real," she snapped. "You can't skateboard."

"I can too," I said, and boy, I sure wish I'd kept my trap shut. She screeched to a stop, pressed down with her foot, flipped the skateboard up into her hands, and thrust it in my face.

"Prove it," she demanded.

Oh why, oh why didn't I put a cork in it? She saw my hesitation, and yes, I'll admit it, that made me angry, which was enough for me to make a decision (in an instant): I'll fake it. I swiped the skateboard from her hands. "Pff. It's small," I said, trying to sound all experienced. "And I usually—"

"Blah-blah-blah. The usual excuses. C'mon, Skater Girl. Bust a move."

Okay, I thought, *I can do this. I mean, I'll just go from one street corner down to the next, and then I'll stop and pretend I'm bored—like I have nothing to prove—and I'll give her back the skateboard or maybe drop it on the ground right in front of her like it's so beneath me.*

"Tick-tock, C-Dawg," she snickered, eyeing me with her creepy pink eyes.

Okeydokey, I thought, *this is it, I'm doing it.* I put one foot on the skateboard and gave myself a forceful push with the other. I was off! Oh my God, it was easy. Wheeeeeeeeee! *I'm free, I thought, look at me go. I'm Skater Girl! I'm fonky. I fly like the wind. And I only brake for rainbows. Ha! Why didn't anyone tell me this was so much fun?*

"Doin' okay, C-Dawg," cried Albino Girl behind me.

I dared to look back. She was running toward me. *Oh, no you don't*, I thought, *you're not catching up with me.* I gave myself a really hard push with my foot this time and—woo-hoo!—I flew even faster down the street. Oh my God. So. Much. Fun. And. Then. I. Realized. That I was in the opposite lane and a Red Bull delivery truck was blasting its horn and coming right at me. Ahhhhhh!

"Look out, C-Dawg," screamed Albino Girl. I looked up. She was bounding through the air. Oomph! She gave me a push and— holy crap!—I went flying in the other direction and right onto a side street. I saw the Red Bull truck whiz past with the slogan, "It Gives You Wings!" on the side (*who needs wings*, I thought, *I've got a skateboard*). I was still on the board, but I was slowing down. *Phew,*

125

I'll be able to stop in a sec, I thought, *and without killing myself*, and then I made a shocking realization. Albino Girl saved my life, she actually did a nice thing—for me—which means that I, Cindy Bixby, brought about real and positive change. I've been a catalyst for good. I felt the breeze whipping through my (probably tragic) hair. I felt joy. I closed my eyes. I spread my arms out. *I am a force for good*, I thought.

"Hey, C-Dawg," hollered Albino Girl behind me, "I sure do hope you have a stunt double."

Now what on earth does she mean by that? I wondered. I opened my eyes—and I screamed. I went over the edge. N-o-o-o-o-o-o! I was suddenly plunging straight down the steepest street in Ronkonkomo County.

"H-e-e-e-e-e-e-l-p!" I cried.

Bam! I hit something hard. I had reached the bottom of the hill. I had flown off the skateboard. My face was flattened on the hard, grassy ground of Fairfield Park. I didn't move. I wondered aloud if I had broken any bones.

"Is that a bruise?" asked a little boy standing over me.

"Uh-uh," answered another. "That's a slut mark. My sister gets 'em."

"Eeeow. Slutty girls shouldn't be allowed in the park."

"Back off," cried Albino Girl, running up breathless. I was still facedown (if I didn't look at anything, I reasoned, it would all go away); I could hear the boys gasp, no doubt at Albino Girl's freakish appearance, with her long white hair and pink eyes.

"Your friend's got a slut mark," proclaimed one of the boys to Albino Girl.

"That's right. She's a slut. A big one. Now get lost before I give you a slut mark too!" That seemed to do the trick. They scampered away, and Albino Girl grabbed my elbow, and pulled me up. "Break anything?"

"I don't think so," I said.

"Where's my board?"

I shrugged. Who knew where it went?

"Fine. You're buying me a new one."

"Wait, hold on," I mumbled. I was still a bit winded and dizzy. "Maybe tomorrow we'll . . ."

"Now!"

Disoriented, I followed her to Heinous, a dirty, hole-in-the-wall skateboard shop, but before we got there, she took my hand, led me down a dead-end alleyway, doffed her shoes, hiked up her tartan plaid skirt, pulled off her green-and-red-pepper-patterned thigh-high stockings, and hurled them at me.

"Here. Use these. You're embarrassing me."

Quick thinking on her part. I tried my best to tie them around my neck (anything to hide my slut mark).

"An oblong knot?" she shrieked. "Are you serious? What are you—my granny?" She demanded that I bend down, then she batted my hands away and tied the stockings around my neck in a surprisingly fashionable four-square buckaroo knot. "Holy shit," she chuckled. "You've got to do something about your hair. It's so . . ."

"Tragic, I know, thank you," I retorted impatiently. "Can we please just move?"

At Heinous, I wasn't the least bit surprised when she picked out the most expensive item there, an eighty-six-dollar Blind brand skateboard with a picture of their trademark skull-boy creature brandishing a huge gun amidst flowing red blood. I used my Visa Buxx card (which Dad had given me for emergencies) to pay for it.

"Dag!" exclaimed Albino Girl as she held the skateboard in her hands. "I'm gonna fuckin' kill this puppy."

"Why do you always do what Meri says?" I interjected boldly. "Is it for the money? Or something else?"

She looked up at me; her pink eyes gave away nothing. Then she looked back at the skateboard, and I almost thought she was going to thank me (ha, silly me), but instead she said, "You can keep my stockings. Just don't get off by sniffing them or anything weird like that." I was about to say that I'd be happy to burn them when she hurled the skateboard down and in one swift movement leaped on it, sped out of the store, and flew down the street.

"Anything else?" asked the lanky, overly cosmeticized, faux-punk guy behind the register. I was about to say no (of course), but something stopped me. I'm tempted to say that a lightbulb went off above my head, or a bell chimed *ding!* but it was actually a lot simpler than that. I just knew what I wanted—in an instant.

"I'll take that one," I told him, gesturing to a "Zero Punk" brand hot-pink board.

I didn't ride the skateboard back to my jail cell at Chappaqua (I'm not that dumb). I held it tightly under my arm in the shiny red and gold Heinous bag. Did I want to learn to skateboard? Was hot pink really my color? So many questions.

A frosty breeze whipped against my face, giving me the heebie-jeebies. I was in the supposedly "hip" section of Ronkonkomo (two whole blocks). There were used clothing stores, a leather apparel boutique, a tattoo parlor. There was even a small movie theater, the Hollywood Twin, that played double features. I looked up at the marquee. In Cinema 1, the double feature was *Mary Poppins* and *The Exorcist* (the programmer, I decided, must think he's a real card); in Cinema 2, it was a Christian Bale double feature, *American Psycho* and *Batman Begins* (I'd seen *American Psycho* on cable; Lisa thought it was "fierce," but I thought it was just like a *Friday the 13th* movie, only more pretentious). I'm not sure why, but a voice inside me seemed to say, "What the heck, let's go, it's almost ten to six and *Batman Begins* starts at six" (it's not like I had anything better to do).

Cinema 2 was practically empty. The floors were unbelievably sticky, and when I put my elbow on the armrest it stuck to a wad of purple gum. Gross. *Batman Begins* started. I'd seen it before, and at the time I'd thought the opening sequence—where Christian Bale learns how to become some sort of Fu Manchu warrior—was maybe just a bit long and repetitive. But not this time. This time I was riveted. Oh my God, I couldn't tear my eyes from the screen. The movie seemed to be speaking to me. Directly.

"You've tried to fight, but now you must journey inward," whispered Liam Neeson to Christian Bale. "Now. There is no turning back. Journey inward. To what you really fear."

Oh my God, oh my God, oh my God, I thought. Is that what I have to do? Journey inward? In order to fight Meri? I was so spellbound that my jaw was open and a piece of popcorn was hanging off my lower lip.

"If you devote yourself to an ideal," continued Liam, "you become more than a man. And that is what you must do. In order to defeat your opponent."

I gasped audibly. What exactly is inside me, I wondered, and could I really become more than just plain ol' Cindy B.? Is that why I bought the skateboard? My eyes opened wider, and I took in every single thing Liam said. I knew it then (and I know it now), he was personally instructing me on how to bring Meri down.

"Theatricality and deception are powerful agents," he advised. "The will is everything. To master the fear of others, you must first master your own."

I'm not sure what happened next, but I must have dozed off because—*swoosh!*—I was suddenly airborne in a black leather outfit on my hot-pink skateboard, whizzing through space past star fields and galaxies. I ducked—*ayeeei!*—as a meteor and a planet rushed past. They each had flashing neon signs. One said, "Follow the money!" The other said, "Fight a bee, sting like a bee!" Then—*yeeeooow!*—I zoomed up to Saturn, with its rings glowing. On the largest ring, lettering whirred around and around in a circle, just like it does on a news zipper on a skyscraper. The same phrase flashed over and over: "C-Dawg in the Hizzie! C-Dawg in the Hizzie!"

Bang! A pimple-faced usher whacked his flashlight against the back of my seat, waking me up. "If you wanna see the next show, you have to pay for the next show," he reprimanded.

I shook myself awake groggily. The theater was empty, the house lights were up—and my board was gone! Holy crap. I bolted up, looked around, and screamed, "Excuse me, have you seen my skateboard?"

"What? That belongs to you?" he chuckled disbelievingly. He stepped to the front of the theater and retrieved my Heinous bag. I swiped it from his grubby hands, and please, I am not a nasty person—I mean, I could have told him, "Up yours, you pizza-faced jerk! Your mother's mustache!"—but instead I just fixed him with a supermean glare (just like Liam would do). That's right, buddy, this skateboard is mine.

"Um, er," he mumbled, clearly psyched out. "The crapper's just past the concession stand."

It was cold and windy as I walked back to Chappaqua. The streets were weirdly empty, the darkness pulled me into its long, open hands. It felt familiar. *I'm so tired of being alone,* I thought. Then it hit me! Loneliness is my greatest fear. "That's it," I whispered aloud.

To master the fear of others, you must first master your own.

Oh God, I thought, *Liam is right.* All my life, I've hardly had any real friends, much less anyone to talk to. But it got worse, because I'd only recently had a taste of what it's like to have wonderful, close friendships—all my wonderful friends at RU and Alpha Beta Delta. Then along came Meri. She took it all away, cruelly, leaving me alone—trapped in a dark cave. If I master my loneliness, I realized, then I can win against Meri. Or to put it another way, if I can come to see that being all alone isn't that bad—if "just me" is okay—then I have nothing to fear. I can do anything. I can risk anything. Because the worst that can happen is I'll be alone again. I'll be Cindy in the dark, and I already know what that's like.

As I turned down the street toward my Chappaqua jail cell, I wiped a single tear from my cheek (I hadn't even realized that my eyes were welling up). But I wasn't sad. I was happy to be walking in the brisk, cool air by myself. It was refreshing. In fact, I was in such high spirits that I barely noticed the dozen wrapped red roses at my door. *Something's definitely wrong*, I thought, because I'm not the type of girl who gets a dozen red roses from anyone, unless it's some sort of prank.

I carefully unlocked my door and gently kicked the wrapped roses into my cell. Nothing. They didn't explode. No toxic gas poofed up. *If these are from Meri*, I thought, *they must have thorns*. I peered closer. Nope. Not a single one. There was an envelope attached to a small gift box, too, which was taped to the plastic wrapping. I opened the envelope and pulled out a card. On the front, there was a cartoon drawing of a little dog with big, sorrowful eyes and his tail between his legs. I opened it. There was writing: "Sorry I left a mark. I'll control myself next time. Yours, Cliff (aka Kurt)."

I unwrapped the gift—and I laughed out loud. Along with the roses, Cliff had sent me a small bottle of L'Oréal Medium Warm Light Concealer. Oh my God, so sweet. Are one-night stands usually this thoughtful?

I'm in bed now, and as I'm writing this, it feels like I'm looking at a black mirror image of myself. I know what I look like, but in the mirror, I look somehow different. I feel different too. I'm seeing the future: I've mastered my fear, and my brain is spiraling down a skinny black line to an underground tunnel, where everything's dark and shadowy and fierce. This, I realize, is where Meri lives; it's the only part of her brain that she uses. Should I stay here? Should I learn to ride a skateboard? And if I'm going to fight a bee, should I sting like a bee? Why not? I've tried everything else. Liam says, "If you devote yourself to an ideal, you become more than a man." That makes sense, and this much I know for sure: Cindy can't win the fight against Meri. But maybe, just maybe, C-Dawg can.

Hmm. C-Dawg. That doesn't sound right. Let's see. I'm tough. I'm fierce. I'm dark. Oh my God! That's it!

I'm Dark Cindy.

NOVember 11

Dear Diary:

My knees are badly scraped, my butt's throbbing it's so sore, but who the heck cares? I'm going to bring down Meri and return to Alpha Beta Delta. Woo-hoo! This morning when my eyes popped open I still felt fuzzy and halfway in my dreams. All night my head was flooded with black rivers and dark murky clouds that seemed to bubble and sizzle against a thin red sunrise; all that blackness, and yet something was being born, something was beginning. Dark Cindy was emerging.

It took me a sec to realize that the darkness in my room wasn't from my dream. It was five thirty in the morning, so it wasn't light out yet. *It's Saturday*, I reminded myself, *it's morning*. I'm not sure why, but I felt compelled to do it. I flung my covers aside, and within minutes I was dressed, outside, and ready to give it a go. I slapped my hot-pink skateboard to ground. *Do it*, I told myself, *practice makes perfect*, while at the same time less helpful thoughts popped into my head, like *I am officially kooky* and *I don't feel pretty right now* and *I should floss more* and *Hold on, what did Cliff mean when he wrote that he'd "control himself next time"? Next time?* But thank goodness for Mr. Dee, my eighth grade social studies teacher, who once assigned the class to write a research paper about Thomas Jefferson. I remembered something inspiring Jefferson once said: "It is part of the American character to consider nothing desperate." *Darn right,*

I thought, *and there's nothing desperate at all about being at a rinky-dink community college parking lot with a hot-pink skateboard just before sunrise* (a stretch, I know, but I went there).

I leaped on the board and flew through the parking lot. Yippee! It was still dark, but pools of light from the surrounding street-lamps guided me. *Hey, not bad*, I thought as I skillfully tore down a center aisle between a row of parked cars. *Ooofff!* My elbow hit the outside mirror of a parked minivan, which threw me off balance and—*whoosh!*—the skateboard shot out from under me and I fell backward onto my behind. Hard. Ouch (to put it mildly). *Okay, clearly this isn't a good idea*, I thought. But I didn't give up. I tried again. And again. And again. I realized that I was fairly good at riding the board in a straight line. It was the turns that were killing me (and my knees and my hands and my arms and my butt).

I tried turn after turn, and each time I fell splat. On the eighth try, my left knee was bleeding and skin was scraped on my lower palms. The streetlamps were dimming just as the sun was skimming the horizon. *This is it*, I thought, *I'm going to nail it.* I rode slowly in a straight line, aiming for the end of the lot, where I would make my turn. *Speed into it*, I told myself. I pushed really hard with my right foot and then leaned with my other to make the turn—which is when I hit the curb and shot off the board, flew into the air, and fell face-first onto the (poorly manicured) lawn. It was spectacular (in all the wrong ways). I spit out a mouthful of grass. And heard muffled laughter. What?

I craned my neck around. It was Jahmal, Chappaqua's gruffly handsome parking attendant, standing at the far end of the lot—and he was laughing at me! Not cool. He must have just arrived. I picked myself up—I was beyond humiliated—and looked around for my board. Jahmal chuckled again. He was pointing at a beat-up hatchback to my left. My board was behind it, upside down, its wheels still spinning. As gracefully as I could, I picked up the board, tucked it firmly under my arm, threw my head back huffily, and stalked toward my jail cell, and really, it would have been a great exit, but I tripped on a jutting rock and my right shoe flew off and I fell to my knees. You meant to do that, I told myself. I stood there a moment on my knees, my back straight—as if I do this every time I finish practicing, like I'm meditating—then swiped my shoe, stood up, and continued walking, and while I might have believed my little playacting routine, the muffled chortles I heard from behind told me that Jahmal did not. *Oh, stuff it, Jahmal*, I thought. Okay, so I wasn't Dark Cindy yet. I was, I don't know, Beige Cindy, or maybe Taupe Cindy (both of them feeble, indecisive colors that a lot of designy types in *Vogue* seem to favor these days). But still, everyone has to start somewhere, right?

There was a nip in the air by the time I darted back to the parking lot. I was late, it was just after ten, and I didn't want to keep Lindsay waiting, because who knew what sort of responsibilities she had to attend to for Viva Veterans Day.

"Cinde-e-e-e-e-e-e!" squeaked a familiar, high-pitched voice. I was so thrilled. It was Sebastian! Lindsay had brought along Sebastian and—oh my God—Sheila Farr, too. "Group hug," Sebastian squealed, jumping up and down. My heart leaped. I was so happy to be among true friends. We were all ready to step into Lindsay's Porsche when she suddenly screamed, "Wait! Hold it. You guys are going to freak." She eagerly popped her trunk and leaned in to grab something. "I wanted to wait until we were all here. Just us. Oh, you'll love it, I know you will." Then she pulled out a long rectangular box, closed her eyes for a moment (for strength), took a deep breath, and told us, "This is from Auntie's collection. I just got it yesterday from Mother. It's really old. She told me if I lose it, or if anything bad happens to it, she'll pull out Auntie's eighteenth-century guillotine. And use it on me. And I don't think she was kidding."

"Tsk. That would be most unfortunate," said Sheila.

Lindsay whipped opened the box. Sheila gasped, her hand clutching her bosom; Sebastian screamed (loudly); while I was frankly just speechless. Its brilliance was overwhelming. This was better than the hennin hat, better than the (fake) tiara (and surely better than the guillotine). In the box was an ancient white-gold scepter, and at the tip of it was a large five-pointed star encrusted with sparkly diamonds and faceted topaz beads. Lindsay held it out triumphantly. She was a fairy princess with a magic wand (and an umbrella). Giggling with delight, she brought it down to Sebastian's shoulder.

"I dub thee fabulous," she intoned.

"It's official!" he shrieked. Then she brought it to Sheila's shoulder.

"I dub thee a star."

"Thank you, my dear," responded Sheila sweetly. "It's redundant, but always welcome." Next it was my turn.

"I dub thee . . ."

"Dark Cindy," I blurted.

"Oooh, I like that," gasped Sebastian. "Dark Cindy."

"I like it too," said Lindsay, who peered at me knowingly; I could tell she was picking up on something.

"Kind of scary, kind of sexy," continued Sebastian. "I see spandex, I see leather. Mmm. Yes. Very fembot." We piled excitedly into the Porsche, we were on our way to Rumson, and I have to admit, I was really nervous. This would be my first time there since I was so shamefully exiled.

"My dear," Sheila whispered, leaning in to me. "Remind me to give you a quick makeup tutorial one day soon. You're blotchy. There's a large blotch here. . . ." She used her moistened thumb to rub some of the concealer from my neck, then paused, only fleetingly stunned. "Oh, I see. Never mind."

"Cindy's got a slut mark!" cried Sebastian. Oh, darn it. Now they knew. I tried to explain. It was something I would never do again. Never, never again would I have a one-night stand.

Sebastian snorted. "Yeah, right."

"Be nice," scolded Lindsay, swatting him.

I wasn't even interested in Cliff, I told them. I mean, a guy with a love patch? And nipple rings? Who gave me a slut mark? And tried to make up for it by buying me roses and concealer?

"He actually bought you concealer?" asked an astounded Sheila. "My, my. The young'uns blossom nicely these days."

"I got a slut mark from a boyfriend once," Sebastian declared merrily. "But it wasn't on my neck. Get it? Get it?"

"Please," admonished Sheila, "show some integrity."

"Integrity?" he joked, pretending this was something new.

"Yes, my dear boy. A lamb you led to slaughter a long time ago. But try."

"So did he go down on you?" Lindsay asked me—and sucked back a gasp, immediately regretting that she had brought this up publicly. I shrank back into my seat. All eyes were on me. Did I have to answer? And I knew what Lindsay was thinking, but was "going down" on a girl really some sort of litmus test for a "good" boyfriend (or a one-night stand)? I don't know why, but that made me angry.

"Yes, he did, but so what?" I proclaimed. "He's a nice guy. Okay? He's an artist. He's a painter. And he's really talented. And his upbringing was terrible—my God, it was awful—but he's out there, he's doing his art, he's risking everything, which I think is kind of heroic. And . . . and . . ." I was struggling to explain. Why didn't they get it?

"Go on," whispered Lindsay, whose eyes were as wide as saucers.

"We had a good time, okay? And it wasn't just the sex, which was great, but he, he . . ."

I sputtered to silence. Now they weren't just looking at me, they were gaping at me with a mixture of shock and strangely escalating joy. Sheila patted my knee. "Yes, my dear. Sometimes, if you're lucky, it's about more than sex."

"Right," I said, anxious to bring the conversation to a conclusion. "But it's over. It was a one-time thing. So that's that." Sebastian grinned, and he was about to say something—who knows what—but Lindsay silenced him with a fiercely cautionary glare.

As we drove up the street to RU's campus, my heart rose expectantly. Despite the chill, the day was bright and the trees blazed with dazzling golds and reds. I had stepped out of the dark cave, I was in the land of the living. I was free. Okay, I was on a day pass, but still.

"Do I look okay?" I asked excitedly.

"Of course," said Sebastian. "You look the way you always do."

That's not what I wanted to hear (though what did I expect?). Still, the way I "always" look was obviously just fine and dandy to my friends. How great is that? After we parked Lindsay's Porsche, we strolled together past the Great Lawn toward Alpha Beta Delta. *I'm here*, I cried to myself, *I'm back*. Everything was so fresh and bright. My smile was widening to the point that my skin hurt. Even things that used to annoy me—like the show-offy couples macking publicly—were now warmly familiar. A couple of students were playing Frisbee and Hacky Sack, still others were sitting around a tree with steamy hot drinks and open study books, and two burly RU gardeners were happily raking up fallen leaves. Then, without warning, I had a seizurelike attack of anguish, because no matter how cheerful my surroundings and my friends were, I was here as a visitor. My happiness was a cruelly double-edged sword; it lifted me up, it pulled me down. My insides searched frantically for a middle ground. *Yes, this is a nice place to be,* I thought, *but I can't stay.*

"What are those girls doing?" asked Lindsay. We all turned to look. A group of fashionably dressed girls were moving from one group of students to the next, and quickly circling around students who were just strolling by. Lickity-split they looped around us, chattering randomly and in unison, "Whatever! Whatever? Whatever-whatever-whatever. Whatever."

Then they struck poses like models on a runway while gesturing to their clothes and accessories, "Whatever windbreaker. Whatever sheepskin. Whatever-whatever. Whatever cardigan. Whatever raglan. Whatever? Whatever. Oh my God, whatever-whatever-whatever."

It took me a sec, but I recognized these girls. They were all members of the Campus Evangelical Crusade. They were modeling Meri's line of Whatever Clothing.

"Is this viral marketing?" yelped Sebastian.

More like A-bomb marketing, if you ask me, I thought. We were surrounded, we couldn't escape. With a flourish, they whirled off, leaving behind two girls, one of them a stunning African-American girl with long, stick-straight hair who thrust her hand in front of us and displayed quite the flasher on her ring finger.

"Whatever Chastity Rings. Whatever-whatever. The word of the Lord keeps impurity at bay. Okay? Okay. Whatever. Whatever-whatever. Whatever Fashion dot com." *Poof,* she was gone, leaving behind just one girl.

Sebastian screamed, "Doreen?"

Oh my God, there was Doreen, Bitch Kitty herself, head to toe in Whatever attire. She rolled her eyes impatiently.

"Look, I get paid for this, okay? And I could use the moolah. So back off."

"But a Chastity Ring?" I asked.

"Fuck yeah. Kind of awesome, don't you think?" she said, holding her hand out proudly. "I wear it all the time now, and let me tell you, I've never gotten so much action in my entire life." She squealed in mock protest. "No. Don't. I'm saving myself!" Then she burst out laughing. "Guys sure do go for that virgin shit. Unfuckingbelievable. I'm thinking of Japan for spring break. You know, for the operation? Totally new hymen. I think they use goatskin."

"Gross," exclaimed Lindsay.

"Besides, the ring's pretty. Don't you think?"

"I think it's the height of hypocrisy that you're wearing it," Sheila stated, which didn't sit well with Doreen, who angrily scoffed, "Whatever!" And she was off.

Alpha Beta Delta was a buzzing beehive of activity. Sisters were everywhere, making last-minute Viva Veterans Day preparations. In the kitchen, there was a whole crew of girls I'd never met before, nearly all of them in slacks, loose-hanging shirts, and Birkenstocks.

"Bobbie's friends," Lindsay told me. "They're helping with the food preparation. It's going to be an all-vegan Mexican feast." Bobbie herself trounced in and pulled me—*uumpf!*—into a close, firm, hard hug (I think she even cracked my back).

"Damn it, we've missed you, Bixby!" she bellowed. But there was no chance to catch up. Bobbie was wanted out front, and Lindsay, too. Shanna-Francine was close to hysterical, since everything had to be dead-on perfect, and she needed their help with the elaborate themed yard decorations. Before they took off, I asked Lindsay if I could use her computer to check my e-mail (of course she said yes). Then I found myself momentarily alone in the kitchen with the Birkenstock girls, who were moving with blinding speed. And yet, once they were certain that Bobbie was out of earshot, they whispered furtively, "I don't like her." "Neither do I." "She'll break Bobbie's heart." "You know she's a LUG." "Oh my God, so LUG." "She thinks she's pulling a fast one." "Please, she's not fooling me." I was astonished. They were obviously talking about Shanna-Francine—and in a nasty, derogatory manner. Still, I was confused by at least part of what they were saying, so I loudly (much louder than I had planned) asked, "What's a LUG?"

The Birkenstock girls turned around and looked at me like I was some sort of uncouth gate-crasher or something. Finally, one girl brusquely informed me, "LUG stands for Lesbian Until Graduation."

"Oh," I responded. I still didn't understand, but she continued, her anger building.

"A LUG is a girl who becomes involved with another girl, then breaks her heart. She stomps on it, shreds it, cuts it into pieces." The other girls nodded grimly in agreement. "And all because our little LUG was just 'experimenting,'" she added acidly. "You know, she was just 'finding herself.' Get it now?"

Wow. Now I was mad. How dare anyone think badly about Shanna-Francine, who's probably the purest-souled person I know? I leaped to her defense.

"Uh-huh, I think I get it. There are rules of the heart. Strict rules. Your rules. And if people don't follow your rules, then they're bad people. Well, you know what? I think that's conformist. Yeah, I do." I fumbled, trying to think of something that would slam my point home. "In fact, I think you're all starting to sound like . . . like a bunch of meat eaters!"

I heard stunned gasps when I spun out of the room, and while it's true that I still don't know how I feel about Shanna-Francine being "that way" with Bobbie (I keep picturing the sex part) (gross!), I also don't believe anybody has a right to tell someone whether or not their feelings are genuine. A voice abruptly *ka-boinked* into my head: *You're right, Cindy, that would be harsh, kind of like a girl who rejects this completely awesome guy because she doesn't think her mom would approve.* Oh my God, oh my God, oh my God, I really didn't have time to think about things like that.

I barreled up the stairs to Lindsay's room. Tamari and Pumpkin

Seed followed me (they've gotten awfully plump). I was hoping
and praying that Mark had sent me more diary entries. I logged
on to Sheila's account, opened her in-box, and almost leaped for
joy when I found this:

From: <sugarrush@aol.com>
Date: 11 November
To: <misssheilafarr@yahoo.com>
Subject: RE: RE: (no subject)

Hi Sheila:

Hey, no prob at all. I've sent along two more diary entries.
I would have sent more, but I'm busy exploring the holo-
graphic wisdom of speaking in tongues. Did you know African
drums talk?

My hands talk too. In fact, they're starting to feel awe-
somely sonic as I type this to you. To you. To you. My
hands. My finger. Tips.

Up with trees!
Mark
HTML Attachment (MSWord Document) [*Download File*]

Quick as lightning, I downloaded the document, hit print,
then logged on to my own account (which I hadn't checked in forever). I couldn't believe how many unread e-mails I had. Then I
saw that they were all from the same person:

Dark Cindy

Sender	Subject	Date
lissa@lissabixby.com	You can't IGNORE ME!!	11/04
lissa@lissabixby.com	Ahhhhhhh!	11/07
lissa@lissabixby.com	Hasta la pasta, Marietta	11/08
lissa@lissabixby.com	Ian Somerhalder is FINE!	11/09
lissa@lissabixby.com	Catch me if you can!! He-he!!	11/10

God only knew what Lisa had been up to, but I figured I might as well print out all of her e-mails and quickly read them.

From: <lissa@lissabixby.com>
Date: 4 November
To: <cindybixby@yahoo.com>
Subject: You can't IGNORE ME!!

Dear Sis:

Why didn't you talk to Mom yet? What is up with you? Why are you never online? Marietta is. Killing. Me. Oh my God, you are soooooo selfish!

Would Jamie Lynn abandon Brit-Brit at a time like this? Huh? Would she? Would Jessica tell Ashlee to get lost? And what? Take a douche? Huh? You think she'd do that? Pul-ease. And here I am, your sister—needy, helpless, AND a star—and? AND? What are you doing? What could be more important?

I went into your room tonight and stabbed your stuffed monkey plush toy. Twice. With a scissor. So there. You are such a meanie.

Hating U (and your little monkey, too!),
Me

From: <lissa@lissabixby.com>
Date: 7 November
To: <cindybixby@yahoo.com>
Subject: Ahhhhhhh!

Dear Sis:

No thanks to you, but L. Lo's peeps are finally off my back.
I guess given all her probs—girlfriend has got to learn to
drive!—she wised up and told her lawyers to get real. L. Lo?
Sue me? Her BFF? S-o-o-o-o dumb.

Mom made me sign this humongo document, and supposedly it
says that I agree not to step within one hundred feet of L.
Lo (or else!), but hello, can you say Robertson Boulevard?
Like, I'm all about shopping at Lisa Kline, and of course L.
Lo shops there, and Paris, too, and that skanky little
broomstick known as Nicole Richie, but I am s-o-o-o-o over
even THINKING about Nicole these days. Eeeow.

Meanwhile, school is PURE HELL (not that you care). Everyone
keeps bugging me and wanting to be my friend, and I totally
understand, but I'm like, "Read my blog, I don't have time."
Okay, so meanwhile, there's no VIP seating in the cafeteria,
and I'm like, bummer. But I deal. And no, Mom hasn't started
my Zone at Home lunch delivery, and I'm like, that's a
bummer too. But I deal.

So then I sit at an empty table and I'm hoping no one will

bother me and I try to eat my (yech!) Salisbury steak and then *flash-flash!* Somebody takes my picture right as I'm lifting my fork to my open mouth—which is wrong, okay?—and I know it's going to end up in the tabs with some dumb-ass headline like "Lissa at the Trough!" or "Lissa Sucks Up Salisbury!" SUCH a bummer. But I deal. Then I look up and all these girls are LOOKING at me and I say to myself, I say, "Lisa, chill. Just eat. Don't look at them. Their lives are sad and empty."

Anyhoo, I'm eating my Salisbury steak, and it has these big pieces of chopped onion, and I really wasn't feeling the onion thing, so I picked up a piece of onion and, I don't know, I just threw it over my shoulder . . . AND RIGHT AFTER THAT, like a split second after, practically every girl in the cafeteria picked up a piece of onion from their Salisbury steak and threw it over their shoulder. Just. Like. I. Did. And I'm like, whoa.

But I'm like, I get it. But I want to make sure. So I took a few peas in my hand—and I threw them straight up into the air. Oh my God. You should have seen it. Every girl. Everywhere. Peas. Flying. Straight up into the air. And they're all looking at me, like, "You are s-o-o-o-o the supercoolest and you're s-o-o-o-o famous, so we'll do anything you do," and I'm like, awesome, this could be really cool.

So later after fifth period I'm walking down the hall and I'm thinking, let's see how far this can go. So I reached up into my blouse and supercasually unhooked my bra, then pulled it out and held it in my hand to my side and kept

walking—tra-la-la la-la—as if I'm like, you know, holding a
dog leash or something. No biggie. Right? Two secs later
every girl in the hallway pulled out their bras without
saying a word—no joke—and they just walked supermellow (like
me), with their bras dangling from their hands (the guys
couldn't believe what was happening!).

Then I stepped outside and I pulled out a lighter and
torched my bra and tossed it in the Dumpster and walked
back inside. I mean, why not? Right? I just have to be me.
Then *poof*. Big-time. There's like so many bras, and they're
all on fire, and the Dumpster's this huge, freaky bonfire
from like *War of the Worlds* or something. Only its bras!
S-o-o-o-o cool.

And then MAJOR bummer! Principal Flack totally grabs me and
PUSHES me into his office and he's yelling at me, and Mrs.
Menefee (remember her?) (that hippie-dippy guidance counselor
with hairy armpits), eeeow, she tries to "bond" with me and
be all "down" and she's asking me if I was trying to make
some sort of bra-burning feminist Betty Friedan statement or
something, and I'm like, Betty WHOOOOOO? Is she Betty
Crocker's sister? Hahahaha!

She keeps talking-talking-talking, and Flack keeps yelling-
yelling-yelling, and I didn't know what to do, so I say,
"Guess what Jack Black told me? He grew up in a sex commune.
Gross, right? I think he was trying to hit on me—but I was
DEF not interested. I mean, maybe if he was Colin Farrell or
something. Love. Him. S-o-o-o-o cute. Have you seen his sex
tape? I did. His thingie points to the side. Really. It
curves. Like a question mark."

I'm home now. I was SUSPENDED! Can you believe? Mom is pissed. So is Dad. But I didn't do ANYTHING wrong. What's wrong is Marietta. What's wrong is I haven't heard back from LLB. Doesn't Ringo miss me? Did they write their lyrics yet? And record them? I need a follow-up to "Touch my Daisy" n-o-o-o-o-w! Lissa mashes LLB! It's gotta happen! They have my tracks down already. WTF is the hold up?

I hate you for not e-mailing me back.

Lates,
Moi

P.S. I sewed up the little stab wounds on your monkey. Okay?? I even gave him extra stuffing. He's fine. He said so. He said, "Monkee fee-wing wee-wee good" or something like that. So e-mail me. Or call me!!!!

I have to hand it to Lisa. She imagines, she plans, she conquers. I don't have a single doubt that she'll somehow end up back in Hollywood—or Texas, or New York City, or wherever it is she wants to go. Maybe Lisa once again has something to teach me. Maybe I need to do a little more imagining and planning in order to really conquer Meri.

I was just about to read the rest of her e-mails when I noticed Tamari and Pumpkin Seed. They'd been sleeping (they seem especially expert at this activity), but suddenly, and in unison, their heads popped up and their ears insistently crooked this way and that, as if they were receiving some sort of Morse code signal. I've read about animals picking up on natural disasters before they actually happen (both dogs and cats are said to be able to sense an oncoming earthquake seconds, sometimes minutes, before humans do), and after they perked up, I heard a familiar pavement-slapping sound. I gulped. They were picking up on an unnatural disaster, not a natural one. I flung the pages, whipped the curtain aside, gazed out the window—then pulled my head back, just a bit, so I couldn't be seen.

There they were, the St. Eulalia posse and Albino Girl, casually breezing toward Alpha Beta Delta, whirling around on their skateboards. *Go out there and tell them to get lost,* I thought. And that's just what I did. I bolted downstairs, stepped commandingly out the front door, and was just about ready to run across the street and give those girls a good tongue-lashing when I heard a violent whirring above me. Dirt and papers flew, my hair was blown in every direction. I ducked inside for cover. A helicopter was landing. The rotor blades gradually slowed—though they still whipped threateningly—then the cabin door popped open and out swept Meri, half-smiling, holding a cocktail glass with a greenish-looking liquid. Albino Girl and the St. Eulalia posse circled around her as if they were satellite moons orbiting their planet. I got a good look at everything by peeking through the front door mail slot. As usual, Meri was strikingly put together, and her head was held high. She wore large Chanel sunglasses, a scarlet knee-high Diesel sheath dress, a long gold chain necklace with an amethyst jewel, black net stockings, and incongruous, but somehow fitting, heavy black combat boots. Slung over her arm was a slick black leather jacket (it was cold out, but the sun was shining brightly), and over her shoulder, an impossibly huge Dior handbag (who needs the gym, I've often thought, when you can use those massive Dior bags as free weights?). Her look had a fussy, too-perfect sheen; she was a movie star ready for action. I was surprised in one sense. Her outfit almost seemed "rocker chick," or something that Paris Hilton might wear if she had a genuine sense of style (an oxymoronic observation, I know, but it made sense to me), and I wondered also why she wasn't wearing clothes from her Whatever line, though she probably felt that she was above such plebeian promotional efforts. Why not leave that to the "lowly" CEC girls (and Bitch Kitty)? From the corner of my eye, I also noticed barbed wire. I wasn't sure what I was looking at—I was too nervously engrossed by Meri—but I sure found out by the time the party started.

Poor Shanna-Francine. She tries so hard. She had meant Viva Veterans Day to be a true celebration of Latin American veterans' contributions to the military throughout the ages, but she also (unfortunately) wanted to make a "statement" about America's blatant racism. "The first slaves in the Americas were imported from Spain," she had told me. "And our current political effort to demonize Mexicans who cross our borders is only making matters worse, even though Mexicans are only taking labor-intensive, menial jobs that American workers don't want anymore."

She may be right (I had no reason to think she wasn't, and while I haven't done as much reading on the matter as she has, even I had to admit that all the border patrol talk on the news lately smacks of something foul). But being right about something, no matter what it is, is a far cry from being able to skillfully make that point at a party (of all places). Just before it really got going, Shanna-Francine bounced up to me and thrust a video camera in my hands.

"Here!" she exclaimed. "You were so good at documenting things before. I thought you'd like to do it today, too. In fact, it's an order from your president."

I was touched. It had been my idea to document our fund-raising and celebratory efforts so that we'd have something positive to show the Intersorority Governing Council when we appear before them in December, and here was Shanna-Francine, cheerfully ordering me to continue my camerawoman efforts—as if everything was the same, as if I really was still a sister.

But jeez Louise, once I aimed the camera, I didn't know where the heck to point it. The house was quickly crowded with Latin American war veterans of all ages, as well as their husbands, wives, and children, and while most of them looked bewildered, a few were obviously steaming mad. And who could blame them? At the front of the house, guests were greeted with rolls of glinting barbed wire looped across a rented eight-foot high fence, flashing red lights, and a group of sisters dressed in combat gear with fake machine guns and German shepherds on leashes. It was a makeshift replica of the U.S.-Mexican border. Guests streamed in, astonished at first, handing over their invites, which were in the form of expired green cards. A large flashing sign above said: WELCOME TO MEXICO! VIVA VETERANS DAY!

Inside, the living room had been turned into a garish eye-popping mock-up of a Mexican border party town, like Tijuana, with Mexican flags, hanging piñatas, two booths meant to be illegal pharmacies selling discount Viagra and Xanax, as well as several sisters lewdly dressed up as Mexican prostitutes ("*Oooh, papi chulo!*" they cried. "*Ven aquí!*"). Okay, so maybe the guests could have forgiven the excess and regarded the party as a "statement" about how Latin Americans are unfairly marginalized in society, which is what Shanna-Francine intended, and yet there was one thing they could not forgive, probably best expressed by an aging veteran who cried out, "*Este comida sabe a miedra de perro!*" which I later learned roughly translates to "This food tastes like dog poop!" but I actually didn't need the translation, because he angrily spat a bit of his overstuffed vegan taco into his (Mexican-flag-patterned) cocktail napkin. The point was made. The Birkenstock girls had blown it. *Uh-oh*, I thought abruptly, *where's Meri? What the heck is she doing?*

The crowd was getting angrier, despite Lindsay's desperate attempt to entertain them by performing folklorico dance moves in a near-cartoonish Mexican peasant dress (while wielding her auntie's scepter), and it took some effort to bob above their heads in order to scan my surroundings. At the foyer, I saw a grim-faced Dean Pointer shouldering forth with David Martinez, the vice-chancellor of student affairs, who looked ashen and traumatized, as if someone had just stabbed him in the heart. But no Meri. My panic was rising. Where was she? I raced to the kitchen. Nothing. No Meri. I bolted to the back porch. There was no one (save for the Mexican-American veteran tending to her ailing six-year-old son, who was retching up his vegan tostada into a planter). Now I was confused, and I didn't like it. Nervously, I ran back into the living room—and yelped.

"Looking for someone?" she whispered breathily. "What happened to your neck? Eileen told me it's a slut mark. I find that hard to believe."

"What are you doing here?" I gasped.

"I'm enjoying the party. Aren't you?" She gestured to the increasingly unruly crowd, and she laughed—lightly, airily. "I didn't even have to do anything this time. You girls are amazing." Then she squinted her eyes; her mind was processing something, you could almost hear *click-click, click-click*. "I suppose there are flickers of truth in what Shanna-Francine has tried to do here today." She sighed. "But there's no excitement in that truth, and no clarity, either. Tsk. What a shame. It's an embarrassment, actually. My respect for her is shattered." Darn it, she was right (about the party), and, oh, how I hated her for that.

And then, for reasons I didn't immediately grasp, she brushed her fingertips lightly against her arm. "Smart girls wax their hair off," she intoned softly, gazing lovingly at herself. "It's best to start at age thirteen. Never shave. If you regularly wax without shaving, by the time you turn thirty-five or so, you'll only need to wax once every five months. When I was a little girl, Cook spoiled me. He made me my own special wax with sugar, water and fresh lemon nimbu juice."

"I think you should leave," I boldly, if nervously, told her. "Now. Unless you want me to throw you out." Oh God, I can't believe I said that. I was trying to be Dark Cindy and heed Liam's wise words, and Mamacita's, too, and to my short-lived delight, she was actually taken aback. She raised an eyebrow, as if assessing my newfound daring. Then she chuckled.

"Nice try, little bow-wow."

My mind raced. That's it? You tell her to get lost and she does nothing? What's the point of being Dark Cindy, or trying to be, if it doesn't change anything? Then it hit me. Not dark enough. Fight a bee? Sting like a bee! Meri had already turned around. She was striding into the crowd. And that's when I furiously charged forth, grabbed her shoulders from the back, and pushed her hard—"Hey! What the . . . ?" she gasped—right out the front door. She spun around immediately, her hair seeming to flare out with indignation.

"I'm a black belt, Cindy. I've studied karate. In fact, I studied for twelve years with the renowned Sensei—"

"If you really did," I interrupted, "then you know that karate can only be used for self-defense."

"Very good, sempai Cindy. Aikido is the way of harmony. So go on. Make your move. Give me an excuse. I dare you."

"I want you to leave," I said, trying to contain myself.

"What? You come in peace? Aw. But I don't. And I'm staying. Oh, and fair warning, if you so much as touch me one more—"

"Blah-blah-blah. The usual boring threats," I quipped, gritting my teeth. *It's time to let Meri know what's really going down*, I thought. *She needs to know, right here, right now, that she's dealing with a new kind of Cindy.* "Look at me," I told her, my anger tightly coiled. "I have nothing to lose anymore. And neither do my friends."

She half smiled, whispering, "There's always more to lose."

"You're not listening. Don't I seem different? Look at me. Go on. What do you see?" She made a mockingly elaborate show of peering at me, then impatiently shook her head, clearing her thoughts. Something was bothering her. She seemed genuinely concerned. She sighed heavily.

"Cindy, let's stop this for a moment. Okay? And I'll be honest with you—because I think somebody should be. You want to know what I see? All right. I see someone trying on a new coat, but it doesn't fit very well. Do you understand what I'm saying?" My heart skipped a beat. Was I really so transparent? "I see someone with a jumble of ideas squirreling around in their noggin, but they haven't been worked through. I see a fluffy toy poodle trying very hard to be a Rottweiler. It's sad, really. Fly back down to earth, Cindy—it's safer down there—and yes, there's always the possibility that if you soar up higher, you'll reach something. But I doubt it. And I think you do, too." She was gutting me. Not physically, but with words. I struggled to respond, but she wasn't finished. She smiled warmly, as if she were offering me her most heartfelt sympathy. "I'm used to being worshipped, Cindy. Lots of girls have tried to emulate me, but it never works out. My behavior was born out of my own spontaneous need for it, and in other people's hands, well, let's just say that a copy isn't much fun when the original's around. The best thing you can say about these girls is 'Look, she reminds me of Meri,' and what's the point of that? And you. Look at you. You have the guts to try to be something you're not—that's something, I suppose—but the end result is ludicrous. Stop, Cindy. Enough. You'll always be what you've always been. A needy little good-girl who wants an A. Now, don't worry. I'll give it to you. But for effort only."

It took me a second to realize that I was hyperventilating, but not from nervousness or anxiety. My brain was fritzing out because I didn't know what to do next. Diamonds glinted. Meri flinched.

"I dub thee Dullsville," said Lindsay, her singsongy voice dripping with sarcasm, bringing her scepter to Meri's shoulder. "And please. Fishnet stockings? Are you for real? Which side of the block are you working? Uh-oh. Phone's ringing. Hello? It's for you, Meri. It's Tara Reid. She wants her outfit back. Like, now."

Meri's face hardened. Oh, boy. Criticizing her fashion was surely a big no-no, and then—oh my God—Lindsay grabbed Meri's arm and pushed a stack of documents in her hand.

"I'm officially serving you," she said. "Daddy's suing you for destroying auntie's hennin hat. It's a priceless historical artifact." She gestured to the papers. "Oh, and I posted them on *The Smoking Gun* and sent a copy to the university press. Bad publicity, Meri. Something you can't control. And yeah, I know, pretty small potatoes, but you know what? I'm going to enjoy every stinking minute of it."

Wow. Dark Cindy? How about Dark Lindsay? Meri smiled— oh no, this can't be good, I thought—then held the papers up to Lindsay's face and viciously ripped them in half. My eyes popped out of my head. Lindsay was stunned, and while I'm sure she would have found her footing and fought back, Meri was already turning to walk away. Now that I look back on it, maybe there is hope for Dark Cindy. My mouth opened. I cried out, "Wrong move, Meri. Just wait, I'll bring you down. In fact, I'll destroy you."

She kept moving. But I continued hollering—and she stopped dead in her tracks.

"Then where will you be? Huh? Let's see. Hey, I know. You'll be living with a construction worker. In Queens. And taking care of his incontinent dog and his grandmother you'll have to bathe.

How does that sound? Huh? Want to play games, Meri? I'll wipe the floor with you."

Oh my God, oh my God, oh my God. Does she know? Does she recognize the words from her own diary? She stood there motionless—her back was to me and Lindsay—then spun around and pushed her face right up to mine. Ahhhhhhh! I wanted to scream. My heart was pounding, but I gave nothing away. I smiled—just slightly. *Click-click, click-click.* She was processing. Something wasn't right, but she didn't know what. Her icy eyes drilled right through me, and jeez, I almost thought she was going to put her hands on my head and do a Vulcan mind-meld or something. But it wouldn't have worked. Why? Because I was following Liam's advice. Deception is a powerful agent. The will is everything. I willed myself to give back nothing. Just emptiness. *Naw,* I thought, *send her an image,* and I did. Look at the "good-girl," Meri. She's blasting forth on a hot-pink skateboard wearing a fierce leather mini, stiletto boots, fingerless black gloves, and in her right hand—*crack!*—she has a whip. Woo-hoo! I'm not sure if she saw it. She suddenly rolled her eyes and murmured testily, "Whatever."

And off she went. My hair blew back, and so did Lindsay's, and we held up our hands to protect ourselves from all the flying debris. Meri's helicopter was ascending. As it curved toward the horizon, I caught a glimpse of her gazing out the window; her face was granite, her eyes red with fury. Something was wrong, and she still couldn't figure it out. The whirring blades became a distant sound. The helicopter vanished in a faraway cluster of dark clouds.

Wow. A flood of relief washed over me. No, scratch that, it was more than relief. I felt strangely transformed. I had stood up to Meri. Successfully. I even used a weapon—words from her own diary, which I flung in her face—and nothing bad happened. Not a thing. In fact, she didn't even try to retaliate. And there I was. I was still standing. I had made a choice. I didn't back down. Instead of cowering in fear, or running away (which is what I would normally do) I had dared to change my behavior, and because of that—eureka!—I got a brand-new result. In a small but significant way, it felt like I'd won.

"What the heck just happened between you two?" asked a confused Lindsay.

I was only half listening to her. Right then and there, Dark Cindy was born. If I were a conventional superhero, I would have run into the nearest phone booth and—*poof!*—leaped back out wearing a slinky skintight costume. But I didn't need that (and I've always thought that was more of a boy thing, actually). My transformation was subtle; it was real, because it was happening inside me, and while I was definitely tickled by the idea of running around in a hot leather mini and cracking a whip, I also knew that those things were just icing on the cake, they were window dressing. Meri was right (again). Why should I be a copycat? Who wants to be a Meri clone? Mamacita was right too. Fight a bee, sting like a bee, sure, but no two bees are alike. Dark Cindy is special because there's only one Cindy. Period.

"Meri's a scuzzy hellpig!" exclaimed Lindsay, though it was pretty hard to take her seriously in that ridiculous Mexican peasant outfit.

"C'mon," I said. "You need to get out of those clothes."

A half hour later, the dust had cleared. The party was over, and it was an official disaster for Alpha Beta Delta. Several sisters were dazedly cleaning up. Lindsay and I helped. Under the cover of her umbrella, we carried several overstuffed garbage bags to the side of the house, where we tossed them in the Dumpster. From the porch, we heard soft crying. It was Shanna-Francine. I started to go to her, but Lindsay stopped me.

"It's okay," she whispered. "Bobbie's with her." A sudden, blood-curdling scream took us by surprise. Inside the house, a sister cried out, "Meri!"

Quick as bunnies, we ran around to the front. *What now?* I thought. Did Meri pop out from hiding? Did she somehow parachute out of her helicopter? But we didn't make it inside. We didn't have to. There she was, incredibly, just a few feet from the house, strolling up self-assuredly. At the front window, sisters were peeking out, gesturing fearfully.

"Let's roll," I said grimly, and walked right up to her. *Why should I let her near the house?* I thought. *Whatever business she has, she can deal with Lindsay and me.* The three of us stood in the middle of the street. Meri smiled, flipped back her thick raven hair, and cheerily whispered, "Hi, girls."

"What do you want?" I commanded.

"You're a scuzzy hellpig!" cried Lindsay.

"Stop it," I scolded. Name-calling, I knew, wasn't going to get us anywhere. I turned back to Meri. "Well?"

"Oh, it's nothing I want," she said cagily. "I just happened to be in Dean Pointer's office. See, I thought he might want a lift somewhere, and helicopters are so much fun. Anyway, the dean was there, and Mr. Martinez, too. We all had a nice cup of tea. Jasmine tea. It wasn't very good, but then there's nothing better than Cook's homemade Oolong downy pearls. She imports select raw branchlets and leaves from the Fijian province. As a child, I helped her wrap the pearls in soft silk mesh to dry by the—"

"Get to the point," I demanded. I mean, jeez, if I'd let her go on she might have given us a lecture on every conceivable floral tea going all the way back to the Ming Dynasty.

"Don't worry, little bow-wow, there's a point," she said, then pulled out a sealed white envelope. "Here. I told the dean I'd do him a favor and bring this over." Before I could take it, Lindsay hurled aside her umbrella, snatched the envelope, and got ready to rip it in front of Meri's face.

"Ah-ah-ah," she warned. Lindsay froze. "Not a good idea. I mean, go on, rip it to shreds. But it won't change anything." I pried the envelope from Lindsay's hands and glared hotly at Meri. She chuckled lightly and gave me a wink. I was oh-so-tempted to startle her like I had before, but something inside me commanded: *No, don't. Wait. Look at all the diary pages and know exactly what you're doing with them first.* I watched her walk away. There was nothing special about it, and yet there was. Meri can take an ordinary gesture, or even an everyday stroll across the street, and make it seem scarily triumphant. I almost admire her for that.

In the house, I gave the sealed envelope to Shanna-Francine. It was addressed to her.

"Burn it!" fumed Lindsay, who really was starting to get out of hand. "She's a pisshole! She's vomit! She's a blister on her uncle's ass!"

"Lindsay!" I cried. I mean, enough with her newfound potty mouth.

"You want me to open it for you?" asked Bobbie gruffly, putting her arm around Shanna-Francine. She was trembling, but she shook her head no. "Okay, then. Just do it. I know you can. Get ahold of it like a bulldog and rip it open."

Shanna-Francine took a deep breath, closed her eyes, and tore it open. It was a letter on official RU embossed stationery. Her eyes scanned it intently, and almost instantly she struggled for breath, her eyes welling up.

"What is it?" implored Bobbie. But Shanna-Francine couldn't speak. Her mouth opened, like she was about to scream, but out came an ear-splitting screech, causing Tamari and Pumpkin Seed to run terrified under the couch. Then she covered her mouth in horror, dropped the note, and ran up the stairs. *Boom.* We heard her door slam shut. Bobbie picked up the note and read it out loud. It was seemingly benign. Both Dean Pointer and David Martinez were "requesting" Shanna-Francine's presence at the dean's office tomorrow at twelve thirty p.m. to discuss her "problematic presidency" and "thoughts about the future direction of Alpha Beta Delta."

"Jeez, that can't be good," said Lindsay.

Bobbie gave her a withering glare. "Oh, good observation, Linds. And for that you win the porcelain hairnet." She stomped upstairs after Shanna-Francine.

Despite Lindsay's invitation to stay the night, I insisted that she drive me back to Chappaqua. I was on a day pass, and I didn't want to get Shanna-Francine into any more trouble by breaking the rules and staying the night. As Lindsay drove—spouting more harsh expletive-deleteds (Meri seems to have turned her into a truck driver)—I gazed straight ahead, trying to concentrate and keep my thoughts ahead of Meri. Obviously, I realized, the meeting tomorrow had been orchestrated by Meri. But what exactly was the result she wanted? And why, I also wondered, did Mr. Sugarman previously assure Mom that nothing bad would happen to me right before Dean Pointer booted me from RU? Then it hit me all at once. Follow the money.

It started in Newport. When Meri was twelve. She wanted the family to move. Her father had refused. And she "dropped the documents in front of him, the ones I was able to secure last week." Follow the money. Meri's ability to toss about astounding amounts of cash—surely more than most wealthy heiresses do— is directly related to the documents she was somehow able to obtain when she was twelve. Meri is blackmailing her own father. The documents, and her no doubt continued threats of public exposure, enable her to control the entire Sugarman fortune— even to this day. And yet, as important as this piece of the puzzle might be, I was still frustrated. After all, it had been staring me in the face when I first read the diary entries, so it wasn't exactly news.

"Oh my God!" I exclaimed out loud. Lindsay shrieked, and gripped the wheel.

"Where are they? Are we being following again? What's going on?"

No one was following us. I had just been bonked on the head with a stunning realization. Perhaps, I realized, one piece of the puzzle—namely, Meri's blackmail and her hold on the Sugarman fortune—would make a lot more sense if I were able to figure out what other puzzle piece it connected to.

"Why did Meri decide to go to RU?" I asked, more to myself than to Lindsay, who shrugged.

"It's a good school?"

"Nope. Uh-uh. It's not about RU. It's about being at RU."

"Huh?"

"Think about it. She has the money, the power, the ability to influence anyone."

"Okay. And?"

"She could have gone to college anywhere. Right? In fact, it would have made more sense if she went to the Sorbonne. Like Jackie O."

"I don't get it."

"I don't either," I murmured gravely, but I knew I was onto something. Something big.

"Want to get a drink? Thinking about Meri makes me want a fucking huge-ass cocktail."

I agreed, but we made a deal. No more smutty language. "It doesn't become you," I told her. "What would your auntie think? You have her beautiful scepter and you're running around using such dirty language."

Lindsay sighed. "You're right. Fuck me. I mean, oh . . ."

"Darn it. Try that."

Lindsay shook her head. "Not the same."

"Oh, doggone it."

"Better. Sort of."

"Stinkers. Crud you."

"I like crud you."

"You bet your sweet aunt's kisser."

"Yeah! And your uncle's greasy cornhole!"

"Lindsay!" I screamed.

"What? I didn't use the *F* word."

"Okay. You're right." We agreed. She can be angry and naughty—and not resort to the *F* word. Or the *S* word. Or the *A* word. It seemed like a good compromise.

"Meri just makes me s-o-o-o"—she grimaced—"so freakin' mad." The anger in her eyes was there, but a kind of grief bubbled just beneath the surface, and I didn't have to ask why. "Bud's going to get sprung," she abruptly told me, smiling faintly. "You'll see." I smiled back, nodding my head, and I pushed the image of a jail-house wedding (and seedy conjugal visits) out of my head.

It was Aireoke Night at Swingles. One after another, drunken RU college students took to the makeshift stage at the far end of the dance floor and played invisible electric guitar to a variety of guitar-heavy songs (Jimi Hendrix, for obvious reasons, was a fave selection). Maybe it was the cocktails Lindsay and I were drinking, or maybe my mind just needed a break from thinking about Meri, but some of the Aireokers were actually kind of amazing; it really did seem like they were playing—you could practically see the guitar being strummed and furiously fingered in their hands—and a couple of the guys had the swivel-hipped sexy rock star moves down pat. Which reminded me of Lisa. After she saw Britney madly strum the air guitar in her video for "Do Somethin'," she played Aireoke practically day and night for about two weeks, singing "Do Somethin'," even at breakfast, which definitely got on Mom's nerves.

"Lisa, no playing guitar at the table," she said, trying to placate her by referring to the phantom instrument as if it were real. "Put it away."

"Why don't you d-o-o-o-o-o-o-o somethin'!" shrieked Lisa, singing the lyrics and strumming wildly. "I see ya lookin' at me, like I'm some kind of fre-e h-e-eak . . ."

"Lisa . . ."

"Whatcha gonna do when the crowd goes ayo!"

"Young lady . . ."

"Why don't you d-o-o-o-o-o-o-o somethin'!"

Sitting next to her, I yanked her arm and made an elaborate show of "grabbing" her guitar and "banging" it several times on the table. "There," I said. "It's broken. You can't play it. And can you please not play it on the bus anymore? It's embarrassing."

"Oh, please," she guffawed. "You? I'm the one with the reputation."

"A reputation and a rash."

"Bite me!"

"Both of you, stop it!" Mom scolded. We continued eating our cold cereal in silence. But after only a few bites of her Strawberry Blasted Honeycomb, Lisa shoved her hand under the table, whipped it back up, and triumphantly proclaimed, "I have a spare!" There was nothing we could do. She couldn't be stopped. "Why don't you d-o-o-o-o-o-o-o somethin'!" she shrieked, strumming like crazy.

"Next up," called the Aireoke announcer, "it's Aer Lingus!" The crowd applauded wildly—expectantly, even—and Lindsay and I glanced at each other. Who at RU would be silly enough to have an Aireoke name like Aer Lingus? The opening guitar licks from Janet Jackson's "Black Cat" blasted. The crowd screamed. And, oh my God, out flew Sebastian, shaking it this way and that, speckled in gold and silver glitter, strumming his ax like a pro. Lindsay and I screamed and cheered (I think I spilled half my cocktail on someone). It felt good to laugh and have fun. Sebastian struck a final shoulder-vamping pose, whispered "Hot-cha!" seductively into the mic, then scampered off the stage to tumultuous applause (and a rose thrown by a cute guy I'm assuming was the new "hot CSP" he'd e-mailed Sheila about). I couldn't wait to see who was next.

"Ladies and gentlemen," cried the announcer, "up next, Whammy Bar!" The audience really screamed this time—and it was mostly girls' screams. Nickelback's "Animals" detonated from the club's speakers. The girls' screams grew even louder (several of them were openly swooning), and I was honestly surprised by how little I cared.

Keith wasn't wearing a shirt, his pumped-up chest and ripped abs were glistening with sweat, and the top button of his (too) tight jeans was undone, giving a peek-a-boo glimpse of his treasure trail (he obviously wasn't wearing underwear). He looked like one of those strategically mussed-up Abercrombie & Fitch models (the ones they try to make look all "tough," even though you can tell it's such a pose), and I so don't mean this in a spiteful way, but even though he was live and right there in front of everyone, he looked airbrushed. And to be honest, he wasn't that good on air guitar (really) (I'm not just saying that) (his strumming was okay, but his fingering never seemed to match the song) (and I'm not being overly critical) (I don't think) (no, I'm not), but he compensated, as he always does, by showing off his physique (anybody who says that guys aren't as vain about their bodies as women are is really kidding themselves) (big-time).

"We can go now," said Lindsay anxiously, which was very sweet of her, but so unnecessary. I'm not going to say I didn't feel anything by watching Keith wriggle half-naked up there (with all those girls squealing and reaching up for him). I felt a pang, definitely, but it was dim, and it was mingled with thoughts like, *Was it just the sex?* and *Was I really in love with him?* and *Was being wanted by someone who's so popular the real thrill?* and *Will I actually know true love when it comes along?*

"And people have the nerve to call me a slut," sniped a voice next to me. It was Doreen, who'd swept up with a cocktail, resplendent in Whatever fashion. "I mean, look at him. Why doesn't he just whip it out and hang a hat on it?"

"Or a cowbell," added Lindsay.

"What is it with guys these days? I hooked up with this dude the other day between classes, he takes off his shirt, and like, his chest hair was trimmed."

"No. Really?" I asked.

"Uh-huh. Shaved. And prickly. Ouch. Then he takes off his pants and his CKs, and his pubes—oh my God—like a topiary bush. I didn't know whether to blow him or fertilize him. Then he has the nerve to tell me that I'd look really sick with a boob job. And I'm like, dude, these are real, okay? They're fucking famous."

"All over town," deadpanned Lindsay.

"Damn right. What the hell happened to real men? And I know what it is, too. They watch too much porno. We're all supposed to get boob jobs now. We're all supposed to have these big, squishy Gummi Bears instead of breasts. Well, I for one do not need a boob job."

"I don't think you do either," I said. "I don't think any girl does."

"And forget anal bleaching. No way."

"That's disgusting," gasped Lindsay.

"See? That's what I'm talking about. And it's all thanks to those stupid porno stars. Now we're supposed to cut up the goods and slap on new parts. We're supposed to pimp our own ride. Literally. Well I'm not doing it. I'm Doreen Fucking Buchnar, goddamn it. And that should be enough!" Lindsay burst out clapping. And I'll admit, I did too. It's silly, maybe, but in her own way, Doreen had made a declaration, a call to arms for (slutty) girls everywhere, and I actually agreed with it. Why should any (slutty) (or otherwise) girl have to be anything other than what she already is? Lindsay brought her scepter to Doreen's shoulder and said, "I dub thee Doreen, Real and Braless."

Doreen smiled, then sighed heavily. "Oh, well. What comes around goes around, right? When you sleep around?"

"I don't sleep around," I said.

"Neither do I," said Lindsay.

"I'm thinking of putting my kitty on ice, if you want to know the truth."

"Really? That's wonderful, Doreen," and I meant that. Maybe not sleeping around, I thought, would help her discover that she has so much more to offer—besides meaningless sex. But then this was Doreen.

"I mean, at least for tonight," she harrumphed. "Look at this place. There's not even anyone worth flirting with here. Sebastian's the only one with real chest hair." Her eyes went back to Keith. She was angry (or heartbroken?), and she snapped bitterly, "Big stud on campus. You know, he never went down on me."

Lindsay shrieked, then burst out laughing.

"I don't think that's funny," said Doreen. "In fact, it was frustrating as hell. What's so funny?"

"Nothing!" I blurted. I really didn't want to swap bedroom stories with Doreen (eeeow!) (though I'll admit to feeling kind of "validated," as they say on *Tyra*, because that meant Keith doesn't go down on any girl) (which is his failing) (and not mine).

Keith was finishing up—and what a finish it was. He struck the final chord and leaped off the stage and into a throng of adoring (and semirabid) female fans. For the briefest second he caught my eye—and I screamed. Oh my God, was I seeing things? In the crowd, just near the stage area, was Patty. She was bopping to the music, then she vanished behind the stage and out the back entrance. *Cut her off at the pass*, I told myself. I ran outside the bar's front entrance, sprinted to the back. It was empty and desolate. There was no one there. Was I imagining things?

"Patty," I cried out, but nothing answered except the *thump-thump* from the bass inside the club. It seemed to throb in the pit of my stomach. "Oh, Patty," I whispered to myself. I stepped back to the front and Lindsay burst out of the club.

"I saw her too! Did you find her?"

I'm definitely not one for speeding, but as Lindsay and I rode back to Chappaqua, I told her to step on it. If there was even the slightest chance that Patty might show up tonight at my jail cell, I wanted to be there.

"RU's rehab is open twenty-four hours," said Lindsay. Maybe, she explained, if Patty showed up, I could call her on her cell, and she'd dash over in her Porsche and we'd force her to go back to the rehab.

It's two a.m. now. I've woken up twice. No Patty. I've left the door unlocked just in case. Oh, Patty, where are you? There was a little note pushed under my door when I came back tonight. It said, "Thinking of you. Cliff." Why did that make my heart leap? It's so sweet. Just thinking about Cliff makes me smile. And feel relaxed. He's so smart. And talented. And we were never at a loss for words. And I love his lips. And his love patch. Something must be really wrong with me. Are CSP's supposed to make you feel this way? And can I turn it off (so I don't get hurt)? I have to go to sleep. I'll channel Dark Cindy. She'll tell me what to do.

Dark Cindy's already told me what to do about Meri. Follow the money. I think I've just about got it all figured out. Honest. I've taken a cue from Lisa. I'm imagining, I'm planning, and soon, very soon—I'll conquer. I should be back at RU in a few days! Ha. You can't stop me now, Meri.

NOVember 12

Dear Diary:

Today's Sunday, so I didn't plan on waking up too early. Or let's put it this way, I sure as heck didn't plan on waking up at five thirty a.m., but for some reason, my eyes popped open. Panic gripped me. I had the distinct feeling someone was watching me. *Crunch-crunch-crunch.* I sat up with a start. Patty was sitting cross-legged on the bed, chomping on Mucho Nacho Snack Chips, her eyes bugged out, her hair madly whirling and sticking out in multiple directions, as if it were searching desperately for every possible avenue of escape.

"There is no point in overvaluing one's lost innocence," she whispered intensely, allowing Mucho Nacho chip crumbs to dribble onto her grimy black sweater. "Once it's gone—*poof!*—that's it. Pretending it isn't is romanticizing the self." *Crunch-crunch-crunch.* "Which may cause mood and dissociative disorders not otherwise specified."

I didn't move an inch. I was captivated. She was continuing our last "session" together, and it's true, I do want back what Meri has stolen: my innocence, my carefree outlook (no matter how lonely it left me at times), and most of all, my once-unshakable belief in the decency of everyone around me.

"Of course, mine is a minority point of view," she continued in hushed tones, feeding herself more Mucho Nacho chips. "UCLA psychiatrist Dr. Jeffrey Schwartz writes in *A Return to Innocence* that aspiring to innocence is the 'highest of human accomplishments,' but I, Patty, say tiddlywinks. Nonsense. Pigs with wings." *Crunch-crunch-crunch*. "Don't we want to develop into thinking, feeling adults?" *Crunch-crunch-crunch*. "I think we do. God forbid we get caught up in Dr. Schwartz's goofy line of cheese—this fantasy of adult innocence. 'The highest of human accomplishments.' Please! Phooey!" *Crunch-crunch-crunch*. "Does he actually expect us to push aside our natural desire to know ourselves? And the world around us?" *Crunch-crunch-crunch*. "In all its beauty and ickiness?"

She was making sense (kind of), and it made me sad. I told her about a dream I had the other night—I didn't even write it down because it was so brief. I was working as a fry cook at Long John Silver's. They fired me. And before I left, I opened my employee locker and took back all the things that belonged to me. And they were all childhood objects: my recorder from third grade, my teddy bear, my favorite ballerina picture book.

"Mmm. Yes. Kind of obvious, but yes," she said. *Crunch-crunch-crunch*. "The desperation to reclaim what is lost is both touching and poignant."

I also told her, reluctantly at first, about Meri's diary pages, the birth of Dark Cindy, and the strange—I don't know what else to call it—"transformation" I felt when I confronted Meri yesterday. How I wasn't scared. And how I didn't cower in fear. I didn't run away. I stood my ground. And she didn't, miracle of miracles, retaliate. Patty screamed with joy (loudly), and threw her arms up, which sent Mucho Nacho chips flying in every direction.

"Oh, joy!"

Wow. I didn't expect that kind of response. She could tell I was dumbstruck. She took my hand and attempted to be calm, but she was so excited there were tears forming in her eyes.

"Oh, Cindy. Oh, this is wonderful. You had a Corrective Emotional Experience."

"Um. Oh. I see."

"No, you don't. Oh, sweet Cindy. All your life, your conditioning has caused you to run when faced with obstacles. Your fear guided you. Perhaps this was caused by an attachment disorder—let's see, let's see, we'd have to dig deeper. Did your mother hug you enough as a child? Did you feel consoled or anxiety-ridden in her presence?"

"Um. Er."

"Forget that, forget that. For now. Don't you see? All your life your conditioning has caused you to expect disaster, or even punishment, if you stood up for yourself. But you did it! This time you did it. And you weren't punished. An old, unhealthy pattern of behavior was destroyed. That's a Corrective Emotional Experience. There was no disaster. That's why you felt, how did you put it?"

"Transformed?"

"Yes! Oh, Cindy." She pulled me into a hug. I realized that I had tears in my eyes too. Then she abruptly pulled back. She looked deadly serious.

"Hold on. Dark Cindy. Atypical? Pathological? Cognitive distortion? Impulse-control disorder not otherwise specified?"

"What are you saying?" I yelped. "What's wrong with Dark Cindy?" Her eyes glazed over, and her body seemed to deflate, as if a big balloon had been pricked and was going *sssssssss*. She mumbled, "I'm afraid our time is up for . . ."

Boom. She fell back flat on the bed, which was now littered with Mucho Nacho chips and crumbs. *Do it now*, I screamed to myself, *you might never get another chance.* I raced out of my jail cell, and while I had to run a whole block in order to get a signal on my phone, I got through, and within minutes, Lindsay and I startled Patty by gently taking her hands and pulling her up off the bed.

"Huh? Wha?" she murmured, still half-asleep.

"We're going for a ride," said Lindsay at the top of her lungs as if Patty were deaf. Patty's eyes bulged. She panicked.

"Ride? Where? No!"

It was so sad. We really had to grip her tightly—and yank her with all our might, too—in order to get her out of my jail cell and into the backseat of Lindsay's Porsche, which she had parked at my door. Patty screamed, "N-o-o-o-o-o-o-o-o!"

I think she knew where we were taking her. Lindsay floored it, and Patty flung herself in horror against the window, her hands pressed against the glass, as if she were in a paddy wagon on her way to the pokey. Sitting next to her, I tried my best to be reassuring.

"Patty, you're addicted to Skinny. You need help. That's why we're doing this."

"N-o-o-o-o-o-o!" she wailed. "I'm so close. My breakthrough is coming. I know my curative factors, I can facilitate my own dialectic."

Maybe she could, I thought. Patty's so smart. Maybe we were doing the wrong thing.

"Skinny makes me skinny," she sputtered with an errant giggle. I almost laughed along with her. Okay, news flash, I realized, you are not doing the wrong thing. As we neared RU's rehab center, she pressed herself against me like a small child. Her body was shivering. "My problems are fascinating," she whispered, choking back a sob, seeking reassurance of some kind. "Aren't they?"

"Yes, they are," I told her softly.

I'm back in my jail cell now. It's seven a.m. I should go back to sleep, but there's so much to do. Where to start? Then I saw the stack of printouts on the floor next to the bed. *Okay*, I thought, *first things first*. I still hadn't finished reading Lisa's e-mails.

From: <lissa@lissabixby.com>
Date: 8 November
To: <cindybixby@yahoo.com>
Subject: Hasta la pasta, Marietta

Dark Cindy

Yo Sistah!

I am SO out of here. Ha! My agent Jennifer called. I have
meetings to go to in New York City. And get this. TRL wants
me on their sh-o-o-o-o-o-o-o-w!! Y-e-a-a-a-a-a-ah!!
Unbelievable, but not really. TRL needs me!! And so does
Quddus. Hot. He's from Canada. Which is whatever. IMHO. But
I forgive him for that.

Mom and Dad were being total weenies about it—at first. They
didn't want me to go 'cause Dad's busy with work and Mom
doesn't want to miss the Winter Flower Show at the Marietta
Park Conservatory 'cause she has some dumb flower in the
show. What. Ev. Er.

But Jennifer rawks. And so does Frederick. They told them
that Jennifer will be right by my side no matter what happens
(yeah, right!), so I'm FLYING. OUT. TWO. NITE. Y-e-a-a-a-ah!
Meetings. A little B2C. N-WHY-C. Par-t-a-a-a-a-y! I hear
Diddy's got a sick crib. Nice. I wonder if I'll run into L.
Lo? "Hey, guuuurl, look at me, yo. Steppin' back. A hun-did
feet. Ha-ha-ha-ha. Love the new tat." I know we'll hug and
kiss and totally hang. Lissa + L. Lo = World on
Fi-ya! But how to avoid Ashlee. Zzzzz. Thoughts? Suggestions?

I know why you're not answering my e-mails now. You're
jealous. Oh, Sis. Don't you know I wuv you? It's twue. And
like, I'm famous, I know, and that must be s-o-o-o-o-o hard
on you 'cause you're not, but Sis, think about it, families
with two famous sisters—it never works out. One is always
hotter than the other (except for maybe the Olsens, but

171

they're totally creepy). And Sis, I think you're hot,
'cause, you know, we're blood and I have to, but would other
people think that? I really don't want you to get hurt.
Just, like, live through me, okay? I understand.

We Be Blood,
Mwuah!

From: <lissa@lissabixby.com>
Date: 9 November
To: <cindybixby@yahoo.com>
Subject: Ian Somerhalder is FINE!

Dear Sis:

NYC loves m-e-e-e-e-e-e!! Of course. So many meetings today.
Jennifer and I met with these cool CD company peeps. They're
in. No more singles. They want a whole CD!!!!! I was, like,
completely calm. I was all biddness. Yes, I told them, I know
exactly what I want to call my first CD. *Nympho*. And they
were like, wow, do you mean that literally? And I'm like, play
the game, Lissa, and I said, "Oh my God, no, that would be
s-o-o-o-o-o crass. It's like, wanting to be a nympho for life
and for living—and to save trees and fight breast cancer. Shit
like that." So they nodded yes, uh-huh, mmm-hmm. They bought
it. Tee-hee. CD people are dumb. I mean, hello? I'm Lissa.
What do they think I'll do with *Nympho*? Ha-ha-ha-ha. They'll
thank me later. *Ka-ching ka-ching.*

Me and Jennifer walked out of the meeting and we were on the
street and I screamed, "Woo-hoo! Gimmie props, baby. Did I

whale on the sucker or what?" Then we went to more meetings.
MTV. The TRL peeps. Behind-the-scenes guys. What am I going to
sing? And I told them. I have a hot new single. It's called
"Ghetto Grrl." It's like, a hot new mash-up with LLB. And they
were like, wow, will LLB be there? And I say I don't know—I
mean, if they care about their career they will be (I didn't
say that, though)—but I'll def have their tracks backing me.
Like on the real single. We wrote it together, I told them.
Ringo thinks I'm cute. And they were like, wow.

Jennifer was kinda pissed at me about that. We walked out of
there and she said I still don't have the tracks from LLB,
but I totally calmed her down. I said, "Jen. Chill. I'm on
it." Then we went to this publishing place on Sixth Avenue—
where they actually make books—and we met with this editor,
Julia, who was s-o-o-o-o cool, and she has like this bitchin'
view outside her office and really great shoes. And get this:
She wanted to talk to me about a book . . . about my life!!

"Awesome," I said. "I'm all about writing. I should definitely
write it all by myself. Like, right from my mouth. You so
want that. Have you read my blog?" Julia looked kind of funny
for a sec, then said, "Yes, actually, I have." Then Jennifer
said to her, "Ghostwriter?" and Julia nodded yes. So cool!!
Ghostwriter! Like, Poltergeist Pen! Love it!! And it so makes
sense. I'm Lissa. Why should I be an *ordinary* writer?
More meetings, more meetings, more meetings, and then I
thought, *Whoa. When do we shop?* It was late afternoon
already. Jennifer kept up with me. Kirna Zabête, Mayle,
Catherine Malandrino. Ever. Ree. Where. New York is cool,
'cause you can shop and shop, and like, throw all your shit

in a cab and keep going. So later I jumped in a cab by myself
and screamed, "Butter!" And I was off. *Phew*. I mean, why did
Jennifer have to follow me ALL DAY? Right? Am I right?
Butter's in Brooklyn. High-high-high-end couturier. Jelly's
just down the street. Shoes. Oh my God. I bought six pairs.
wOOt! Then a voice whispered behind me, "If you do that again
I'll handcuff you to my wrist." I turned around. Holy shit, it
was Jennifer, and she was smiling really nicely. And she
winked. Ha-ha-ha-ha. What a kidder. "Wow. I totally thought
you were in the cab with me," I told her. "Forgives?"

We had dinner at this place called Cowgirl Hall of Fame, and
the New Yorkers, man, they were so pretending they didn't know
me. Which was cool. And then we went back to the Soho hotel
place where I'm staying and Jennifer—get this—said, "Good
night." Ha. Like it's lights out for me at nine o'clock? Get
real. Then she left. And I went to the bar.
And. Time. Stood. Still. There he was. Ian Somerhalder. All.
Alone. Oh my God. So. Fine. So I go up to his bar table and
sit, 'cause, like, we're both famous, so we both need a drink.
Right? "'Sup, bitch," I said. And he said, "Do I know you?" *Be
cool*, I thought, *this is what New Yorkers do. Remember? From
the restaurant?* "No, you don't," I said–wink- wink–"And I
don't know you, either"–wink-wink-wink–"But here we are.
Whatcha drinkin'?" He told me he was drinking Coca-Cola, and I
said with what, and he said just Coca-Cola, and I thought,
right—we don't want anyone to know we need a drink every now
and then 'cause we're, like, so majorly famous. Gotcha.
B-e-e-e cool.

When the barmaid came up, I told her I wanted a Coke. "A
famous one," I said–*wink-wink*. "I don't think I know how to

make that," she said. Too funny. New Yorkers crack me up. Then she sorta gasped. "You're Lissa, right?" Wow. Uncool. But I said yes, and she said she'd be right back and walked away and whipped out her cell phone.

I sighed. *Sigh! Heavy sigh!* "Sorry, Ian," I said. "She's probably calling the tabs"-*sigh! heavy sigh!*-"And the bloggers. We are *so* all over the place tomorrow. Gawker. Page Six." "Do I know you?" he asked again, putting a lot of emphasis on KNOW. At least he gets how it's played. Thank God. And did I mention that he was cute???

And then-I couldn't believe it-he stands up and calls out, "Jennifer," and then he gives a big hug . . . to MY agent! WTF? Where did she come from? "Do you have a client staying here?" he asked all friendly-like. Oh, they talked and talked and talked-apparently, they both rocked out at Level V the other night (with Julia!) (does everyone know everyone in New York?). Jennifer didn't mention my name, 'cause she's a New Yorker too, so she knows how to play it, but she gripped my hand. Ouch! Real hard!

Then she pulled me away from Ian-n-o-o-o-o!-and past the barmaid . . . and actually slipped the barmaid a big-ass wad of cash. "I have eyes and ears everywhere," Jennifer told me. "And I promised your parents. If there's trouble, I'm putting you on the first plane back to Marietta. You can't drink here. You're underage. Go up to your room and go to sleep. Now."

The NERVE of that woman! Ian was waiting for m-e-e-e-e. We were going to have Famous Cokes together. And it was ruined

because of Mom and Dad!! And her!! Ahhhhhhhh! "I'll double
your commission," I said. "For two weeks." It's all about
commission for these agent people . . . but she actually said
NO! What is WRONG with her?? Does she actually think I'll put
up with this? I'm Lissa! I'm in bed now, but word, it ain't
gonna play out this way tomorrow night. Watch. Just watch.

Like, I'm so PO'd,
Moi

From: <lissa@lissabixby.com>
Date: 10 November
To: <cindybixby@yahoo.com>
Subject: Catch me if you can!! He-he!

Dear Sis:

Colin Farrell wants me. All. Night. Long. I can't tell you
why I know this, but trust me, I know. I know what hotel
he's staying at. And I know how to sneak out of my hotel
without Jennifer knowing. Oh my God, I'll do anything
Colin wants. En. Nee. Thing. 'Cause he so cute! Tonight's
the night. I'm going to lose my virginity . . . to COLIN
FARRELL!! Maybe I'll have his baby. He's waiting for me.
I'm leaving right now. Tell ya about it later. Next time
you see me, I'll be . . .

Colin's new GF!!!!!!
Me

P.S.: Delete this e-mail IMMEDIATELY. The tabs find out
EVERYTHING.

I didn't even wait to finish her last e-mail. I threw the stack aside, ran outside, and tried to get a signal on my cell. Darn it, it wasn't working.

"Whoa, you look stressed," said a voice next to me. "And it's so early on a Sunday." It was Cliff. I yelped.

"My sister's in trouble. Can I use your cell phone?"

I was so wrapped in myself that I didn't even notice (at first) that he was wearing this cute jogging outfit—a plain, slightly paint-spattered sleeveless T and gray sweatpants—and he was running in place, being totally patient with me as I waited for Lisa to pick up.

"Hello?" answered a voice I didn't recognize. Then I heard screaming in the background.

"H-e-e-e-e-e-e-l-p!" shrieked Lisa. "Help m-e-e-e-e-e!" Oh my God. My heart sputtered. Who was on the phone? What was happening to my sister?

"Who is this?" I cried. Was it a kidnapper? Had someone kidnapped "Lissa"? Was it Colin Farrell? Or Jack Black? Or maybe L. Lo?

"Is this Cindy Bixby?" asked the unfamiliar voice.

"Yes. Who's this?"

"H-e-e-e-e-e-e-l-p!" screamed Lisa again. Oh my God. I couldn't take it.

"What are you doing to my sister?!" I shouted. That got Cliff's attention. He stopped jogging in place.

"Cindy, this is Jennifer, your sister's agent," she said supercalmly. "Your sister's doing quite wonderfully. Would you like to talk to her?" She handed the phone to Lisa, who practically shattered my eardrum by screaming, "H-e-e-e-e-e-e-e-l-p m-e-e-e-e-e!"

I actually had to pull the phone away for a sec. But I was determined to get to the bottom of things. "Did you have sex with

Colin Farrell?" I demanded. "You're in so much trouble if you did. And I will tell Mom and Dad."

"Oh, Colin." She sighed. "Sweet lover. Do I have to go into it now? Read my blog."

"Lisa . . ."

"All right. Jeez." She sighed heavily, then she gasped. "You're not recording this for the tabs, are you?"

"Lisa . . ."

"My own sis! Selling me out! Ahhhhhh! I'll sue! I'll sue!"

"Lisa, if you don't tell me what happened with Colin Farrell right now, then I'm taking all your pictures from fifth grade—you know the ones, with the braces, the headgear . . ."

"Oh my God . . ."

"Your pockmarked face from chicken pox . . ."

"Oh my God, you bitch . . ."

"And I'm selling them on eBay. Maybe I'll even make com-memorative plates. And mugs. And T-shirts. Think anyone will want to touch your daisy after that?"

"You wouldn't!"

I let silence be my answer. I could hear her squirm. She told me everything. Yes, it's true, she did sneak out of the Soho place she's staying at, and somehow she made it over to the nearby Hotel Gansevoort. Colin Farrell never knew what hit him. He was on the rooftop pool getting in some laps.

"It's, like, amazing. Totally enclosed in glass," Lisa told me. "And heated. And open all year round. For Colin. Just Colin."

I doubted the last part, and after enduring her gushing "Blop Mag" descriptions—he was wearing a "Loose 1.5" Aussibum swim-suit, she said, there was a black cross tattoo on his left arm, and his eyes were "like, dreamboat brown"—I snapped, "Lisa, I'm call-ing Mom. Right now."

"Okay, okay. I'm just setting the mood."

She continued. After finishing his laps, Colin stepped out of the pool, took a swig of his Amstel Light, and reached for his towel. Only it wasn't there. It was behind him. In Lisa's hands.

"Hi," she said, posturing coyly.

"Why, hello there, darlin'," he said with a wink, and I guess Lisa almost fainted dead away. For reasons I can't quite fathom, he actually talked to her for a minute or so as he dried off with the towel. He is not, he told her, seduced by Hollywood.

"Oh my God, me neither," she said. "I'm like, all about me. And the universe. Do you want another towel? Let me get you another towel." She swiped his, gave him a clean one, and was just about to tell him her thoughts on *Alexander* when she felt something hard and cold around her wrist. *Clink!* "What the . . . ?"

"Jennifer!" exclaimed Colin. He hugged Jennifer, who'd popped up and clamped a handcuff around Lisa's wrist. Lisa was more than outraged. But what could she do?

"Why the bracelets?" asked Colin, gesturing to the handcuffs holding Jennifer and Lisa together.

"It's for a role!" blurted Lisa. "It's research."

Jennifer let that slide, and after bidding good-bye to Colin— they made plans to meet up at Cielo next weekend (jeez, who doesn't Jennifer know?)—she dragged Lisa to the elevator and down they went. And when Jennifer made a move with her hand, Lisa tearfully protested, "I'm keeping the towel! Don't touch it!" The towel, she told me proudly, has never left her side. She sleeps with it. She watches TV with it. She also carries it neatly folded in her purse wherever she goes, and sometimes pulls it out and pets it. "If you're nice to me, I'll let you sniff it," she said. "It totally smells like Colin."

Eeeow! I mean, no offense to Colin Farrell, but eeeow!

Unfortunately for Lisa, the towel isn't the only thing that follows her around. Ever since the Colin incident, Lisa begins each day at her hotel by being handcuffed to Jennifer, who discreetly uncuffs her before meetings, then—*clink!*—on they go again. And the hotel staff is on to her.

"I swear I was just looking for the ice machine!" she wailed, describing an incident in which hotel security found her in the basement near the boiler room, running for the exit. "Everyone's so mean to me!"

"Bye, Lisa," I said. Obviously, everything was under control. "And give Jennifer my best."

"Your best? She's insane! I'm her prisoner! Help m-e-e-e-e. . . ."

Click. I'd heard enough. I handed the phone back to Cliff. "Thank you. Emergency over."

"I'm glad," he said with a smile, then kissed me on the cheek and jogged to the street. Just like that. Casual. Easy. As if we were a couple or something. *Keep the focus,* I told myself, and within minutes I was at the parking lot with my hot-pink skateboard. I still couldn't do a turn without falling off the board and scraping my knees, but my speed was improving. *Whoosh!* I flew from one end of the lot to the other.

Oh my God, this is Dark Cindy in training, I realized. Unfortunately, Dark Cindy had a snickering little peanut gallery. There was Jahmal—again—watching as I botched another turn, flew sideways off the board, and slammed into a parked Camry. Ouch. It wasn't especially funny to me, but I guess I've become Jahmal's morning entertainment. He was holding his sides, he was laughing so hard.

Keep trying, I reminded myself. Sunday is a day of rest, but not for Dark Cindy. There's too much to do, and the plan for my return to RU is already formulated. And it's ready to begin today.

But now I had the remaining printouts to look over. I was confused when I looked at the first one. After all, I'm receiving her diary entries all out of order. But I figured it out: The first entry I read was written after Meri forced her father to move from Newport, and before they moved to Virginia and Palm Beach. She was thirteen years old.

Hullo:

Mark is rude. Last night at dinner, he flatulated at the table—and right as Cook was serving my brioche crab melts.

"We do not flatulate at dinner," I scolded.

"What am I supposed to do?" he asked, looking dumb.

"You simply hold it in," I instructed. "Then you let it pass slowly through your ribs."

"Flat-chew-late," he chuckled, suddenly finding the word oh so funny. Father laughed along too. I shot him a glare. And he was silent. Father's getting the hang of things. Thank goodness.

I've grown used to Wina. The wedding was lovely, considering. It was 100% organic. I wasn't particularly supportive of this idea, but since Wina was so earnestly dead set, I thought, *What's the harm?* I allowed it. The invitations were printed on slate gray recycled paper. Very gauche. Guests arrived at Greenwich Park Beach at the Clambake Area, where they were greeted with organic beeswax candles and a bar made out of wine barrels and purple tellin seashells. Tacky. Honestly, I know Wina's from San Francisco, but it was all just a bit much. The tabletops were decorated with pineapples, Indian figs, and muskmelon. The entrée, which I strenuously advised against, was chorizo-crusted cod with corn cakes and spiced cranberries. I also voiced my objection when Wina decided to walk barefoot during the wedding ceremony on the rocky beach, but she insisted. As the evening unfolded and the sun set, I thought, *Jesus Christ, this is just too "Kumbaya."* And then, to my horror, I heard:

> *Kumbaya, my Lord, kumbaya*
> *Ohhhh, Lord, kumbaya*

Several of Wina's San Francisco friends were gathered
around the campfire, strumming guitars, singing "Kumbaya."
It was just too much. I quickly excused myself, then ran
behind a dune and vomited. It was an involuntary action, of
course, but there was a certain emphatic quality about it that
pleased me. Not very Connecticut, I know, but given the
circumstances of the evening, certainly understandable. I
stepped back out and father greeted me.

"Are you okay, Meri?"

"Yes, I am. I hope you're happy."

"I am happy, thank you." Then he hesitated awkwardly. "I was
actually hoping you might have a special wedding gift for me."

We gazed at each other unflinchingly. He looked away first.
Oh, Father. Did he actually think I'd give him the original
documents? As a wedding present?

"My gift to you," I said evenly, "is my continued assurance
that they're in a very safe place. By the way, I'll need the
helicopter tomorrow. Josette and I are going shopping at
Trump Tower."

In the meantime, I've grown used to Greenwich (thank God I
decided against Westport!). Lady Arlington's School is
acceptable, and there's a certain playful competitiveness in the
neighborhood that I find amusing. For instance, several girls
my age have set up lemonade stands outside their estates, and
one of them, Kimberly von Koffi von Klondike
Hollingsworth—of the nouveau Von Koffi von Klondike
Hollingsworths—likes to boast unbecomingly about how much
she makes with her lemonade stand.

It was easy to put a stop to. The next day I opened up
fourteen lemonade stands in the neighborhood, each of them
manned by a young boy or girl under the age of eight. They
were happy to work for me. I paid them in jellybeans (I also had
them fill teabags with grass and sell them as chamomile tea).
And I was happy to collect a tidy sum from all the booths—and
let Kimberly know about it. How? Simple. Versalink owns all

the local papers on the Eastern seaboard, and the next day they each carried a front-page photo of me holding up a wad of cash before one of my booths with the headline: SUGARMAN HEIR TURNS LEMONS INTO GOLD! The article went on to say that I donated my earnings to the Uganda Children's Charity Foundation, but I bought two pairs of Ferragamo slingbacks instead. I'm so proud of me.

Jackie O. once said one should always pretend that there's a red carpet spread out before you; you must always stand tall and assume people are watching your every move. I don't have to assume this anymore. I know.

The next entry seemed to be later—in Virginia—right before Meri demanded that her father move the family to Palm Beach. Meri had just turned sixteen.

Dark Cindy

Hi:

Have you missed me? I haven't written in a while. I took a trip
yesterday. I rode a private Versalink jet to Newport. It's silly, I
know, but I just wanted to check up on the goods. Figuring I
might run into someone I once knew, I took off all my jewelry
and wore dark sunglasses, a plain white Gap T, an ordinary black
V-neck cardigan, tarnished denim CKs, brown Cole Haan boots,
and a thin, light blue glitter scarf. I looked like a Mall Girl who
was trying too hard. No one would dare expect that of me.
Briskly I strolled to the Newport National Bank, gave them my
safe-deposit box number and secret security number, and was led
by a guard down a long corridor. He dutifully retrieved my box
and set me up in a private viewing room. He didn't even ask to
see my ID, which I thought was lax, but still, everything's
behind lock and key, and the only ones who know the box
number and the secret security number are the bank and me (and
you, my dear little blog).

It gave me such pleasure to hold the documents in my hands.
I've checked privately with attorneys. True, the statute of
limitations is nearly past, and yet Father could still be hurt
should these documents ever see the light of day. Very badly, in
fact. Board members don't take too kindly to corporate
espionage. I doubt the taxman would be all that approving
either. It was silly of Father to leave them just lying around on
his desk so many years ago—sloppy, in fact. Details are important.
Jackie has taught me that. She's also taught me that loose lips sink
ships, even with those closest to you. For instance, even Jack
couldn't penetrate her carefully cultivated exterior. "My thoughts
are my thoughts, Jack," she once told him. "And they wouldn't be
mine anymore if I told them to you. Now would they?"

I put the documents back in the box, and I knew then that
enough was enough. I don't have to come back to Newport

anymore. They're here, as they always will be, and they'll continue to serve me whether I physically see them or not. I stepped outside. The sun was blazing. All you could see was hot blue sky.

My town car was waiting, but I told the driver to follow me. I wanted to stroll. I hadn't been to Newport in some time, and it's loomed so very large in my mind these past years. And yet I was surprised by how small, even insignificant, it appeared to me now. It was plain, yet pleasantly picturesque, like a familiar mare. I couldn't recall exactly what prompted me to leave Newport, though I'll never forget the satisfaction I felt when Father realized he had no choice in the matter. The look on his face when I dropped those documents before him. Oh, too much! I think that's when I was really born, and not so coincidentally, when I was first able to control both my destiny and the great Sugarman fortune, which is rightly mine. For that alone, Newport will always hold a special place in my heart.

"Meri, is that you?"

I turned around. I wasn't too thrilled that I'd been recognized, least of all by Elke Sommerville, a somewhat dim, galumphing girl who was nevertheless slavishly devoted to me at Miss Grayson's. When you're admired, as I am, devotees come in all varieties. I've always graded mine. Some, like the wonderfully good-spirited Helen Theodorakis, warranted a A+ (Greeks, and generally all those of Mediterranean descent, are terribly smitten with me, given their shameless aspirational desires; I give them something to work toward, and while they'll never reach my heights, they make a good go of it). Elke, on the other hand, was a definite C–.

"Elke, is that you?" I said with a dull inflection that communicated only faint interest.

"What are you *doing* here?" she squealed like an infant. "And, oh my *gawd*, what are you wearing?"

Okay, that made me angry. Caught in front of Elke Sommerville—in Cole Haan boots!

"Just a quick visit. But I'm afraid I'm running late. You

understand. Bye now." I strolled to my town car, and she followed, or waddled, actually, eager to bathe in my spotlight—if only for a moment more.

"Gosh, I sure do miss you, Meri. We all do." Then she tittered (like a bird). "Remember 'Bloody Meri'? Wasn't that a gas? Oh! We still talk about it. 'Bloody Meri! Bloody Meri!' Ha-ha-ha-ha-ha!"

I was not amused. A great anger foamed in my mouth, and my first instinct was to slap her across the face—openhanded, and with great force—and yet, does anyone even superficially interested in the human condition need to be told *not* to respond, in any way, to the likes of Elke Sommerville? It's no great accident that we don't care if people like her live or die, and while it might be preferable that she was, in fact, deep-sixed, her very banality makes it seem a foregone conclusion.

"Aren't you a funny bunny," I said, then vanished in the town car. On the plane ride back, I felt pain—a sharp, stabbing pain. Now I remember why I left Newport. Oh, I was just a child. A gentle child. Unfortunately, it may be time to leave Virginia, and it's all Pru's fault. Damn that fucking Pru.

Pru had been one of my finest devotees. She was an unattractive girl with a rough complexion and facial features that seemed to contradict each other wildly—big, dopey eyes, one slightly larger than the other; a surprisingly fine aquiline nose; oddly mushed-up lips that look as if a collagen session had been abruptly cut short. She aspires to be a scientist of some sort one day, and when I first met her, she was wearing a short dress over a shrug with Thalia jeans from Kmart. Despite her family's wealth, she had obviously been spending too much time amidst the test tubes. I took pity. And I had yet to add a scientist type to my collection, so I was intrigued. I gave her a complete makeover, had her purchase several useful pieces from the Jil Sander collection, and took her to see Antonio for a flattering new haircut that had the effect of reshaping her unremarkable head. I was touched when she also dyed her hair a lustrous raven, matching mine.

Everyone was impressed by my efforts (of course), even Timothy. I was still seeing Timothy at the time. He's the school's star soccer player, unusually handsome, and possessed of enough smarts to realize that being with me was a very good thing. I cheered him on at all his games, I sang his praises, and I gave him a far better time than he deserved, that's for sure. What other girl could fly him in a private jet to Rio for Carnivale (that was a fun trip)? Or tie his arms and legs to the bedposts and be skilled enough not to leave marks? Timothy had it all.

When I stopped by Timothy's manse last week to surprise him with plans for a trip to Ixtapa, I was shocked beyond belief to find him on the living-room couch—with his hand wriggling up Pru's Jil Sander blouse. I could have stormed in. I could have acted "furious" or "heartbroken." But instead I pulled out my pocket-size Panasonic D-snap. It's lighter than a pack of cigarettes, and quite handy for such occasions. I took aim, zoomed close, and hoped for the best. After all, what's the point of a "capture" if you aren't capturing anything?

I only had to send the AVI files to a few key students that night (anonymously, of course) (Mark helped with that) (between bong hits). The next day everyone was giggling and pointing at Pru and Timothy and quoting some of their favorite lines. There was the moment when Timothy was having his way with Pru. She was bent over the ottoman, crying out breathlessly, "Call me Meri! Call me Meri!" Better still was when Pru roughly straddled Timothy and he squealed, "Uhhhh! Call me Meri! Call me Meri!" The cherry on the cake arrived when Pru, perhaps understandably stunned and disappointed, blurted out, "Already? That's it?" Predictable, yes, but always good for a chuckle in these circumstances.

I got the result I wanted. Timothy's new nickname around town is "Meri"—the guys are having fun with that one (God bless dumb jocks)—and practically all the girls now regard Pru as cheap trash. Everyone was sympathetic toward me. I had been wronged. By a nothing girl. A plain girl. A zilch. I should have been satisfied. And outwardly I was. But there was a fly in the ointment. Though no one said it out loud, they thought it: Meri is not infallible. Meri is not perfect.

For the life of me, I still cannot comprehend the notion of Timothy wanting to be with Pru . . . and not me. That Pru had betrayed . . . me, of all people; the me who had transformed her from a plain, nothing girl to a (moderately) acceptable one, the me who demanded so little in return beyond simple devotion, and yes, all her term papers, thrice-weekly runs to the dry cleaners—and okay, when I walked Tazio, our Great Dane, I had her pick up his excrement (but this was only because my immunologist instructed that my allergies might improve if I refrained from such activity). Is that too much to ask? I have so much to give, and my heart is open.

The other day I asked Gilberto to take me up in the helicopter. I had no particular destination in mind, and as we swept gracefully over rolling hills and into town, I sipped my Mojito and popped several Provigil. I suppose I was feeling sorry for myself—an unacceptable activity, to be sure—so I sought solace with Jackie, dear Jackie, who once said, "Never allow yourself to be sentimental. It backfires." That cheered me greatly. The incident with Pru and Timothy, I knew, would simply blow away and be forgotten—like last week's supermarket tabloid. My reputation was secure. I happily returned home (instructing Gilberto to fly low over town, which startles pedestrians and never fails to lighten my spirits).

Yesterday at school I expected the dumb jocks to continue razzing Timothy, which is as it should be. But Timothy, perhaps attempting to defuse the taunts and jeers, arrived for the day in a fitted white T-shirt with black cursive writing that blared: "Call Me Meri!" This caused much amusement for everyone, and Timothy, having planned for such a reaction, came prepared with over a dozen "Call Me Meri!" T-shirts in various sizes and colors. By lunchtime, "Call Me Meri!" T-shirts were everywhere. Even Pru wore one. Timothy and Pru were now part of the joke. They were participants. I felt a shudder from my head to my toes. My efforts to humiliate them had backfired—badly. I had calculated poorly. I had failed. I now know the ghastliness of being a figure of fun, for while the face-saving joke, as it were, wasn't aimed directly at me, I was its collateral damage.

I didn't go to school today, and this evening, after I'd enjoyed my fourth Bellini, I overheard Cook's new aide de cuisine commenting on my "Napoleonic insecurities," "unpredictable rages," and "exquisite style." Well, one out of three, I suppose, but not good enough. I promptly informed Cook that she will need to find a new aide de cuisine—by tomorrow morning— then strolled to my private bathroom to freshen up. It had been such a long contemplative day. I turned on the lights—and screamed! Mark came running.

"Ants!" I gasped, gesturing to the loathsome little creatures that were marching in disgusting zigzaggy patterns across the sink. Mark chuckled. How dare he! He knows that ants disturb me to my core. Furious, I made up my mind. We're moving. Mark protested—in that drawn-out "whoa dude" way so common to hash heads—but I barely paid him any mind. Father was equally unmoved by the idea, but too bad. We're moving. Tomorrow. I hear Palm Beach is lovely this time of year. Father actually dared to suggest that we might have to sell our summer manse on Squabble Lane in Southampton in order to financially accommodate my demand. I laughed. Nice try, Father. No, scratch that. Dumb, Father. Very dumb.

Mark joined me on a soaring farewell-to-Virginia helicopter flight. It was just past one a.m. The helicopter's whirring rotor blades were like music. *Whip-whip, whip-whip.* Mark toked on his one-hit. I popped a dexy. Would I miss Virginia? I thought. Not really. The lights that twinkled below me were entirely generic. It's not *where* I am that makes life special, I realized, but the fact that I, Meri Sugarman, *am* there. Mark coughed, then mumbled, "You can't do this all the time, you know. Just move every time something goes wrong."

I chuckled softly. "I can *do* anything I want."

"But what about college? What happens then? It's only four years. What are you going to do? Go to, like, ten colleges?"

He was right to bring this up. In fact, I've often thought of it myself. I still don't know where I will go to college, but I'm fairly certain that I won't be going to more than one.

Right now, I suppose one could regard me as a rough draft; a sketch by Michelangelo that is yet to blossom into a fully realized masterwork, such as the Sistine Chapel or David. By the time I reach college, I will be perfect. Jeweled. There will be no need to move. And I will be more equipped to deal with any conflict, great or small, that may come my way. Each morning when I awaken, I feel more *me* than ever before. There is still a crucial piece missing, of course, a fragment of understanding that escapes me, but if I find the college near to the One Who Will Complete Me—the one whose very presence will facilitate my truest excellence—then I'll be a rough draft no more. I must do more research. So far, my investigations have narrowed down the possibilities to either North or South Carolina. Once my research is complete, I'll chose the appropriate college and bide my time. Matters such as these must be handled delicately. It may take two years, perhaps even three. Patience is vital. In the meantime, college will be my springboard. My gloriousness will take flight. And then everyone will know—and they will see. There is only one Meri Sugarman. And she is perfect.

Wow. Okay, it's official, Meri Sugarman lives in cuckoo land. She's their reigning queen. And I don't think I need any kind of degree to figure that out. And yet, do the entries provide me with any real ammunition to use against her? I'm still not sure. Maybe. They definitely won't impact my plans to return to RU. That's going to happen. Follow the money. My plan is perfect. I know it's going to work!

After I finished reading the entries, it was still early in the morning, and I suddenly realized I had a call to make. I felt bad that I hadn't made it earlier. Stepping outside, I found a signal and reached Pigboy, Patty's football-player boyfriend.

"I'm already here," he told me reassuringly. "Lindsay told me."

Oh, thank God, I thought. Pigboy was at Patty's bedside. She's detoxing, and apparently it's not pretty (to put it mildly), largely due to the fact that she's still in deep denial about her problems with Skinny. But this time I think she'll make it. Pigboy's not leaving her bedside. Thank God for Pigboy.

It's about twelve noon right now and I'm awfully tired. I think I'm going to take a nap. In a half hour, Shanna-Francine will be meeting with Dean Pointer to discuss her "problematic presidency." I hope she's okay. I've just got to have faith in the future. In my heart, I know everything will turn out all right. For all of us.

November 13

Dear Diary:

Ahhhhhhhhhhh! Oh my God, oh my God, oh my God, oh, my God! I can't take it anymore. This can't be happening! Meri Sugarman is president of Alpha Beta Delta! Again! Why didn't I see this coming? I can't write. This is too much. Oh, I hate Meri Sugarman. I hate her!

November 14

Dear Diary:

Everybody's ready. Me, Lindsay, Shanna-Francine, Bobbie, even Professor Scott. Tomorrow's D-Day. After it's all done, I'll return to RU. And Alpha Beta Delta, too. Ha. Can't stop me now, Meri. Dark Cindy's on the move.

November 15

Dear Diary:

I still shudder in horror when I think about the phone call that woke me up Sunday night. How I was able to get a signal in my room is still a mystery, but I jerked awake when I heard Lindsay say rat-a-tat fast, "Are you sitting? You should be sitting."

"I'm lying down on my bed, actually."

"Oh, good. Stay down. Don't get up. Oh my God, don't even sit up. Prostrate yourself. Flat on the floor. Like a nun."

"What's going on?" I shrieked. Now I was worried. She explained everything—in excruciating detail. Apparently, when Shanna-Francine returned to Alpha Beta Delta from her meeting with the dean, she looked like she'd just been flattened by a semi.

"Get her some water!" roared Bobbie, who led her gently to the couch and calmly (for Bobbie) asked her what had happened.

Shanna-Francine mumbled, "I'm . . . I'm . . ."

"Just lay it on the line. C'mon. I know you can do it."

"Oh my God," Lindsay gasped. "What is it? Tell us."

Shanna-Francine burst into tears. And she told them. When she met with Dean Pointer, none other than Sister Nellie Oliverez was on speakerphone. Sister Oliverez is president of Sigma Gamma Lambada, the national intersorority governing council in Vero Beach, Florida, and at first, her mellifluous voice calmed whatever initial fears Shanna-Francine might have had about the meeting.

"You've been such a fine little trouper," she said. "And I think I speak for all the sisters at Sigma Gamma Lambada when I say that your efforts to modernize Alpha Beta Delta, and sorority life in general, have been nothing short of groundbreaking. I was impressed with your decision to drop the traditional hazing rituals—which has, as you know, caused us to receive so much unfair press over the years. Tsk. So unfair."

"I changed it to New Member Assessment," blurted Shanna-Francine hopefully.

"Yes, that's right. What a wonderful idea that was. You must be so proud." Huh. So far, so good. Shanna-Francine looked up at Dean Pointer, who was plopped before the speakerphone, legs casually crossed, smirking between loud sips of coffee. "But Shanna-Francine," continued the sister, "we both know that you've also stumbled. Badly. And on more than one occasion." She went down the list. And it was a long one. The Cookie Booth fiasco. The Hour of Silence disaster. And on and on and on—all the way to Viva Veterans Day. According to the sister, both Sigma Gamma Lambada and RU had been flooded with literally hundreds of calls and e-mails demanding that the governing council and RU officially revoke Alpha Beta Delta's charter.

"Oh, please, you can't," Shanna-Francine wailed, and pleaded with the sister to give her another chance. Alpha Beta Delta, she reminded her, has been a venerable institution at Rumson U. for decades.

"I am sorry," said the sister, her honeyed tones still intact. "But it's the end of the road for Alpha Beta Delta. You and the girls will need to vacate the premises immediately for RU's North Center Dormitory. I believe the house will be used for graduate students from now on, isn't that right, Dean Pointer?" The dean agreed, not even bothering to hide his satisfied smile. "Shanna-Francine, please, I ask you to use your esteemed leadership abilities in these final hours for Alpha Beta Delta. Go peacefully. And encourage your sisters to do the same. It's the right thing to do."

"And if you don't, I'll have campus security bodily remove each and every one of you," said the dean snidely, rubbing salt into the wounds.

"Oh my God, I was speechless," Shanna-Francine told the sisters back at Alpha Beta Delta. She even blurted to Sister Oliverez, "Oh my God, I'm speechless."

"Of course, there is one other possibility," said the sister softly. Shanna-Francine's eyes practically popped out of her head. A way to save Alpha Beta Delta? For real? She was all ears. "Our world is changing, Shanna-Francine," said the sister. "And we cannot have a house that runs counter to the values and beliefs that the majority hold so dear—nor one that operates so openly against the values set forth by the Greek community at Sigma Gamma Lambada. In fact, both the dean and I are determined to take any and all necessary action against any Greek organization at RU that goes against these values. Now, that said, I believe there's a way we can all achieve our goals."

Her plan, no doubt approved and suggested by Dean Pointer—and orchestrated by you-know-who—entailed the following: (1) upon Shanna-Francine's agreement on behalf of the house, Alpha Beta Delta would immediately and officially become RU's first Evangelical sorority house. Several girls from the CEC were prepared to move in that day; (2) all previously planned Alpha Beta Delta events, including a performance of *The Vagina Monologues* to benefit Planned Parenthood and groups that fight domestic violence, which Shanna-Francine had scheduled for after Thanksgiving, would be canceled; (3) Shanna-Francine must relinquish her reign as president of Alpha Beta Delta, effective immediately; (4) an election for the new president of Alpha Beta Delta would take place first thing Monday morning, and

Shanna-Francine must recuse herself from consideration; (5) all the girls currently at Alpha Beta Delta, including Shanna-Francine, may stay at the house, but must pledge to abide by all of Alpha Beta Delta's new rules, bylaws, and moral codes of conduct.

Shanna-Francine was stunned. She murmured, "Well, we have plenty of room in the house."

"Of course you do," said the sister. "The number of girls who have pledged to new sororities nationwide is dwindling. Which means, of course, that there are fewer members paying dues."

"Oh, I see," said a shell-shocked Shanna-Francine. "So this isn't about morals. It's about money."

The sister (uncharacteristically) snapped, "Don't be a smart-mouth, Shanna-Francine. What this is about is retaining a place for women at colleges everywhere who want to be in a sorority. I think we can all agree that this is a truly important and noble objective. So which is it, dear? Are you the sister who brings down the curtain on Alpha Beta Delta, or the brave and farsighted sister who opens a new day for Greek life and a new dawn for Alpha Beta Delta?"

"So what did you say?" Bobbie roared. Shanna-Francine forced a grin and glanced at her watch.

"Um, they should be here in thirty minutes."

"Evangelical girls?" gasped Lindsay. "What are they like?"

"Like every other girl." She shrugged. "I met a few of them before I left the dean's office. They were waiting outside. They really want to be in a sorority. They're really excited. I mean, I don't know, I liked them. They're sweet. There's eight of them coming."

"We'll be outnumbered!" wailed Lindsay.

"We can't look at it that way," Shanna-Francine insisted. "These are nice girls. And okay, none of us are born-again, or anything like that, but what's the big deal? We all have a belief system. And we all deserve respect. If I've stood for anything as your president, it's for the conviction that all cultures and all beliefs must be allowed to flourish freely."

"Uh-huh. But do they believe that?" asked Bobbie grimly.

They didn't have time to argue the point. The CEC girls had arrived. They were tentative, even sheepish, at first, as they stepped past the foyer and into the house with their suitcases and belongings. A few of them had trunks that were loaded in their cars parked out front. Lindsay and the gang were wary. No one was saying anything. But God bless Shanna-Francine. She threw her arms out and winsomely blurted, "Oh my God, you guys, welcome to Alpha Beta Delta!"

Resistance was futile. Shanna-Francine's eyes twinkled, her smile was infectious, and her frizzy hair, which had previously drooped, seemed to spring magically to life, its wild tendrils gesturing merrily in every direction. In no time at all, everyone was gathered in the kitchen, and while the CEC girls obviously weren't used to politically appropriate snacks, they were game. And one of the girls, Karla Mae Marshall, a stunning African-American girl with long stick-straight hair—I saw her selling Whatever clothes on my way to Viva Veterans Day—was positively elated when Bobbie single-handedly hefted her heavy trunk from her car and then carried it up the stairs to her room.

"Wow. You're really strong," exclaimed Karla Mae.

"Thank you," Bobbie bellowed. "Hey, you ever heard of Barbara Cartland? I'm thinking you might have, 'cause her books are enshrined at the Slipper Chapel in England. Did you know that?"

"No, I didn't," said Karla Mae—and really, who on earth would know this besides Bobbie?

"You can attend Mass and then go to their memorabilia room," Bobbie explained excitedly. "It's famous. Tons of her books are there. And did you know? Barbara publicly protested against removing prayer from school. And spoke against infidelity. And divorce."

"I had no idea," said Karla Mae. "That's fascinating." It happened in an instant: Bobbie had triumphantly bridged the culture gap. With Barbara Cartland.

Downstairs, Lindsay and the gang were helping the other CEC sisters carry in their belongings.

"Are you the umbrella girl?" one of them asked, gazing wide-eyed at Lindsay. Lindsay was unsure how to respond at first. But then she figured, heck, might as well be honest and start off on the right foot.

"I've had hundreds of umbrellas over the years," she stated calmly. "But these days, I prefer my limited-edition indigo lace-patterned Stella McCartney."

"It is her!" gasped another CEC girl. "You know, you girls are kind of famous."

"We are?" asked Lindsay, exchanging a nervous glance with Shanna-Francine, who shrugged, cheerfully blurting out, "That's so cool. Now we can all be famous together."

Everyone was delighted. It was all going so well. Then a screeching voice called out, "Hey! Careful with that suitcase! It's got a pebble finish. Don't you dare fucking scuff it."

"Doreen?" exclaimed Lindsay. "What are you doing here?"

"What do you mean, what am I doing here?" she snapped. "I promote the Whatever line. I raise money for the CEC. I'm a member. Jesus fucking Christ, what's your problem?"

Lindsay yanked her aside. "Don't you think you're being a little hypocritical?"

"No, I don't," she responded testily, pulling her arm back. "I was brought up Catholic. Bet you didn't know that."

"I don't think it's quite the same thing."

"Oh, really? You don't think? Well I sure as hell don't see you dunking your fucking head in a pool of water and crying out

'Hallelujah.' Hypocritical. Please. I'm the only honest one here."

"Doreen . . ."

"I want to be in a sorority, goddamn it. Everyone knows it helps you in the business world. Everyone. When you're out job hunting, and you tell all those women you're interviewing with that you're Greek—pow!—head of the line. Why the hell should I be denied? Huh? Think I'm not good enough? Is that it? Oh, and news flash. Mary Magdalene was a whore. Did you know that? Big-ass whore. Says so in the Bible."

"She was a repentant whore," corrected Lindsay.

"Oh, right, so now we're getting technical. I see. Well isn't that convenient for you." She called out to the CEC sisters, "Girls? Help me out here. Mary Magdalene. Big-ass whore. Right?" This caused a lively discussion. Was Mary Magdalene a (repentant) big-ass whore? Perhaps, yes, but then careful study of the Bible, pointed out one CEC girl, reveals that Magdalene is never actually referred to in the Bible as a prostitute, or even a fallen woman, and has long been confused by some readers with the female "sinner" in Luke who's forgiven by Christ for "loving too much"; but another girl pointed out that Pope St. Gregory I explicitly proclaimed in 591 that Luke's female "sinner" was, in fact, Magdalene; while Karla Mae, who'd by now come downstairs, said that in 1969 the Church declared once and for all that Luke's female "sinner" and Mary Magdalene were two entirely different people.

"Whitewash!" Doreen cried. "C'mon, guys. You can't kid a kidder."

"Wait a sec," blurted Shanna-Francine. "I thought there were eight girls coming over. I'm only counting seven. Where's the—" She was interrupted by a thunderous whipping sound. On the phone, Lindsay paused and said, "Do I have to tell you the rest?"

"Yes," I responded grimly.

"Okay. But you're sitting, right?"

"No, I'm not. I'm standing. And I'm pacing. Go on."

To Lindsay, Meri's helicopter looked like a giant bug as it landed in the middle of the street in front of the house. But even more disconcerting was the response from the CEC girls, who excitedly ran outside, calling out Meri's name—as if they were welcoming royalty. Meri swept out of the copter, decked out resplendently.

"What was she wearing?" I asked.

"Oh, I don't know," whined Lindsay. "What does it matter?"

"It matters!" I exclaimed. Meri's fashion choices, I knew, could tell one what mood or strategy she was aiming for; like her Boho chic look when she was at Chappaqua, or her favored Chanel when she was feeling particularly confident. It's the only element of Meri's personality that's a consistent giveaway.

"Okay, let's see," said Lindsay. "She was definitely in Chanel."

"Uh-oh."

"Uh-huh. She looked pretty amazing, actually. She had on a cream white blouse, a blue Chanel cropped jacket—I think it was blue—with this gorgeous white-and-yellow-gold diamond pendant necklace, and let's see, a black knife-pleat skirt—I think it went to her knees—and, okay, this I remember: seriously hot stiletto thighs. Oh, and a huge black Chanel bag. Huge. And Purrfect. Of course. She was holding on to him with a leash. Scared the heck out of Tamari and Pumpkin Seed."

I wasn't impressed. Either I'm used to Meri's outfits by now, or she was up to something. Sure enough, she was up to something. She greeted several of the CEC girls with a kiss to either cheek and intoned delicately, "A cropped jacket over a simple blouse or shirt gives you a sexy silhouette—and without showing any skin."

This was met with much approval by the CEC girls, who want to be sexy and cool, like any girl, but not so sexy that they depart from their beliefs. Meri was playing to her audience. And according to Lindsay, they ate it up.

"Oh, I forgot. Her eyes," she said. When Meri took off her sunglasses, all the CEC girls oohed and ahhed over her custom-made diamond-encrusted mink lashes. She barely acknowledged Lindsay, Shanna-Francine, or Bobbie. And before anyone knew what was happening, two tuxedoed servers from La Residence, North Carolina's finest French restaurant in Chapel Hill, blew into the kitchen with silver domed serving platters. Dinner was served. Courtesy of Meri. And it was spectacular. She even had workers install a large Swiss-import espresso machine.

"Only thirty Olympia Creminas come to the United States each year," she breathily informed the girls. "But I think we're worth it. Don't you?" And then there was the Hearthware i-Roast, a high-end coffee-bean-roasting machine, which was fine-tuned to create Meri's own custom blend, "The Sugarman Roast." Dessert consisted of artisanal cheeses, lemon-poppy cookies, and huckleberry sorbet. After dinner, Kir Royales with Blackberry Puree were served in the living room. The CEC girls were dazzled.

"She sure laid it on thick, didn't she?" I sneered.

"Yeah, and it worked," said Lindsay ominously. Later that night, Lindsay stepped into Karla Mae's room, ready to convince her that Meri's a loon (and a dangerous one). Karla Mae was unpacking her belongings, listening to a swooning soul song on her iPod. Lindsay stopped short. Karla Mae's eyes were brimming with tears, though she was smiling faintly. Next to her bed, she was setting up a shrine of sorts. There were pictures of two black women whom Lindsay didn't recognize, and next to them, a picture of Christ.

"I'm sorry," said Lindsay, stepping back.

"No, it's okay," said Karla Mae. Lindsay commented on the nice pictures, and Karla Mae gently took her hand and brought her close to them. "The first one, that's Anita Baker. She was Mama's favorite. Practically every day, 'On My Own,' 'Piano in the Dark,' all of her songs. Mama said Anita was touched by

God's grace." Then she pointed to the picture in the center. "That's Mama. Before she got sick."

"She was beautiful," said Lindsay. Karla Mae wiped her nose.

"She was. And I was rotten. Rotten to the core. Typical jerky teenager. Always out drinking, running around with boys. And Mama." She sighed heavily. "It felt like everything she said to me was so mean and so critical. She criticized my clothes, who I hung out with, everything." She paused, her voice lowering to a hush. "When she got sick I was a mess. I couldn't take it. And she was even more critical. Twenty-four seven. I didn't realize it at the time, but she wasn't really criticizing me."

"She wasn't?"

"Uh-uh. She was trying to advise me, to prepare me."

Lindsay asked tentatively, "How did she die?"

"Heart disease. Coronary . . . microvascular something or other."

"I'm so sorry."

"Thank you," Karla Mae whispered, then smiled, remembering. "She knew when she was going. She had all of us gather around her hospital bed. And she told me to play 'Body and Soul.'"

"By Anita Baker?"

"Yeah. That was her absolute favorite. 'Body and Soul.' She was listening to it right before she went. She took my hand and she pulled me real close. And she whispered, 'Karla Mae. Promise me. Promise Mama you'll accept Christ as your Lord and Savior.' And I did." She smiled, gesturing to the picture of Christ. "I was born again." They stood there a moment before the pictures, and Lindsay suddenly realized what song they were listening to. Anita Baker was singing rapturously,

We are whole, body and soul
Don't leave me out in the cold
Just love me, body and soul

"Have you ever heard her?" gasped Lindsay to me on the phone. "Her voice, it's like, beyond beautiful." Lindsay helped Karla Mae unpack her clothes, and when the moment was right, she said, "You do know Meri's completely insane, right?"

"Wait," said Karla Mae. "I thought the crazy one's that Cindy girl. That's what I heard."

Lindsay grew impatient. "Listen to me. Meri's a psychopath."

"Oh my God," Karla Mae exclaimed. "You're the Psychology Girl! I didn't know Umbrella Girl and Psychology Girl were the same. That's so cool. You're, like, doubly famous."

"I hope you cleared everything up," I said. But Lindsay didn't get the chance. Karla Mae asked if it was okay if she played "Body and Soul" again, and of course Lindsay said yes. As they listened to the song, Lindsay told me, it just didn't feel like the right time to get into Meri, and I can't say I blame her.

"She has the coolest iPod thingie too," she said.

"She has an iBuzz?" I screamed. "Like the one Bud got . . ."

"No, no, no." She laughed. "It's an iBelieve. So cool. It snaps right on top of her iPod shuffle and makes it look like a cross. She wears it around her neck."

They listened to "Body and Soul" once more, and afterward, it was time for bed. Lindsay sweetly brought her scepter to Karla Mae's shoulders. "I dub thee Karla, Body and Soul."

"I can't believe Meri is back at . . ." I couldn't complete the sentence.

"I know," said Lindsay. "Get some sleep. Don't worry. We'll figure this out tomorrow."

I woke up extra early Monday morning. D-Day was coming. I needed to be ready. And frankly, I didn't care that Jahmal was already at the other end of the parking lot stifling a smile (okay,

I cared a little bit) (okay, it really annoyed me) (a lot). *So what if he's laughing?* I thought. *His laughter has no effect on what you're trying to do. Let him laugh all he wants.* I'm not sure if that qualifies as a Corrective Emotional Experience, but I sure felt better.

It was time to get ready for class. After a quick shower, I got dressed, packed up my knapsack—and nearly jumped out of my skin when my cell phone rang. The caller ID said it was Lindsay. *Oh God,* I thought, *it can't be good.* I answered, but all I got was static, and then the connection cut out. Oh, damn the bad reception at Chappaqua! I ran outside and tried dialing her.

"Hello? Cindy?" she screamed. "Oh my God, you . . ."

The line cut out again. Ahhhhhh! I ran around the corner, tried again.

"Cindy!" she wailed, then I heard more static, then: "Mariah Carey! It's awful, she . . ."

Again I was cut off. I couldn't stand it. Something about Mariah Carey? That definitely wasn't good news. Finally, standing behind the huge cafeteria Dumpster (the smell was overpowering), I got through. At first all I could hear was singing. Oh, God, no! It was Mariah:

> *If you believe in yourself enough*
> *And know what you want!*
> *You're gonna make it happen!*
> *Make it happen!*

"Cindy, can you hear me?" shrieked Lindsay. "Hold on." It sounded like she was running outside. Her breathing was labored. And then: "Okay. Better?"

"Better," I said, my heart thumping.

Then she blurted it out: "Meri Sugarman is president of Alpha Beta Delta."

I stood there, stunned. It was a gorgeous, brisk November day, but in the stillness of that moment a million other thoughts—all of them morbid and terrifying—swarmed around me. Blackness gripped me.

I'm in a dark cave all by myself and I'll never be happy because I'm here, I'm trapped, and if I try to crawl out, it'll somehow makes the cave bigger and bigger and even darker than before. I hear singing. I hear Mariah. Oh God, not Mariah. And faintly in the distance I heard "Bow-wow! Woof!"

"Cindy? Are you there?"

Lindsay told me everything. The arrival, bright and early that morning, of Dean Pointer; the call for an immediate vote for president (which the dean would monitor); the desperate scramble on the part of Lindsay, Shanna-Francine, and Bobbie to find a worthy opponent (they settled on Bobbie); the crushing vote, in which every single CEC girl voted for Meri (even Doreen, that dumb slut); the delirious celebration breakfast (prearranged by Meri, no doubt), with poached eggs, smoked salmon toasts, pear bruschetta, champagne, and "Sugarman Roast" coffees, lattes, and espressos; and the pièce de résistance, an all-new pledge book, solemnly handed out by Meri and supposedly vetted by Sister Oliverez, and, according to Lindsay, pretty straightforward stuff—except for one tiny little bylaw buried in the back, which read: "You must always obey the orders of your president or face immediate expulsion from the house."

And the inevitable Mariah. Meri picked "Make It Happen" as the official house song and ordered all the girls to listen to it (a relatively humane) eight times in a row in the living room. Strangely, no one seemed to mind, and by the third spin, a few of the CEC girls were even tapping their toes and singing along.

"Incredible," I gasped.

"I've really got to get back in there," Lindsay said, her panic rising. "I think it's going to play two more times, and if she finds out that I'm—"

"Go, go," I said, then I shouted out, "Wait! Get everyone together. You, Shanna-Francine, Bobbie. We've all got to meet at lunch."

"Cindy, I've really—"

"Listen to me. One o'clock. You know where."

"Okay."

"Promise?"

She clicked off—and the click seemed to echo ominously in the dark cave. *Hold on,* I told myself. *I am not, in fact, in a dark cave all by myself; I am directly behind the cafeteria Dumpster and it smells like vomit.* Was this another Corrective Emotional Experience? Should I be keeping track?

In Professor Scott's class, I made a "To Do" list for D-Day, which I decided would be the next day, Tuesday the fourteenth, from twelve noon to one or two p.m. (I didn't know how long it would take, but I was figuring it wouldn't be longer than an hour). There was a lot I needed to accomplish after Professor Scott's class. I wrote:

1. Meet with Patty at RU's rehab at noon. Give her M's diary pages.
2. Lunch meeting at Long John's with Lindsay, Shanna-Francine, and Bobbie. Outline plan of attack. Assign duties.
3. Call Dad. Beg him to load up Visa Buxx card.
4. Go to (supposedly) "hip" two-block area of Ronkonkomo and buy all necessary supplies.

I looked up from my desk. Professor Scott was giving a lecture on *Maggie: A Girl of the Streets* by Stephen Crane, a brilliantly grim short novel in which a hard-luck Irish girl in the late 1800s is disowned by her family and turns to prostitution. The class was numb with indifference (Demi Moore hadn't yet made of a movie version of it, after all). And yet, what struck me most was Professor Scott. He was lecturing with real passion, real excitement—his arms and hands gestured wildly as he made his points, like he'd suddenly become Italian or something—and he didn't seem to care one hoot that no one was paying attention. *Something's happened to him*, I thought, *but what? Has Professor Scott had a Corrective Emotional Experience too?* Then I realized, *Oh, Cindy, you ding-a-ling, don't forget Professor Scott!*

Ouch! I was suddenly thwacked in the back of my head by a sharp pencil tip. I whipped around angrily.

"Here," said a guy who had moist toast or bagel bits encrusted between his teeth from breakfast (why don't people brush?). He handed me a note. I opened it. It read:

I miss you!
xxoo
Cliff

I jerked my head up. He had turned around. He was gazing at me so sweetly. He must have painted in the morning, because there was a thin streak of purplish paint on his left cheek. Involuntarily I mouthed, "I miss you, too." Oh my God, oh my God, oh my God, oh my God! What the heck was going on? I said it (or mouthed it) so I must have meant it. Right? I sat there with my jaw hung open like a total spazz.

"Class dismissed!" Professor Scott cried out. The class filed out, including Cliff, who just smiled at me—plainly and gently—and I heard, "Is there anything wrong, Cindy?"

I clamped my mouth shut. Professor Scott was walking toward

me. He had a spring in his step. He was concerned about me, which was nice, but it wasn't interfering with his otherwise cheery, and unexplainable, good spirits. He sat across from me.

"You look like someone who's in . . ." He paused, smiling inwardly. "Well, I don't want to get too personal."

Oh no. He knew! I blushed. *But wait*, I thought, *what does he know, because I sure as heck don't know what I know, at least not about what he thinks he knows that I allegedly know.* Then I looked up at Professor Scott; his beaming face, his lightened spirits.

"Is anything wrong with you, Professor?" He looked away for a sec, like the cat that ate the canary (was Professor Scott in love?) (and was she over twenty-one years old) (for once?) (eeeow!). Then he exclaimed abruptly, "I'm being published!"

"Wha—what?"

"Oh, Cindy. Cindy!" He dashed to his desk, swiped his (sadly) raggy briefcase, chuckled giddily as he rifled through it, then proudly handed me a sheet of stationery. "I just got it yesterday. I can't stop looking at it."

I scanned the letter hungrily.

Dear Mr. Scott: Congratulations. The editorial committee at Fireplace Perennial have read your manuscript, *Beautiful Cherry*, and unanimously agree that it's a very fine and beautiful coming-of-age story. We'd like to publish it. Please call me at your earliest convenience, and do have your literary agent contact me as soon as possible. Again, congratulations. We look forward to working with you.

I screamed: *"Ahhhhhhhhhhhhh!"*

"Don't rip it!" he shrieked merrily.

Then we both screamed: *"Ahhhhhhhhhhhhh!"* It was all unbelievably euphoric—bursts of fizzy candy were tingling inside me—and God help me, I threw my arms around the professor and gave him the biggest hug, because as much as I may have (privately) made fun of Professor Scott's literary ambitions in the past, boy, oh boy, he sure showed me, didn't he, and I'm so glad he did.

"Professor," I enthused. "Oh my God. Book tours. Signings. Your picture on the back flap. Your book—in actual bookstores."

"I know, I know!"

"Did your agent call the editor yet?"

"I don't have an agent!" he yelled, and that seemed hysterically funny to us both. We screamed: "*Ahhhhhhhhhhhhhh!*"

"But I'll get one, I'll get one," he said, gasping for air.

"Of course you will. Oh, Professor." For an instant, I saw Professor Scott as a young man—a young boy, even—bursting through his middle-aged face: his eyes, so joyous; his cheeks, chubby and flushed; and his smile, pure bliss. Then I noticed his lined forehead, his aged, slightly sunken eyes, his coffee-stained teeth, and I thought, *Wow, he so totally deserves this (along with a better health plan with dental).*

"What's up with you?" he suddenly asked. His smile was easy and generous. "What did you want to ask me? Anything. Anything at all."

"I . . . I . . ."

How could I explain? Especially now? I wanted to tell the professor about my plan to return to RU and Alpha Beta Delta—and include his return to RU as part of the package. But why would he care now? He's going to be published.

"Cindy, tell me," he insisted.

And I did. Everything. The whole plan, the outcome I was hoping for, and how it would undoubtedly make you-know-who very unhappy.

He quickly snapped, "So you're sticking it to Meri. That's great!"

"I . . . I . . ."

"I'm in! Let's bring her down. Fantastic. I'm in!"

"Professor . . ."

"Cindy, I'm going to be a published author. Right? And I'm a professor where? At Chappaqua Community College?" He was right. That didn't exactly have a tony literary ring to it. "Okay, forget that, that's elitist. I'm not that way. No, no, no." He gripped my hand tightly. He was so heartfelt. "Cindy, listen to me. Here's the thing. I loved teaching at RU. It was my home. For decades. And I loved my students." *And loved them and loved them and loved them,* I thought (yuck!). "Meri took that away from me. I want it back. Please, Cindy. Won't you let me go home? Please?" Then he smiled. "Have pity on a soon-to-be-published author."

"Can I ask you something, Professor?"

"Anything. Anything."

"How many girls at RU have you slept with over the years?"

Uh-oh. Pop goes the balloon, I guess. But I had to know. I mean, what would I be "bringing back" to RU? The professor crushed inward; shame rose to his cheeks. He intoned meekly, "Between us?"

"Of course." And I meant that.

He whispered, "Barbara O'Brien."

"The older woman at your party?" I remembered her. She was the one who flung her arms around me when I first arrived and screamed, "So you're the latest!" I should have known right then. I'm slow sometimes (all right, a lot of times).

"She's not old," whined the professor defensively. "She's only in her midforties."

"Okay, fine," I sighed. Whoopsie. Age = touchy subject for people over thirty. "So who else?"

"You promise . . ."

"Yes. I promise. I swear. How many more?" He cleared his throat, cupped his hands nervously in his lap, looked down at them. Then he mumbled, "Mmmumats mmmumit."

"What?"

"Mmmumats mmmumit."

"Professor, I'm sorry. You're going to have to speak up."

He did—just barely—and said, oh so softly, "That's it."

"Excuse me?"

"That's it. No one else. Just Barbara."

"What?" I couldn't believe it.

"Please, you promised!" he wailed. "Think of my reputation! Think of my manhood!"

"Gosh, I'd really rather not, Professor!" I gasped in shock. "I mean, no offense. But what about your cherries? 'I have a jar of cherries, I've kept them through the—'"

"I know my own poem," he grumbled. Poor Professor Scott. The truth came out. The sad, saggy truth. Yes, years ago (decades, more like), he was working as a professor's assistant while completing his master's at RU. And he caught the eye of freshman lit major Barbara O'Brien. They had an affair, and a pretty tempestuous one, if the professor was to be believed.

Nightly, in bed, they would discuss Austen, Flaubert, the poetical works of Shelley, and one night, as he recited a poem by Keats ("Asleep! O sleep a little while, white pearl," to be exact) he surprised her by poem's end. He placed a ring box in her hand. He had found true love (and he'd emptied out his entire savings and taken out a loan for the engagement ring too). Barbara looked at him with disbelief. She opened the ring box—and darn her, because I don't think this was right—she laughed. Not a mean laugh or anything, but a truly startled and surprised and flat-out this-does-not-compute laugh.

"This isn't for me, is it?" she asked.

It was, of course, but the professor was too shocked and dis-combobulated to speak.

"Tsk, Scotty," she continued softly. "You don't marry your muse. The relationship between an artist and his muse is too sacred for that."

Oh, brother! Yes, Professor Scott was (and is) caught up in his own baroque, sometimes near porny, notions of romance (when I think of Professor Scott "in love," I see doilies, baby's breath, frock coats and bustles, frankincense and myrrh; I see him somewhere in a bower endlessly reciting impromptu couplets, and his maiden, poor thing, clearly at her wit's end, forcibly crushing him with a kiss—if only to shut him up), but Barbara, well, she took the cake. She really did think she was going to be a great artists' muse (as in plural artists).

"You'll have so many muses," she cooed to the professor. "I'm just your first."

Ick, ick, ick. But sad, too, because the professor bought it hook, line, and sinker. As the years passed, there were plenty of innocent young freshman girls, his cherries, who were dazzled by his mind (as I was) (and still am), and thrilled to spend time in his company and be taken out for drinks and dinner where they would listen, endlessly, about the daily struggles he encountered while writing his "great novel" (one that I, for one, didn't even think existed) (did any of the other girls? I wonder), and inevitably, the professor would bust a move, as he had with me (eeeow!), and be "rebuffed," "cruelly denied."

And yet, the girls did not abandon him. They didn't pity him, exactly; in some small way they understood him, and as the years passed their friendships deepened and they regarded him with even more fondness, as the kindhearted, slightly dotty literary intellect who first introduced them to swooning romance and didn't ruin it, entirely, with one mangy, sad little kiss.

"So you see . . . ," said the professor, his voice trailing off.

"Yes," I said. Then I glanced at my watch. It was just after eleven. I jumped up. "Professor, I'm sorry, I have to go."

"Of course," he said listlessly.

I raced to the door, then turned around. "D-Day is tomorrow. You in?" His eyes lit up like a Christmas tree.

"Of course."

"Oh, and congratulations again on your book, Professor. That's just awesome news." I ran outside. I didn't have much time. If I didn't catch the bus, I'd be stuck. But there it was. People were climbing on board. It was just within reach. I ran faster. Faster. Its doors were closing. It was starting to pull away. N-o-o-o-o! From the corner of my eye, I saw a violent whirl of white. *Whoosh!* Albino Girl swerved forth on her skateboard, rocketing onto the street. The bus screeched to a stop. Was she trying to get herself killed?

"Motherfuck!" she screamed, waving her fist at the bus driver, then gesturing to a posted sign. "'Kids at Play,' asshole. Get it?"

I flung myself against the bus, banging on the door. Reluctantly the bus driver opened it—*phew!*—and we took off down the street. *How much does Albino Girl know?* I wondered. Had she been listening outside Professor Scott's classroom? Oh God, does she know about D-Day? I looked out the bus window. Albino Girl was vanishing in the distance, whirling in circles in the middle of the street. She wasn't following me. Or so I hoped.

When I stepped off at the bus stop just outside RU, I glanced at the list I had written up in Professor Scott's class.

1. Meet with Patty at RU's rehab at noon. Give her M's diary pages.

Oh, darn it! I wanted to kick myself for not thinking things through. What if someone saw me on campus? What if, God forbid, Meri saw me? Oh, why didn't I wear a wig, or at least dark sunglasses—or something? I needed to think fast. I whipped out my cell phone and dialed. Thank God she picked up.

"Miss Farr? It's me. It's Cindy. I really need your help."

Sheila Farr had recently moved off campus, just a few blocks away, to a small converted garage apartment that the home owners rented out to students.

"*Entrez, ma cherie,*" she murmured, gesturing me in grandly. Her place was a riot of rococo; Marie Antoinette threw up in here. There was chiffon, there was lace, as well as a large beach towel with a candy-colored portrait of Marilyn Monroe hanging precisely over a window, her face brightly illuminated by the sun shining through.

"Now, what are we going for, dear?" she said, gently holding out both my hands, assessing me critically. "Betty Boop? Marlene? Please don't say Cher. Are you hungry? I've got fried chicken. Would you like a bromo?"

I tried to explain—this didn't have to be complicated, and I was in an awful hurry. I just needed not to look like me. That's all.

"Tsk. You're not fun at all. But all right. Fine. Just remember . . ."

"There is no greater star than Sheila Farr," I said with a grin. "In all the stars and heavens above, she's the one we truly love."

She tittered, squeezing my cheeks. "What a wonderfully strange girl you are."

To say that I didn't look like myself by the time I stepped timidly onto the campus of RU would be, like, a huge understatement. Wonderfully strange? Maybe. I was in a plain brown topcoat, a slightly oversize bertha-collared cream blouse, a black skirt that went just past my knees, and black T-strap pumps. So far, so good—nicely nondescript, in fact, which is what I wanted. But what would people make of my jeweled cat's-eye sunglasses? Or my teased-out auburn fire Sizzle Wig from the Raquel Welch collection?

And then there were my breasts. They were strapped over my own under my blouse in an industrial-strength bra. They were birdseed bags. And they were huge. I'm talking torpedoes. And unlike a traditionally stuffed bra (or silicone), they had some serious jiggle. I even got a few horse whistles from a group of guys passing by. *Wow*, I thought, *guys are easy; you jiggle, they come.* That made me smile, so I straightened my back and held my head high. I would never again have breasts this astounding, so why not work it?

Jiggle-jiggle-jiggle. I made my way across the Great Lawn toward RU's rehab. More guys were looking at me. This was too much. *Jiggle-jiggle-jiggle.* Another guy looked up from the girl he was macking on, and she angrily turned his head back. Ha. *Jiggle-jiggle-jiggle.* I felt like, well, a movie star, but a dumb one, and there was something oddly liberating about that, and I imagined myself saying to an interviewer, "Oh, but I enjoyed posing nude for *Vanity Fair*. It was, like, so artistic." I laughed inside, because even if I actually did have real "bodacious ta-ta's," as Bud likes to say, I could never be a dumb movie star, because I'd be way too self-aware of all the silliness that went along with it. I'd make fun of it. And guys don't want that (unless you're Pamela Anderson) (but she's the lone exception).

And then, oh my God, I nearly screamed and fell face-first, because just a few feet in front of me, encircled by a group of fawning girls, was none other than Gloria Daily. Holy shit! Or was it Gilda? I couldn't tell. *Keep walking*, I told myself, *and don't you dare jiggle.* I held my head low and scurried past, hearing snatches of conversation:

". . . cut it in half for good behavior. It was all so silly," said Gloria (or Gilda), which meant that her little stint in prison was very much over. But what froze my blood most was when another girl said, "That's so cool that you'll be back at the house. Did you miss Alpha Beta Delta?"

I gulped. Meri Sugarman and Gloria Daily—together again. This time with Evangelicals. Thank God no one noticed me as I scampered into the rehab wing of RU's medical center. I heard gales of screaming, sputtering laughter. I didn't even have to ask where Patty's room was, I just followed her laughter. What on earth was so funny? I stepped to her doorway. Pigboy was seated next to her bed, chuckling; Patty was sitting up and barely able to talk, she was laughing so hard, though she was trying. In her hands she held an open book, *Shine*, by Star Jones Reynolds.

"Listen to this," she squealed. "It's about her husband. 'The first time he held me in his arms sexually, it was almost frightening!'"

"For who?!" chortled Pigboy. "Did you scare him, Star?"

"Wait, wait, this is better. 'We learned to make love without intercourse.'"

"Oh, man, you know he taught her that. That's how he got out of it." Patty exploded with laughter.

"Hi, guys," I said. They looked up. They were confused (of course). "It's me. Cindy." It seems there are a few things that can get bigger laughs than Star Jones Reynolds. Namely me. I explained, and quickly—I had only twenty minutes to get to Long John's.

"I want to be a part of D-Day," Patty harrumphed.

"Don't worry," I assured her. "You have a more important role. I've got something for you. Diary pages."

"From you? Oh, Cindy, I'm touched. Building an alliance of trust with your therapist can—"

"No, they're not mine." I paused for a moment. Could I say it? She caught my eye. And her jaw dropped.

"No!" she exclaimed. "Oh my God. Gimmie-gimmie-gimmie." She snatched Meri's blog entry printouts from my hands, gleefully scanning them. "Where did you get these? 'My name is Merial Sugarman. My hair is pretty.' Oh my God. Oh my God. This is gonna be way better than Star Jones."

I asked Pigboy to walk me out.

"How is she doing?" I asked, because I honestly couldn't tell. Her face was still pale, but there was a bit of color in her cheeks, and her eyes did seem focused. She was starting to look (and behave) like the old Patty. But was I being too optimistic?

"The detox is rough," said Pigboy, his voice held low. "But she's a fighter. She's doing good."

I felt a "but." There was something he didn't want to tell me. "And . . . ?" I asked. He squirmed, uncomfortable.

"Okay, but I don't get all of it. She's been seeing a psychiatrist."

"That's good. Right?"

"Right. She loves it. And she's taking some pill called Zyprexa."

"I don't know what that is," I said, and I sure as heck didn't like the sound of it.

"And after that, they'll be starting her on lithium. She's been diagnosed as bipolar."

"What on earth is that?" I yelped.

"I don't know exactly," he said, his frustration rising. "Some brain chemical thing."

I covered my mouth in shock. "Is—is she going to be all right?"

"She'll be fine," he said. "I talked to a nurse. She just needs to 'stabilize.' Something like that. Oh, Cindy, don't cry." I didn't even realize there were tears in my eyes. He pulled me into his arms.

"She's so lucky to have you," I sniffled.

"I'm not going anywhere," he whispered. "C'mon, you gotta get going." He led me to the front, gave me a wink. "By the way, nice rack."

"Do I look like a dumb movie star?" I asked impishly.

"The dumbest," he said with a grin—and then his face abruptly dropped.

"What?" I gasped.

"You're leaking," he said, pointing to my feet.

Oh no. I must have jiggled too much. Birdseed was trickling from beneath my blouse to the floor. I readjusted frantically. "How's that?" I asked.

"Walk a little bit," he said. I quickly strolled up to him and back. "No leak. You're good."

I walked-ran (and jiggled just a bit) (ha!) across the Great Lawn. Dark clouds were forming. It was going to rain. A group of birds swooped in a graceful arc against the troubled skies. I think they were crested swifts, or maybe wrens. Actually, they were wrens, and I knew this because one of them was dive-bombing—holy moly!—right at me. I screamed! I ducked. *Whoosh!* It lunged at my feet and eagerly pecked where the birdseed had continued to trickle from my blouse to the ground. I desperately kicked. "Shoo, bird, shoo," I commanded. It fluttered away. *Phew.*

I was walk-running a little faster now. I looked up at the sky. The birds were gone. Thank goodness. But strangely—and ominously—I could still hear them. *Tweet-tweet! Tweet-tweet!* I whipped around. Ahhhhhhhh! They were coming right at me. All of them! I ran for my life across the Great Lawn, but they flew faster and faster, and they were all around me, flying, pecking at my feet, and—oh my God—my birdseed breasts. I cried out, "H-e-e-e-e-e-l-p!" *Flutter-flutter-flutter!* They were everywhere—with their nasty little bills, their scratchy little claws. *What's in these darn seeds,* I thought, *heroin?* I fell backward—*oomph!*—flat on my back. All I could see were wings and beaks. *Flutter-flutter-flutter!* Then I thought, *Hold on, is this really necessary?* I angrily batted my arms and stood up, pulled out my blouse, reached inside, unhooked my industrial-strength bra, and allowed the birdseed bags to plop to the ground. The birds amassed on them ravenously. "I hope you choke," I scolded furiously. "Little rats with wings." Then I walked off. I'm fairly certain that I made quite a spectacle of myself on the Great Lawn. Oh, well. So much for being a dumb movie star.

I arrived at Long John's early enough to change back into my regular clothes. Lindsay, Shanna-Francine, and Bobbie came right on time, and after we ordered two Variety Platters for the table (Chicken Planks, fried shrimp, clams!) (yummmm!) I laid out my plan of attack. Shanna-Francine was confused.

"But that just gets you back in the house. How do we bring down Meri?"

I assured her she had nothing to worry about (which was over-confident, maybe, but I needed to convince myself more than anyone else). I was working with Patty on that, I told her, and hopefully—if I can get just a few more blog entries from Mark—I'll be able to destroy Meri so completely that nothing she tries will ever be able to hurt us again.

"What about Gloria?" asked Shanna-Francine nervously (she was holding Bobbie's hand tightly). "She's back, you know."

I knew this, of course, and yet everyone agreed that Gloria is only as powerful as Meri is. I laid out my entire plan, gave each of them their assignments, and told them to be ready tomorrow.

"Wait," Bobbie announced gruffly. "Can't do it tomorrow. That's my volunteer day." Bobbie, it seems, has finally declared her major: She wants to be a veterinarian—the telltale savage little bite marks on her fingers were evidence of her attempts to feed the squirrels outside the house—and she now volunteers every Tuesday at a local animal shelter.

"Shouldn't be a problem," I hastened to reassure her. "We'll do it Wednesday." I would need to alert Professor Scott about the change. Everyone was thrilled to hear that he had a publisher for his book.

"I can get him an agent," enthused Lindsay. "Auntie used to vacation in Morocco with Bibi Baldwin." Bibi, she explained, is the biggest literary agent in the biz, who foreswore nude sun-bathing for Mystic Tan spray tanning upon the untimely death of

Lindsay's beloved aunt. "She looks like a big, dark, overripe orange now," she said. "I'll call her. She owes me. I let her keep some of Auntie's ashes. She mixed them with glitter and threw them in the air on the dance floor at Les Bains in Paris. Give me the professor's number."

"Why don't I just beat the crap out of Meri?" Bobbie roared.

"Yeah," cheered Lindsay. "And put her in a tunic from Wal-Mart. And shoes from Payless. And take her for a cut and color at Fantastic Sams. She'll die. She'll just die."

"I will so never forgive her," added Shanna-Francine softly, and given her enormous capacity to forgive and her truly astounding reserves of empathy for all mankind, this was quite the proclamation. For the second time today, someone said to me, "Oh, Cindy, don't cry." It was Lindsay. But I couldn't help it. I was so touched by my friends' unconditional support. Still, Shanna-Francine was worried.

"What if this doesn't work?" she blurted nervously. "What if it all blows up in our faces?"

"Don't worry," I told her. "The will is everything. To master the fear of others, you must first master your own."

"Oh my God, that's so profound," she said.

"And remember," I added, "theatricality and deception are powerful agents."

"Oh my God. You sound like Yoda. Or a fortune cookie." I couldn't take credit, of course. I told them about my incredible experience with *Batman Begins*.

"Christian Bale is so deep," Lindsay whispered reverently. "I've seen *Swing Kids*, like, a billion times. Did you know his father was married to Gloria Steinem?"

"He's a vegetarian, too," said Bobbie.

"And he supports Greenpeace," added Shanna-Francine.

We all took a moment to collectively sigh. Christian Bale-

Christian Bale-Christian Bale. Something for everyone.

I was off. I still had so much to do. On the bus back to Ronkonkomo, I called Professor Scott, who said Wednesday was fine for D-Day. Actually, he told me that any day was a good day if it entailed bringing down Meri, and he thanked me profusely; Lindsay had already called to put him in touch with Bibi Baldwin. Then I did something I've never done—but I had to do it. I called Dad at his office.

"Cindy?" he asked breathlessly. "Is something wrong? Are you okay? I'll get on a plane. I'll be right there."

It's so nice to have a dad like Dad. I assured him that nothing was wrong, per se, but I did need a teensy favor (okay, not so teensy): I needed him to add a few thousand dollars to my Visa Buxx card. And I would so pay him back—with interest, if he wanted. Incredibly, he didn't ask why I needed it. My card would be reloaded, he said, within the hour. And, he added, I would not need to pay him back. Gosh, I was Miss Waterworks all day; my eyes welled with tears again. I may have a sister who's bonkers (to put it mildly) and a mom who's, well, very momlike (and always ready to give me her opinion, even if I haven't asked for it) (and I love both them both, don't get me wrong), but Dad is just pure love and support (in the best sense).

And he's true to his word, too. The Visa Buxx card was reloaded by the time I reached the would-be "hip" strip of Ronkonkomo (and cursed myself for not bringing an umbrella, because a light rain was falling). I stepped into Cloak & Dagger, a home surveillance and security shop. I had my list. I knew exactly what I wanted:

- Several Micro-Ear Communicators, with state-of-the-art parabolic circuitry
- A Bug Detector, the size of an iPod, with silent LED displays and warning indicators

- An ultra-compact Pen Camera with transmitter, which hides a camera, transmitter, and mic in a plain-looking pen
- A palm-size Micro-Voice Disguiser, which fits over any phone or cell phone mouthpiece (it can even change a woman's voice to a man's) (and vice versa)
- Envelope X-Ray Spray, which turns normal paper momentarily transparent, enabling you to see the contents of an envelope

It all didn't add up to as much as I thought it would, so I thought, what the heck, and had the clerk add Mini Night-Vision Goggles, a Telephone Tap Detector, an infrared flashlight-size Heat Scanner (which detects body heat up to a thousand feet), and an Air Taser. I wouldn't need all of these things for Wednesday, of course, but who knows, they might come in handy later. *I'm Spy Barbie for real now!* I thought. But when I stepped onto the street, oh my God, a bolt of lightning fractured the sky, thunder crashed, and I realized, no, Spy Barbie is for kids. I'm Dark Cindy. Then I was hit by a torrential downpour. *Okay, there are worse things*, I thought, and I dashed down the block toward the bus stop, staying as close against the storefronts as possible so I'd get a bit of shelter from their awnings. But then it poured even harder and the wind whipped in every direction. So much for the awnings. I was completely soaked. I ran faster, clutched my bags close, and held one just above my head, slightly obscuring my view. I saw red lights flashing; the bus was pulling away. *Oh, crap*, I thought, *run faster*, and I bolted forth and—holy moly—almost knocked someone clear off their feet and onto the ground. Then he cupped my face and gently pressed his lips to mine and the rain poured harder and—oh! oh!—I felt a fluttery rush in my heart and I thought, *to heck with the bags*, and without thinking I let them drop to the ground and wrapped my arms around him and returned his passion and almost went crazy-gaga when I felt his telltale love patch grazing against my lips and my chin.

Then I pulled back. Every girl wants to be kissed in the rain (don't they?) and whisper sweet nothings, but when I gazed slack-jawed into his (naturally) smoldering eyes, all I could think of to say was, "Wow. I'm really getting wet."

Cliff drove us back to Chappaqua. We were both soaked to the bone, and he had the heat on full-blast. I tried to speak: "I . . . I . . ."

Oh, but how could I say it? Why is it that heroines in movies know just what to say? And when? I tried again: "I . . . I . . ."

"You don't have to say anything if you don't want to," he told me. But I wanted to. And then I thought, *Why candy coat? My feelings are (always?) (sometimes?) valid, and who cares if I sound like a doofmeister, because that's nothing new, right?* So I blurted out, "I don't have casual sex."

I cringed. I couldn't believe I said that. *Oooh, mistake-mistake-mistake!*

"Neither do I," he responded quietly.

Huh? Trick response? Hold on. No. Keep going!

"And I don't like drugs. Including pot."

"That's cool. I've been meaning to stop. Makes it hard to wake up in the morning." *What? Really? Keep going!*

"I'm totally insecure about seeing a guy I know my mom wouldn't approve of, which I know is completely lame."

"What about your dad?"

I gasped. I hadn't thought of that. Or had I? But thinking of it right then and there I realized, practically in an instant: Dad is pure love and support.

"I really want to be with you, Cindy," he said, placing his hand on mine. "If you're into that." *Who wouldn't be? For crying out loud. Have I been blind as well as deaf? Wait, hold on. Slow down.*

"I'm, um, definitely into that, but can we hold off on the sex for a bit? And just, I mean, I . . ." *Oooh, dumb-dumb-dumb. Why did I say that? No insta-sex, he's outta here!*

"Cindy, I just want to be with you. I think you're awesome.

And if you're not feeling the sex right now, I'm totally down with taking it slow. As slow as you want." *Ahhhhh! All the right answers! What now?*

"You're such an amazing artist, and I'm just . . ." I fumbled. *Oh my God, am I in third grade now? Where's my sippy cup? Why does this guy make me so spazzy?* He turned toward me and smiled (and I melted), and he said,

"Everybody can be an artist." He grinned. "Want to make some art together?"

We parked the car, and he led me to his art studio jail cell. The rain had stopped. In one hand I was holding my bags, Cliff was holding my other hand, and I thought, *I just laid down a few hard-core Cindy Laws (for lack of a better phrase) on this guy, and he didn't run away.* I felt strangely free—wheeeee!—which was (slightly) confusing because I also felt more warmly connected to Cliff than ever before (which wasn't a problem, exactly, it was a paradox) (I once read that a problem you solve, a paradox you live with).

In his studio, Cliff threw down two long, rectangular pieces of canvas and backtaped the edges to a large plastic drop cloth. "Let's make art," he said, smiling. He poured deep red acrylic paint on his rectangle, and swirled and brushed in some pearl blue, then mixed it with magenta, while I swirled and brushed a soft green, a brilliant pink, and a dark bronze on mine. It was like finger-painting, but on a really large scale. So much fun!

I chuckled. "I don't think I'm making art, but I'm having a great time."

"No, you'll see," he said. "This isn't the art. We're the art." Then he took off all his clothes—every single stitch—and I stood there shocked as he bent down and pressed his entire body out flat, face-first, onto the colorful panel. "Your turn," he mumbled, chortling, and I found myself laughing too—and throwing off all my clothes and then pressing my body down against the cool, sticky paint. "Okay, we just have to hold it like this for a bit," he murmured. "Try to keep still."

"For how long?" I asked, trying not to move my mouth too much (I didn't want to create a mushy face on my canvas). "Mmmgumphmmph. I've never tasted acrylic paint before."

We laughed. We couldn't help it. And after a bit, he said, "Okay. Real slow. Press your hands down to give you leverage and come up on your knees." Oh so slowly we rose, and I gasped. There were my face and body on canvas, their impression outlined against a lively swirl of color. I loved his painting too (of course) (he has a slight outtie, so he had a better belly-button impression on his painting than I did). But then I thought, Crap, we're covered in paint.

"We can't go into the men's or women's shower stalls like this," I gasped.

"Hmmm," he said, his expression saying, "Whoopsie." Oh, I wanted to kiss him right there (but my mouth was already full of paint, so I stopped myself), and then I thought, *What the hey, it's nearly dark outside, and no one's ever in back of the jail cells.* I grabbed his hand and whisked him out into the bucketing rain. We screamed and laughed—the rain was so cold—and then we ran to the back of the jail cells and jumped up and down and used our hands to rub the paint off of each other's bodies. And he kissed me. Sweetly. "This was a good idea," he whispered in my ear.

"You think?" I said. "I'm freezing my butt off."

He gasped. "I have a couple of electric blankets in my room."

We screamed, running as fast as we could to his jail cell room (his other one) (where he sleeps), and after we dried off, we both shivered with delight under the slowly increasing heat from the electric blankets. And we made an impromptu dinner on his hot plate: hot dogs, buns, and some prewashed salad with dressing from his cube refrigerator. And we talked and talked about everything—about the music we love, our lives, and what books we like (he's a reader too!) (yeaaaah!). It was getting late.

"I have so much to do in the next few days," I said, more to myself than to him. I caught his eye—and he must have sensed something.

"You can tell me anything you want," he said.

"I . . . I . . ." But I couldn't. It all seemed so complicated; Meri, Gloria (and Gilda), Albino Girl, D-Day. "Can I talk to you about it in a few days?" I asked. He assured me I could (he's so understanding) (I'm not sure if I would have been. I think I would have been like, what's the biggie? Did you kill someone?). He even lent me an umbrella and gave me the warmest kiss at the door. I have a new boyfriend! I screamed to myself. I gathered my bags and ran back to my jail cell, and within minutes I was under my covers— and I couldn't stop smiling.

I have a new boyfriend, I have a new boyfriend, I have a new boyfriend! Gosh, I wonder what the paintings will look like when they dry. Then my phone vibrated on my dresser, and I flipped it open and my entire body clenched. I had a text message.

TEXT MESSAGE
In North Carolina, Indecent Exposure can land u in jail for
6 months + a $500 penalty. Should I report u?
FR: M. Sugarman
NOV. 13, 11:46 p.m.

Oh, I hate Meri Sugarman! Obviously Albino Girl was watching (in the rain, no less) and reported back to her. I felt so violated. And I wanted to text back "Go ahead. I dare you," but I stopped myself. *Don't let her know anything,* I thought (plus, what if she called my bluff and I ended up in jail for six months?). I pulled the covers up. The phone vibrated again. Oh, darn her. I flipped it open.

TEXT MESSAGE
I'm now president of Alpha Beta Delta. Does that make you
sad? :)
FR: M. Sugarman
NOV. 13, 11:48 p.m.

I gritted my teeth. I wanted to text back so bad. Then I heard
Liam's voice: "The will is everything." I angrily buried my head in
the pillow. My phone . . . yep, you guessed. I flipped it open.

TEXT MESSAGE
Miss me? Wanna come over and scrub my toilet bowl? Ha-ha-ha-
ha! Bow-wow! Woof woof!
FR: M. Sugarman
NOV. 13, 11:51 p.m.

What the heck, I thought. I furiously texted her back.

TEXT MESSAGE
Roll over and die! I'll be happy to make your funeral
arrangements. Kiss-kiss. :)
FR: Cindy Bixby
NOV. 13, 11:53 p.m.

Ha! I felt so giddy. I immediately turned off my phone and
tossed it to the floor (I didn't need to see her response). It took me
a while to get to sleep. Why? Because I felt really bad about sending that message. I honestly don't want Meri to die, and I certainly
don't want to plan her funeral. I just want her to go away. And she
will. Dark Cindy will make sure of that.

When I woke up Tuesday morning, I wasn't Cindy anymore. I was Dark Cindy. I just knew it. *Oh yeah?* I said to myself. *Prove it.* In the parking lot, I slapped my skateboard on the ground and blasted past a line of cars to the curb and—*whoosh!*—I made the turn! Oh my God! I couldn't believe it. I really did it. I wanted to jump up and down and scream for joy, but then I thought, *Dumb luck, do it again.* And I did. Again and again. Each time I successfully made the turn. Then I hopped back on the skateboard and tore around the parking lot, around and around, going faster and faster, between cars, around cars, whipping this way and that—each time passing a flabbergasted Jahmal. I even gave him a wave. Ha. Didn't think I could do it, did you? C'mon, buddy. Check my spot and dig my swirl!

When I finished, I used my foot to flip the board up—and I caught it in my hands. Nice. I guess Jahmal couldn't help himself. He burst out clapping at the other end of the lot. Cindy might have been taken aback by this—or angry that he was only now being supportive—but Dark Cindy just gave him a wink and strolled on. It was a watershed moment. Beige Cindy finally turned Dark.

I skateboarded to each of my classes. At one point I wondered if the final transformation of Beige to Dark Cindy had anything to do with Cliff. Does love (or heavy like) give one the confidence to boldly confront life's most difficult obstacles (such as Meri)? I decided it sure couldn't hurt, but I wasn't ready to give love all the credit. Dark Cindy was born within me. During my last class, I figured I might as well turn on my phone and see if Meri responded to my awful text message last night. She hadn't. Interesting. Cause for celebration? Not by a long shot, I decided. Don't let your guard down.

I slept better than I have in weeks last night. Strangely, when I woke up this morning, my first thought was: *Star Jones. Gastric bypass surgery? Or daily high colonics? Discuss.* I wiped the sleep out of my eyes. I must have been dreaming about Patty. Then I screamed—like, really screamed—because I suddenly realized why I had slept so well. It was 11:40 a.m. and I had set my alarm clock for seven. Crap-crap-crap! This was not a good way to start D-Day. I had twenty minutes to get ready. Lindsay was picking me up at noon. I threw on my clothes, gathered my Cloak & Dagger bags, and caught sight of myself in the mirror. *Okay,* I told myself, *you do look tragic, but does Dark Cindy give a flip? Nope. Get crackin'.*

I flew out the door to the parking lot and was frantically searching for Lindsay's Porsche when I heard a car motor rev. I jerked around. Two figures in the front seat of a Camry ducked down. Oh my God. It was both of them. Gloria and Gilda. Lindsay's Porsche screeched up, and I saw Albino Girl in the distance, speeding up on her skateboard. "Hurry," I wailed, piling inside. Startled, she hit the gas and we flew down the street. I looked in the rearview mirror and saw the Camry gunning forth—then violently come to a halt when Albino Girl clumsily swerved before it.

"They're getting sloppy," I said as the Camry and Albino Girl vanished in the distance.

"What's that greenish stuff on your ear?" asked Lindsay, then she gasped. "Erotic body paint! Bud and I do that too. Doesn't it taste yummy? We use strawberry and chocolate. Have you tried the glow-in-the-dark kiwi? So fun. He rubbed it all over my . . ."

"Is everybody ready?" I asked, desperate to change the subject. They were, she assured me. Bobbie picked up Professor Scott— she told Meri that she was on her way to a small construction job to make extra money (very believable in Bobbie's case)—while Shanna-Francine is supposedly at her first class of the day. But everyone was at Long John's, raring to go.

"Is this really necessary?" asked Shanna-Francine at the restaurant when I handed them their Micro-Ear Communicators. "I mean, why don't we just use our cell phones?"

"Because it's so much cooler this way," squealed Lindsay excitedly.

"Aren't taser guns against the law?" asked Professor Scott nervously.

"Not in North Carolina," I assured him. "As long as you're over eighteen."

We were ready to go. Everyone had their supplies. Looking both ways as we stepped out of Long John's, Lindsay and I leaped into her Porsche, Professor Scott and Bobbie climbed into Bobbie's Chevy Avalanche pick up, while Shanna-Francine strolled nonchillingly on her way to Alpha Beta Delta. We were off. "Testing one-two-three," I whispered.

"Wow, I can really hear you," Shanna-Francine giggled. Everyone else could too. Thank goodness.

"I wish Bud was here," sniffled Lindsay, which prompted an ear-splitting chorus of *aww*s and encouraging sentiments. Moments later Lindsay and I were stealthily making our way near the dean's office when we heard Shanna-Francine whisper, "Going in." She was striding into Alpha Beta Delta.

Then Professor Scott mumbled, "She's moving, getting in her car," which meant that the professor and Bobbie were already in front of the dean's house and had spotted Louella, his wife, on the move.

Lindsay and I hunkered down behind a lawn hedge (with shade from a leafy tree) (which was good for Lindsay) right across the street from the dean's office. Like clockwork, he strode out on his way to lunch. Lindsay murmured testily, "Look at him. Smug little jerk."

"Shhh," I warned her. He walked to his private parking space and—what? Since when does the dean drive a Mercedes-Benz SL? I chuckled inwardly. Follow the money. This really was going to work. I pulled out my Micro-Voice Disguiser.

"Can I do it? Please?" begged Lindsay.

"This isn't a game, you know."

"I know, I know, give it to me." She grinned, pulling it from my hands. She clicked it on and spoke through it. "Do I sound like a man? Like a manly man?" We both erupted in giggles—then quickly shushed ourselves. It worked. She really did sound like a man (who was maybe slightly constipated). She snapped it over her cell phone mouthpiece and dialed, once more sounding just like a man when she spoke with Mrs. Juergens, the dean's harried assistant, pretending to be a Homeland Security agent.

"Yes, ma'am, you'll have to vacate the premises immediately. It could be toxic. Mmm-hmm. We're not sure if it's rice or—"

"This is just like the University of Texas!" screamed Mrs. Juergens, referring to a recent scare in which a university dorm was allegedly sprinkled with a deadly contaminant. Lindsay didn't have to say much more. Whiz-bang, Mrs. Juergens was out the door and in her car and speeding down the street within seconds.

"Poor thing," I whispered.

"I believe it's ricin, not rice," said Professor Scott instructively in our ears. "And by the way, did we all know? Today in 1918, Victory Day was celebrated for the first time in Britain to mark the end of the First World War."

"Can't stop teachin', can ya, Teach?" ribbed Bobbie good-naturedly. In fact, there was a lot of chatter in Lindsay's and my ears: Professor Scott and Bobbie, who were parked in front of the dean's house, discovered a mutual love of golf and planned on hitting the greens together, while at Alpha Beta Delta, we could hear intermittent voices from Shanna-Francine and various sisters, which were easy to ignore until we heard one voice say very clearly, "Where's Lindsay?" It was Meri.

"I think she's at Long John's with Cindy," answered Shanna-Francine nervously.

And then, chillingly, we heard: "Look at this kitchen floor. Who wants to do a little handsies-kneesies? Well? I prefer a volunteer."

"Hurry," I whispered to Lindsay, grabbing her hand. She balked. She was opening her umbrella. I furiously shook my head no. The last thing we needed was to be spotted because of her spectacular indigo lace-patterned Stella McCartney. The sun was shining brightly, but I held Lindsay's hand and she kept her head down low as we scampered lickity-split across the street, into the lobby, and into the dean's waiting area.

"We're in!" shouted Lindsay. I clamped my hand over her mouth. Then I whipped out my Bug Detector and waved it slowly around the room. Nothing. The LED indicator stayed in the green zone. Next I pointed my infrared Heat Scanner at the dean's closed door. Also nothing. No one was in there. I mouthed "Stay here" to Lindsay, opened the door, crept inside, and gently closed it behind me.

I knew I would have to work fast; it probably wouldn't take Mrs. Juergens long to realize that she was the victim of a hoax. *Okay, first things first,* I told myself, and I waved the Bug Detector around the room. Uh-oh. The indicator turned bright red when I brought it near the phone. My mind reeled. Is this a leftover bug from Meri's earlier days, or a new one? I was about to reach for the phone, when I thought, *Don't touch it! If it's new, leave it, or she'll know you're on to her!*

I was beginning to perspire, and I could still hear voices in my ear, including poor Shanna-Francine, who was very convincing when she blurted out, "Gosh, this is fun. I've actually missed handsies-kneesies."

Frantically, I rifled through all the dean's drawers and went through his papers. Nothing. Oh, darn it, darn it, darn it. I also found a few unopened envelopes, but with my handy-dandy Envelope X-Ray Spray, I quickly determined that they didn't contain anything I needed. I ran my hands over his computer keyboard. Like an idiot, the dean hadn't logged out (thank God), and I double-clicked desperately. Nothing. But an idea occurred to me. A good one. I opened his Quicken application, and from the File menu I clicked Open Recent. It was all there. All of his deposits and payments. Oh, think, think, think, when were you booted from Alpha Beta Delta? Then I remembered.

"Today is National Bittersweet Chocolate with Almonds Day" Meri had intoned breathily. Was that on the sixth? The eighth? Somewhere around there? I recklessly scrolled up. And there it was. On November 7.

Date	Description	Debits	Credits
11-07	*CHECK DEPOSIT AT 11:46 CITIBANK RNC		$850,000.00
11-08	*CHECK #4523 RALEIGH MERCEDES	$172,050.00	

Bingo! I pulled out my ultracompact Pen Camera and made sure I got a good shot of the screen. But would this be enough? I wondered. It didn't say where the money came from. Oh, darn it to hell. I would need his bank statement and canceled checks, that I knew for sure, and I was just about to go through his papers again when my ear nearly exploded from a voice screaming, "What the fuck are you doing here?"

"Waiting for Mrs. Juergens," mumbled Lindsay nervously.

Oh my God. I didn't have time. I had to act fast. I charged to the door and whipped it open. *Ka-bam!* Gloria spazzed violently and crumpled to the floor out cold—because I had just shot her in the chest with my taser gun.

Lindsay gaped. "That was beyond freaky."

"Everyone on alert, they're onto us," I whispered intently, grabbing Gloria's wrist and feeling her pulse (it was racing). Then I turned desperately to Lindsay. "Any ideas?" We obviously couldn't carry her outside in broad daylight.

"I've got it," she exclaimed. "Mrs. Juergens has been here for, what, at least two decades? How can she stand it, right?" She ransacked Mrs. Juergens's desk drawers. "Ah-ha," she cried, triumphantly pulling out a silver flask from the bottom drawer.

"Hurry," I said. While Lindsay unscrewed the flask ("Eeeow, it's schnapps," she squealed), I bent down toward Gloria and opened one of her eyes. It was blue. "Gloria has brown eyes," I gasped. "This is Gilda."

"Yeah? Well, she's one hell of a sloppy-ass drunk, that's for sure," tittered Lindsay, and poured a bit of schnapps on Gilda's mouth and her blouse, then pressed the flask into her hand. "Look. Oiled up on schnapps. What a loser."

"Alert," barked Bobbie in my ear. "Louella is coming back. She's one and a half blocks away."

Oh no! My impromptu plan was to make a quick trip to the dean's house, but how could I do that now if Louella was returning home? I coolly explained to Bobbie. Was there anything she could do to hold her up?

"I've got great insurance," she growled.

"Wait!" I cried. But it was too late. Ow! Lindsay and I winced when we heard Professor Scott shout. Then we heard a long screech and a muffled crunching sound. And a moment later,

Bobbie's voice, "Phew. I'm so glad you're okay, ma'am."

"Better hurry, Cindy," whispered Professor Scott.

"No kidding," Lindsay wailed, and gestured to the window. Mrs. Juergens was walking across the street to the office—and she didn't look happy. Lindsay whipped around. "Cindy, oh my God, don't you dare shoot her!"

"Who's shooting who?" gasped Professor Scott in my ear. Oh, jeez, all these voices, and only split seconds to think.

"Meri's on the phone in the living room," whispered Shanna-Francine. "I can hear her. She just said, 'Go in after her.'"

I didn't have to ask who. Out the window, I saw Gloria on her cell phone charging right past Mrs. Juergens. And right behind them was Albino Girl, veering up on her skateboard.

"Oh shit, we're fucked," cried Lindsay, but quickly added (given her promise not to be a potty mouth), "I mean, darn it, we're screwed, we're stiffed."

"No, we're not," I said. I grabbed Lindsay's hand, yanked her out of the office, rushed down the hall to the back entryway, swung open the door—and screamed.

"Nice try," sneered Gloria. *Ka-bam!* She spazzed and crumpled to the ground.

"Lindsay!" I exclaimed.

"Why should you have all the fun?" she said, wielding the taser. Then she frenziedly dumped a tiny one-ounce bottle of powder onto Gloria's face. "Look. We're fine. She OD'd on Ralph Lauren's Romance."

We were off. As we swerved away in Lindsay's Porsche, I saw Mrs. Juergens on the ground—oh my God—entangled with Albino Girl. "What is her problem lately?" I gaped.

"Hormones. Got to be."

"You know how you make a hormone?" I heard Bobbie ask gruffly in my ear. "You lay her but don't pay her. Ha-ha-ha-ha." That got a few groans from everyone—and a sucked-back gasp, too. We could hear Meri asking, "What's so funny, Shanna-Francine?"

"Um, just thinking of the old days," she babbled. "Gosh, we had fun then, huh?"

"What's that on the floor?"

"Oooh. I think it's a jellybean," Shanna-Francine cried. Then we heard nothing. Then we heard a heartbeat. *Thump-thump-thump-thump*. Then strange squishy sounds.

"She swallowed it," Lindsay gasped. "The ear communicator thingie. Oh my God, we're, like, eavesdropping on her large intestine."

"We just exchanged insurance info," whispered Professor Scott. "Our truck's fine. Louella scraped her knee. We're parking her car in her driveway and taking her to see her doctor."

Keep moving, I told myself grimly, and just as Lindsay and I screeched around the corner to Dean Pointer's house, we passed Bobbie's Chevy Avalanche going in the other direction; Bobbie was riding in front with Louella, and Professor Scott was in the back. He actually gave a small wave and mouthed, "Good luck."

It was a cinch getting into the dean's house. The front door was locked, but Lindsay easily pushed open a first-floor window in back. "What are we looking for?" she asked as we tiptoed into the living room.

"A bank statement. Canceled checks."

We searched methodically—and quickly, because who knew how much time we had. There was unopened mail in the kitchen (but no bank statements), a stack of bills on an end table next to the rocker in the living room (but no bank statements), along with a brand-new flat-screen TV that wasn't there the last time I was here (guys are so predictable when they get a little money—a flashy new car, a new TV. B-o-o-o-o-o-ring.) (what did Louella get? I wondered).

"Keep looking," I instructed Lindsay. Then I scampered down the hall and discovered that the dean has a quaint little home office. Perfect. I shuffled carefully through a stack of papers on his desk. Nothing. Then I spotted a lone envelope on the armrest of a Barcalounger. I swiped it. It was from Citibank. It was a bank statement. The postmark read November 11. And it was unopened. I hesitated for a sec. If I opened the envelope, I could be convicted of mail tampering, which is a federal crime. *Yes, that's correct*, I thought, *and you could also be sent to the pokey for breaking and entering and tasering a pair of psycho twins (probably), so go for broke and rip it open already.* I tore it open. Canceled checks tumbled to the floor. I fell to my knees. I found it. I held it in my hands. Then I heard a scream and a shocking, forceful tinkling crash from the living room.

Dean Pointer was not a happy man. After Lindsay tasered him (she was getting a bit too trigger-happy for my taste), we sat him up in a chair and tied his hands behind his back. He awakened groggily. The phone rang. Lindsay, to my astonishment, picked it up.

"Hello?"

"Give me that phone," barked the dean.

"May I ask who's calling?" She covered the receiver. "It's Mrs. Juergens. Are you in?"

"Give me that—"

Lindsay shushed him and brought the phone up to his face. "Don't say anything silly," she warned, holding up the taser with her other hand. "Or pow."

"Hello, Joan," grumbled the dean weakly, clearing his throat. "Fine, how are you? Oh, it's, um . . ."

Lindsay whispered, "Your niece. I'm visiting."

"My niece. She's visiting."

"You have to go. I'm ovulating."

"I have to—what?"

"Hang up. Bye, Joan."

"Bye, Joan."

Lindsay clicked off the phone. "See? That wasn't so bad, was it?"

"What the hell is the meaning of this!" bellowed the dean. He was beginning to get his strength back. I pulled a chair up opposite him and calmly laid out the reality of the situation. As I did, Lindsay reached into her purse, opened a small container, and—what the heck?—began applying mint mask to his face.

"I'm only doing this because you have combination skin," she told him.

"That check could be for anything," snarled the dean as I held up the incriminating canceled check from Sugarman Industries.

"You took this check as a bribe," I said sharply, but evenly. "To keep Meri happy. And to keep me out of RU Isn't that right?"

"Gosh, that's not very nice," said Lindsay, gently working the mask in. "Try not to move your mouth too much."

The dean scoffed. "You have no way of proving what that check was for. It could have been a loan."

"Right. Think Mr. Sugarman will back you up on that?" I asked. "Or Meri? And gosh, what about Uncle Sam? Does he know about this 'loan'?"

He smirked. "Fine. How much do you girls want?"

"Oh, I don't need anything," said Lindsay cheerfully. "I'm loaded."

"I don't want your money either," I told him. "You're free to spend it on cars, TVs, hookers . . ."

"Get out of my house!"

Then the oddest thing happened. Both Lindsay and I looked up at each other; in our ear communicators, we both heard what sounded like a toilet flushing. Lindsay covered her mouth in shock.

"Poor Shanna-Francine," we heard Bobbie whisper. "I hope it wasn't like passing a kidney stone."

"Are we through here?" snarled the dean.

"Not quite," I said. "We haven't talked deal yet. And, Dean, don't even think about double-crossing me. Not this time." As I continued, Lindsay blew delicately on the dean's face to dry his mask, then stepped to the bathroom and returned with a damp washcloth, which she used to gently remove it. "Here's how it goes. I keep this check and your bank statement, and I won't tell anyone if—and I mean if—you do the following. I'm allowed to return to RU and Alpha Beta Delta."

"Fine," he groused. He didn't seem to care.

"And I have immunity," I added.

"Which means what?" he snapped.

"It means that if I do anything to Meri, anything at all—and I plan to do quite a bit—you won't report me to the intersorority governing council or any other authority. It'll be as if nothing ever happened. Nothing at all. Understand?" My words sank in. He seethed.

"Fine. Get out of my house. Now."

"I'm not done yet."

"Please hold your head still," tsked Lindsay, who was now skillfully working mousse into his hair.

"Patty Camp will be able to return to Alpha Beta Delta," I continued. "No matter what Meri says." He rolled his eyes, agreeing. I was about to continue my demands when a thought occurred to me. "Hey, I'm just curious," I asked. "Do you know the dean at Duke University?"

He snickered. "Why? You want a date?"

"Just answer me."

"Yes, as a matter of fact, I do. We're old golfing buddies. Not that it's any of your business."

"Mmm, I think it is." Maybe, I thought, there could be some benefit here for Cliff, too. I mean, why shouldn't he get a full scholarship next year?

The dean hollered, "Are you out of your mind? You really think I can tell him how to run his own goddamned university?"

Lindsay chuckled. "Why not? Cindy's telling you how to run yours."

"Absolutely not," he bellowed. "And that's final." I calmly flipped open my cell phone and dialed.

"Hello? Can I have the number for the Rumson River district attorney's office? Oh, and do you have a direct dial for their white-collar crime division?"

"Okay, okay, I'll see what I can do," he sputtered frantically. That didn't sound good enough to me.

"Thank you, operator. Yes, you can connect me."

"All right! I'll make it happen!"

I flipped my phone closed. "One-year scholarship, guaranteed, with a full living stipend."

"Fine. Get out."

"One more thing. Effective immediately, Professor Scott is back at RU."

"What?" he shouted.

"Oh, thank you, Cindy," whispered the professor in my ear. Then he chuckled. "Throw in tenure. See if he goes for it."

"And you're giving him tenure."

The dean fumed hoarsely, "That dirty, no-talent . . ."

"That no-talent's first novel is being published by Fireplace Perennial. Professor Scott. Tenure. Agreed?" The dean struggled against the rope, then finally sighed. He was a beaten man.

"Agreed."

"Louella's bandaged," Bobbie whispered in my ear. "We're headed back to the parking lot."

"Wait!" cried the dean. "What happens if Meri's father asks for his money back?"

Hmm. I hadn't thought of that. I shrugged. "Not my problem.

Oh, and see my pen? The one sticking out of my blouse pocket? It's a video camera. Smile."

Lindsay fluffed his hair. "You have the thickest, curliest hair, Dean Pointer. It's like fusilli."

"Lindsay, we need to go."

"You have to untie me!" protested the dean.

"I don't have to do anything," I said with a smile.

"Try it with a dab of pomade," advised Lindsay, hastily rearranging his hair. "Brush it forward. See? Just a hint of Caesar." I grabbed her hand. It was time to move. The dean seethed.

"I'm ashamed of you, Cindy. You used to be such a nice girl."

"Really?" I said. "Well now I'm a better girl." And with that, Dark Cindy hip-swung her way out and slammed the door shut. Hot-cha!

November 16

Dear Diary:

Meri's in her room now. What a baby. I hope she's crying (though I doubt it). She's for sure hand-washing her blouse—or maybe she threw it away. I was lucky that it was white. Ha. With all the new CEC girls, I'm sharing a room with Lindsay now, which is such a blast. We're having the supercoolest PJ party ever. We made popcorn and Cosmos, and right now we're on the bed. She's carefully dabbing ultrafine Black Crow glitter dust over my wet neutral toenail polish and "communing" with Ani DiFranco while I'm writing this (I'll be using Royal Blue glitter dust on her toenails once I'm done).

First thing this morning, I slipped a note under Cliff's jail cell door. Artists sleep late, and I didn't want him to think I'd abandoned him or anything, because I knew I'd be gone by the time he woke up. I wrote:

Dear Cliff:
I'm free! I've left Chappaqua. I'm back at RU.
And I already miss you!! Call me.
xxoo
Cindy

Wait, I thought. *Too mushy? Darn. Too late. It's already under his door.* I lugged my trunk and several bags to the parking-lot curb. Jahmal gazed at me oddly. I blew him a kiss good-bye (I can't believe I did that). He actually blushed, and that made me blush (I never noticed how handsome he was before) (maybe because he was always so busy laughing at me). I had a few minutes before Lindsay's arrival, which gave me a moment to take stock. Something didn't feel right.

I felt different, sure, but did I look any different? I felt like Dark Cindy, I had a (fairly) good handle on my emotions these days, but I was still the same old dreary-looking Cindy B., with perpetually tragic hair and clothes by OshKosh and Old Navy. Were my transformed insides enough for my (hopefully) triumphant return to Alpha Beta Delta?

"Dark Ci-i-i-i-indy!" screamed Sebastian, and broadly waved, his head hanging out of the passenger side of Lindsay's Porsche as she swerved up.

"Ready to ditch this hellhole?" Lindsay said with a wink. They helped me stuff my belongings in the trunk and backseat, and boy, I was more than ready to kick off (and how). Take one last look, a voice inside me said. My eyes gazed through the grimy haze. I could see the ugly airport-hangar-type buildings, the nondescript jail cell dormitories, and a small group of students in the midst of a humiliating Polo Flat-Racing tournament. I almost felt sentimental. *This place has served me well*, I thought. *I never want to come back, but I did turn over a new leaf here.* I shivered. It's always oppressively hot at Chappaqua, and yet I've always felt so cold, I guess because I've been frozen inside with fury and anguish and loneliness and tears that kept choking in my throat. *You can go now*, I thought. *You were in a dark cave all by yourself, you were trapped, but now you're free. Go!*

Lindsay blasted down the highway. It was warm out today, so she had the roof up. The wind whipped through my hair. I felt naked, unprotected—and that terrified me. *But the dark cave was safe!*

I cried to myself. Then I thought, *Of course you're scared, you haven't finished your work yet.*

"What kind of clothing do you think Dark Cindy wears?" I blurted out to Sebastian.

He gasped. "Do you mean? Are you saying?"

"Yes."

He shrieked with delight—and so did Lindsay, who screeched off the highway. Sebastian took me shopping. And shopping. And shopping. He's very good at it. And really-really fast. "Forget that. No. No. Yes. Eeeow. No. Yes." And gosh, he really did have a handle on what Dark Cindy should look like. "The hair," he murmured (sympathetically, but with obvious disapproval). He shook his hands through my tragic locks. "Do you trust me?"

"Of course."

Clip-clip here, clip-clip there. I stared at myself in the mirror at the hair salon. My new do was "beyond fierce," according to Sebastian, and oh my God, he was right.

"Go into the bathroom and change," squealed Lindsay, who was beside herself with excitement. *Don't look in the mirror,* I told myself as I put on my Dark Cindy outfit; *just feel it, be it.*

"Ready?" I called out to Sebastian and Lindsay. Their screams of anticipation told me they were. I closed my eyes, took a deep breath. "Devote yourself to an ideal," Liam whispered in my ear. "That is what you must do." I was ready. I opened my eyes, pushed open the door, and strode right out. And. There. Was. Complete. Silence. Lindsay covered her mouth in shock. Sebastian's jaw was dropped, but ever vigilant, his eyes critically scanned me from top to bottom—like a laser beam—making sure everything was just right.

"Do you want to look in a mirror?" asked Sebastian.

I smiled inwardly. "Naw."

Meri didn't know what hit her. It was a busy day at Alpha Beta Delta. There was major construction in the kitchen—Meri was paying workmen to transform it into a château-style French kitchen, with maple countertops, a blond slate floor, and other "château-chic" amenities—and since it was lunchtime, she had ordered all the sisters to change into work clothes and prepare to get dirty. Real dirty. She wanted the front yard completely dug up and turned into an elaborate *jardin français*, or French garden, and all the sisters, even Bobbie and Shanna-Francine, were slavishly digging and planting and sweating, while Meri, imperiously supervising their work and glancing at a picture of a seventeenth-century château for reference, gave orders.

"You there," she called out to a CEC girl who had just finished planting an intricate plot of French poppies. "I've decided I want them irregularly spaced. Pull them up and start again." Then she stared off into space; an idea was forming. She whispered delicately, "Gnomes. Garden gnomes. A whole army." Shanna-Francine was sweaty; she had just finished planting an array of orange and purple mums, and her clothes and face were caked with mud. But Meri didn't care. She was delighted with the result. "Aren't they precious?" she cooed. "Giggly. The happiest of fall blooms. Wait. Pull some up and put them in a vase. On my night-stand. Remember, girls, the decaying sweetness of fresh-cut flowers is one of life's purest pleasures."

Incredibly, none of the CEC girls seemed to mind being treated like slaves. In fact, according to Bobbie, they enjoyed it. They just don't "get" Meri. To them, she's a life mentor, a superior being, and they're happy to do her bidding (except for Doreen, who's ingeniously arranged for various cheer squad members to call her whenever it's time for really heavy chores) ("Fuckin' A, man, I'd love to help, but I got practice. Later.").

A few blocks from the house, I asked Lindsay to pull over. If Dark Cindy was going to make an entrance, she had to do it right. It had to be *pow!*

"You're not scared? You're not freaked?" she asked nervously.

I didn't respond. My mind was racing ahead. Lindsay pulled off, and I stood there in the center of the street for a moment. "There is no turning back," urged Liam. *Damn right*, I thought. I slapped my hot-pink skateboard to the pavement and kicked off, shooting like a missile down the street. Then *whoosh!* I swerved around the corner. Alpha Beta Delta was at the end of the street. *Go faster!* And I did. I blasted through the cool autumn air, whipped in front of Alpha Beta Delta. And suddenly everything felt like it was going in slow motion. My black Harley-Davidson stiletto boot smashed down on my hot-pink skateboard and it flew up into the air—right up past my totally sick black leather mini, my black wrapover blouse and bomber jacket, farther up past my face, past my short, spiky black hair, and then *bam!* I caught it in my hand with my dope black fingerless gloves. I grinned inwardly and said, just loud enough for you-know-who to hear, "It's so nice to be home."

Then I hoofed it right past Meri and into the house. Hot-cha! Shanna-Francine later told me that everyone's eyes were on Meri at that point. She stood very still, but her face seemed to disintegrate and then ghoulishly reform itself in seconds, blending into a smooth mask of frightening oneness. The sun's autumn angles glinted off her eyes and they lit up like a bonfire. She swiped a large sharp pruning scythe, then stalked to the front door—and was blocked by Bobbie, who held out a cell phone and intoned gruffly, "Better call the dean first."

Meri flinched; she was ready to push past her, but Bobbie leaned in and gravely told her, "Be smart. Make the call."

A few minutes later, me, Shanna-Francine, Bobbie, and Lindsay were gathered in Lindsay's room—and we heard a hair-raising scream that seemed to explode from the bowels of hell. Then we heard sickening jabs and stabs.

"Oh my God," squealed Shanna-Francine. "She's killing evangelicals!"

We ran to the window. It was quite a spectacle. The CEC girl were clustered nervously together, watching in awe. Meri had a pickax, and she was swinging savagely, gouging apart the just-completed French garden. Poppies and mums were flying. Natural Welsh slate, which had been carefully laid for the winding walkway, shattered against her hurling ax, sending jagged pieces soaring. The garden was destroyed. Meri stood upright. The ax drop from her hand. She closed her eyes. Then she smiled—just slightly—whispering loud enough for the CEC girls to hear, "Traditional English gardens have herbaceous borders. A hand-thrown rhubarb forcer and a wooden beehive add charm and function." Then she opened her eyes and breathed deeply, wiping her hands, seemingly satisfied. "We'll start tomorrow."

Who knows what the dean told Meri. Early in the evening, I heard her scream in her room, "I don't care if he's en route to Rome! You tell him it's his daughter. Do you hear me? If I don't hear back from him by tomorrow morning, there'll be hell to pay. You hear me?" Uh-oh. How would Mr. Sugarman react to the news? I wondered.

Gloria was in the kitchen, barking orders to all the girls (I knew it was Gloria from her brown eyes). Meri was having them make a ridiculously complicated dinner—lobster with udon noodles, bok choy, and citrus; oyster chowder with salsify and bacon—and everyone was lending a hand. Except for me. When I stepped in the doorway I thought, *I have immunity, I don't have to do a thing.* Then I heard several of the CEC girls whispering, "She's the crazy one, right? Yeah. Uh-huh. I hear she blows up toilets." That's when I saw poor Bobbie quartering slices of bacon (she looked like she was about to throw up). I gently took the knife from her. "I'll do that," I said.

"No, you won't," Gloria snapped.

"What difference does it make?" I retorted hotly. I didn't see why vegetarians, like Bobbie and Shanna-Francine, should be made to do any type of food preparation involving dead animals. It's just not right. Gloria fumed and tore out of the room. *Boom-boom-boom!* We could hear her running up the stairs to Meri's room. Then *boom-boom-boom.* She came back down, pointed at Shanna-Francine, and bellowed, "You! Grab those lobsters and throw them in the pot!" Shanna-Francine gasped.

"No. I—I won't do it." Terrified, she backed away from the enormous pot, which hissed with boiling water.

"Haven't you read your new pledge book?" reminded Gloria with a smile. "Orders from your president must be obeyed. Or would you like to pack up and leave now?"

Shanna-Francine is so brave (braver than I would have been if I was a vegetarian) (which I'm not). Trembling, she lifted the cover off a large plastic box filled with water—and two very live lobsters.

"I'm waiting," huffed Gloria.

Shanna-Francine slowly put her hand in, then jumped back with a squeal and buried her face in Bobbie's chest. "I can't, I just can't," she wailed. "They look so happy."

"You'll do it now or you'll pack your bags," barked Gloria. "Which is it?" Everyone was horrified, and spellbound, too. What would she do? She looked up from Bobbie (who was holding her so sweetly) and caught my eye. It was as if she drew strength from Dark Cindy. She wasn't going to give up the fight. Not now. Not when we were all so close. She slowly disentangled herself from Bobbie and stepped up to the box.

"Would you like me to say last rites?" asked Karla Mae, which was awfully nice of her.

"Yes, please," Shanna-Francine sniffled.

"Oh, for God's sake!" cried Gloria.

Karla Mae crossed herself and quietly recited, "Through this holy anointing, may the Lord in his love and mercy help you with the grace of the Holy Spirit. May the Lord who frees you from sin save you and raise you up."

"Amen," said the CEC girls in unison.

She was done. It was time. "But—but what if they're Hindu?" whimpered Shanna-Francine.

"Do it now!" screamed Gloria, and Shanna-Francine—whiz-bang!—reached in, grabbed the lobsters, and hurled them into the pot. Oh my God, oh my God, oh my God! They screamed. "Eeeeeeeeeeee!" And I mean literally screamed. It was high-pitched, like a baby seal, and it was earsplitting. Their little claws flailed desperately, and one of them made a brave leap. *Crack!* Gloria smacked it back with a metal spatula. They screamed louder, louder! And then, without warning, we were engulfed by an awful, eerie silence.

Nobody moved. All we could hear was the water boiling. Then we shrieked in horror! One lone lobster claw violently shot up, reaching in vain for the heavens, then just as suddenly slumped back down, finally succumbing to its hot, roiling deathbed. It was done.

Dinner was served. Everyone was seated in the dining room, including Meri, who studiously ignored me, as if I wasn't even there. The CEC girls, braced for something horrible, no doubt, kept looking back and forth between us and—understandably— only picked at their lobster. After dessert I realized that it was time for Dark Cindy to throw down the gauntlet. What was I waiting for? I broke the silence.

"I'm so glad to be back," I said to everyone with a slightly fakey smile. "And please, I'd love to make everyone cocktails. You can sit right where you are. I'll do everything." Dead silence. Gloria whipped around to Meri, who shrugged at her, murmuring, "Whatever."

In the kitchen I worked fast, combining all the ingredients in a large pitcher. In the living room, Meri was lightly conversing with the CEC girls while I calmly poured my concoction into one cocktail glass after another, slowly working my way to Meri at the head of the table. I was getting closer. Only a few more cocktail glasses to go. Oh my God, oh my God, oh my God, oh my God. Can I do this? Should I do this? "Fashion is in a soft, girlish mood again," said Meri. "Lovely taffetas, ruffles, pale chiffon gowns. Which means it's time to bone up on our etiquette. It's time to let everyone know how beautiful we all are."

Now! I screamed to myself, and then I "accidentally" tripped, and the pitcher flew from my hands and struck Meri right in the chest—*splat!*—right on her soft off-white Chanel blouse, splashing it with at least half a quart of Bloody Mary cocktail. Everyone gasped. Meri sat there, stunned.

"Oh, I'm such a fuddy fingers," I cried, swiping a cloth napkin and making a good show of trying to dab it up. "Tsk. Bloody Mary mix, all over you." Then I gasped, as if the idea had just occurred to me, "Bloody Mary. Get it, you guys? M-e-r-i? Bloody Meri! Ha-ha-ha-ha-ha-ha!"

Bobbie gasped. She got it. She exclaimed, "Bloody Meri!" Which prompted more scandalized gasps and whispered refrains of "Bloody Meri. Bloody Meri. Bloody Meri." Meri sat like a statue. Her eyes were wide, and yet it didn't seem as if she was looking at anything in front of her. I could only imagine that—in those few brief seconds—she was transported back to Newport. She was twelve. Dennis was waiting for her outside the pharmacy. Then she stepped out. And she heard a little boy shout delightedly, "Look, Mommy! There's Bloody Meri!"

She bolted up from her chair, covered her mouth as if she

might vomit, then ran from the room and up the stairs. *Boom-boom-boom*. We heard her door slam. No one knew what to do or say—except for Karla Mae, who glared at me furiously.

"That was mean," she said. Then she directed her gaze at all of us—me, Shanna-Francine, Bobbie, Lindsay. "All of you. That's what you are. You're just mean and nasty." She stabbed her fork into her plate, took a hearty bite. "And this lobster tastes awesome." Then she pushed back her chair and went up the stairs to Meri's room, presumably to console her.

I smiled at Gloria, who was beyond angry. We seemed to communicate telepathically. And I told her: *Sorry, bitch, I've got immunity*. Does Meri know that I've read her blog diary? I doubt it. I played it too well. And it worked wonderfully. I unnerved her (to say the least). She's a little bit off balance and vulnerable now, which is exactly where I want her. And to think, I'm only just beginning.

November 17

Dear Diary:

"Bud Finger, at your cervix."

Oh, dear God. Some things never change. I was in the discharge room at the Rumson River Minimum Security Facility. Lindsay was too nervous and excited to come inside herself. She was waiting out front in her Porsche, so it was up to me to go inside (amidst all those dirty criminals), find Bud, and lead him out to "the future Mrs. Finger," as Lindsay likes to call herself now. When Lindsay got the call this morning from John Hadity, Bud's lawyer, I thought somebody had died; she nodded her head vacantly, her expression was blank, and she kept going, "Uh-huh. Uh-huh. Okay. Uh-huh. Thank you." Then she hung up and, oh my God—*poof!*—it was like some hot, bright glowstick had just cracked open inside of her. She was lit up. Then she grabbed both my arms and screamed at the top of her lungs, jumping up and down, joyously crying and laughing and shrieking, "I love Bud Finger! I love Bud Finger!"

It took me a few minutes to calm her down. She told me everything. All charges are being dropped against Bud. Everything. He walks. A deal was struck. And oddly enough, Lindsay has Meri to thank for that (inadvertently), since one of the government's primary pieces of evidence against him, namely the recording from Lindsay's tiara that had been sent to the FBI anonymously by

Meri, was deemed "inadmissible" by the judge on the grounds that it was "illegally recorded and obtained," which meant that all the evidence the FBI subsequently found because of the tape could not be used in the trial. Lindsay screamed with delight, "Inadmissible!"

Bud lucked out. Big-time. But he did have to cut an unusual deal. For the next five years, and possibly longer, he'll have government-installed spyware on his computer—if he even thinks of illegally downloading or burning anything, they'll know—and he's forbidden from using any other computer, public or private.It seems like a small price to pay (though this may restrict Bud's fondness for visiting naughtygirlsswallow.com and candysclimaxcorner.com) (gross!).

"Gimme a little squeeze," Bud said with a grin in the discharge room. Ugh! He pulled me into his bony arms and hugged me really tight, and after a second it felt like his puny little waist was hump-hump-humping against me so I pushed him back and slapped him across the face.

"Knock it off."

"Miss me, Cindy? You look sexiful. What happened?"

"Did you really propose marriage to Lindsay?"

"I love Lindsay," he said with sudden sincerity. "I want to be with Lindsay forever. Like, all monogamous and shit." Aw. And yet, this was Bud, so he had to ruin the moment, of course, by grabbing his crotch and adding, "Yo, the tubesteak is taken. Bud's bazooka is off the market."

"That's disgusting."

He giggled with that obnoxious hyena laugh he has. "Spank you very much. I know you missed me, Cindy."

"Can we go now?"

"You want it. You know it." Then he spun around, doing a Hammer-time jig, singing:

U can't touch this
Break it down
U can't touch this
I told ya
U can't touch this

He was beyond happy. For a fleeting moment, I was happy for him too. I mean, he's gross and yecchy and pond scum and twerpy and stinky (and so many other things), but he does love Lindsay, he wants to be "all monogamous and shit," and that has to count for something (right?).

"Yo, hold up," he said, pulling a small can from his knapsack. "Word. Just a quick blast of Axe across my abs and I'm ready to roll."

"You don't have abs, Bud." He ignored me, pulled up his shirt, and gave a few squirts (does any sane girl in this world need to be warned off the bug-spray smell of Axe?). As it turns out, Bud now has abs, an honest-to-God six-pack. I'm not kidding. I guess he worked out while behind bars (what else is there to do?), and eeeow, I so wish he didn't catch me staring, because then he did a little shimmy-shake right there in plain view of everyone, undulating his abs at me.

"Yeah, baby. Bud's brisket. Hot. Sssss."

Bud and Lindsay's reunion was like out of some old-time Hollywood movie. I walked out with Bud and he was suddenly alert, his eyes searched—yearning, pining—and at the other end of the lot, Lindsay whirled around, her umbrella held high, her face brightening. She gasped. He gasped. Then they ran like two star-crossed lovers across the parking lot. She leaped into the air—like a fairy princess in flight—and he caught her in his arms and lifted her into the air and twirled her around and around. She threw her arms out freely, extending the umbrella, her hair flowing in the wind, and I swear, I'm not joking, I heard music soar, angels sighed, and since this involved Bud I waited for the whoopie cushion, but it didn't happen because they stopped twirling, she sank languidly into his arms, and they gazed lovingly into each other's eyes, and just as their lips were about to meet, the umbrella came down, slowly, demurely, blocking my view.

In the Jaguar, Lindsay and I excitedly caught Bud up on all things Meri. "Whoa," he said. "She's fucked."

"Almost," I said, and I could feel the excitement building inside me. In fact, I've been excited all day, mainly because of how my morning started. After I finished applying Royal Blue glitter dust to Lindsay's toenails last night, we were ready for bed—but Dark Cindy wasn't. She had a few things to do. It was late. Meri had gone back downstairs with the CEC girls. And I snuck into her bedroom. What's the use of having immunity if you don't take advantage of it? Made sense to me.

This morning I woke up extra early, walked quietly up the stairs, and waited outside her door. I just had to see it. Or at least hear it. I waited patiently. Meri's alarm clock went off. I could hear her stirring. Then she gasped, "What the . . . ?"

I smiled. So far, so good. Last night, I had taken four small packets of grape Kool-Aid and sprinkled the dusty granules lightly between her sheets. I figured that even Meri sweats when she sleeps—we all do—and from her sudden gasping wail, I knew it had worked. The Kool-Aid had become moistened and gotten into her pores, which meant that most, if not all, of her body was now the color of a big, ugly, purple grape. Ha. But I didn't get to see her right away, because she rushed to the bathroom. I heard the water running and her squeals of frustration. *Go to the toilet*, I giggled to myself, or as Bud would put it, *Dude, time for a morning movement.*

There was silence for a moment. Then another wailing scream.

Tsk-tsk. Poor Meri. I had tightly stretched Saran Wrap over her toilet and under the seat—it's a catch-all (gross, I know) (but effective, I've heard)—and, yes, I had also moistened the seat with Icy Hot. Ouchie-wowchie. I could hear her stomping furiously across the room to the door. I leaned against the wall opposite, smiling slightly. It was just too easy. Dark Cindy was amused.

Then she swung open the door and—*ker-splash!*—the old bucket-of-water-above-the-door trick, only I updated it by mixing in a bit of Bobbie's Swedish mashed potato mix to give it that extra bit of gross, gooey texture. She stood there screaming like a banshee. She was completely overwhelmed. She couldn't believe what was happening. And she was wet and she was gooey (and a shocking shade of blotchy purple). But I still wasn't done. Not quite. I held up a fire extinguisher and blasted her. Whoa! She flew backward onto her behind. She was beyond shocked. In a part of her mind, this just didn't compute. I put the fire extinguisher down and calmly stepped up to her.

"You are so dead!" she screamed, spitting out a bit of murky mashed potato. I gave her a wink. And I said just one word: "Immunity."

Then I made a kissy-kiss sound and hightailed it out of there. And yes, I know, what I did was all very gratuitous, but it felt good, and more important, it let her know that I knew no boundaries. Not anymore. The gloves were off. And true, I never would have been able to pull that off normally. But for Dark Cindy it was a walk in the park.

"Holy shit," gasped Bud. "You're really asking for it." But I don't think so, because anything Meri thinks she might do to me, well, it can't possibly match what I have in store for her. I'm meeting with Patty tomorrow. It's all about the details. Meri will finally go down. The only thing that rattled me this morning was Karla Mae. I like her, she seems like a sweet girl, but she wasn't to thrilled when she found out what

I had done to Meri. She cornered me in the kitchen.

"I think you're petty and childish," she snapped. "And I'm ashamed to be in the same house with you." I stammered for a moment, because she was right, but how could I make her understand?

"Karla," I hesitated.

"Karla Mae," she corrected, eyeing me with contempt.

"Right. Look, I know you're new here and everything, but . . ."

"But you're the crazy one. Yeah-yeah-yeah. I know all about you."

"No, actually, you don't. I know it doesn't seem like it, but Meri's completely insane." That got a laugh.

"Uh-huh. You keep telling yourself that." Then she leaned in and said huffily, "Men have loved darkness rather than light, because their deeds were evil. John 3:19." Holy moly. She was condemning me with the Bible. I stuttered back the only thing I could remember from Sunday School.

"Um, do not judge, or you too will be judged. Somewhere in Matthew. I think."

She chuckled derisively. "Gee, where'd you pick that up? From a doily?" She stalked out—but paused at the door. "Oh, and by the way, it's Matthew 7:12. You should read the Bible. It's been known to bring peace to nutcases like you."

I've been thinking about what Karla Mae said throughout the day; during my classes, when we picked up Bud, and later at Kristy's Bottoms-Up Lounge, a pole-dancing lounge, which is where Bud wanted to go right after his release (of course). I kept running it back and forth in my mind: Men have loved darkness rather than light, because their deeds were evil. Is Dark Cindy too dark? Have I abandoned the light? Lindsay's delighted screams distracted me. She and Bud were drinking cocktails and laughing and cheering on the pole dancers (who I have to admit were skillfully slinky). When Bud went to get more drinks, I asked her, "Don't you think this is demeaning? I mean, to you? That he wants to be here?"

"But he wants to be here with me." She smiled brightly, then gestured to the pole dancer. "Think I could do that?" Oh, brother. The last thing anyone needs is for Lindsay to start shaking her moneymaker at Kristy's Bottoms-Up Lounge. It was late afternoon by the time I dropped them off at Bud's dorm (they were tipsy, so I insisted on driving), and they were all excited to play some sort of game with whipped cream, cling peaches, oysters, and a "Ms. Piglet" inflatable party pig (I didn't ask). After they took off, I was barely two steps away from the car when a voice suddenly boomed, "Cindy!"

Pigboy charged up to me. I gasped.

"Patty? Oh my God, is she okay?" He grabbed my hand, rushing me toward a dormitory building.

"She's great," he said. Before I knew what was going on, he had brought me into a dorm room, and I was hit with a wall of joyful screams. I blinked twice. So many guys, and all in Abercrombie & Fitch.

"Cind-e-e-e-e-e!" shrieked Sebastian, pulling me to the TV. "It just started, you haven't missed a thing." I still didn't know what was going on until I looked at the screen—and held back a gasp. There was Lisa on *TRL*, flirting shamelessly with Quddus. I couldn't believe it—but then again, I did. She imagines, she plans, she conquers. It's as simple as that. Quddus asked her if she ever feels competitive with other pop stars.

"Get real," she chuckled, rolling her eyes. "Britney's bloated, Madonna's ancient, and Beyonce's way too busy with her clothing line. You guys, like, so need me."

"What about Ashlee?" he asked.

Lisa exploded with laughter. "Oh, man. You kill. That's good.

You're funny. You're so cute. Want to go out sometime?"

"We hear you've been partying with Colin Farrell. Any truth to that rumor?"

Lisa sighed heavily. "Colin. Sweet lover. But please, my personal life is so incredibly personal! I so can't comment on all the hella good times we've had. And, oh my God, don't even ask me about Ian Somerhalder—and Jesse McCartney and Young Jeezy and Robbie Williams and Orlando Bloom and Aaron Carter and Fiddy and Tupac."

"Wait. Tupac's dead," he said, confused. It only took a millisecond. Lisa burst into tears.

"Like, it so sucks, doesn't it? Please. Please. Allow me to grieve in private. It's so hard being famous. I feel, like, so vulnerable. Put your arm around me. Hold me close. No, closer. Are you wearing CK One? Is that a hickey?"

"Your sister's really something," said Sebastian. What could I say to that? And yet it felt like the worst was yet to come when Quddus asked, "Is your family proud of you?"

"Proud?" she exclaimed. "They worship me. I, like, boggle their minds. Hey, I want to give a shout out to my awesome sister, Cindy Bixby, at RU. Yo, Sis, you rock!" Sebastian and the group exploded with whoops and cheers, and at first, I didn't how to feel about my name being screamed on national television.

"You're famous!" exclaimed Sebastian. I guess I am—in a sort of dumb footnote parasitical way—and yet I suddenly felt a lump in my throat. Lisa thinks I'm "awesome"? Who knew? And yet, I guess I always have. And I guess I've always thought she was awesome too. I almost felt like crying. The audience on *TRL* was cheering. Lisa was about to perform her "hot" new single from her upcoming CD, *Nympho*, with chorus and backup vocals sung by Los Lonely Boys (I guess Ringo came through).

"For the first time ever," announced Quddus. "Lissa sings 'Ghetto Grrl!'" Everyone cheered, and the song began. It was actually okay (if mildly dirty) (big surprise), though I didn't understand the Spanish parts. Lisa sang:

> *Yo, check this out,*
> *Yo, tag it hard*
> *My name is Lissa, I'm in the yard*
>
> *Boo-yea, boo-yea*
> *Boo-yea, boo-yea.*
>
> *I'm make you chubby,*
> *I'll make you slide*
> *My name is Lissa, my booty's wide*
>
> *Boo-yea, boo-yea*
> *Boo-yea, boo-yea.*
>
> *I'm so ghetto, I'm so street*
> *I'm so tough, yo, feel dat heat*
>
> *Iz you trazy? Iz you curl? Well I'm your*
> *Ghetto Ghetto Grrrl! Uh-huh! Uh-huh!*
> *Your Ghetto Ghetto Grrrl!*

She shimmied and shook as the voices of Los Lonely Boys piped in with:

> *Es maldita blanca,*
> *Es un centro gran!*
> *No conoce naccas*
> *De un gritto bacca!*
> *Ceremos que es bonita*

Dark Cindy

Pero es un falsificación
Yo, issimos cantos
Por que? No dio la plata!

No es nacca, no es nacca
Que no! Que no!

Lisa kept singing, and then something really strange happened. A few of the guys in the dorm room started laughing, and in the *TRL* audience, at least a fourth of the audience was doing the same thing. I could tell it was throwing Lisa a bit, but she kept going—she's definitely a trouper—and yet, when the Los Lonely Boys chorus came on again, the audience lost it, and so did several of the guys in the dorm room.

"What the heck is going on?" I asked José, Sebastian's "hot-hot CSP" (though he seems to be a bit more than that these days). He explained. And I was flabbergasted. Lisa doesn't speak Spanish (she can barely manage English), and Los Lonely Boys' lyrics roughly translated like this:

Es maldita blanca,	*She's so damn white,*
Es un centro gran!	*She's major mall!*
No conoce naccas	*She wouldn't know a ghetto*
De un gritto bacca!	*From a cattle call!*
Ceremos que es bonita,	*We think she's cute, but*
Pero es un falsificación	*She's wannabe*
Yo, issimos cantos	*Yo, we did this song*
Por que? No dio la plata!	*For a really big fee!*
No es nacca, no es nacca	*She's not ghetto, she's not ghetto*
Que no! Que no!	*No way! No way!*

263

On *TRL* the laughter was reaching a fever pitch, and when the song concluded, Lisa hurled down her microphone and screamed furiously, "What the hell is wrong with you guys? Huh? I'm ghetto! I'm ghetto!" Then she knocked past Quddus and walked off the show. "How bad is this for her?" I asked José desperately.

He started giggling. "At least she wasn't lip-synching." That prompted him and all the Latin boys in the room to practically fall all over themselves chuckling, "No es nacca, no es nacca!" Okay, this was bad. And so unfair. Justin Timberlake goes from being this twerpy, pasty little beanpole on *The New Mickey Mouse Club* to wearing a do-rag and hanging with a "posse" and thinking he's all "gangsta" and "down wit da brown" (oh, and he thinks he's an actor, too) (ha!). Yo, indeed. But then I realized that something more was bothering me, and it was hard to admit. At least a part of me has been inspired by Lisa in my quest to destroy Meri. She imagines, she plans . . . and she belly flops. Oh my God, oh my God, oh my God, oh my God!

Back at Alpha Beta Delta, I stepped into Lindsay's and my room and discovered that Meri (or more likely someone following her orders) (like Gloria) had squeezed toothpaste in all my socks, rubbed Vaseline in every single one of my panties, and used red lipstick to write "You r so dead!" on the large mirror above Lindsay's dresser.

Men have loved darkness rather than light, because their deeds were evil.

I shuddered. Is there any difference between me and Meri now? And given what I'm planning to do, am I the evil one? Before I went to bed tonight, I heard another screaming call from Meri to her father. She still can't get through to him.

November 18

Dear Diary:

Karla Mae didn't even look at me this morning. She's really starting to creep me out. Why were her words still bothering me? Today's Saturday, and she was dressed casually in a sexy black T, which said "Living Proof That God Forgives" with an arrow pointing up to her face, lots of jangly silver cross jewelry, and her iBelieve around her neck. She was off for a meeting with the Xtreme Christianity Hip-Hop Bible Study Group, one of the more "radical" evangelical groups popping up on campus these days ("Jesus was way subversive," they say) (like this is news to anyone?).

"Karla Mae?" I dared to ask as she slung her Whatever purse over her shoulder. "That quote you said yesterday? About men loving darkness instead of light? Where can I find that in the Bible?" I really wanted to see it context. She stared at me long and hard (actually, it was probably just a sec, but her searing glare made me so alarmed that it felt like forever).

She finally said, "John. 3:19. I have a Bible on my dresser. You can look at it. But don't crease the corners. And wash your hands before you touch it." Then she sauntered out, slamming the front door. Yikes. Like I'm going to give her Bible evil Cindy cooties or something? Obviously I'll have to look through someone else's.

"You're gonna start reading the Bible now?" cracked Doreen,

who was sashaying down the stairs in her cheerleading outfit. "That's a good one."

"I'm surprised you've even heard of it," I retorted.

"Look, I'm just trying to get along with everyone. And they're trying to get along with me. By the way, everyone's coming to the game tonight. They're being supportive. Are you coming?"

"I doubt it." I had far more important things to do.

"See? That's what I'm saying. You're not supportive. Everyone here helps. We all have our special skills."

"Oh? What are yours?" I asked. "I'm just dying to know."

Doreen scoffed, then proudly announced, "I can deep throat and teabag at the same time. So there." A sudden scream from the kitchen startled us both. Meri cried out, "Ants! Ahhhhhhhh! Someone get in here! I want this place handsied-kneesied now!"

Doreen forcefully knocked me aside. "C'mon, move it, I got practice." And she was gone. Meri continued shrieking, and several CEC girls rushed into the kitchen. She was making such a commotion, but then I remembered one of her diary entries:

"Ants!" I gasped, gesturing to the loathsome little creatures. . . . Mark chuckled. How dare he! He knows ants disturb me to my core.

I felt bad for the CEC girls. They'd have to handsies-kneesies the kitchen, redo and replant the entire garden (traditional English now instead of French), and go on their daily trek to sell more Whatever clothing to raise funds for their various charities before being granted the "thrill" of attending the football game and watching Doreen cheer. Why were they putting up with this?

I didn't have time to figure that one out. Dark Cindy had a schedule to keep. *Whoosh!* I blew down the street on my skateboard, swerving down the streets. Then I heard a sudden clattering behind me. I whipped my head back. They were coming right at me—Albino Girl and the St. Eulalia posse. *Come and get it, girls,* I thought, and sped like lightning. And so did they. They swerved right up alongside me as I blasted toward RU's rehab center, spinning and circling all around me (like a bunch of show-offs).

"Where ya going?" taunted one of the St. Eulalia girls, hefting her Super Shooter Aquapack squirt gun.

"You even think of shooting me with that thing and you'll regret it," I warned.

"Oooh, I'm shiverin'."

"You should be. Talk to Gloria lately? Or Gilda? One shot with my taser and—*ka-bam!*—you're flat on your butt." I didn't actually have the taser on me, and I would so never shoot a little girl with one (though in the case of this bunch, it was tempting), but they didn't have to know that, right? They just had to believe it.

"All right, ladies, back off," ordered Albino Girl. "I want talk to C-Dawg alone." This didn't go over well. The posse loudly protested that they were supposed to stick together and follow me all day. But Albino Girl got her way (because of her A-type personality? Her scary pink eyes?). They swirled off as fast as they had appeared, and when I arrived at the rehab center and kicked the skateboard up into my hands, Albino Girl snickered.

"Getting' pretty good on that thing, C-Dawg. I like the hair, too. Spiky works for you."

"What do you want?"

Her eyes narrowed. "All right, I'm only going to say this once. So listen up. My allegiances can be bought."

What? I couldn't believe what I was hearing. But I didn't respond. I let her keep talking. "You've already benefited from my help," she whispered conspiratorially. "You can have that and a whole lot more. If you play your cards right." My mind raced. And then I held back a gasp, because I suddenly got it. Of course.

Albino Girl is a whiz on her skateboard. Which meant that she had deliberately swerved in front of Mrs. Juergens (and tripped her too, for God's sake) in order to stop her from getting into the dean's office when Lindsay and I were there; she had intentionally sped in front of Gilda's and Gloria's Camry, allowing me and Lindsay to get a head start when we left Chappaqua; and days earlier, when I had left Professor Scott's classroom and was rushing for a bus to get to RU, it was no accident when she blasted right in front of the bus and brought it to a halt, allowing me to climb on board.

"I know so many things you don't know," she said cagily. "But they're going to cost."

"Cost what?"

"I want cash. Lots of it. And this skateboard sucks. I want a new one. Oh, and I want a pony." I laughed. But she was unmoved. "What I can give you will bring this whole thing to a stop," she said. "Permanently." *What a tempting offer*, I thought, but then I'd already tapped out Dad, and besides, for all I knew she was playing me for a fool.

"I'm busy, Eileen," I said. "And I don't buy anything without sampling the goods. Care to fill me in?"

"Care to pay up?"

"Have a nice day. Give Meri my best." I strode into the rehab center, and boy, was she mad. I could hear her screaming, "Big mistake, C-Dawg! You'll see. You hear me? And Billie Joe Armstrong wants his hair back!"

Rehab isn't pretty. I sat down next to Patty's bed and it was obvious she wasn't well. Her brow was sweaty, there were dark circles under her eyes, and she seemed beyond exhausted. "I have my good days and my bad days," she murmured hazily. "Thank God for Jesse. And you. Oh, and everyone."

"I can come back another time," I said. Her recovery, after all, was more important than any of my problems. She suddenly laughed.

"Call me Meri. Ha. That's my favorite part." She was referring to Meri's blog pages. Then she suddenly became quite serious. "You do see the psychodynamic parallels between you and Pru, right?"

"Um, what?"

"Tsk. Cindy. Okay, let's start at the beginning." She sat up and began explaining eagerly. "On one hand, we have Meri, our happy-go-lucky sociopath with narcissistic personality disorder; her psychotic sense of self-importance, her phobic preoccupation with her own beauty and power, her need to manipulate others for her own selfish needs. I suppose we could toss in dysthymic disorder and borderline, but let's keep it simple. And then we have Pru. Poor little Pru. Classic avoidant personality disorder; she's deeply, and I mean deeply, insecure, socially repressed, and she won't even think of becoming friends with someone unless she's absolutely certain she'll be liked. Sound familiar?" My heart sank.

"Yes," I said. She had just summed up my entire loser-ish life with a few quick brushstrokes.

She patted my hand. "Shh. You're growing, you're changing. We know that. But stay with me. So Meri decides to befriend and even transform our little Pru. But why?"

"I don't know. Out of some strange goodness of her heart?" Even as I said it, I knew it sounded ridiculous. Patty rocked with laughter.

"That's funny. As if she even has one. But no. The true narcissist needs acolytes, disciples. If you're all-powerful, or fantasize that you are, then you need constant admiration. And who better to give that to you than someone who's . . ."

"Deeply insecure," I said numbly. I was getting it. And it wasn't making me feel good.

"And grateful," she added. "Grateful is key. So you see? You are, or were, Pru. And Pru is you. But it gets better. Our little Pru grows overconfident, she scandalizes Meri by going . . ."

"Going out with Timothy," I gasped, covering my mouth in shock. "Just like I went out with . . ."

"With Keith. That's right. Which is why her focus on destroying you is so maniacally intense. Not because you went out with Keith per se, but because your very presence taps into her darkest childhood fears and insecurities. You're a sword stabbing into her one tiny soft spot; a crushing echo of her tortured formative psyche. And that, dear Cindy, is your trump card."

"What is?" I asked. I told her about my fun with the Bloody Mary pitcher. Is that what she meant? She waved me off.

"Child's play. Too easy. You're going to have to go bigger than that. And you do know you'll have to get the rest of her blog, right? Or at least one crucial page. To really end this." I did know that. I had sent another e-mail to Mark, but I still haven't heard back from him. "Keep trying," she urged. Then she giggled. "But in the meantime, this should freak her out." She handed me back the blog pages. She had carefully highlighted key phrases and paragraphs, and she gave me several more pages she had written up: complicated graphs and paragraphs with headings such as "Five-Axis Disorder Exploitation" and "Delirium Implementation" and "Total Schizo-Cognitive Annihilation."

"Jeez. I hope I know how to use all of this," I said, awed by the amount of work she had put into it.

"Oh, you will," she said reassuringly. Then she grasped my hand tightly, warning me, "Watch your back, Cindy. At all times. Remember, Meri's way too smart not to be hypervigilant. Especially at a time like this."

November 19

Dear Diary:

Oh my God, oh my God, oh my God, oh my God! I've been terrified and confused and thrown for a loop every minute of the day.
But I'm getting ahead of myself. Last night I went on a date with
Cliff. A real date-date. He called me after I left Patty at rehab and
we agreed to meet at The Heights, a wonderfully old-fashioned
restaurant just outside Rumson with candles and big booths and a
live violinist. So much fun (and so romantic). Before that, Lindsay
took charge. Cliff is an artist, after all—and so edgy and so cool—
which meant (in her opinion) that I had to dress appropriately, so
she lent me some of her clothes and made me up from head to toe.
I have to say, when she turned me around to face the mirror—holy
moly. There I was in tight, form-fitting black leather pants with a
low-slung Allen B. brown leather belt, rocker-chick Dolce &
Gabbana red T-strap pumps, and a (way too) sheer black
Rocawear top with a plunging neckline that highlighted my
cleavage, which was substantially pushed up by a flirty Agent
Provocateur Abracadabra black lace bra. Then she spiked my hair,
made me up with Serena Williams's Strawberry Rush lipstick and
shimmering eye-shadow, and gave me a bit of bling with a
C.H.A.R.M. gold heart locket and chain. I was stunned.

"I can't go out in public like this."

"Why?" Lindsay grinned. "Afraid everyone will know you have

a figure? Uh-oh. Secret's out." She was right. Besides, Dark Cindy gets to play dress-up and Cindy can't? That didn't make sense. "Oh, and don't tell him about the dean," said Lindsay. "You know, about Duke University? And helping him out with his scholarship?"

"Why?" I asked. "He'll be happy."

"No, he won't," she insisted. "Guys like to be the guy. They're the ones with the penis."

"Excuse me?"

"If he knows what you did, then you'll have the penis."

"What?" I couldn't believe what I was hearing.

"I mean, you're already developing a slight nub."

"I do not have a nub!"

"Gosh, of course I'm speaking metaphorically. You know, because you're so tough with Meri? Which you should be. You have to be. Plus, what if you break up with him?"

"So I'm supposed to keep this big secret? And be all la-di-da, you have the penis?"

We couldn't come to an agreement on that, so I was more than a bit frazzled and confused and self-conscious when the maître d' at The Heights led me to the table. And then my jaw flopped open. Cliff nervously bolted up from his seat. He was in a stiff white dress shirt, dark blue slacks, black leather dress shoes, and—oh my God—a tie! *I have so stupidly blown this*, I screamed to myself. And yet, just a few minutes later we were laughing and holding hands beneath the table. It's funny how things turn out. See, I thought I had to dress up like an "edgy artist's girlfriend," and he thought he had to dress more conservatively, given my comment about my mom's would-be disapproval.

"Maybe we should just be ourselves," said Cliff. I smiled with relief.

"Great idea." Then I hesitated. Should I tell him about the dean? About Duke? I wasn't sure. But I sure as heck knew I had to

Dark Cindy

tell him about Meri. And I did. Everything. From beginning to end. And when I was all through, he whipped out his cell phone and dialed frantically. "What are you doing?" I asked.

"Calling Mark," he said. "You need the rest of the blog thing, right?"

"Wait," I exclaimed, but it was too late. He got Mark's voice mail, and in that "whoa, dude" way they have of communicating, he told Mark to call him back "like, butt-kicking fast."

After dinner, he drove me back to Alpha Beta Delta, and we made out in his car. Yum! I think I'm in love. There, I said it. And, no, not in my old "my love, my sweet, my everything!" sort of way—that seems so foreign to me now, and kind of hysterical—but in a newly warm and tender and wonderful way that makes both of us feel loved and respected for who we are, differences and all. And he didn't bust a move, and he didn't ask to come inside, because he knows I want to take things slow. "I love your lips," he whispered. Oh God, and I love his. So much. Cindy <3s Cliff. Ha. He even walked me to the door like a real gentleman. Thank goodness everyone was out at the football game. He gave me one more good-night kiss, then stepped back to his car. We were both grinning like fools. "Hey, don't worry about Mark," he called out. "I'll get him on Monday. He never answers his phone on weekends. And I know just what to tell him."

I panicked. "Cliff, what do you mean?"

"Do you trust me?" he asked. And in that instant I knew. Yes. Oh, yes-yes-yes. I, Cindy Bixby, aka Dark Cindy, trust Cliff Haven, aka Megatalented Artist and Superhandsome Guy, completely. A leap of faith? Maybe. But I listened to my heart. "Yes," I cried happily. "I do." And he was off. I was about to turn around to put my key in the door when I noticed the garden. Oh, those poor CEC girls. It was flawless. It was English. There was even a perfectly manicured herbaceous border.

273

In Lindsay's and my room, I hung her clothes back in the closet and noticed all sorts of new sex toys (still in their original packaging). I guess Lindsay's been saving up for her reunion with Bud. There were Bad Girl Activity Cards, a leopard-print blindfold, a see-through nylon bodystocking catsuit. There were even a whip—a genuine whip—and for reasons that I swear were completely nonsexual, I took it out, let it fall loose in my hand, then let her rip. *Crack!* I had to laugh, and not just because it was silly (or because I seemed to have such natural skill with it), but if I had imagined just a few months ago that I, loser Cindy B., would have a talented artist-boyfriend and be cracking a whip in the privacy of my own room, I'd have thought I was bonkers.

Turning out the light, I climbed into bed and was just about to fall asleep when I heard all the girls returning from the game downstairs. My heart began thumping. After a moment I realized that Lindsay wasn't with them (she had probably gone back to Bud's dorm room). I was all alone in the dark. *Boom-boom-boom.* Someone banged on the door.

"Sleep well, little bow-wow," sneered Gloria in a sickeningly sweet singsongy voice. That's the last thing I remember from last night—and the first thing I remember from this morning. *Boom-boom-boom.* Someone was banging on the door. What the? "Hey, Bixby," hollered Gloria. "The dean wants you in his office in twenty minutes. Chop-chop. Golly gee, I hope you're not in trouble." Her malicious laughter punctured my soul. *Oh no,* I thought, *has the dean somehow double-crossed me? Again?*

I felt like a wreck as I whizzed across campus on my skateboard and made my way into the dean's outer office. Mrs. Juergens wasn't there, but the door to the dean's office was slightly ajar, and I could hear teasing, fluttery laughter.

"Thank you, Dean. I moisturize at least three times a day." I swallowed hard—*just get this over with,* I thought—pushed open the

274

door, and stepped into the office. There they were, cozy as could be. The dean was standing tall behind his desk, and Meri was on it, literally, posed on the edge in a girly, slightly slutty blue and white embroidered smock-waist dress (she wasn't wearing a bra), a dazzling blue-onyx necklace, with her legs demurely crossed and dangling in sheer stockings and light blue Lanvin pumps. And the dean couldn't take his eyes off her (I'll be the first to admit that Meri has great legs) (darn her).

"Good morning, Cindy." She winked. "Sleep well?"

I was silent. *Just listen*, I thought. *Don't negotiate, don't say yes or no.* "Meri woke me up this morning," said the dean, looking for all the world as if he was quite happy that she did. "And she's told me about some of the troubles you two have been having lately." He looked at me, expecting me to say something. I remained stone silent. "Meri hasn't been able to get ahold of her father yet," he continued. "And naturally, before involving other parties, she came to me." *Oh, darn it*, I thought, *here it comes, here comes the devastating double-cross.* "So I've made a decision." He smiled. "I want you both to get the hell out of my office. Now. And I never want to see either of you again."

"Pardon?" murmured Meri with a sunny smile and a practiced eyelash flutter. What was going on?

"You heard me," he said, stepping to his door and decisively swinging it wide open. "Get out. Both of you. You have immunity"— he pointed at me, and then he pointed at Meri—"and you have immunity. So go at it. I don't care if you two kill each other. But if I so much as hear a peep or another whiny complaint from either of you, then that's it, you're both out. And I don't care what you do to retaliate. You hear me? Now get the hell out of here." I didn't move an inch. I was too shocked. No double-cross?

"You're making a big mistake, Dean Pointer," said Meri with a smirk, swinging off the desk and slinging her blue and white

Fendi bag over her shoulder. "As I seem to recall, you took—"

"A bribe?" he sneered. "I sent back every goddamned penny."

"How noble of you," she fumed. "And ill-advised. Just wait. When Father gets back, he'll have your ass in a sling. Then he'll stretch it so wide you'll be able to fit the entire cast of *Friends* up there."

"That's disgusting!" I gasped.

"And you," she seethed, turning on me. "More hot air from a dying gasbag? Well? What do you have to say for yourself?"

I was terrified, I was stunned, but I yelped, "Gosh, I don't know, Meri. But all that blue and white? Don't you think you're a little match-y today?"

Oh, no! I criticized her fashion! She vibrated, there was a fiery, earth-splitting shift in her eyes, then she screamed— "Ahhhhhhhhhhhhhhhhhhh!"—and violently swung her Fendi bag into the dean's trophy case, shattering the glass, then swung it again, sending a file cabinet toppling to the floor, its folders and papers spilling out like guts. Then she was gone—*poof!*—leaving hurricane-force devastation in her wake. I stood there trembling. The dean whispered tightly, "Get out."

By the time I returned to the house, I wasn't too surprised to hear screams of "Handsies-kneesies!" But later, when Meri held a meeting to plan a nighttime tiki-inspired beachside charity party—charity to be determined later, of course—she was all creamy, cooing smiles. The party will be this coming Wednesday, the night before Thanksgiving, and while one CEC girl mentioned that she had planned to fly home on Tuesday night for the holiday, Meri smiled and softly commanded, "Change your flight plans," and there was no doubt that she would.

Karla Mae volunteered to be in charge, and though Shanna-Francine offered to help, Karla Mae deliberately ignored her. There was some mention that it might be too cold for such an event on the beach, but everyone agreed that it's been unseasonably warm lately, and besides, they would have heating lamps at the tables. After dinner, Karla Mae and another CEC had kitchen clean-up duty, and I said I'd be happy to help. They didn't say no. We stood there silently washing and drying and scrubbing down the counters, and I felt relaxed, because Karla Mae was playing "Body and Soul." She's right. Anita Baker's voice is truly lovely. But not to everyone.

"Who put this music on?" asked Meri.

"I did," said Karla Mae.

Meri chuckled good-naturedly. "Anita's so old-school. At times she recalls Marvin Gaye or the Chi-Lites. And yet being a being throwback is so easy. And some might say trite. The revisionist soul of, say, an Alicia Keys or a Leela James is infinitely superior. Don't we all agree?" Uh-oh. Under any other circumstance, Karla Mae would have been in complete agreement, and yet Meri's criticism must have felt like a direct (and vicious) assault on her mom. She abruptly blurted out, "No, we do not agree," standing her ground just as Anita hit a soaring, heartbreaking high note. She grinned in triumph. "Okay? When Alicia can do that, you let me know."

Meri gazed at her uncomprehendingly, then shrieked, "Someone turn this garbage off!"

"Garbage?" Karla Mae gaped.

Gloria bolted for the living room—and Karla Mae anxiously charged right after her. I could hear a terrible struggle; the volume blasted, then silenced, then blasted. A sudden plastic-crunching *cra-a-a-ck* startled everyone.

"You bitch!" wailed Karla Mae. "You're buying me a new nano! You fucking bitch!" Then we heard her stifling tears as she raced up the stairs.

Come bedtime, Lindsay and I turned down the comforter and

were talking in whispers about what happened with the dean when we were startled by a loud *boom-boom-boom* on the door. I sighed heavily.

"Go away, Gloria." I really have had enough of her. But I was ignored. The door swung open and then just as quickly shut. Karla Mae leaned against it. Her face was stoic. Her voice was firm.

"I'm in," she said evenly.

"In what?" yelped Lindsay.

I shushed them, leading them both to the bed. We turned off the light and lit a candle.

"What's going on? I'm scared," jittered Lindsay.

Karla Mae whispered angrily, "I finally get it, okay? And I'm telling you, if I have to do one more round of handsies-kneesies, I'll scream."

"Do the other girls feel that way?" I asked.

"No." She sighed. "Unfortunately not."

"That's a real shame," I said. I began thinking, thinking. Then it occurred to me. Follow the money. I quickly explained the situation. "We need an expert on computers."

"Not Bud," begged Lindsay. "Oh God, if he goes to the gulag again I'll die."

"Please," harrumphed Karla Mae confidently. "Show me a server I can't crack. Just show me." It took Karla Mae several hours on Lindsay's laptop—we all sat tensely on the bed in the dark illuminated by just the candle and the glow from the computer screen—and by the time she hit on the right server and opened the right series of password-protected files and folders, our eyes were completely bloodshot. But there it was. Proof. All the money raised by selling Whatever clothing and merchandise, intended expressly for various CEC charities, was being funneled into three different private accounts belonging to you-know-who.

"And right back the money goes," said Karla Mae furiously, ready to hit the keyboard.

"No," I urged. "She'll know. Print it out. You can show the other girls. Don't change anything. Please."

And then a wonderful idea suddenly came to me. I explained it to Karla Mae, and she searched diligently. But this time she was stumped.

"Hmm. I see she has cookies for it. I see the password. But when I try to bring it up it says, 'Page not found. The URL you have entered is incorrect.' Usually that means it was deleted by the owner." My heart hydroplaned and crashed. Oh God. She knows. She knows someone's been looking at her blog and she shut it down.

"But we have the pages," said a confused Lindsay. "And Patty's notes. What's the big deal?" I was too shocked to explain.

"Can you tell exactly when it was shut down?" I asked. Karla Mae typed and searched. And typed and searched.

"Looks like tonight," she tsked. "Around ten thirty. Right after Meri . . ."

"Went up to her room." I shuddered, then desperately asked, "Is it cached?" It was, but only the log-in page, which was useless at this point. "Oh God, we're in trouble," I said, but Karla Mae didn't think so. She collated the Whatever pages she had printed out and assured us: By tomorrow afternoon every CEC girl will have a brand-new perspective on Meri—and be ready to do something about it too. Then she paused, looking at me and Lindsay strangely.

"You two sleep in the same bed?"

"It's kind of a full house these days." I shrugged.

"So you guys aren't . . ."

"Of course not," I gasped. Oh my God, how could anyone think that? Lindsay, of course, found this hysterically funny, and I had to push a pillow over her mouth in order to muffle her giggles.

"But Shanna-Francine. And Bobbie," whispered Karla Mea tentatively. "They're . . ."

"Lesbians. Yes," I said. I couldn't believe how casually that kerplopped out of my mouth. Karla Mae tsked with disapproval.

"God doesn't approve of that."

"Wait, I don't understand," said Lindsay. "Whose God?"

"God God."

"Your God?"

"Um, yeah."

"Okeydokey, then it's settled," she concluded happily. "We are definitely not introducing your God to Bobbie and Shanna-Francine." Karla Mae smiled wryly. No doubt she had many arguments up her sleeve for that one, but there were greater evils to conquer, and Karla Mae, I'm starting to learn, is nothing if not stunningly practical.

"All right," she said warmly. "It's settled." Before she stepped out, she added, "Oh, and Cindy. I have another Bible quote for you. It's a whole lot better than the one I told you before. 'Be of good courage, and He shall strengthen your heart.' Psalms 31:24."

"I like that one," I said. I was so touched, and I really did wish I knew the Bible better in order to discuss it with her properly, but I did know a wonderful passage from Euripides. "'Danger gleams like sunshine to a brave man's eye,'" I quoted.

"Amen and gesundheit!" said Lindsay with a grin. Karla Mae closed the door quietly, and Lindsay fell asleep almost instantly, her face beaming with hope for a better, Meri-free future. But I didn't feel so confident. In fact, I felt a rush of paranoia. I leaped out of bed, whipped out my pocket-size Bug Detector, and ran it across every single solitary surface in the room. Nothing. The LED read-out stayed in the green zone. Then I used my

Telephone Tap Detector. Nothing. There were no bugs in the room. And yet I felt even more jumpy and terrified than before. Was someone listening outside the door? I yanked out my infrared flashlight-size Heat Scanner and nervously pointed it at the door. Nothing. The scanner was picking up body heat from bedrooms many feet away, but not outside the door. It's quarter after four now. I have a class at eight. *Page not found. The URL you have entered is incorrect.* Oh God, I wish I could sleep. Now even Dark Cindy is scared.

November 20

Dear Diary:

Professor Scott is back! At first I was confused and shaken, because I'd assumed Dean Pointer would renege on everything he'd promised once he sent the bribe back to Mr. Sugarman, but there was Professor Scott, so alive, so invigorated. As he stood before the class and lectured (quite beautifully) on *What Maisie Knew* by Henry James—a lesser-known, but I think wonderfully complex, James scenario in which a passive young girl finally attempts to stand on her own two feet—I realized, yes, Dark Cindy hasn't won yet, and Meri remains as formidable as ever, but at least something worthwhile has come out of this.

I wanted to talk to the professor after class, but before I even got out of my seat, a group of eager students were crowded around him (and yes, they were all girls) (a man can dream, I suppose, and I wondered for a brief second who the new fantasy "cherry" might be) (yuck!). I caught his eye. He mouthed, "Thank you," and I could see the gratitude beaming from his face.

I strode out onto the Great Lawn. What am I doing? What am I doing? What am I doing? There was a messy collision inside my brain. *I have so much to accomplish, and so little time, and I'm still waiting to hear from Karla Mae to see if the CEC girls are on board.* Karla Mae was a crazy whirlwind this morning—she has so much to do to prepare for the Charity Beach Party—and she barely even acknowledged me. Did last night even happen? I wondered. And then there's the matter of Thanksgiving. Lindsay wants me to fly up with her and Bud to her parents'. "Oh, please," she insisted. "You've got to be there when we tell them we're engaged." Everything is happening so fast. My phone vibrated. I flipped it open.

"Hurry back here," whispered Karla Mae. "She just left the house." *Click! Holy moly*, I thought, *she must have talked to the CEC girls.*

I whipped across campus on my skateboard, but I almost fell *splat* when I heard the unmistakable whirring of rotor blades above me. I looked up—and there she was in a helicopter swerving above me, her face a terrifying mask of determination. I had to look away because I would have fallen off my board. I whipped around a corner, blasted down a street, then—*whoosh!*—it felt like the helicopter was right on top of me. And it was! I jerked around. The world seemed to be tilting sideways. Meri's helicopter was diving down at an angle as I frantically pushed faster on my board. . . .

. . . *I happily returned home, instructing Gilberto to fly low over town, which startles pedestrians and never fails to lighten my spirits. . . .*

I wanted to scream, but the sound of the blades—*whip-whip-whip!*—was too loud, the wind was threatening to hurl me off my board, and all I could see were crisscrossing blades, a quaking sky, cars' grilles exploding right toward me, and Meri's face, spinning sideways, upside down, her smile spreading into a skeletal grin, her eyes detonated with glee. But Dark Cindy wasn't afraid. She didn't want to scream. *Focus*, I told myself, and I tore around the corner and saw Alpha Beta Delta at the end of the block and kept it in my sights, even as I felt the force of the rotor blades pounding on my back and then—*zzzwapp!*—it felt like the entire helicopter bounced right off me. I looked up. It soared at a tilt into the clouds just as I arrived in front of the house. *Phew.* Dark Cindy may have saved me, but I was completely shaken.

The house was unnervingly quiet when I stepped in, and then I heard muffled chuckles. In Lindsay's and my room I found Bobbie, Shanna-Francine, and Lindsay tittering over all the new sex toys she had purchased, and Karla Mae, visibly mortified, standing to the side. Bobbie gamely grabbed the whip. "I like how this feels," she bellowed happily, giving it a clumsy swing. I rolled my eyes and swiped it from her.

"Like this," I instructed. *Crack!* Shanna-Francine's jaw dropped.

"I won't even ask how you know how to do that," she whispered. "But I'm starting to feel all tingly."

"What's this?" asked Karla Mae, and we were all startled by an insistent beeping sound. My eyes popped out of my head. She was holding my pocket-size Bug Detector—and the LED readout was in the red! Oh my God, oh my God, oh my God. I made a fierce, insistent shushing sound with my finger. Karla Mae was confused, but everyone else got it. Lindsay immediately piped up, "I so have to get a new alarm clock," and she took the Bug Detector from Karla Mae and popped out the batteries, silencing it. "Gosh, I'm hungry. Anyone want to go to Marie Callender's?"

At Long John Silver's, Lindsay cheerily used her scepter to dub her hush puppies "sinful but delicious." Karla Mae was all business.

"You've got everyone," she said grimly. "And not just the girls in the house. You've got all the CEC girls, and all the guys, too. Everyone's just itching to help."

"Do they know what they're up against?" bellowed Bobbie.

Karla Mae snorted. "Please. We fight against abortion clinics. You think some rich bitch with good skin is going to scare us?"

"Atta girl," Bobbie cried, and gave her a forceful smack on her back (nearly causing her to upchuck a Chicken Plank). I admired Karla Mae's fighting spirit, but at the same time I thought, *Behold the confidence of the inexperienced.*

"Where was she going in her helicopter?" I asked.

"Probably meeting with her father," said Shanna-Francine. *Not good*, I thought. *Not good at all. Disastrous, even.* And more troubling, on the way to Long John's, I had called Cliff, who told me that he'd left Mark countless detailed messages and still hasn't heard back. Whatever we were going to do, we had to do it fast. Thanksgiving is the day after the Charity Beach Party, and a lot of girls are leaving for home right after it's over (including Lindsay and Bud) (she's still bugging me to come with her). And who knows what Meri will be able to accomplish when she goes home for Thanksgiving (no one knows if she is, but we have to assume the worst).

I tried to clear my head. I passed out the blog pages marked up by Patty, as well as her complicated pages with graphs and psychological ammo. We flipped through them, desperate for inspiration. Karla Mae grinned devilishly (though she probably wouldn't want me to put it that way).

"Okay, girls, I think I've got it. Order up some more hush puppies. This may take a while."

By the time we left Long John's, I was feeling a teensy bit more optimistic. We can definitely destabilize Meri, at least temporarily (thanks to Patty and Karla Mae), though we'll have to work awfully fast. And yet I couldn't help but feel that we're already defeated—and I so don't want to be defeatist, but Meri did pull down her blog. Now there's no way I can get the critical information I need.

"Maybe she printed it out," said Karla Mae.

"I doubt it," Bobbie put in. "She just moved the whole thing to another site." Oh my God, that seemed very likely. And if that's the case . . . then what?

"Hey, ladies, did you hear?" asked Doreen, sashaying up to us. "Latest report from Denmark. The female brain shuts off during orgasm. And I quote: 'An area governing emotional control is completely deactivated.'"

"Wow. What if you're faking?" asked Lindsay shyly from beneath her umbrella, then quickly added, "I mean, not that I ever would."

"What happens in a man's brain?" asked Shanna-Francine.

"Men," scoffed Doreen. "Their brain scans showed, let's see, how did they put it? Oh, yeah. 'During orgasm, men experience an activation of their pleasure-reward cortex.'"

"Wait a sec," I said. "So we give in and they get off? That seems so unfair."

"Aw. We deactivate each other, honey," cooed Bobbie to Shanna-Francine (I thought Karla Mae was going to scream in horror at that one).

"Speaking of deactivating," said Doreen, "I'm on my way to watch the wrestling team practice. Anyone want to come? It's great research. I tell you, nothing like a little Greco-Roman action to help you pick out just the right bedwarmer for the night. Trust me, it's foolproof." We declined, and Doreen was happily on her way. I turned to Karla Mae.

"You didn't tell her . . ."

"Of course not," she scoffed. "Besides, Doreen's on the side of whoever's winning. And that won't be Meri." I hope she's right. The sky was darkening. Unconsciously, I began searching the skies . . . for what? A helicopter? An incoming missile? I warned all the girls that we have to assume the entire house is once again bugged. We have to be careful. We can't afford to make any mistakes. Not one.

November 21

Dear Diary:

Meri likes to call the girls who make dinner for the house her Kitchen Bitches. "You, Kitchen Bitch!" she'll call after one of them, and no one really likes it. Tonight, she had the Kitchen Bitches make steak tartare—which is basically raw ground beef with onions and a raw egg plopped in the center. I thought Bobbie was going to throw up, and there was a tense moment at the table when Meri whispered pointedly, "You're not touching your steak tartare, Bobbie." And then, "Jackie first enjoyed steak tartare while studying at Université de Grenoble in France. It was an unhurried time in her life, and she enjoyed becoming acquainted with the pleasures and traditions of the countryside." A moment passed, and then, "Don't you like steak tartare, Bobbie?"

Bobbie gulped. "I'm a vegan, Meri."

"Oh, that's right. I forgot. A vegan. You don't know what you're missing. Would you like to know what you're missing?" The table was silent as Bobbie contemplated her answer. Meri delicately lifted a forkful of the bloody-looking raw beef mixture to her mouth and swallowed. She dabbed with her napkin. Then she tittered. "Dinner's always so much fun at Alpha Beta Delta. Don't you girls agree?" And everyone did—heartily—hoping Bobbie had caught a break. And she had. *Phew.*

Today no one could figure out where Meri flew off to yesterday, and she didn't return until late this afternoon, which was good luck for all of us. It gave us time to put our plans into action, even though we had to keep an eye out for Gloria—and Gilda, too, who followed after us when me, Shanna-Francine, Lindsay, Bobbie, and Karla Mae met for lunch in the cafeteria. She gazed at us suspiciously from a corner table (I only knew it was Gilda because the afternoon sun glinted off her blue eyes).

I'm amazed at how organized the CEC girls are. I was frankly worried about how much we all had to do to make tomorrow go smoothly, and yet they executed their top secret duties with complete precision. Still, if even one girl peeps by mistake—in front of one of Meri's acolytes, or in the house, given that she's probably bugged every room again—then that's it, we're done.

After lunch I strode over to the rehab center to check up on Patty. Her mouth seemed to be running a mile a minute, which was, she told me, typical, given her newly diagnosed bipolar condition.

"Classic symptoms in the manic phase include self-esteem that shoots through the roof, spastic motor activity, and quickened speech," she told me rat-a-tat fast. "Sometimes patients in their manic phase are misdiagnosed as schizophrenic." She suddenly burst out laughing. "Schizophrenic! Schizophrenic! My psychomotor's going really fast. Lithium takes time to kick in. Kick in. I'm an incredible person. Fantastic. I'm huge."

"You are," I murmured, slightly stunned.

"Dark Cindy could be indicative of a split somatoform state," she told me speedily. "Specifiers are mixed. The patient seeks escape in an alternate persona with psychoaffective melancholic features caused by acute stress disorders. Stress. Meri. Stress. God, I'd kill for a lude."

I had a lump in my throat as I stepped away from Patty's bed, and I guess Nurse Gertie could tell I was upset. She stepped up to me and gently put a hand on my shoulder.

"She's going to be fine," she told me. "And I'm glad you're helping."

"Helping? How?" I asked lamely.

"You're here." She smiled. "You're being supportive. You'd be surprised how many people abandon their friends and family when they're in the midst of battling a chemical brain disorder." She chuckled ruefully. "They sure don't take off when someone has their leg ripped open in a car accident or requires critical surgery."

"I would never abandon Patty," I said, and I meant it.

"Good," she said. "And remember, her condition is treatable. She will get better." Tears welled up in my eyes. She pulled me into a hug. A dam had burst. I was scared for Patty, I was scared for myself—because I know all too well that no matter what condition Patty is in, her mind is always working, and I wondered, Does Dark Cindy have psychoaffective melancholic features?—and I was scared for the girls of Alpha Beta Delta, too, because they're all following my lead, and if everything blows up in our faces tomorrow then it'll be my fault, and if that happens, Meri will be stronger than ever.

But psychoaffective melancholic features or not, Dark Cindy took over. For the rest of the day, I was beyond decisive and focused. And a little information from Bobbie helped calm my nerves. Before dinner, she heard Meri screaming on her cell phone upstairs. It seems she did not see her father yesterday, because she was shrieking at his assistant to keep tracking him down.

"Then where did she go?" I asked. Bobbie figured from all the Nolita shopping bags and a matchbook from the Royalton Hotel—which Meri used to light her joint while supervising the Kitchen Bitches—that she must have gone to New York City for a little retail therapy.

"She'll need lots of therapy after tomorrow," I said with a grim chuckle. As for Lindsay, she finished everything she needed to do for tomorrow extra early, which meant she had time to supervise the workmen who arrived to (I kid you not) install a stripper pole in her bedroom.

"If you can't lick 'em, join 'em," she said, grinning. "Besides, it's a great workout. Watch." I guess Lindsay picked up more than a few tricks by observing the girls at Kristy's Bottoms-Up Lounge, because—wow!—round and round she went on the pole, her legs extending, her body shimmying and shaking. "This is the firefly," she said, slink-swinging down the pole with one leg hooked around like a sexed-up firefighter. Then she demonstrated more moves. "This is the corkscrew. This is the ballerina." Then she whipped around the pole and hung upside-down, her legs spread wide. "This is the helicopter." I was absolutely speechless. "Do you think Bud will be impressed?" she asked.

"I think Bud is the luckiest guy in the world," I told her.

After dinner Meri made everyone watch the motorcade assassination of John F. Kennedy at least fourteen times. Tomorrow, she told us solemnly, is the anniversary of JFK'S death. That's not the only anniversary it'll be, I thought covertly. If everything goes right, then I'll be celebrating November 22 for a long time to come.

November 22

Dear Diary:

Oh my God, oh my God, oh my God! I'm writing this on an airplane. And no, I don't see any aerosol cans or golf clubs or fishing poles or drills or any of those phallic thingies, because Cliff is seated right next to me (and no, I don't mean to say that Cliff is a phallic thingie) (strictly speaking) (I just mean that he's right next to me so I'm not completely schitzing out) (not yet, anyway).

"Handsies-kneesies!" Meri cried this morning.

"Boy, I'd love to use her head as a mop," grumbled Karla Mae, but she put on a brave front when she joined Shanna-Francine and two other CEC girls who were ordered to scrub down the bathroom on each floor.

Soon after, Meri swept downstairs in an all-black Chanel ensemble. She was in mourning for Jackie. "I'm not sure if I'm up for a party tonight," she said.

"Sure you are," insisted Lindsay, who dutifully served her a cup of Sugarman Roast coffee. "You're just tired. Pop a dexy." Meri's eyes narrowed suspiciously, and she kept them narrowed as she took her first sip, staring intently at Lindsay. "Besides," babbled Lindsay nervously, "you can't disappoint everyone who's coming. And it's for such a good cause." I probably should have kept my mouth shut, but I couldn't help it. Dark Cindy took over. As I sipped my own coffee, I murmured,

"What is that 'good cause,' Meri? Have you decided yet?"

She didn't answer. Instead she waited a moment, then airily intoned, "I'd like to start a podcast. My words are worthy, after all. I am quotable."

"'The surest way to make a monkey out of a man is to quote him,'" I said with an acid grin, citing Robert Benchley. Lindsay shot me a glare that said, stop playing with fire! But I really didn't think I was, and Meri, true to form, wasn't taking the bait.

"Halle Berry has six toes on her right foot," she whispered, taking another sip.

"That's a rumor," tsked Lindsay, who was just as confused as I was in terms of where Meri was going with this.

"Keanu Reeves is married to David Geffen," she continued. "Richard Gere has sex with gerbils. Lindsay Lohan is anorexic. Ciara is a post-op transsexual. Tom Cruise enjoys homosexual intercourse. Hillary Clinton is a lesbian. Lou Reed is dead. And yes, Elvis is alive." She smiled—just slightly—and continued, "The powerful and influential, such as I, are frequently targets of erroneous stories and gossip. With a podcast, I can separate truth from fiction."

"What truth? What fiction?" I asked. "The rumors of your death are greatly exaggerated? You don't look anorexic to me. Does anyone really think you're a transsexual?" Lindsay shot me another glare. I chuckled inwardly. I was giddy. I was scared. I mean, if Meri didn't go to the party tonight, then what? But then I thought, *I have immunity, I should be acting confident and smart-alecky.* She would know something was wrong if I were nervous. Meri smiled with satisfaction and put down her cup.

"A podcast. What a wonderful idea." With that, she was off. She seemingly floated up to her room and closed the door, and I was happily resigned to the notion of her staying up there for most of the day, but then some things are obviously too good to be true. Fifteen minutes later we were all startled by a sudden bloodcurdling scream and the cry of: "Everyone downstairs in the living room! Now!"

Jeez Louise, I thought, *it's barely ten a.m. and no one has classes today. Does she ever give anyone a break?* And even though it wasn't for very long (a few days at best), why did Karla Mae and the CEC girls put up with her? *Follow the money*, I reminded myself. They thought she was one of them, they believed she was contributing enormously to their cause. And God bless them, they kept playing the part to a T. With Shanna-Francine and the gang, Karla Mae and the CEC girls bolted downstairs and lined up in the living room like a group of little tin soldiers. For my part, I sat lazily on the couch, still nursing my coffee. I swiped an *Elle* to flip through so I'd look really bored. *Boom-boom-boom.* Meri tore down the stairs with Gloria and then slowly paced back and forth, back and forth.

"Who's good with computers here?" she asked flintily. *Uh-oh. This isn't good*, I thought. I had assumed someone missed a spot on her bathroom floor. Computers? What was this about? "Are you?" she asked, pushing her face in front of Karla Mae. "How about you?" she continued, peering keenly at Bobbie.

"What's going on, Meri?" asked Karla Mae daringly. Meri ignored her. I had my nose buried in *Elle*, but I knew she was talking to me when she whispered, "It was you, wasn't it?"

I yawned, playing it up good. "I don't know what you're talking about, Meri," I said, and I honestly didn't. "Besides, I'd much rather grease your toilet seat with Icy Hot. Maybe next time I'll use Super Glue." Then I laughed and laughed. Suddenly, without warning—oh my God!—I was knocked to the floor and Meri was on top of me and she was squeezing her hands around my neck and wailing maniacally, "Where's my blog?! What did you do with my blog?!" Everyone was screaming, and for a second it felt like everything was turning fuzzy, and all I could see were swirling black dots, but in that moment I realized, holy crap, if Meri didn't pull down her blog, then who did? And cripes, if I can't get my hands on that one crucial page, I'm totally and completely screwed, and then I thought, *Hold on, there are maybe more important things to be concerned about right now, like breathing.* I was suddenly coughing and gasping for air. Bobbie was holding me in her arms. Karla Mae and Lindsay (and Gloria, of all people) were holding Meri back.

"I want everybody's laptop in my room right now," she seethed. "You'll get them back after Thanksgiving."

"No, that's dumb," said Karla Mae. Meri's eyes widened in disbelief—and so did mine, and so did everyone else's, and I thought, *No, Karla Mae, now is not the time to be defiant. It's too soon.* "If someone messed with your computer," she said calmly, "you need to get some computer wonk over here to look at it. Besides, I need my laptop today. We've got more than a hundred people confirmed for tonight, and I still have lots of prep work. And so do all the other girls here. The dean is coming. And I heard through the grapevine that Sister Nellie Oliverez is coming too. You know, the president of Sigma Gamma Lambada?"

Meri's eyes widened even more. "Then what the hell are you all doing just standing there?" she fumed, yanking her arms loose. "Get to work." She stalked back upstairs, and I breathed an immense sigh of relief. Karla Mae had covered spectacularly. She gave me a wink—and thank God Gloria didn't catch it.

"I'm watching you, little bow-wow," she sneered. "And if you think you're going to—"

"To what? I don't have to go to the party, remember?" I yawned. "I have immunity. So get out of my face." Shanna-Francine sucked back a gasp. But I just shrugged, flipping through *Elle*. I didn't see Gloria step away, but I sure heard her. She clomped out of the house and slammed the door hard. *Too bad for her*, I thought. I continued paging through *Elle* until an article caught my eye, or rather, the title of the article: "Now You'll Really Knock 'Em

Dead." Dark Cindy allowed herself a smile. Just a slight one.

Darkness fell. I was in Cliff's car as we made the long drive to the Cape Fear coastline. It was still unseasonably warm, and when I looked out the window I could see that the wind was turbulent, there were whitecaps on the waves, and the sky was turning from a sheer, glossy blue to a hard, foreboding black. Something churned in the pit of my stomach.

"Are you okay?" asked Cliff. I didn't have an immediate answer. Shanna-Francine, Karla Mae, and the rest of the sisters were already on Wrightsville Beach, one of two barrier islands on the Cape Fear coastline, cagily setting up the party, lying in wait. They were ready. But was I?

"I'm okay," I said, pulling down the sun visor to check my hair in the vanity mirror. I was startled by my cold, calculating stare. This is Dark Cindy you're looking at, I realized, and I almost laughed—and not pleasantly. Where did Cindy go? Where's the girl who believes in the inherent goodness of virtually everyone around her? *She won't help you now*, a voice whispered in my mind. I swallowed nervously. Something was terribly wrong, and I couldn't put my finger on it. Then I gasped, "Mark Sugarman!"

"What about him?" asked Cliff.

Oh my God, I thought, *of course!*

"Mark is the one who pulled down Meri's blog," I exclaimed. "Which means he's got to—"

"Whoa-whoa-whoa," cautioned Cliff. "I still haven't heard back from him. We don't know that."

But Dark Cindy knew. There were now two intriguing possibilities. Mark either pulled down the blog to protect his sister, or he pulled it down in order to help me. Either way, I figured, I still had a shot. I felt myself breathe deeply for the first time in days. I could see the terror rising within Meri, I could feel her clenched-up panic, and for a moment I reveled in all the deliciously awful possibilities to come. *This time,* I thought, *little bow-wow won't just bite. She'll go straight for the kill.*

As we neared the Wrightsville Beach parking lot, Cliff extinguished his headlights. Even though Meri wasn't due to arrive for at least thirty minutes or so, we didn't want to take any chances, and we had to assume that Gloria or Gilda, not to mention Albino Girl and the St. Eulalia posse, were already there.

We tiptoed gingerly from the parking lot to the sand. We saw torch lights in the distance, and we could hear the *thump-thump-thump* of slightly annoying Caribbean-tinged New Age-ish music, which was just right. While Meri would be walking from the parking lot to a footpath that led her down to the party, we were sneaking up from behind it by way of the beach. In the distance, a flashlight beam flashed twice, then was extinguished. It was the all-clear sign. Out of the darkness, Lindsay rushed up (God bless her, holding her umbrella aloft). "Follow me," she whispered urgently. "We've got the perfect spot for you." She grasped my hand, and I grabbed Cliff's, and we were off, seemingly flying along the coastline until we were nearly blinded by festive lights—intense reds, dark purples, glittering indigos. I saw all the decorations, too, which were meticulously arranged for maximum effect.

"This table has a charmeuse tablecloth," said Lindsay. "You'll be able to see right through it." Quick as bunnies, me and Cliff lifted up the tablecloth, which hung right down to the ground, and crept beneath the table. Lindsay was right. Through the tablecloth's floral-lace markings and stitches, we had a dotty, pixilated view of the entire gathering. There had to be more than a hundred people. It looked like any beach party anywhere. Shanna-Francine, Karla Mae, and the rest of the sisters were happily mingling with the guests; Sebastian and Sheila Farr (in a glorious white turban) shared Greyhound cocktails; and Bud was goofily booty-bumping Bobbie in time to the Caribbean New Age-ish music. I guess she wasn't particularly amused, because she booty-bumped him back—hard—and he flew sidelong-*splat* to the ground (and laughed, of course). I heard a vibrating buzz right next to me. Cliff whipped out his phone and looked at the caller ID.

"It's Mark," he gasped. Now we would know for sure. He opened his phone, and yet I couldn't hear a word he was saying because there was a loud murmuring and a sudden expectant rustling in the crowd, and when I looked through the lace-patterned tablecloth, I could see her.

Meri was smiling—just slightly—as she slowly and confidently descended to the party. Gloria and Gilda were on either side of her, but honest, you barely noticed them because Meri was so undeniably jaw-dropping. This was her South Beach cocktail attire. Blink once and you could see how perfectly she'd mesh with a vivid Miami sunset: her fire engine red Pucci cashmere sweater, her gargantuan mirror-reflective Dior sunglasses, her orchid drop earrings, numerous gold cuffs, countless rings and necklaces—all of them studded with multicolored crystals and precious stones—the Byzantine medallion belt that wrapped around her canary yellow, sleekly hip-hugging Cavalli pants, her crimson Blahnik sandal pumps, and in her hand, a small, but dazzling gold Chanel clutch. *Oh my God*, I thought, *it's starting!* I gulped hard. *Meri so richly deserves this*, I thought, *for all the horrible things that she's done to me, and for all the heartache and pain she's caused my friends. There comes a time when you just have to stand up for yourself. And fight back.*

"Hi, Meri," said Karla Mae in a soothing, obedient tone. She took Meri's hand, leading her into the throng. "You'll be happy to hear, we've already raised quite a bit of money. And everyone helped with the decorations. Oh, wait, I almost forgot. You didn't get an invitation." She casually handed one to her. Meri took off her sunglasses. "It's nice, isn't it?" asked Karla Mae. "It's made of slate gray recycled paper." This didn't seem to register one way or the other for Meri.

Oh, darn it, I thought. *Okay. Okay. Calm down. This is only the beginning.*

Half-amused by Karla Mae's overt attentiveness, Meri allowed her to lead her around to various sections of the party, where she helpfully gestured. "All our torches use these wonderful organic beeswax candles. Nice touch, don't you think?"

"I suppose," uttered Meri, not committing one way or the other.

"Oh, and this we made special. We worked on it for two whole days. See? We made the bar out of wine barrels, and then we decorated it with purple tellin shells. Don't you love it?" I couldn't see too well, but I swear I saw Meri's mouth open and just as quickly shut, as if some vile, slimy life force had nearly leaped right out of her. She muttered apprehensively, "I—I'd like a cocktail." It was happening. Meri's mind was disassembling. She was on a beach in Greenwich. With her father and Wina and all those guests from San Francisco.

"Oh, but wait," enthused Karla Mae, leading her farther in. "Look at all our table decorations. See? We used pineapples, Indian figs—and look—cute little muskmelons." Meri involuntarily yanked her hand away, but Karla Mae pulled it back, grasping it, leading her even farther in—and even closer to the table where Cliff and I were hiding.

"Bobbie helped with the cooking," she said, her voice becoming slightly tart and singsongy. "But I came up with the menu. Doesn't it smell good?"

"I want a cocktail now," said Meri. Her breathing seemed erratic.

"Doesn't it look scrumptious? Corn cakes. Spiced cranberries. And for our entrée, chorizo-crusted cod."

"What's going on here?!" she shrieked abruptly. She backed away fearfully—and bumped right into a group of partygoers, all of whom were circling around her. "What are you all doing?"

"Hey, what the fuck is going on here?" cried Gilda from the back of the crowd, where Bobbie was pushing her back.

"Aw. And we thought you'd be proud," tsked Karla Mae. "We've raised so much money. But gosh, we'd like to raise a bit more." On cue, the crowd silently separated, revealing a diminutive lemonade stand. "Isn't it darling? Would you like to work it for us?" She forcefully grabbed Meri's hand. "Here. I'll pay you in jellybeans." Then she dumped a pile of them into Meri's hand. A jagged fissure seemed to crack across Meri's forehead. Her hand fell numbly, allowing the jellybeans to scatter.

She stuttered, "You—you didn't . . ."

"We didn't what, Meri?" asked Karla Mae sweetly. "Raise enough money? Here." She once more grasped Meri's hand and mashed several tea bags into her open palm. "I filled them with grass. Shh. You can sell them as chamomile." Meri violently slapped her hand back. Uh-oh. Her fury instantaneously bubbled up, dousing her fear—her anger was now in full and fiery bloom.

"Which one of you has it? Who has it? My blog is private!"

She whirled around and found herself encircled by all the sisters and all the guests, everyone openly grinning at her; silently, ominously. The Caribbean music was hushed. All you could hear were the gentle lapping waves and Meri's sudden, shrieking, echoey, gut-wrenching cry: "You're all dead! All of you!"

Then someone else screamed. Loudly.

"Ohhhhhhhhhh! Pru!"

Meri spun around in horror—and the crowd separated just for her, revealing Cliff grinning on top of me on the table as I threw my arms out and wailed, "Ahhhhhh! Call me Meri! Call me Meri!"

Then we flipped over and I mock-mounted him, and he gyrated beneath me and roared loudly, "Call me Meri! Call me Meri!"

Meri sank to her knees and wailed—a horrible, anguished wail—but it was quickly drowned out by all of the partygoers, who cheerfully chanted, "Call me Meri! Call me Meri!"

Then one by one the girls removed their tops, the guys took off their shirts—and then Meri could see: Everyone was wearing

T-shirts emblazoned with the slogan, "Call me Meri!" And right then I hopped off the table, and Shanna-Francine handed me a guitar. I gazed down at Meri and whispered, "This is for you, Meri. It's special, just from me." I strummed lightly and gently sang,

Kumbaya, my Lord, kumbaya

I felt a soft, warm rush as I saw Meri's face crumble before me; it was like a landslide. All her defenses trickled away, revealing a gnarled, quivering child. She was ugly and exposed and naked. Her truths were laid bare. Her power had been spiked. There were even tears, and they flowed when all the sisters and all the partygoers joined me as I sang,

Kumbaya, my Lord, kumbaya
Ohhhh, Lord, kumbaya

Meri ran. She blazed like a freight train up the footpath and into the night, and that's when all hell broke loose, because we had so little time. I was so confused. Lindsay was screaming one thing, Cliff was hollering another. Less than an hour later I was at the airport and boarding a plane bound for Glorieux, a wealthy suburb near Toronto, with Cliff, Lindsay, and Bud, and frantically using the plane's phone to reach Mom, who didn't understand why I wouldn't be coming home for Thanksgiving.

"Has anyone called asking for me?" I yelped.

"I think so," answered Mom. "Yes, I think so. A nice girl named Gilda wanted to know if you'd be home for Thanksgiving." Oh my God, oh my God, oh my God.

"You told her I'd be there, right?"

"Of course, but where are you—"

"Mom, I have to call you back. And if anyone calls—and I

mean *anyone*—I'm coming home for Thanksgiving." I hung up, and then it was Cliff's turn to dial. He'd talked only briefly with Mark when we were hiding beneath the table on the beach. Mark told him he'd printed out Meri's entire blog before he took it down. I needed only one page, Cliff told him, and Mark promised he'd fax it to us. Frustratingly, Cliff only got Mark's voice mail this time, but he handed the phone to Lindsay, who recited her father's fax number. *Think, think*, I told myself. I swiped the phone and dialed Karla Mae. "Is she back at the house yet?" I asked.

"Nope. Totally silent here. And I haven't heard any helicopters, either."

"I'm going to Marietta. If she asks. For Thanksgiving."

"If she even shows up."

"Is Purrfect still there?"

"Yeah. He's in back with his automatic feeder."

"Then she's coming back," I said. I couldn't imagine Meri leaving Purrfect alone on Thanksgiving, even though she now delegates most of his care (she seems to be bored with him these days) (maybe because cats are even more narcissistic than she is). "Can you stall her somehow?" I asked. "I mean, before you leave for Thanksgiving? If she shows up?"

"How?" asked Karla Mae helplessly.

Think, think!

"Do you know Jesse?" I asked. "Patty's boyfriend?"

"Pigboy? Sure. Why?"

"He's majoring in entomology." I didn't have to explain. She knew exactly where I was headed. "He's staying with Patty this weekend. She's not an outpatient yet."

"I'm on it," she said. "And Cindy? May God bless you and yours during this lovely Thanksgiving holiday."

"God bless you and yours, too, Karla Mae."

Click.

November 23

Dear Diary:

When Lindsay told us that Glorieux, Canada, was a "nice suburb," I took this to mean that it's actually a very wealthy enclave. I also assumed her home would be quite large when she mentioned that it was "comfortable." After all, Lindsay was born of Canadian royalty, but unlike Meri, she's not the least bit ostentatious. A nice limo driver picked us up after midnight at Toronto Pearson Airport, and it wasn't long before we were whisked into a darkly magnificent winter wonderland. I was holding Cliff's hand as I gazed awestruck out the window at the gently rolling hills, the towering evergreens, the huge snow-laden oaks.

"We're almost there," said Lindsay excitedly as we turned up a small road. "This is our driveway." *Okay,* I thought as we drove for at least ten minutes more, *this is definitely the world's longest driveway ever.* And it was so pretty. Rows upon rows of sugar maples and paper birch trees lined the brightly moonlit path, and I held back a gasp when I saw a large house to my right.

"What a beautiful home," I said.

"Thank you," said Lindsay with a smile. "We built it special for Hank. He's our landscaper. There's a fireplace in his bathroom. Isn't that fun?"

"Ooo, yeah," said Bud with a guttural groan. "Nothing like a warm crapper in the morning" (gross!). Lindsay playfully slapped him. Then she perked up.

"Here we are, guys. Be it ever so humble . . ."

Surely she was joking. This wasn't a house, it was a castle! Okay, so maybe not a castle, exactly, but wow, all those towering columns, the delicate friezes, the flying buttresses. I nearly burst out laughing, it was so outrageous. "Are you sure you have room for all of us?" asked Cliff with a wink. Lindsay winked back.

"Sorry, but you two are going to have to bunk in the same room."

"Madame and Monsieur Cunningham," as we were told by Christophe, the Cunninghams' imposing, aging, and dryly amused butler (he seemed to be in some joke that only he knew the punch line to), were already "retired and doing God knows what for the rest of the evening," but he insisted we partake of a "little snicky-snack" before bed—which turned out to be a gargantuan spread with imported cheeses, breads, wine, and champagne—and, he continued, if we wanted to "indulge" before bed, we were welcome to use the courtyard Jacuzzi, though we would need to make our decision now instead of later so the appropriate towels, robes, and "warm fuzzy footsies," as he put it, would need to be retrieved. I politely declined—really fast—and I hope no one thought I was being rude or anything, because while it might have been nice to relax with Cliff and Lindsay in a Jacuzzi (I've never actually been in one), there was the (not so small) matter of Bud, who cried out spastically, "Woo-hoo! Free ballin' in the hot tub! Oooh, baby. Hot. Sssssss."

"Your bedroom is on the right at the end of the hallway," Lindsay told me and Cliff. The "hallway," as she called it, seemed to go on for a good half a mile, and I thought Lindsay was joking at first when told me to use my skateboard. "I'm serious," she said. "I used to ride my tricycle up and down this one all the time."

"I'll race you," Cliff said with a grin.

"You're on," I cried. *Whoosh!* I flew down the hallway on my board. "Ha! You'll never catch me now," I giggled. *Oomph!* He grabbed me from behind, then lifted me right up in his arms and stepped on my board and—oh my God!—pushed off. It was way too romantic. Besides the fact that he's obviously strong ('cause I'm no little peanut, that's for sure) (and I felt kind of blobby from all the cheese and bread and champagne), he was also incredibly coordinated. He even managed a quick kiss as we sped toward our bedroom door, and I thought, *Wheeee! I'm a princess*, even though I know that's not a good thing. Patty's warned me on more than one occasion that Swedish cognitive psychotherapy studies show that girls brought up on fairy tales are more likely than not to be overly submissive and victims of domestic abuse because "classic princess characters, like Snow White and Cinderella, are templates of female disempowerment" (but then that's the Swedes for you, and I'm not really sure what that means, except to say that their studies obviously didn't take modern influences into account, like "Lara Croft," or even Kelly Clarkson). Oh, what the heck. I felt like a princess—there, I said it—and jeez, I was practically in Cinderella's castle, so when Cliff carried me to the gigantic four-poster bed and started macking on me, I did what any good and proper princess would do. I took off his clothes. Then I took off mine. And I discovered that making love with a guy you're really-really into can be a whole lot of fun in a bed big enough to get lost in.

Fax machine! I thought when my eyes popped open this morning. My phone was vibrating too. I had a text message. I anxiously flipped it open.

TEXT MESSAGE
Turkeys get killed on Thanksgiving. Even in Canada.
Happy Thanksgiving, turkey. Die slowly. :)

Dark Cindy

My first thought (besides *Holy crap, how does she know I'm in Canada and not in Marietta?*) was, *Is this from Gloria or from Gilda?* I flew out of bed and found Lindsay, who led me straight to her father's office fax machine. Nothing. Then I ran back to my bed, leaped on top of Cliff, and begged him to call Mark again. He did. And left another voice message. Aaarrrrgh! *One page! That's all I needed!* I grabbed Meri's blog pages, the ones Patty had marked up, and searched frantically, hoping it was really there and I had just missed it. I read:

Briskly, I strolled to the Newport National Bank, gave them my safe-deposit box number and secret security number, and was led by a guard down a long corridor. He dutifully retrieved my box and set me up in a private viewing room. He didn't even ask to see my ID, which I thought was lax, but still, everything's behind lock and key, and the only ones who know the box number and the secret security number are the bank and I (and you, my dear little blog).

No, I didn't miss anything. She didn't type them in this entry. Damn. But the fact that she'd typed "the only ones who know the box number and the secret security number are the bank and I (and you, my dear little blog)" means that she once did write them down . . . in her blog. I just needed that one page.

"But won't you need a key, too?" asked Cliff. Oh my God. I'm so stupid! And here I thought I could just waltz into the bank, give them the safe-deposit box and security numbers, open the box, and finally—once and for all—strip Meri of her power by seizing every single document she's used for decades to blackmail her father. Follow the money. That's what Mamacita said. And she was right. For Meri, money is power, and I wanted to take it all away.

Permanently. And yet I didn't even think of a key. Stupid-stupid-stupid! By now Lindsay and Bud had hopped on the bed too, and Bud said, "Yo, hold up. If she doesn't have the blog anymore, then she doesn't have the numbers, right?"

"That's an assumption!" I cried.

"Wait," said Cliff. "He could be right. Look. She says at the end, 'I put the documents back in the box and I knew then that enough was enough. I don't have to come back to Newport anymore.'"

"Which means what?" I wailed. I was so exhausted by it all. Lindsay gasped. Oh, everyone was getting it except me!

"They could be right, Cindy. I mean, she wrote this when she was sixteen. That's almost what? Six whole years ago? She's supposed to remember her exact safe-deposit box number and a bunch of security numbers for all those years?"

"This is Meri we're talking about." I grimaced.

"That's right," added Lindsay excitedly. "The same Meri who thought her blog was totally private all these years. Even though her own brother was reading it all along."

Okay, there she had a point. Even Meri herself once wrote, "Though no one said it out loud, they thought it: Meri is not infallible. Meri is not perfect." But still, I would feel a whole lot safer once Mark faxed that page. I was in half a haze all during Thanksgiving. At first I wondered why the Cunninghams were even celebrating Thanksgiving—it's not a Canadian holiday—but Lindsay reminded me that her father is American. I was dazzled by Mrs. Cunningham, or Madame. She was slim, like Lindsay, and impossibly glamorous and poised—just as you expect royalty to be—but yet so down to earth (and with the most enchanting French-Canadian accent).

Then we heard a voice boom, "Is that my little bobbysoxer in there?" In strode Mr. Cunningham. He lifted Lindsay in the air and twirled her around (kind of like Bud did after he got out of prison) (but so not in a sexual way) (which would have been creepy) (but it wasn't, it was cute). He was big, like a linebacker, with large, ruddy cheeks, a twinkle in his eye, and a thick Southern accent, too. "Did ya'll go hot tubbin' last night?" he asked. "Did ya' go nekkid? Me and the missus always like to go nekkid." Madame Cunningham tittered, girlishly smacking his shoulder.

"Darick, arrêt!"

"Uh-oh. She's speakin' French," he said with a wink. "That means I've either been really bad or really, really good." That caused Madame to giggle even more. I was beginning to get something. I looked at Mr. Cunningham, then I looked at Bud—back and forth, back and forth—and I thought, *Maybe, just maybe, if Bud washes his mouth out and stops wearing capri pants, he could become (maybe) half as respectable as Mr. Cunningham.* Then I looked over at Lindsay, who was beaming, and I thought, *And people say I have an Electra complex?*

Bud and Mr. Cunningham got along famously (they played hand after hand of Spit before we ate) (any card game that requires its players to periodically cry out "Spit!" is apparently "all righteous" with Bud). Cliff and I were inseparable (when I offered to go to the kitchen and get more wine, Madame surreptitiously whispered to me, "Your boy. He's a keeper"), but poor Lindsay was obviously nervous. Today was the day she was going to drop the bomb: She's engaged to Bud. I figured it probably wouldn't be all that big a deal, given the behavior and personalities of Madame and Mr. Cunningham, but who knew? This is Bud Finger we were talking about. Lindsay. Lindsay Cunningham. Mrs. Lindsay Finger. And their three adorable little Fingers. I just didn't see it.

I stepped away for a moment to call Karla Mae and wish her and her father a Happy Thanksgiving—and get an update on Meri, too. Karla Mae took care of everything before she left for home. She found Pigboy. He jimmied the lock to the RU ento-mology lab. He jimmied the lock to Meri's room. And just before Karla Mae left the house to take a taxi to the airport, she heard a hair-raising scream from Meri's room. "I put them everywhere," said Karla Mae. "In all her drawers. All over her closet. In between all the bedsheets. All over the floor."

"On the toilet, too?" I asked.

"Everywhere in the bathroom." I could almost see her proud smile. And why shouldn't she be proud? Thanks to her (and the RU entomology department), Meri had arrived in her room and found it crawling with thousands upon thousands of ants, wrig-gling throughout all her clothes and her panties and her books and her bedding. At the very least, I figured, it stressed her out. "Ants disturb me to my core!" she had written in her blog. Aw. Dark Cindy allowed herself a chuckle.

The Cunninghams have two cooks, and the Thanksgiving meal was delicious, but what I enjoyed most of all was the warm and easy laughter (and Cliff gently cupping his hand into mine beneath the table) (and the Macintosh Toffee! Yum!). When we shared after-dinner drinks, Lindsay cheerfully exclaimed, "Bud and I are engaged!" Madame tittered and giggled when she heard that one. Ha-ha-ha-ha-ha. And so did Mr. Cunningham. Ha-ha-ha-ha-ha. "No, really," insisted Lindsay. "Bud and I are going to be married." Ha-ha-ha-ha-ha. Oh, *mon dieu*. What a joker their daughter was. Lindsay's brow furrowed. "You guys, I'm, like, really serious. We're engaged. We're going to be married." The laughter halted. Mr. Cunningham jerked his head around, glared at Bud—his brow was knitted furiously, his eyes were bulging out of his head—then bolt-ed up. His chair flew back—*ka-bam!*—and Bud screeched, and, oh my God, he ran! He flew down one of the mile-long hallways, and Mr. Cunningham charged right after him, and all we could hear was Bud's echoey, wailing scream: "Ahhhhhhhhhhhhhhhhh!"

It was all so sudden. Madame stood up too, brought her hand to her forehead, stifled an infinitesimal sob, then flew into the kitchen like a wounded nightingale. Lindsay ran after her. Christophe politely leaned in. "More Macintosh Toffee, mademoiselle? You seem partial to it." I was about to answer when I heard a gunshot. Holy crap! One Finger! Over and out! Cliff and I ran down the hall. We heard another gunshot. And another. *This is so not good*, I thought. We found them in the Cunninghams' immense library (complete with a mounted moose head) (Bobbie would not approve). *Bam-bam-bam.* Mr. Cunningham was firing his hunting rifle at Bud's feet. Bud was leaping up, jerking aside, anything to avoid being shot, while also grabbing very nice first-edition books and hurling them defensively. *Thwack!* He hit Mr. Cunningham in the head. Oh no. He cocked his rifle. *Bam-bam-bam.*

"Gosh, is this really safe?" I asked meekly. Mr. Cunningham whipped around—and I screamed. Cliff held me in his arms. Cliff and Cindy. Killed in Canada. News at eleven.

Mr. Cunningham gruffly intoned, "You. You're a good girl. My daughter says you're her best friend. So what do ya think? Ya think my daughter oughta marry that snot-nosed little punk over there?" Bud was about to say something. Mr. Cunningham swerved the rifle back. "Don't," he ordered grimly. Then he turned back to me. "Well?"

Hmmm, I wondered, *what to say?* There were so many answers I could have given him (so many filthy ones) (because Bud is, after all, filthy to the core). "Can I pass?" I asked politely.

"No, you may not," he grumbled. "This ain't a bridge game. I'd like an answer. Now." *Oh, brother*, I thought, *why me? Because he knows you love Lindsay, that's why.* I had a sudden flash. I saw Lindsay and Bud in the prison parking lot; their joyous expressions, her hair fluttering, her umbrella held aloft, and okay, Bud's greasy hands squeezing her behind (eeeow!).

"All right." I sighed. "I think Lindsay and Bud should be engaged."

"What?" hollered Mr. Cunningham.

"Until they graduate from college," I added. "I mean, honest, Mr. Cunningham, they really and truly love each other"—I couldn't believe I said that, but it's true, I wasn't lying—"but like, what's the big rush?"

"You're not answering my question," he growled.

"No, I'm not, because I don't think it's really my question to answer," I boldly told him. He raised an eyebrow, but I kept going. I'm not sure why, but I could feel myself getting angrier and angrier. "Lindsay should decide who she's going to marry. Not me. Not you." I gestured toward Bud. "What are you going to do? Shoot him? I mean, sure, that might make me happy. . . ."

"Cindy!" yelped Bud.

"But do you think it'll make Lindsay happy? Jeez, Mr. Cunningham, you're the best Thanksgiving host ever, but if you think I'm going to play Showdown at the Cunningham Corral—I don't know, it's just so dumb. Put that rifle down. And you—put down that book. It's a first edition. Now both of you, look at me. I want you to play some Spit. Right now. Play some Spit and talk to each other. And listen." I took a breath. Bud and Mr. Cunningham, I realized, really do deserve each other. "Now, I'm going to walk out of here and go find Lindsay, so if you guys want to mud wrestle or slap each other around, or whatever it is you do that'll make you feel all he-man, go right ahead. Just don't draw blood, don't use that rifle, and don't come looking for me, because I'm not answering any more questions or giving any more opinions. Except to Lindsay. And that's how it should be." Then I stalked off. Cliff followed me, and he whispered, "Wow!" He put his arms around me and kissed me on the neck. "Where'd that come from?" *Now he knows Dark Cindy*, I thought. *Is that a good thing or a bad thing?*

"The fax machine," I gasped. "Let's check again real quick." We raced down the hall (I could hear echoey cries of "Spit!" coming from the library, which made me smile) and turned the corner into the office. Nothing. The fax machine just stood there, its empty paper tray sticking out like a tongue going "nyah-nyah." "I don't have a good feeling about this at all," I murmured fearfully. Cliff whipped out his cell phone and hit speed-dial. When Mark picked up, I could hear music blasting from the receiver and his voice happily (drunkenly?) shouting, "Cl-i-i-i-i-i-iff!"

That's why I'm on a plane (again!). I didn't think we could actually do it at first, but Lindsay just rolled her eyes and gestured at her surroundings. "C'mon, you guys. Look at this place. I grew up here. Don't you think I can afford a few measly plane tickets?" In the seats in front of me, Lindsay's sleeping, Bud is snoring (and so is Lindsay!) (oh my God, I can never ever tell anybody that) (maybe it's the turkey), and Cliff is sleeping too, leaning against the window (and not snoring) (but his mouth is hanging open and it's so cute). Mark had told him, "Cl-i-i-i-i-i-iff! There're no fax machines at Burning Dude!" Then he laughed and laughed. And hung up.

All we have to do is meet up with Mark, get the blog page with the numbers, and that's it, Meri's done for. Cliff said it should be easy to find Mark. He and his friends are in their own communal theme camp (which means what? I wonder), called "Camp Snitch" (I won't even guess). I just looked over at Cliff (still so cute), and gazed farther out the window. Is she out there? On her broomstick? Is she following me? Or is she one step ahead? If Meri gets the pages before I do, she'll have all the power—she'll be able to do anything—and given what I've done to her in the past forty-eight hours, holy moly, that's it, I am "so definitely dunzo," as Lisa would say. I'm starting to feel queasy. I don't know what to do with myself. Actually, that's not true. What I really want to do is run into the cockpit and scream, "Step on it, already!" But I probably shouldn't do that.

November 24

Dear Diary:

The sun was just rising when we arrived at Burning Dude, but the party was still going strong. Naked and semiclothed partyers were everywhere, and music was blaring from all directions. In the middle of a scalding-hot Nevada desert, and surrounded by the white dunes of Sand Mountain (the dunes are famous for the loud "whispering" sounds they make when the wind sweeps past), Burning Dude was throbbing with music and art and dancing, and from what I could tell, lots of drugs and alcohol. The art was astonishing. There were huge, colorful floats and installations: a gargantuan, vividly colored hamburger, immense wooden chairs seemingly arranged at random (they were meant, I think, to suggest some kind of social interaction), a glowing, fourteen-foot-high croissant, a towering steel-and-bronze dragon that shot actual fire from its mouth, and at the center of the gathering, at the top of the highest dune, "The Dude," a twenty-foot-high structure of a man made entirely of wood, its arms outstretched in welcome.

"Whoa." Bud grinned, taking in his surroundings and all the partyers. "Makes you just want to rip off your clothes and run free, doesn't it?"

"Don't," I told him hastily. I so didn't mean to be a party pooper or anything, and I totally understood how anyone (and not just Bud) would want to run free in such a dizzying, liberating atmosphere (though I, for one, would not run around naked) (but that's me), but jeez, we were here for a reason.

"How do we find Mark?" I asked Cliff anxiously. I was operating on so little sleep. My head was spinning with images of sand, streamers, Meri on a broomstick, giant croissants, and Lindsay's fingers working mousse into Dean Pointer's hair. Cliff took charge. Thank God. He couldn't reach Mark on his cell phone (again!), but he was ready to take off and look for him, or more specifically, "Camp Snitch." He told Lindsay and Bud to do the same. "You don't want me to do anything?" I asked. He kissed my cheek.

"Nope. You're the only one who didn't get any sleep last night," he said. "Wait here. Relax." They took off, vanishing in a swirl of sand and streamers. Exhausted, I sat down next to *The Chakra*, a giant, ever-changing light-sculpture garden. Its colorful beams intermittently blinded me. I was getting woozy. All those colors, all that sand, all that white hair. I bolted up. Was I imagining things? Was it a mirage? I cried out, "Eileen!" Then I heard a sudden, terrifying, booming sound—which I later learned was an especially loud "whisper" from Sand Mountain. A churning tornado-like blast of sand whipped up before me. Then it settled. And there she was. She looked frail, ravaged even. Her face was lightly flecked with a fine layer of sand, and long lines streaked down from her eyes. She'd obviously been crying, but you wouldn't have known it otherwise by the way she addressed me.

"Jeez, where the hell have you been, C-Dawg?" she griped. "I've been up half the night looking for you."

"What on earth are you doing here?" I gasped. *Albino Girl may be many things*, I thought, *but first and foremost she's a little girl. I don't care how tough she thinks she is, she shouldn't be here. This is wrong.*

"What do you think I'm doing here?" she retorted. "Playing hopscotch? I'm not dropping acid, that's for sure, even though half the bozos here keep offering it to me."

"Oh, Eileen," I shuddered. I bent down and took both of her hands in mine. She didn't resist. "She's here, isn't she? Where's Meri?"

"Who knows? I don't care anymore. I'm finished. She can bite my weenie. To hell with her." Then she held back a sniffle; her eyes were glassy with tears. "She was supposed to hold my hand. She promised. We were supposed to stay together."

"I'm getting you on the first plane back to Rumson. Okay? I promise." She burst out sobbing. Just like that. And she wasn't faking. It was heartbreaking. I pulled her into a hug. "You're going home. Don't worry. I'm not leaving you."

"I don't like her anymore," she murmured.

"I know." She pulled back and wiped her eyes. Then something strange happened. The old Albino Girl reappeared. Tough. Grim. Unforgiving. "You should know everything," she said very evenly. "And don't worry, I won't charge you. Even though I still want a pony." My eyes widened. "I know so many things you don't know," she had told me several days ago. "What I can give you will bring this whole thing to a stop. Permanently."

"Shhh. You don't have to tell me anything you don't want to," I said, pulling her back into my arms.

"Oh, but I do," she whispered ominously. And she did. She told me everything. Every secret thing.

"Cindy!" cried Cliff. He ran up breathless with Lindsay and Bud. "Sorry. It sucks. We can't find him. I can't even find Camp Snitch." And then all hell broke loose. Lindsay screamed, Cliff whipped his head around, rotor blades whirred in the distance, and a shattering booming "whisper" sank into the pit of my stomach.

"She's leaving!" wailed Lindsay. I grabbed Albino Girl's hand

314

and we ran toward Meri's helicopter as it soared triumphantly into the blazing hot sky. And right below it was Camp Snitch, a makeshift camp and art installation with large pictures of Judas, Richard Nixon, Benedict Arnold, and other famous snitches and liars, as well as an interactive display with a typewriter where guests and passersby could feel free to type, or "snitch," on themselves or others. The inside of the camp was ransacked. Papers were strewn about everywhere.

"Look at this," Bud sputtered, gesturing to the typewriter. A long roll of paper spun out from it. Partyers had typed hundreds upon hundreds of their snitches, including "My boyfriend held up a HoJo's and got away with it. Nadine," and "When I was a kid I stole medicine from my parents' bathroom so I could play Nyquil Truth or Dare with my buds. Awesome fun! Paul," and "Terri lies on her expense reports. Anonymous," and "My boner points to the side. Like a question mark. Colin." At the very top, the last snitch read: "I'm a bad, bad girl. Meri."

November 25

Dear Diary:

I haven't had time to breathe in the last twenty-four hours. At Burning Dude, it was obvious that whatever blog pages Mark may have had—*poof!*—they were gone. Meri had them now. After I saw Albino Girl off on a flight to Rumson, Lindsay laid down the law. "We're not giving up," she declared hysterically, waving her umbrella about for emphasis.

"Aw, but aren't you tired, buttercup?" asked Bud.

"Tired? You bet I am." Then she turned to me. "I dubbed thee Dark Cindy. Remember? Would Dark Cindy give up?" My heart was sinking, my mind was ground to mush. But yes, I remembered. Devote yourself to an ideal. And you will defeat your opponent. I felt a surge of adrenaline. *I can't give up now*, I thought, *I can't let her win*. I could feel my teeth grinding; I was formulating a plan. *Cindy's my little bow-wow. Woof woof!* Oh, no you don't. Not this time.

"When's the next flight to Newport?" I asked.

Bud gasped. "You don't mean . . . ? You don't think . . . ?"

Cliff laughed appreciatively. "Let's roll, Dark Cindy." We were off.

It was late afternoon when we arrived in Rhode Island and hopped into a cab outside Newport State Airport. There wasn't a moment to spare. Lindsay flung my skateboard and knapsack into my lap, then whipped open her own suitcase, searching for her Treo smartphone. Out popped her coiled-up whip and leopard-print blindfold. "Oopsie," she said with a grin, finally finding her phone.

"I'll take that," I said, grasping the whip. Bud held the blindfold up to me and Cliff.

"If you guys ever want to borrow this, no prob. The other night, so cool, Lindsay blindfolded me and put red lipstick all over my—"

"I've got it," announced Lindsay triumphantly, her fingers flying over her keypad. "Driver? Newport National Bank. 400 Thames Street. Between Fourth and Mill."

"And step on it!" I wailed, unsure in the moment if I was speaking to a cab driver or an airplane pilot (did I really break into the cockpit?). To my amazement, the driver listened. Oh my God, he drove wham-bam fast. In no time at all he screeched around the corner of Mill Street to the top of Thames Street.

"Numbers are descending," Cliff cried out. "It's at the end of the block." A shattering whistle blasted suddenly. The driver hit the brakes. We all flew forward. A large delivery truck was backing out of an alleyway. Car horns honked all around us.

"Can't you go around him?" I cried to the driver, even though it was obvious he couldn't. Cliff grasped my hand.

"It's okay. We're almost there." *Thump-thump-thump*. My heart was exploding out of my chest. I couldn't breathe. *Thump-thump-thump*. My body felt all tingly. *Oh my God*, I thought, *I'm going to faint, I'm going to die*. I gripped Cliff's hand tighter, I took a huge gulp of air. *Thump-thump-thump*. Then I screamed, "I can't wait!" I jumped out of the cab, threw down my board, and flew down the street. *Cindy's my little bow-wow. Woof woof!* I couldn't even see. Wind charged up into my face. Then I jerked to the side, narrowly missed smashing into a telephone pole, and kicked off faster, faster. *Whoosh!* A blue convertible jutted out from a parking lot and—oh my God!—I leaped up into the air, soared over the car, and landed right back on my board as it flew out from beneath the car. *Holy moly, that was close!* I could see the bank. At the very end of the block. *Go faster, faster!* Then I saw a telltale figure stepping out onto the street, clutching a large manila envelope. I cried out hoarsely, "Bloody Me-e-e-e-e-ri!" She jerked around, her thick raven hair horrifically awry, her mouth furiously agape. Then she ran like the dickens, tearing around the corner, and I kicked off, faster, faster. *Whoosh!* I spun around the corner and there she was—racing for a town car, the passenger-side door flung open. I cried out, "N-o-o-o-o-o-o-o-o!" Then I dropped my right hand down, let it fall loose, jerked it back up in a wide arc, and flung it with all my might. *Crack!* The tip of the whip struck the back of Meri's neck. Her entire body spasmed. The manila envelope flew from her hands. She fell to the ground—then leaped right up and lunged for the folder. *Crack! Crack!* I got her in the thigh, the shoulder blade. Her body jerked in a seizurelike motion. *Whoosh!* I spun around to the envelope and snatched it. Behind her, Lindsay, Bud, and Cliff ran up. They were horrified.

"Cindy, don't!" screamed Lindsay. I suddenly realized that I stood poised, ready to strike Meri again. She was hunched over pathetically, on her knees, clutching her sides, huffing and puffing gutturally. She crooked her head and gazed up at me. Her face was expressionless, but her eyes told the story; they were overflowing with rage. I looked back at her and silently mouthed, "Bloody Meri." In a flash she leaped up, dove into her town car, and—*vroom!*—vanished down the street. And that was that.

I visited Patty in rehab this afternoon. "Have you spoken to Mr. Sugarman?" she asked.

"Not yet," I said. She leafed through the documents, shaking her head.

"You have a decision to make. A moral decision."

"I'm not giving these back to Meri," I gasped.

"Of course not. This brings Meri money. Money makes the world go around. Especially Meri's."

"That's so ugly. That this all comes down to money and power."

"Oh, Cindy. It doesn't. Really. It comes down to you. To that nice, sweet, innocent girl from Marietta."

"I'm not so innocent," I said sadly. "Not anymore."

"That's right." She smiled sweetly. "You're all grown up now. I mean, I could talk your head off about various postpartum specifiers and interepisode conversion criteria, but let's keep it simple. When Cindy couldn't do the job, Dark Cindy stepped in."

"Yeah. Pretty pathetic, huh?" I felt so messed up.

"No, Cindy, it's lovely. Because that nice, innocent girl and that tough, take-charge woman are one and the same. It doesn't have to be either/or. Introduce them to each other." She handed the documents back to me. "Then you'll know exactly what to do with these papers."

The sun had already set by the time I stepped out of the rehab center. I strolled lazily across the Great Lawn. The streetlamps were just coming on, illuminating a light snowfall. I closed my eyes and breathed in, clutching the documents to my chest. When I opened my eyes I could barely focus. Something misty appeared beneath a streetlamp. Then it vanished. Then it emerged right before me. "Hello, Cindy," whispered Meri delicately. It was cold out. She held herself tightly in her fur coat. And she smiled knowingly. "Let's cut to the chase," she said softly. "How much?" I didn't answer. I could tell she was on edge, even though she was trying to play it oh so cool. She involuntarily leaned in, as if she wanted to grab the documents. I flinched.

"You think these are the only copies I have? You must think I'm really dumb."

"Oh, I don't think you're dumb at all, Cindy. In fact, I have a feeling you'll play this just right. See, we can have our cake and eat it too." She paused, then whispered, "So how much?"

"Would it shock you to hear that this isn't about money?"

She smiled. "Well, look, it's not like we're going to be best girlfriends or anything. But we can certainly have détente. You've earned that. At the very least."

"I want you to leave Rumson," I told her calmly. "Go away. Finish out college at the Sorbonne. Or Yale. Or Harvard. Just go."

"Or what? You'll give those documents back to my father? I'm a very resourceful girl, Cindy. You should know that by now. Do you think I even need them?"

"Probably not. But I also know that you absolutely hate to be degraded, embarrassed, or humiliated in any way."

She rolled her eyes and sighed impatiently. "'Bloody Meri.' That was so many years ago. But props to you for using that. For using all of it. You've been a very worthy opponent." She stared at me. She was waiting for me to cave. The snow was falling thicker. Her skin seemed to turn bluer and bluer, as if her body were synchronizing with the icy air. This time I was the one who smiled. And I said, "Meri Sugarman, bastard daughter of Nancy Forbes. Correction: Meri Sugarman, bastard daughter of a convicted killer. Actually, a serial killer, if we're to believe all those pesky newspaper accounts. Gosh, Randy and Nester should have a field day with that one. Sort of a human interest exposé."

Meri quivered—just slightly. Everything Albino Girl had told me made sense. Why didn't I see it before? Meri had written in her own diary:

I'd like to meet my real mother. I know that if I wanted, I could force Father's hand. He would tell me where she is if I really wanted to know. But it's fine for now. I enjoy the mystery, not to mention keeping Father on edge.

And later she wrote:

So far my investigations have narrowed down the possibilities to either North or South Carolina. Once my research is complete, I'll chose the appropriate college and bide my time. Matters such as these must be handled delicately. It may take two years, perhaps even three. Patience is vital.

Meri did take her time. Now I knew why she came to Rumson (instead of Jackie's beloved Sorbonne), and when she was forced to do community service in October, she finally introduced herself to Nancy while delivering meals to the aged. I chuckled inwardly. Psycho daughter finally meets psycho mommy. Ha! What a reunion that must have been.

"What happened, Meri?" I asked with a grin. "He knocked her up, I know that. Dumb move on her part. I'm sure she got a payoff, but she didn't marry him beforehand. Tsk. She could have collected a whole lot more. But then I guess she wised up. Marrying all those rich old men who 'suddenly' died."

"You can't prove any of this," she whispered. She seemed to be in a trance. She wasn't quivering anymore. She was standing absolutely still.

"Sure I can," I said. I held up the documents. "I'm going to bilk your father for all he's worth. Then I'll grease the right palms. Oh, look. A birth certificate. Then I'll give Nancy a huge chunk of change. Huge. And Randy and Nester will interview her. Aw, she'll be so happy. It all comes down to money, Meri. Money and power. So what do you say? Paris for Christmas? Graduation at the Sorbonne? Sorry I won't be able to join you in Capistrano. But, please, do give Nancy my best."

Meri left Rumson tonight, but I'd like to think that she just evaporated right there in front of me on the Great Lawn. It certainly seemed that way. After I'd had my say, the snow slowly thickened around her. Her face became dense and brittle. A tiny crack gave way. Then another. And another. Then she was nothing but tiny snow white particles. A great wind blew forth and off she went, hoping against hope to reassemble somewhere new, but for now, retreating behind all those billowing curtains in her mind. Maybe now she'll set them on fire.

I started my own fire. Right there on the Great Lawn. When I was certain I was alone, I introduced Cindy to Dark Cindy, and I made my first real grown-up decision. I dumped the documents into a metal trash can, struck a match, dropped it, and watched everything crinkle and burn and finally levitate—all those blackened little pieces of paper. They were gone. It was done. *Gosh, what the heck are you standing here for?* I thought. *Cliff's coming for dinner and he's bringing over the "artwork" you guys did together.* Woo-hoo! *Maybe,* I thought, *we can make some more.*

About the Author

Born in Texas and educated in New York City, M. Apostolina is the author of *Hazing Meri Sugarman*, *Meri Strikes Back*, and *Dark Cindy*, all of them from Simon Pulse, an imprint of Simon & Schuster. Don't forget to check out www.mapostolina.com.